The Sleuthing Adventures of Tennessee Muffcat Mansker Presents:

THE VOICES

Book 1

L.A. STEPHENS

TouchPoint
Press

THE SLEUTHING ADVENTURES OF TENNESSEE MUFFCAT
MANSKER PRESENTS: THE VOICES by L.A. Stephens
Published by TouchPoint Press
Jonesboro, Arkansas
www.touchpointpress.com

Copyright © 2015 L.A. Stephens
All rights reserved.

ISBN-10: 0692591877
ISBN-13: 978-0692591871

Editor: Ashley Carlson
Cover Design: Colbie Myles, colbiemyles.com
Author Photo: Leslie Kemp Phillips
Cover Photo: Model Credit to Leslie (MiMi) Buchanan Prow

Visit the author's website at www.lastephens.com

First Edition

Printed in the United States of America.

To my Tutu. Until we can ride the moon.

This book was a labor of love. Many friends jumped at the opportunity to have their names or likenesses used for the making of this series. First and foremost, I'd like to thank my editors Benee Knauer and Ashley Carlson for their hard work and dedication. Benee, it was a long process in development, years, as a matter of fact. Thank you for not giving up on me and my vision for the series. Ashley, thank you for your patience with my comma errors and for your willingness to go the extra mile in making sure all the final details were perfected! I also would like to thank my private investigator, Big M (Michael) Sands, my graphics and social media guru, Adam Marsh, and my little brother, Johnny, who assisted in some of the legal aspects regarding the last will and testament of Leighanna. To my husband and son, who patiently waited for me to finish a paragraph before speaking (hey, I am not a multitasker, what can I say?) To all of my friends at Cole and Garrett Funeral Home that assisted with embalming procedure terminology, many thanks. Last but not least, my grandmother Anne, my Tutu, who passed away during the book's completion, there will never be another book lover like you, my dear. To my mother, sister, cousins, friends, and neighbors who might have felt that they needed to move to Canada after the release, I hope you never acquired your passport. It might be a crazy little book with a lot of content that is scandalous, but what else would you expect from your Lele? Love to all and many thanks for never giving up on me.

Prologue

Voices can motivate. They can alarm, influence, shock, and haunt. But those voices that come from inside your own head? Well, those can change your destiny.

You hear the voices, don't you? Be honest now. We all hear them. That little one that tells you not to eat that last biscuit. The song on the radio, with that mindless refrain that really grates on your nerves and bugs the piss out of you for the entire day. It settles into your head like an unwanted visitor. You can't get rid of it. That last conversation you had with your father before they killed him during the "routine procedure," nothing to worry about. They really get you good. They play over and over, on a loop.

But what about the other voices? The ones that try to impart their perception into your sense of morality, your future, the viability of your success. How do you distinguish which ones to listen to? Or do you even? Do your voices exasperate you; do they drive you to take action? Are they real? They *are* in your head. How do you differentiate the ones worth a listen? How do you recognize the ones that are trying to tell you right from wrong? Do you listen and take action, or dismiss them and do nothing?

I could always turn mine off with a little vodka and a splash of juice. Just like flipping a light switch and watching the cockroaches scatter to the wind, my voices crawled back into the walls with the aid of a stiff swallow. Returned to the souls to whom they belonged. All of that changed in September of 2012. Sure, the vodka could still slow the voices down for a nanosecond, but what started to unfold in my head was a story I was not sure I wanted to hear. We all have our demons; you might well have already guessed the nature of mine. But when the psyche of a murderer decided to colonize my mind, there was not a cocktail to be found strong enough to tune him out.

Nanny always did say that I had a demon on one shoulder and an angel on the other, but this voice was coming from some place that was pure evil. It somehow connected to my very soul; oh yeah, he wanted his story to be told. At first, it wasn't clear why he wanted to steal my stream of consciousness. And then the first body showed up on my embalming table. His voice and the voices of his victims all but paralyzed me that autumn. Daily living became a challenge. Sleep was impossible. The flashes of brutality and violence overwhelmed every sense of my being.

I did not become a psychic detective by choice. It was more like through corrosion. Those irritating voices that inhabited and stalked, those demons that haunted me, they led me down a new career path at the ripe old age of forty-one. Just as I was thinking I could finally let out a deep breath and kick up my feet.

Chapter I

I should have known that the job title of mortician would make it onto my resume eventually, seeing how my granddaddy owned a funeral home and I, myself, could speak to the dead. Being a Southern born and bred spit-fire, I never was good about listening to anyone who wanted to lend me advice. Of course, I should have listened to Nelley Needlemire. Nelley was my first childhood "voice." She stuck around the first time until I was eleven, when the discovery of boys set my underwear on fire with puberty-induced hormones. Nobody ever saw it coming, well nobody that is but Nelley. Muffcat Mansker, a funeral director. Let's face it, definitely not the most glamorous profession in the world, but the vocation pays the bills, allows for me to keep the family's B&B afloat, and supports my shoe habit. It really would not do my life justice to call it ordinary, nonetheless, up until last week it was pretty damn close. When you take into consideration that I started hearing voices at the tender age of three, that my name is associated with female private parts, and that currently the boys and I live in a fish bowl, it's a wonder I have not been institutionalized. Yet.

*****

My hometown sits just eighteen miles north of the capital of Tennessee, two miles off of I-65, but Parrottville has always been light years away from the metropolis they call The Music City. The latest community gossip in the fall of 1974 was that my daddy had taken over as president of our hometown bank, ousting his own daddy, and it was causing a little hostility in the Mansker family. It seemed that Gran's purchase of Simon's Family Funeral Home in 1971, the year I was born, was causing him way too much stress. It was obvious to everyone the pressure of running two businesses and living with Nanny at the family's B&B had spread Gran a little thin. The bank examiners were scrutinizing Gran's lending practices at the bank, and my daddy was a fine choice as a replacement president, or at least that is what our mother told us. We moved from a tiny cabin on the grounds of Granddaddy's home, The Three Waters, into a regal residence on Phillips Drive. Our new house sat on a big corner lot smack-dab in the middle of our community on the Davidson County side of the line, only a mile away. It was centuries apart from the pre-Civil War plantation Granddaddy purchased from the Needlemire family in 1951. According to Tilly Jean Sanders, the head of the local DAR (Daughters of the American Revolution) chapter, it was the right side of the tracks for Daddy's young and influential family. The move was to give us a fresh start, or so that is what Daddy said. But seeing how I was told to leave my imaginary friends behind, I wasn't as excited about it all as my older brother, Tommy.

My sister, Lenore, was just a few months old in August of 1975 when Momma finally settled on the regal Queen Anne-style residence with the gigantic front porch and stick detailing in the gables. Daddy about had a conniption fit over the price tag of a whopping $39,000.00, but as a banker he said he'd given himself the best interest rate he legally could. Our new house sat on Phillips Drive, which intersects with Carr Avenue and Butler Drive, forming a scalene triangle around the beautiful Toss-Knight Park. The house sat smack-dab in the middle of everything, just one block from the Parrottville town square. We were considered privileged to have the address. So Daddy did not understand my tender young pleas to return home to Nelley. He'd figured the gigantic backyard, new swing set, and the addition of three new bird dogs would make me normal. Right!

Nevertheless, The Three Waters is where I have always considered home, ghosts or not. I remember they'd just had delivery of my first big-girl bed, which had a white bedspread with little white balls all over it in a pattern that now reminds me of one at Andrew Jackson's homestead. My bedroom was across the hallway from my parents' on the bottom floor; at the very end of the hall next to the closet where the movers put Momma's vacuum cleaner and our winter coats. On that very first night in our new house, I slept alone for the first time in my life. Momma set up a nursery for my sister, but she was still in a bassinet at the foot of my parents' bed, that sat high off the ground with four posters of red walnut wood. My night started out with just one dead man and a streetwalker named Natilda, but things rapidly grew more disturbing.

This old man, Fredrick, was wandering the hallway, and wasn't happy about it. I thought it was a dream, but my reality and nightmares have always bled together like a watercolor painting whose artist had a nose bleed. The man in my dream was dreadful. He told me he was dead, and that the hall closet was his personal passageway to hell. Someone wanted him to see what a real family looked like before his soul was forever lost to the fiery pit he was about to enter. He was informed by the Wind Whisperers not to disturb us, but he was scared, and for good reason. He tried to pass the time by keeping me up; he wanted to confess all of his sins. He wasn't good to his wives and kids; then he admitted to stealing money from his business partner for the past twenty-two years. Fredrick said he liked to drink too much and smoked unfiltered Camels, but his true downfall, in his retrospect, was all the pretty women that walked up and down the streets. He told me that one morning, he just knew he had not woken to a normal day. He could still see and hear people that were alive, but he was being chased by shadows. He believed one was under my very own new bed. He said their breaths felt like hot wind on the back of his portly neck and their gasps smelled of death. So he pulled his feet up really tightly, almost to his chest, but his stomach was too big. He asked if he could use the pastel colored gingham-square blanket at the foot of my bed to shelter him. He begged me for a cigarette, but I didn't know anyone who smoked. He pleaded for my water, but my glass was empty. He demanded for me to look into the closet and tell him what I saw, but my hands and feet were heavy because I was, well at least I thought I was, still asleep. I never will forget the date. It was August the fifteenth and Fredrick was hoping he'd get a last minute invitation to some big party, which made sense seeing how it was a Friday night. But the invitation was supposed to come from baby Jesus' mother herself and Fredrick worried she might have forgot about him. I kept telling him that maybe someone made a mistake, and if he prayed to baby Jesus he could possibly get another invite, but Fredrick wouldn't listen. He kept mumbling something about his Sister Paola di Santa Teresa and how it "had to be true." He told me a really long tale about this lavish feast and how every year baby Jesus' mother renews a miracle of mercy where thousands of souls are saved from a city he called Purgatory. Fredrick kept crying out for the Virgin Mary to spare him; he made funny hand gestures while he prayed. When I told him I would pray along with him, Fredrick began to weep.

Shortly after finally getting Fredrick quiet, someone else showed up. She'd been instructed to enter the same doorway the Wind

Whispers told Fredrick to use in order to pass to the other side. Natilda was from the Bronx. She was a slim-framed, pale lady who confessed to being a prostitute, but I told her I didn't know what that meant. I remember loving her earrings; her hair was a bright red, which did not quite seem natural, but it reminded me of the nose of the clown on our local news station. Natilda, too, was seeing the shadow people, who she professed were like herding dogs from hell with no eyes, just big mouths that never closed. She told me they chased and chased and chased her, and that her feet were sore from her high-heeled boots. She took them off then set them under my bed. She admired my Sunday dresses that had just been placed in my closet that very afternoon while asking if I liked to wear headbands. She told me she missed her daughter, who had a better shot with her gone. She liked the summer sun of the South but thought my daddy looked like a slave master. She didn't know why she was there exactly, or where she was going.

Natilda said she heard me talking to Fredrick and thought we might be having a party, so she thought she'd join in. Funny, she called him John, but I knew his name was Fredrick. He just smirked and said he knew her kind. They exchanged war stories; they shared the experience of having attended their own funerals. They went on and on; they would not let me sleep for nothing! I finally worked up the courage to yell to the wind, "they are over here!" Just as if gunshots had hit them, they both jumped out of my bed, then swatted at invisible flies. Natilda was in such a hurry she forgot her boots, but when I awoke the next morning, they were gone.

It continued. Each night, more strangers. Word got out. People who heard about the girl who could see them (that would be me) lined up for hours, begging me to go to all sorts of places that sounded very beautiful. They promised me candy and dolls; one woman even offered to let me try on her mink coat! But I was tired. I didn't want to travel anywhere unless it was in a boat with Wynkin, Blynkin, and/or Nod. When they stopped by, we'd set sail on a shiny sea, but they always felt guilty when I had to touch back down to the sand. I have met a lot of dead people in my life, but these were not the good ones.

My full name is Muffy Catherine Lucinda Tennessee Mansker. My momma named me after her freshman roommate, Muffy Collette Ramburger, and my daddy's mother, Mrs. Catherine Bernadette

Thomas-Mansker. Then she threw in a few extra names to explain my father's Southern heritage and her own mother's immigrant background hailing from the Castilian region of Spain. I was given the nickname of Tennessee Muffcat my very first day of kindergarten at the Parrottville Elementary school. Poor Miss Rizor called roll and about fell out of her damn chair when she read my entire name. Chandra Sue Worsham yelled at the top of her lungs, "I wanna sit next to the Tennessee Muff Cat!" To this very day, thirty-five years later, we are still the best of friends. Chandra is now the Parrottville First Baptist Church secretary; my excessive cussing, love of alcohol, and ability to see dead people has always scared her silly. She won't sit next to me at church, but I love her dearly anyway, even though the nickname she started did make for some painful high school memories.

Not to say, for one minute mind you, that my entire existence has been a splendid party or walk in the park, but I've been told I make the best of what life wants to throw at me. I just never realized that the punches would come so hard and so fast, and that my ghosts would return throughout the decades. Then again, stability does not make for the grandness of tales. And let's face it, I am a drama queen.

Chapter II

After an unplanned pregnancy and a bad marriage to Johnny Glass, I escaped Parrottville with little money, big dreams, and a two-year-old in tow. I defied the odds, made a few waves in the fashion industry under the big city lights of New York City, but with fame and fortune came other problems. My son, Gavin, and I were sharing a studio apartment in Alphabet City when I got the call from Betsy Johnson to join her team. The A-D Avenues were still considered bohemian (make that grimy, dangerous, edgy, and rodent-infested) back then.

My work life was exhilarating and rewarding, but we were crammed into a shitty rathole-of-a-place, and we were counting pennies. I desperately wanted to launch my own clothing line, but the odds were stacked against me. It was a tough decision, but I turned down the offer from Betsy Johnson for a shot at my own line using $2,000 from Nanny's bourbon ball proceeds. Our tiny apartment was where Bluegrass/Black House of Fashion was born. As the head of product development, branding, and marketing, my first year was a complete bust. With only two seamstresses on payroll, negative cash flow, and dwindling distribution outlets, Gavin and I were on the streets in less than eighteen months, and our future was uncertain.

Then I met Sonny Felderbush. Though his division of Cantor Fitzgerald was not into such risky investments, by the time we'd eloped to Cayo Espanto, Belize, my life had changed on a dime. With Sonny's financial backing, my air-conditioned shitkickers (rhinestone encrusted, high-heeled, open-toed cowboy boots) became all the rage and were regularly featured in no less than *Vogue* and *Cosmopolitan*. After Manhattan's style elite grudgingly trekked across the East River to the Navy Yard during the 1994 Mercedes-Benz Fashion Week, Bluegrass/Black House of Fashion's splash onto the world stage caught the attention of a *Wall Street Journal's* "Life & Style" columnist. By the time her piece detailing our Grand Ole Opry-esque hemlines was featured, we'd grossed our first million. In 1996, "The Hillbilly Hipsters," as the media loved to call us, moved into an extravagant showroom and production facility in the heart of the

Garment District. It was sandwiched in between major fashion labels like Carolina Herrera, Oscar de la Renta, Calvin Klein, Donna Karan, Liz Claiborne, Nicole Miller, and Andrew Marc. As a result, the next five years were a blur of fabulously lavish parties and dizzying expansion into fashion-hungry European and Chinese emerging markets. It seemed the publicity and hype, the thrill ride, would never end.

By my thirtieth birthday, life could not have been more satisfying. Sonny and I were deeply, madly, wildly in love. We had just purchased a six-bedroom penthouse in the heart of the financial district in downtown Manhattan. Gavin was enrolled in a private middle school; he made the basketball team and had his future sights set on the Julliard School of Music Undergraduate program. Sonny was at a critical point in his career, but it was to be expected. Cantor Fitzgerald was having a record year when the opportunity to head up the Convertible Securities division fell at his feet. Not wanting to abandon our fashion empire, Sonny pitched the label to a few high-end department stores, which produced a few nibbles. When Saks Fifth Avenue made us an offer that was too good to be true, my bags were already packed for a long overdue vacation overlooking Little Dix's Bay in the British Virgin Islands. Before the ink was dry on the contract, I'd committed to staying on as the creative director for five more years. I was determined to kick back and take a less active role in the marketing efforts.

The eve of Labor Day, 2001 changed everything. That night, I called my mother with an eerie premonition. The intuition came to me in the middle of my two-hour martini lunch with my mergers and acquisitions attorneys from Greenfield Stein & Senior, LLP. It was the briefest flash, just an overhead view of Daddy lying motionless on an operating table.

Momma confessed she did not want to "bore us with the details" of Daddy's outpatient procedure. We fought over whether or not I was drunk or high before she called me an "emotionally unstable drama-seeking diva." When my plane landed at BNA the following afternoon, my daddy was already dead. He suffered an aortic tear to his proximal left anterior descending coronary artery during the ballooning procedure of what was supposedly a routine, "in and out," procedure to stent his arteries. By the time they'd cracked his chest wide open, his widow maker striated, and the surgeon was not optimistic about being able to repair the damage. Four hours of open heart surgery later, his own father had to wheel him out of Saint Thomas Hospital in a body bag.

Even before we could lay Daddy to rest at the Spring Hill Cemetery, I knew there was no way to repair my relationship with my mother. Needless to say, the long time coming validation about my sixth sense was not as spectacular as I'd always pictured. First, Mother refused to admit to anyone in the family that our conversation about my premonition had ever taken place. She even convinced my sister, Lenore, that I had totally lost my mind at Daddy's visitation. By the time I'd hijacked the pulpit at the funeral, my relationship with my mother was caput. I hit the bottle pretty hard for a few days, but the visions kept on keeping on. When Tommy drove us to the airport, I was chasing handfuls of antidepressants and was high as a kite from a five-day vodka binge. After I was arrested at the airport bar for public intoxication and resisting arrest, Sonny had to rent a private Lear to get us back to New York City in time for the acquisition's final negotiations.

As you can see, my fairytale life was beginning to unravel. The Bluegrass/Black House of Fashion negotiations went south, our celebratory trip to Little Dix Bay was cancelled, and peculiar voices that had been manifesting in my head left Sonny siding with my mother in regard to my mental stability. By September 10, 2001, my blissful, soul-feeding marriage was on the rocks. Sonny convinced me to seek the treatment from an old college fraternity brother of his at the Weill Cornell Medical Center on the Upper East Side. Needless to say, that meeting with the esteemed Professor of Clinical Psychiatry never had a chance to take place.

I ran sixteen blocks to Gavin's school in bare feet, with random voices pinging in my ears. The first came from a dishwasher from Windows on the World, the romantic restaurant with the amazing views on the 107th floor of the World Trade Center. Badar de los Santos started our conversation by rambling off his social security number and then proceeded to beg me to call his pregnant wife, Mary Joy, and his loving mami, Bea. Precipitously following that conversation, an engineer with Sun Microsystems, Robert Daniel Guilespie, yelled out his social security number, along with a heartbreaking message. "411-45-2766 Bob Guilespie here from Boston. Tell my team on the 39th floor, God forgive me! Terrorists just flew a plane into our building." Nawaf Alhazmi screamed about jihad and rambled off passages from the Quran; a loner, Andy Arbuckle, concerned about his pet, rattled off the address to his cat's veterinarian. One of Sonny's mortgage bankers, Prescott McCloud, shouted the numbers of an offshore bank account. When I reached Gavin's school, it was an FDNY commander's voice that finally brought me to my knees.

Gavin was, surprisingly, not hysterical when I stormed into his school. The staff had not disinterred the entire truth to the students, but I have always treated Gavin as an adult. We ran from the building without even retrieving his backpack. I swiped a pen from the front security desk and yelled for my son to write down the rapid-fire numbers that were ricocheting around in my head. Gavin complied with my request at first, stopping every few feet to scrawl down yet another number, but when the wave of smoke and ash washed over us, he begged me to stop. "Momma, please! Enough! I just want to get home!"

The next hours were a blur of frantic communication with Sonny's children, news reports of more attacks, and the calls to those numbers that kept drilling into my head. Chaos, craziness, unfamiliar territory, and emotionally charged messages flooded every sense of my being. Every voice wanted to know the same thing, but I didn't feel it was my place to share the entirety of what I already knew: the utter devastation. The unthinkable misery. The cruel and twisted insanity of it all. I told the dead they were gone, but could not fathom how to articulate to them they were stuck, isolated from those that were still living or dead. I already knew before the smoke could clear (that would take weeks) that in that pile of hatred and malice, lay souls that were lost in the in-between. The voices needed guidance to grasp what had just transpired. They needed a mediator, a messenger. I really don't know how to begin to explain it. They were all so desperate for reassurance; they needed to know their voices could still be heard.

By the time we made it to our penthouse, Gavin's arms were covered with social security numbers, partial phone numbers, offshore bank accounts, addresses, New York State driver's license identification numbers, anything the voices felt would identify them. We were still covered in white ash as we tried to call a few of the numbers. The phone lines were jammed. "All circuits are busy.

Please try your call again later." The first mother we reached was furious, livid, confused; she kept demanding for me to stop. Her hopes were still alive and my call was not received the way it was intended, the way the voices hoped my gift could connect them back to their loved ones. Their survivors. After my fifth call ended poorly, I had to focus on my son, his mental well-being, our urgent escape route. At that point, Gavin was more scared of what was happening to me that what we were witnessing on the television. I promised him that we would stop, but had to tell him about Sonny. He kept pointing out the window to the bank of stretchers that had been set up for triage. Those stretchers sat, largely unused.

The smell of burning rubber, paper, flesh was seeping into our windows. I couldn't imagine it would be long before the building would be evacuated. Gavin finally admitted to believing me when night fell without word from or about Sonny.

Once the bridges and tunnels were reopened to non-emergency traffic, we were going to head out, even if planes weren't yet landing in and flying out of JFK Airport. Together, we sobbed and screamed. I took inventory of my son's forearms. Then we scrubbed the madness from his body. I never once called Sonny's cell phone that first night. Looking back, and after discussing it with countless others in my situation, I was the only one.

It was noon before we packed what we could into Sonny's BMW sedan. It took us seven hours to move less than two miles, but we didn't make a stop until Allentown, then Harrisonburg, PA. Our last stop before arriving back home was in Johnson City, Tennessee, where we crashed for a few hours at a distant cousin's apartment.

Nanny and Gran welcomed us back to The Three Waters, with open arms, on September 14, 2001, at 5:13 a.m.

It took some time for us to get settled into the 150-year-old log cabin that had once been my childhood home. Slowly, the voices started to fade into the whistles of the trains and the bubbling of the spring that sat just feet from our small habitat. My frantic pace was ground to a speed that was not familiar but welcomed. I contemplated the numbers the lost souls that had tried so hard to communicate with me but didn't dare dial another number. After a long few weeks, the simple act of making a cup of coffee brought on a whole new meaning. It took three weeks for me to get up the nerve to admit the unavoidable, but once we held a private memorial in the backyard of

The Three Waters for my Sonny, life started to beckon me back to its doorstep. By the time the holidays rolled around, our schedule was centered on family, community, and the First Baptist Church. We were back to, what was hopefully, a safe haven for my son, my lucidity, our future.

Gavin was twelve when we finally got around to enrolling him into the public school system in January of 2002. My all-around great kid seemed to fit in from the get-go. But the family's B&B was crumbling down around Nanny and Gran's feet. Of course, my life desperately needed a purpose. I figured Sonny's life insurance benefits were better shared than hoarded, so I purchased the old place from my aging grandparents. Nanny and Gran remained on the property in the private quarters they had shared for over half a century, while my brother, Tommy, and his wife, Keelie, helped me oversee the multimillion-dollar remodeling efforts. By the time the yearlong project was complete, I'd joined the PTA, bought a few bird dogs, and landed the mansion on the cover of the *Nashville Scene* as "The Best of Nashville's" historic places to visit. In short order (I don't mind saying) The Three Waters was booming again. I oversaw the weddings and special events on the weekends, then assisted Gran with hair and makeup up at Simon's whenever he needed me. The busier my life became, the easier it was to distance myself from the hallowing voices. But my decision to rekindle my romance with my old high-school sweetheart, Duke Danderson, temporarily derailed my trip back to the world of sanity.

By the time Duke Danderson was diagnosed with inoperable colorectal cancer, he only had six months to live. To complicate matters, Duke was married to an old friend, Shelley Danderson, who learned that her husband was embroiled in a scandalous affair when she caught us "in the act" on top of her spouse's dental chair. Their only child, Dylan, was Gavin's best friend at Parrottville Middle School. The affair sent shock waves through our tiny community. The B&B bled customers, my name was mud; even the First Baptist Church's congregation turned their backs on me. Even more difficult for me than the disparaging gossip was watching Shelley Danderson spiral out of control as she tried to cope with the loss and the betrayal of both her backstabbing friend (uh, that would be me) and her dying spouse. Shelley found her solace in the bottom of a Wild Turkey bottle and prescription painkillers before she was ultimately introduced to crank by the street thugs. The day she forced Dylan to drive her Jaguar to the liquor store, Duke packed up their belongings, and they moved into my B&B.

On the day Duke died in my arms, Shelley Danderson was officially a missing person. Under suspicion of being somehow responsible for her disappearance, I quietly wall-flowered into a deep depression after Duke's untimely death. It was followed shortly thereafter by the discovery of his widow's body. My decision to enroll in the John A. Gupton College of Mortuary Science (as the oldest person in my class) was done out of desperation; I needed to somehow find another purpose. With another mouth to feed and my bank account devastated, becoming a mortician was the only career move that made any sense.

The fear of those that had transcended to another place evaporated into the normality of just existing, but this world had another lesson for me to learn. One that would take me down a different path and reinforce a fact that I'd known for years: those living voices can hurt you far more than those that are lost in the in-between.

Chapter III

Sometime between October 8 and the early morning hours of October 10, 2012, forty-two-year-old Tana Jade Filson-Harvat fell victim to an atrocious rape/murder that has shaken Parrottville to its core. Her body was found in her own home, off of Gallatin Road, and the aftermath has left me in a mental fog that shifts between uncontrollable grief, fear, and outrage with myself. Since my employment began at Simon's, we have embalmed suicide casualties, car crash fatalities, even a bobcat attack victim. But nothing in my training prepared me for what Medical Examiner Dr. Larry Biggs was about to tell us.

I kept my composure as he debriefed us on the body's condition, took it all in without question. But as soon as we got her body into the hearse, I lost it. My cries always reminded my daddy of the sound a howler monkey makes: loud as hell and a cross between an air-raid siren and a bad heavy metal guitar solo. Betty could barely hear Gran when he called to inform us the next of kin had arrived. He was already in the arrangement meeting and needed an approximation on our arrival time in order to keep the next of kin from wandering over to the display room during the body transfer. Betty said to give us ten; then she turned to question me about my emotional state. She had never seen me lose it before, and she wouldn't shut up about it. This was not the first peer of mine to make it to our embalming table, she kept reminding me. The timing was not right to share the truth with Betty. She might be my mentor, but Good Lord! Betty Simon can bug the piss out of me like no one else. We had our work cut out for us. We had to get the body safely on the embalming table before I knew for sure if my premonition was for real.

I touched up my makeup in the passenger's side mirror before we exited the hearse. Not wanting my childhood friend's family to be subjected to any more emotionally charged drama, I rolled Tana's body into the preparation room only after Betty took over the arrangement meeting from Gran. Funeral directors with raccoon eyes are an occupational faux pas, as per Betty's "Funeral Etiquette 101."

The family was waiting for us to prepare Tana for a private viewing.

Of course, it was understandable, Mr. Filson wanting to see his only child after such a shocking and horrific trauma, but even I was afraid of what we would see. I don't scare easily. Recounting what the ME shared, what I already knew, it was impossible to unzip Tana's body bag for ten minutes. The voices were back; they'd been haunting me for several months now. But this time they were accompanied by a series of gruesome nightmares, which included my now deceased classmate. Contemplating my emergency vodka, I finally got up the nerve to approach the table. Jacket buttoned, I got scrubbed up. Gloves, mask, Vicks Vapor Rub, breathe. You got this, girl.

Tana's face was still in pristine condition, but the scalpel's incision, which started behind her right ear and crossed her forehead, was visible without her hair. There were two tiny prick marks on her forehead that were concealable with makeup, but her skin was in relatively good condition, given the circumstances. Tana's pretty, light brown hair had been pulled out by the roots. The conversation with the ME revealed that her eyes had been jabbed with Q-tips (found at the scene) and soaked in chemicals. Her eyelids and the skin under her eyes were discolored, but we could cover that up simply enough with cosmetology.

Our newest employee, Sally, who was a recent immigrant from Belize, entered the prep room to assist. She unzipped the body bag down to the cadaver's knees, all the while mumbling under her breath. Tana's areolas and genitalia had been mutilated. The second-degree burns on her thighs and legs verified she had been alive while being subjected to the scalding liquid. We rolled the body over to confirm what the ME had shared. *Jesus Christ*, initials were carved onto her left buttocks, and a handle from a baseball bat was left broken off in her anus. It had been removed and was now in evidence, per the ME, but the damage it left behind was horrendous. This type of injury causes leakage that usually requires an anal plug, but the damage was too prodigious for anything we had in our storage closet. Though there was more horror to uncover yet, it was crystal clear that Tana's embalming was not going to be a standard procedure. We were warned about the 365 postmortem cuts by the ME, but it was my first encounter with this type of mutilation. "Weh kinda sicko di dis?" Sally choked out from underneath her mask. Grey skin gaped. Sally heaved into an open trash container, wiped her mouth with her thick arm, and then rejoined me at the slab. The corpse's breasts had received the majority of the destruction. Aside from the areola disfigurement, at least two dozen slashes started from underneath the armpits then went down into the fleshy part of her chest in a v. Each incision was precisely carved. "This took some time." Sally nodded but made no audible noise. I was afraid this type of case might scare her off. Her willingness to work the weekend was my saving grace. "You OK, Sal? Want to get Hollis for this one?" Sally shook her head, "no."

We continued to examine the corpse. The upper torso incisions were symmetrical in technique; same depth, length, and direction. Each had an identical counterpart on the opposite side of her torso. The infinity sign "∞" was clearly visible just above her pubic region with the letter "J" to the left of the perfectly centered symbol. On the right of the infinity sign, a transverse "J" mirrored and flanked the infinity sign. I observed, "There doesn't seem to be much mutilation past her torso besides the PHS left of her anal cleft." Sally mustered an "Um-hum." There were twenty-four longer horizontal cuts starting below the sternum that got smaller in length as they reached the umbilicus (belly button). The cuts acted as some sort of guide for a scrawling message. The words were written in between the folds of gaping skin, undoubtedly performed postmortem but prior to the incisions, otherwise, the blood and other gastro secretions would have made it impossible to inscribe. My dreams gave me some insight to their relevance, but I wasn't sure if Sally was the right person to share my suspicions with. I held off on my premonitions and stuck to the facts. "Most of the communication has been worn away due to the decomposition of the body." This time, Sally did not respond. I explained the epistle was written for law enforcement, per the ME, then noted the inscription seemed to have been printed in all caps using a black permanent marker. Sally flattened a fold of skin. "Deze autopsy incisions make it difficult fi read bes' penmanship." Sally then read the first few lines out loud in her thick, Bileez Kriol accent. "Look down at me and you see a fool. Look up at me and you see a god. Look straight at me and you see yourself."

After the first few lines, the small print was either indiscernible or Sally had lost interest. She unzipped the body bag farther to expose the feet long enough to make the toe tag identification. After the proof of identity was complete, Sally re-zipped the bag back up to the cadaver's chest. The embalming process was going to be a complicated one. If not for the viewing, we would normally leave the corpse in a body bag and recommend cremation. But this is the South, and many of us Baptists are surefire certain the bodies of the believers will rise up like some sort of zombie apocalypse at the End of Times. I tried to convince Sally that cremation was out of the question. Seeing how she casually refers to her Diocese of Belize City-Belmopan as a part of the Roman Catholic faith, I thought she would understand. "Dis body, hat no resurrection."

There was a lot to do in order to prepare the face, and it was going to take some major ventilation to get rid of the overwhelming stench of death that now filled the room. Betty breached the doorway. "Standard burial." Sally rolled her eyes then volunteered to start the procedure. As she made her way to the storage closet, she huffed, "ih noh mata wey yu do as lang as yu tru to yu bileafs." She noted we were low on embalming gel and that we would need to create a plastic shroud to contain the seepage. I retrieved the duct tape from the overhead cabinet in order to seal up the seams and contour the limbs. The plastic would help mask the odor, but when you factor in the bloating of the corpse, it would make it difficult to fit Tana in the black suit the family had brought for the viewing. I asked Sally to hand it over. While she surgically removed the ME's sutures from the abdominal cavity, I went to work cutting the burial garment up the back.

Betty reentered the room to fill us in on the arrangement meeting. Tana's funeral was to take place the following day, a Friday, which was surprising for our community's Southern Baptist formalities. Typically, Baptists call for a visitation the day prior to the funeral, but according to Betty, Tana's family all lived in the area and they wanted to drag the funeral out over the weekend. She further explained that with all the news coverage, it would be easy for the family to get the word out about the memorial details. Betty needed a time frame on the completion of the procedure. I asked her to give us about an hour, but there was something really bothering me about the viewing. We discussed the situation amongst ourselves. After little debate, we were all in agreement that we could not let Mr. Filson see his dead baby girl without her hair. Betty departed to finalize a few loose ends with the family: musical arrangements, pallbearers, grave-side details. I rejoined Sally and continued with the embalming procedure only after sending two of the B&B's employees over to the wig shop off of Dickerson Road; we needed a light brown bob.

After an hour of blowing industrial fans towards the open doorway and furiously working on the corpse, Betty returned. She informed us that the parents had not been the ones to ID the body at the ME's office. Mr. Filson and his second wife, Feedie, were out of the country on a cruise in the Caribbean and had just touched down at the Bridgetown port in Barbados when they'd received the news. Betty claimed the rumors were already swirling around Parrottville before the blow flies had a fighting chance and that most of Bigg's assumptions about the manner of death had been formulated at the crime scene. She then told us that Biggs had made a quick turnaround in this case, given the grizzly circumstances, because even with car crash fatalities it can sometimes take a few days to complete an autopsy. The method of death was clearly by homicide, but the coroner's office was still undetermined on the true cause. Betty proceeded to relay that Tana's son, Henry, a senior at the University of Tennessee, was somewhat concerned when he could not reach his mother late Tuesday night. When his texts and calls went unanswered well into the next morning, he called his father. Even though the high-school sweethearts had been divorced for over two decades, and both had remarried, Tana had taken back her first husband's name after her second marriage dissolved within a few short years. The discovery of his ex-wife's body had supposedly devastated Graham Harvat. According to police chatter, he had been released after questioning, while not fully being cleared from their suspect list, and he wouldn't be in attendance for the private viewing. Betty found out from Henry that his father had to hire my brother's firm to represent him, but the gossip was leading everyone around town to believe Graham Harvat was not the killer.

Every Tom, Dick, and Harry was supposedly pointing their finger at some indiscernible sicko from our past. Even before we retrieved her body from the ME, there was a great deal of chatter about a note being found at the scene that had allegedly been written on a portion of the deceased's old high school annual. Evidently, the note rhymed or had some sort of poetic feel with religious undertones. With the PHS carved on the body, everyone was speculating that someone from our high school had to be the killer. Betty divulged that a ceramic statue of the Virgin Mary was found near the victim, which was mystifying, seeing the mutilation that lay before us. I was in the meeting at the coroner's office when we retrieved the body, and I knew this fact was never mentioned by Dr. Larry Biggs during our conversation. I had no idea who Betty had been speaking with since returning from the ME's office, but my bet was on Officer McNabb. "Betty, much of the penmanship on the body did not seem religious. I actually think the first three verses were a quote from Charles Manson. There were a long series of arbitrary numbers, but it is beyond me if the digits have any symbolic or religious connection." Betty shrugged her shoulders. "The postmortem inscriptions are a numeric allegory, according to McNabb. Their new homicide detective is working on it. But the TBI will probably take this case over."

There was one word still legible on her gaping flesh that was recognizable from my dreams: Theotokos. But I kept this tidbit to myself for the time being. While waiting on the employees to drop off the wig, my anxiety level increased exponentially thinking about the relevance my dreams could have to Tana's homicide. My mind raced while Sally and I completed the complicated embalming procedure. Not sure if I wanted to scare our new employee away by discussing my paranormal visions, I kept my cards close to my proverbial vest, as so many questions pinged in my head. *Why do I sense this is not the first time he violated her? Who is this boy in my dreams? How am I connected to him?* After a good half-hour of contemplation, I had to go into mortician mode and disassociate. After we got Tana dressed and into her casket, Sally needed a break. She had been at it since 6:30 that morning and professed her blood sugar was getting low. I opted to take over the cosmetology while Sally placed a to-go order from Sammy's Barbeque for a mutton plate.

Unlike Alexx Woods from CSI Miami, I do not normally talk to my stiffs, nor do I call them sweetie, honey, or baby girl. But this time, it was impossible to stop myself. Perched on my metal stool, I tried to get Tana to talk to me. Begged for her to tell me what had happened, to reveal who had done this to her petite body. Nevertheless, my poltergeists — the voices — are not conjured; they simply emerge. While applying her foundation, I apologized for the fact that we had to cut her up even more. Then I went on to recount the old times, like the day we thought it was a good idea to set the fire alarm off in 5th period with my can of Aqua Net and a lighter she bummed from Troy McNeece to get out of our algebra exam. Nothing. Then, I asked her to connect with me one more time, to give me a clue as to the meaning of my dreams. Again, silence. "Do you know him? Who is the boy from my dreams?" Soundless. I begged for forgiveness while applying Tana's eye shadow. Cried out about the fact I did not act on the forewarnings. "Sweetie, I am so sorry I didn't warn you." At that very moment, high school names flooded my brain; the Bubbas, the crazies, the weirdoes. "Who is he?" I named them off one by one. Silence. "How do I find him?" Still, absolutely nil. Then, I revealed my suspicions. Tana's murder was eerily similar to another homicide that forced me into my newfound career, the unsolved homicide of Shelley Danderson. The voices that sent me running back to my little hometown after 9-11 now had another mission for me. But these voices were not rambling off a series of social security numbers. They were banging around in my head; they were somehow connected to the killer, and he wanted me to know his story. There was no way to explain the exasperating details to anyone because I still didn't understand them myself. Some of the voices seemed to be witnesses to his actions. Other times, it was like I was hearing the killer himself. Another very distinct voice, which was authoritative and sinister, sounded like what I can only perceive to be his conscience.

After placing the wig upon Tana's bald head, Betty and I wheeled her casket into the small parlor for a viewing. Betty remained behind with the family while I returned to the embalming room to prep Charlie Phillips. Betty told me later in the day that the wig was not a perfect match, but Tana's parents and her son were thankful before they unanimously settled for a closed casket. It was six p.m. before we called it a day. Betty walked me to my car. Still concerned about my emotional state, she tried prying information out of me about my peculiar behavior. I passed my actions off as being a result of the emotionally draining day. Then, we parted ways.

Chapter IV

I left Simon's an emotional mess. Not able to get Tana's bald head out of my mind, I took a familiar path to the home of one of my best friends. I didn't call before marauding their dinner, just showed up unannounced.

The more vodka that was poured, the more I shared with Pammy and Eleanor. The dam had burst. And the voices were back, Big time. After a ten-year hiatus from the insanity, the dreams and sounds were coming to me in waves. Just weeks prior to Tana's murder, the nightmares started. I explained to my friends that the first was not disturbing. As a matter of fact, it was a welcomed recollection from high school, even though this particular encounter never really occurred. The Tana dream was just one in a long series of unfamiliar experiences that was making normality impossible. Eleanor went into the kitchen and mixed up a few martinis. As my stories began to unfold, we all got settled into the couple's newly remodeled living room in front of their metal fireplace.

Being one of the town's only funeral directors, it is natural to have a relationship with the Chief of Police. Truth be told, Pammy and I go all the way back to Parrottville Elementary school, Mrs. Rizer's Kindergarten. That would be the class of 1976. Eleanor, on the other hand, is a transplant from over in West Tennessee, so I had to catch her up on a few details. I began, "The first dream starts out with me, an awkward teenager, entering my uncle EG's store. Late as usual, Tana and I were to be preparing for an editorial meeting." I had to explain to Eleanor the fact that Tana was, in actuality, the youngest senior editor ever at the *Parrottville Bird Post*. "It was just a typical editorial meeting. This type of partnership was not out of the norm for us, as you know Pammy. We were to be collaborating on an article for her column, *Tana's Takes*. Her column was fashion-driven; everyone read it for the sarcasm. She reviewed the fabulous trends of 1988. From acid washed jeans to aviator jackets, we'd decided to focus on the influence MTV had on our wardrobe choices."

Eleanor and I were partaking in the martinis. Pammy had been on call for thirty-eight hours straight and looked to be almost asleep in her chair. Eleanor seemed enamored with my paranormal encounters but admitted my dreams were hard for her to comprehend. Pammy slapped her face awake and got up to flip on the gas fireplace.

"In the first occurrence of the dream, Tana was waiting in our normal booth at my Uncle EG's store with a notebook in hand. We made our way to the meat counter, my great-uncle making fun of our hair. We ordered bologna sandwiches with extra spicy mustard; then we began to write our editorial. An awkward teenage boy was watching our every move from the booth adjacent to ours. Nothing stood out about him, other than his Sex Pistols t-shirt and the brilliance of his bright green eyes, but his actions seemed uncharacteristic for a teen. We didn't know him. There he sat, alone in a deli booth, writing obsessively and talking out loud to himself. We thought he was passing through town; maybe his parents were somewhere in the store. We giggled at the oddness of his behavior. He didn't bother us but seemed intensely interested in our conversation. He kept rocking and babbling."

By martini number four, I'd moved on to the second occurrence of the dream. "As I made my way to the meat counter to order my pre-interview bologna sandwich, Tana wasn't waiting in our booth. The teenager was present again. This time, he had a McDonald's cup in his hand and was chatting with a frizzy-headed blonde by the deli counter. She was dressed scantily. She didn't go to our school, but somehow, I knew her. She told the boy his eyes were as green as the ocean or something to that effect; then she turned to leave. He stopped her, asked if she liked poetry, and recited a line from one of Shakespeare's sonnets. It went something like this. 'O me! What eyes hath Love put in my head, which have no correspondence with true sight; or, if they have, where is my judgment fled that censures falsely what they see alright?' I tried to look the sonnet up at work today, but we were so busy at the funeral home."

I took a deep breath, followed by a huge gulp of liquor, and then continued. "Anyways, the girl looked bewildered. She pulled something from the pocket of her miniskirt that looked like a joint then told the boy to follow her. The kid and his companion headed towards the exit just as Tana entered the building. He shouted to Tana 'Death is the greatest form of love.' She looked back at the couple before bolted for my table. After Tana had calmed down, she confessed that the kid scared her. Then she got all paranoid, professing the boy was stalking her. She claimed that everywhere she went, she saw him. I told her he was just reciting poetry and that she needed to chill out. We wound up in an argument about it."

I described how the day Tana's body was found, the dream reoccurred for the last time. "Here's where the weird part comes in. Tana was in her booth the last time we met. Instead of going to the meat counter for a sandwich with me, she headed to the restroom alone. I got concerned when I saw the boy again; she hadn't returned. As I went to check on her, the entire store began to transform into what I can only imagine a beautiful Catholic cathedral would look like. I am talking a grand and majestic place. The beer coolers became elaborate stained glass panes of the most brilliant colors. Robed men, transparent I might add, were chanting phrases in Latin and conducting some sort of ancient ritual. Just as I placed my hand on the door to the restroom, Tana busted through the doorway, holding her stomach. She jolted right past me, screaming at the top of her lungs. When I looked into the tiny space to see what had frightened her, there was an underdeveloped fetus in the toilet bowl."

Eleanor's eyebrows went up; her face registered shock. I had to finish, needed to get the rest off my chest. "Petrified, I ran to find my uncle EG, who'd just been behind the meat counter seconds ago. He wasn't there. Realizing none of the robed men could see or hear my pleas for assistance, I knew I was the only live soul in the entire building. While searching the aisles for any sign of Tana, I heard a peculiar gurgle. I followed the sounds. There, lying in a pool of her own blood, Tana was taking her last breath. And scrawling the word 'Theotokos' with her outstretched hand. Don't ask why, but she had on a damn pair of roller skates. She looked up at me and with her dying breath, begged me to find him, to find the Devil. I swear on it. She actually called him Lucifer, Son of Satan, as she pointed to the corner of the room. When I looked, there was a woman hunched over the toilet bowl with her hands clasped in prayer. Just as Tana's soul began to depart Earth, I saw the most brilliant beam of light rain down upon my friend's face. She struggled and fought to communicate with me as her soul was being dragged up towards the heavens. She reached for me, uttering a warning, but my hands slipped through hers as if she were nothing but vapor. As her body faded into a fine mist in front of my very eyes, an angel appeared. Shelley Danderson! I swear on my life it was her. She wasn't emaciated, strung out, haggard … no, she was actually beautiful. As Shelley wrapped her arms around Tana, the boy appeared again. He stood there watching, with a beer in his hand, as the very soul of my friend was taken from her mutilated body. Once the apparitions faded into the ceiling, I looked back over to him. He was still without a lick of compassion on his menacing face; I noticed he had aged. He was wearing an INXS t-shirt and had stubble on his face. He was with a woman that looked like Aileen Wuornos, that serial killer. She had unkempt hair and greasy skin, smoking a cigarette. He threw his head back and extended his hands up and shouted, 'We're not in Wonderland anymore, Alice.'"

I about took Pammy's new chandelier out while mimicking the bizarre reenactment. My friends were starting to question the toll Grey Goose was taking on my mental stability. Pammy about pried martini number seven from my hand. She got up to fix a pot of coffee while Eleanor and I continued to deliberate the meaning of my bizarre dreams.

Two pots of strong, bitter coffee later, Eleanor and Pammy both agreed it was time for me to get back to business as usual. They convinced me that my nightmares were over. That there was nothing anyone could have done to save Tana. Seeing that Pammy is the Chief of Police, her insistence was comforting, yet her body language revealed skepticism. Let's face it; she's never been a fan of the psychic side of my personality.

A heated debate over whether or not Tana would be the killer's only victim then ensued. I knew the murderer would strike again. No question about it. Just couldn't put my finger on who that praying woman hunched over the toilet bowl was. By ten p.m., my friends had to practically drag me to Pammy's vehicle. Eleanor drove my car home while I was forced to get a ride in the police cruiser with the chief. There were a million questions about Tana's murder that went unanswered, but Pammy was sticking to our protocol. The less we shared about our jobs while off the clock, the better as far as she was concerned.

After I relentlessly tried to get her to open up about the investigation, Pammy stopped the patrol car at the bottom of my driveway, turned, then roared in my face. "Muffcat, leave the goddamn investigation up to law enforcement! Yes, we sometimes use professionally trained profilers, but there is not a fucking thing my detectives could make from your goddamn dreams! Fucking Aye! Enough with the incessant questioning."

I stared out the window, as she went on. "I do find it bizarre you had a premonition; however, there is no way a kid did this. The mutilation was way beyond anything we have ever seen before. Now straighten up. Gavin's Jeep is here. Don't forget to grab your keys from Eleanor and don't act a fool in front of your son. If I find out you are snooping into the investigation, you can forget about talking to me. You have no idea the pressure I am under. Now get."

I made it over to Eleanor just before falling face-first into the gravel. Eleanor had mercy on me and helped me into my cabin, but Pammy practically cattle prodded Eleanor back out to her waiting cruiser. Police lights and sirens were blaring down the street, away from my abode, before I could attempt to fully plop my drunk and tired ass onto my couch.

Chapter V

Gavin was still up, watching *Iron Chef.* Though it certainly wasn't the first time my grown son has seen me after a vodka-induced binger, I was duly mortified when my backside missed the couch altogether. Hoping to retain some dignity, I tried to make relatable conversation, but let's face it, I was sloshed. "You hear about Tana Harvat?"

Gavin was eating a protein bar and washing it down with a glass of milk. "Yep. It is all over the news, Mom. Y'all got her up at Simon's?" I slid myself into a seated position. "Yes. Sally and I prepped her today for a private viewing. What's the news saying about her homicide?"

Gavin got up to put his glass in the sink then rejoined me in the living room. "They're not saying much, with the exception of it being Parrottville's first homicide in over three years. They showed a clip of Pammy. She was quoted as saying something about random violence in a town with such a small population, few bars, and a rather quiet existence being relatively rare. It doesn't sound like they have any suspects. They set up a hotline for tips." Gavin made the gesture for drinking, bringing his cupped hand to his mouth and throwing his head back. "You're wasted, Mom."

I ran my hand through my hair and took a pathetic stab at lying. My straight-shooting son plopped down beside me. "Cut the bullshit, Mom. What was it? A seven martini night?" I didn't answer. "Henry told me his mother hit the bar scene pretty hard after her second marriage failed, but after she got the job in HR, she actually slowed down with the partying." *Point taken.* Gavin went on, "the ten o'clock news focused on the fact that she'd sent a text to a friend canceling their dinner plans. They never mentioned her work at the Tyson plant, so I suspect they have cleared the majority of her co-workers. We all know she hung out at those seedy singles bars across the Kentucky border in-between her marriages. CID has a cyber team weeding through her emails and social media activity. From the sound of it, the authorities must think she got mixed up with some online predator or a crazy trucker that was passing through town."

I finally collected enough spit to speak. "Her standards had lowered in the last decade ... I have a feeling on this one Gav. Pretty sure Tana knew her killer. And I have a sense her murder is somehow tied to Shelley's."

32

My boy gave me a peck on the cheek. You're really pulling that psychic shit out again, Mother? C'mon, stick to what makes money. Camille has called over a dozen times. Wanted to know why you weren't answering your cell phone. I said you were stuck up at Simon's. She's pushing the buses up by fifteen minutes for Jimmy Kelley's Friday night for the rehearsal dinner. Needs the bar open at 4:00 instead of 4:30. Said it was open tab, and will settle with you Saturday. Okay, that's all I've got. Now go get some sleep, Mom."

My slumber was peaceful and sound until 4:27 a.m. the next morning. Then the phone rang. It was not the ME, but there was another body for Simon's to pick up. I had hoped that my Friday would be somewhat quiet and that there would not be as much going on up at the funeral home. The Three Waters had a big wedding at the mansion to set up, and I was not even supposed to be on call. I was still trying to make sense of what the man on the other end of the line was telling me. Trying to avoid the unavoidable, I started to realize this was no ordinary call. Another homicide had occurred. That's all my hungover brain could process. My over- indulgence had left my mind in a fog.

Keith Petigro started over with the details about his sister's homicide. The particulars were heartbreaking. He explained how she, Leighanna, my old high school friend, had turned into quite the recluse over the last decade. He said that her mailman, an old classmate of Keith's, phoned him about a foul odor coming from Leighanna's home. Since Keith lives in L.A., he called their mother. But Liza Petigro refused to check in on her estranged daughter, leaving Keith with no choice but to call the cops. It was over three hours before the police returned his call and gave him the horrifying news.

Keith went on to divulge how the authorities suspected his sister's body had probably been lying on her bathroom floor for seven to ten days before the cops made the gruesome discovery. He was catching the first non-stop from L.A. to Nashville; he'd head to the ME's office first, he explained, in order to identify the body. I had known for years that Liza Petigro had disowned Leighanna, but you'd expect a mother that lives less than two miles away to assist in her slain daughter's identification. Oh boy. I knew better than to start prying into complicated family matters (Lord knows I have enough of my own problems to contend with), so I let it go. After offering my condolences, I provided Keith with a few time options for Leighanna's arrangement meeting. He said he'd shoot for 3:00 p.m. then abruptly ended our call.

I called Dr. Larry Biggs' office only to discover he was still at the crime scene. The lab tech had no idea as to the release time on the body. After downing four 200-milligram tablets of ibuprofen and two eight-ounce glasses of water (man, was I in for some stomach upset), I swore off the vodka. It was my normal binger routine. Soon, nausea would set in. The "never again" phase came when I vomited in the kitchen sink. The "hair on the dog" step was next; I knew full well that by the time five o'clock rolled around, the "just one more to calm my nerves" epiphany would come.

After a Liquid Prozac (low sodium V-8 juice with two jiggers of off-brand vodka topped off with copious amounts of Tabasco sauce and lemon juice), I showered, collected the paper, fed the bird dogs, and got dressed. It was still too early to pick up our prep cook, Aunt Maude, but given the fact that my unorthodox day off had just evaporated, she was going to have to hold down the fort at the B&B while the wedding party checked in.

Aunt Maude hesitantly agreed to an early pick up, even though she wasn't happy with the last minute request to go over the wedding's banquet event orders at such an early hour. Gavin and Dylan were not up by the time I was ready to leave, so I left a note for them to call when they woke and locked the door behind me. Leighanna's murder was only mentioned once on the radio during my early morning commute, but I knew the shit would hit the fan as soon as Parrottville woke up to the rumors of another homicide. I turned the news off and tried to concentrate on the wedding's to-do list. That's when the voice started to taunt me, "Hiss, boo, hey you!" It was the very same male voice that had been haunting me for weeks. In the shower, in the autopsy room, when tossing and turning in my bed, sneaking in a late-night snack. Every so often, the most beautiful and poetic words would manifest. His innermost personal feelings of longing and yearning were brilliantly woven into thought-provoking prose, masterfully interlaced with assonance and enlightenment. Other times, though, his words were volatile, enraged rants of impulsive fury that only a tortured conscience could project. Hateful tirades of refutation combated and provoked his hallowing pleas for pity, solace, and peace for his tortuous soul.

The combination of the onslaught of his words and driving through a not-so-safe part of town left me shaken. While I pulled into Aunt Maude's driveway, the voice raged in my head. These were not authentic, well-articulated passages. Damn if he wasn't singing an INXS song in my head. *Here come the world, with the look in its eye. Future uncertain but certainly slight. Look at the faces. Listen to the bells. It's hard to believe we need a place called hell. Devil inside, Devil inside, every single one of us, the Devil inside...*

I knew the lyrics well, but the random string of sentences that came next made absolutely no sense at all. I could hear a young man talking to his pet, a dog named Claw. At first, the one-sided conversation was typical first crush mushy chitchat. His voice was a good two octaves higher than the last unprovoked tirade that crescendoed during my morning shower. This time, the singing was accompanied by a phantasmagoria; a bizarre exhibition of optical effects projected into the landscape. It seemed so freaking real.

I remained motionless as a black Doberman pinscher emerged in the yard. It did not slink out from behind a tree or bush. No, it simply appeared out of the low-lying fog that settled on top of the dewy mix of rye and fescue covering Aunt Maude's tiny yard. The vapors swirled and danced over the top of the wet grass before it began to take on shape. The hellhound was sniffing around a newly formed tree stump, barking like mad; it encircled a clump of dead leaves that had not been there only seconds before. Meanwhile, the words that raged in my head were sappy, heartfelt professions of emotion: complicated, confused, powerful sentiments that unfolded like some glorious sonnet.

Suddenly, a young man approached the dog, the same boy from my dreams. His mouth, startlingly, moved to the verses in my head. Then, two more apparitions appeared. First, a young woman materialized from the clump of dead leaves, her slender silhouette still covered in moss and decay. She stood behind the boy, peering down over his shoulder at something I couldn't make out. And then another female presence appeared, this one much older. Her apparel instantly told me she was from another era. She was concealed in lusterless, dull bombazine fabric; I was able to see a widow's cap atop her tightly corseted silhouette. Her skirt tilted to reveal the petticoat's ruffles matched that of her parasol.

The younger female, now weeping, was scantily clad in a sheer, silver top that barely covered her muddy, milk-toned thighs. A studded, leather belt was double-wrapped around her tiny waist, her over-processed blond hair flowing past the hemline of her blouse.

The boy was kneeling, grasping at a black mass that was sticking up from the thick grass, unaware of his company. Just then, Aunt Maude's neighbor's garage door lifted up. The stump, the intimidating dog, the women, and the boy vanished into the harsh light wafting from the building. I looked over to Aunt Maude's front porch steps. She was nowhere to be seen as a full-fledged, certifiable panic attack started to overwhelm me, making it difficult to breath.

Maudine Abigail Edgefield is known to everyone in our community as Aunt Maude. She's now well into her sixties and still, without question, the hardest worker in my house of nuts. Even given that she no longer drives.

Aunt Maude's employment by the Mansker family all started when the stubborn-headed, fifteen-year-old stepped off a train from Tupelo, Mississippi, toting a newborn on her hip. Aunt Maude has a slim, well-built frame that supports the enormous breasts she conceals under her modest uniform. Her lean legs are always covered with off-white support pantyhose, which are accompanied by a crisp white apron over her black, cotton A-line dress.

I don't remember a time before Aunt Maude's once mocha-hued skin was overtaken by Vitiligo patches. Nanny once told me that before the depigmentation began to spread on the right side of her face, Aunt Maude was one of the most striking women in the entire community. With her crystal clear indigo eyes, humorous wit, not to mention her penchant for gambling, Aunt Maude can still excite and turn the menfolk's head.

But, behind her gregarious personality and folksy charm, Aunt Maude harbors a terrible secret, one that only another alcoholic can understand. Aunt Maude is a slave to her personal demons; she will never stop drinking. It is a well-known fact that Aunt Maude will imbibe almost anything. She has drunk stale beer left over from our catered events, half-empty glasses of wine, mouthwash even, as she strolls around acting like she is cleaning up during our functions. One day, somebody will find her pickled on the floor. There will be no need for embalming her. I will just throw her in her casket then some poor archeologist will find her 1,000 years from now in mint condition smelling of "Cool Vanilla" Listerine.

Regardless of her minor character flaw, Aunt Maude is the best. One of my closest and most beloved companions, and truth be told, the most gifted cook in the entire community. She didn't used to start drinking until about three in the afternoon, but the morning Nanny found her coffee cup full of a first vintage bottle of Duckhorn Merlot, and she acted like she was blowing on it to convince us of the "coffee's" temperature, we knew she had a serious problem. From that day forward, I became her personal chauffeur in return for a few extra shifts on the weekends to cover our dwindling bar revenues.

My eyes darted from Aunt Maude's porch to her neighbor's garage as my mind continued to race, and my blood pressure increased exponentially. Then I spotted the outline of her uniform traipsing down the steps and leading into Jerry's shop. The light behind her silhouette made Aunt Maude look like a bag lady perpetuating a robbery, but I knew what it really meant. I always figured Jerry had fathered at least one of her three children, but Maude never revealed the names of her sperm donors; she just likes to talk about their "hunchin" as she calls it.

I rolled down the window and asked Aunt Maude to quicken her pace, before breathing out a sigh of relief. While hurling profanities at my SUV, Maude attempted to coax her mass of wire-like salt and pepper hair into a bun. She plopped down onto my passenger seat. I was looking forward to one of her usual wild accounts of a sleepless night full of sexual gratification. That humorous distraction never came. Aunt Maude's conversation was as sober as a nun in the middle of Mass, and she sure was pissed as hell at me.

Aunt Maude was seriously scared out of her wits. Jerry had her convinced that there was a madman on the loose in Parrottville. As she continued to fidget with her bun, Maude took nary a breath between details until we reached the back door of the tearoom. Jerry had shared some of the particulars about Tana's postmortem condition that had not been released to the general public. She knew too much about the crime scene: the Charles Manson quotes, the baseball bat, the postmortem mutilation.

It was no surprise there were leaks. Parrottville does not have the most proficient police force in the world (I know, you're stunned), but this was a new low, even by Mayberry standards. One of our old reliable officers was at it again, and my money was on Melvin McNabb.

I was afraid to tell Aunt Maude another body had been discovered as we entered the back door to the tearoom but had to let the cat out of the bag as soon as she turned on the kitchen radio. She attempted to settle into her morning routine but was really preoccupied with the details about the initials on Tana's pubic area and buttocks. She tried to convince me that I needed to go to the police about my premonitions, not even knowing what had transpired the night beforehand. Once Maude persuaded me a shot of Jack Daniels would calm her nerves, I unlocked the liquor cabinet and poured her a stiff highball of vodka and orange juice instead. Then I started to share my most recent paranormal manifestations with my one-time childhood nanny. Unlike the rest of my family, Maude has always believed in my ability to see dead people.

We were still living in the cabin on the grounds of The Three Waters when my first paranormal encounter took place. Momma was busy taking care of Lenore. My brother and I were instructed to walk over to the B&B for lunch, which really meant that Aunt Maude would be babysitting us until Daddy returned home from work. When we made it across the yard to the kitchen, Aunt Maude set me up on the counter in order to let me watch her roll out her famous angel biscuits: tiny little puffs of sweet dough that are wondrously riddled with lard. On this particular day, as Aunt Maude splashed flour down on her work surface, Phoebe, the eldest waitress in charge of the tearoom, collapsed in the middle of the ten dollar "All You Can Eat Catfish Friday Buffet." She never made a sound while setting down her tray filled with hushpuppies before clutching her chest. Phoebe hit the ground with such force that her dentures spat across the brick floor, landing next to a mouse trap underneath the baseboard of the cabinets. While Maude rushed to find Tac, I was left sitting alone on the counter. Just before Tac returned from the dining room with Doctor Horowitz and my daddy, a translucent woman approached me. I remember being startled at first because Nelley simply appeared out of thin air. I never will forget the dress she was wearing. It now can be described as a lilac-colored, tamboured muslin Victorian dress, with a band of tone on tone flowers embroidered at the hemline, but back then, it was good old purple.

Nelley reassured me there was nothing to be afraid of as she floated up to the counter. Her voice was warm with a bright, full timbre; Nelley almost sounded as if she were singing when she spoke. She introduced herself as Nelley Needlemire then extended her hands with her palms up. She asked if I liked to play Pattycake. I remember being enthralled by the fact that my hands went straight through hers, never making the clapping noise like when Aunt Maude and I played the game to pass the time. Just before the kitchen door flung open, Nelley disappeared before my bewildered eyes. I attempted to explain to the crowd that had gathered around, but everyone was focused on the doctor as he made chest compressions and blew into Phoebe's gums.

I recall feeling so sorry for Phoebe after the ambulance departed. Nobody ever retrieved her teeth. Daddy eventually picked me up off the counter; it was all he could do to make excuses to the patrons while I recounted playing Pattycake with a purple ghost. After lighting into Aunt

Maude for filling my head with such nonsense, Daddy used those words that have followed me around like a stray cat for most of my life. He said, "Muffy Catherine, you have a vivid imagination, child." Vivid imagination (ugh) is the way my parents explained away the paranormal for years. I cannot even count the number of times Mother sent me to bed hungry over my sworn confession that my imaginary friends were real. It took some time to learn whom I could trust when it came to my gift. It wasn't until after my experience on 9-11 that Aunt Maude divulged her true reasoning for believing in me all those year. On her death bed, Phoebe Jemima Wessynton, corroborated my story.

Aunt Maude still gets goose bumps talking about how our descriptions of Nelley Needlemire were practically identical. Even though my narrative was from the perspective of a three-year-old, we both remembered the purple dress and Nelley's blond hair, which was pulled back tightly in a bun, with a mother-of-pearl hair comb shaped like a butterfly.

After Aunt Maude downed her screwdriver, we went over the BEO's, ran down the employee schedule, and then reviewed a few changes to the seating arrangement for an upcoming wedding. I agreed to confirm all of the deliveries from the florist and the party supply rental company, but Maude was adamant that we needed to call in some additional part-timers for the wedding set up. I signed off then OK'd the additional staff before departing for Simon's.

I wheeled into Simon's Family Funeral Home to a hell of a commotion. Normally, all the staff takes the back entrance and parks in the rear of the funeral home. But today, half of Parrottville's goon squad was loitering out there, waiting on the body of Leighanna Petigro to arrive. Chief Pammy, and Betty, who never gets to the office this early, were standing outside. Pammy was looking down at her black police boots as I approached the three concrete steps leading up to the covered front porch.

Betty's mouth was moving a mile a minute, but it was impossible to make out what she was saying. Pammy started our conversation just a few seconds before reaching the first step. "I did not want anyone to call you about Leighanna Petrigo without a warning. She is in worse condition than Tana." Pammy's normally wicked sense of humor, for an underappreciated Chief of Police in a small town of homophobes and rednecks, was all business. "Thanks, Pammy. I knew you would call me as soon as the crime scene was secure and you got a chance to catch your breath. I know you've probably been at the scene all night. What the hell is going on around here?" Just as I reached the top step, my heel got stuck. Tumbling backwards towards the rosebushes, Betty caught me by the elbow.

For a sixty-two-year-old woman, Betty Simon packs a serious punch. She has the strength of three grown men and looks like a linebacker in drag. She's well over six-feet tall, with short silver hair that is spikey up at the crown. The little leopard skin glasses she wears right on the tip of her nose were dangling from her silver necklace.

"Muffcat, sorry about the phones. Forgot to have Sal roll the calls over to my cell. We had three more bodies come in after 10:00 p.m. last night. What happened to you taking the day off?"

Pammy and Betty were both trying to steady me because my heel was still stuck in the crack of the top step. Just as I started to answer Betty, the police squad straight from hell rounded the corner with their disgusting fat-ass stomachs hanging over their belt buckles. "What are you boys staring at? Melvin, I saw your police car at Mitzi's massage parlor last night. What does Mitzi do? Lube you down with donut glaze and get the kink out of your fat neck?"

I just could not help myself; I didn't think of the ramifications for Pammy before opening my big mouth. Betty made a beeline for the door, locked it, and then shot me a bird in her attempt to show her disapproval of my endless jabs at our Parrottville's finest dork squad. But, c'mon people, for the love of Pete, we have the saddest clan of goobers for a town of nearly 10,000 people you've ever seen.

Betty had yet to unlock the door for the parade of blue. The chief lowered her voice as she walked me over to the edge of the porch. "Look, Muffcat, now is not the time for you to gloat. Just wanted to warn you about the condition of Leighanna's body. I know how much Tana's postmortem condition upset you. Also, we received some communication that led us to believe the killer might be in attendance at Tana's service today. TBI will have some plainclothes officers here as well as three detectives from my force. Melvin will fill you in. Got a debrief with my lead detective. Expect a media circus. Hey, and Muffcat, please lie low. None of your Long Island Medium bullshit. We are dealing with a psychopath, not some twelve-year-old in an INXS t-shirt."

Pammy pointed over towards her officers that were still waiting on Betty to open the door. Pammy whispered before scurrying away to her Crown Victoria, "No more jabs, especially at Melvin." Once the door to her white sedan was open, Pammy yelled back up to me, "need a decent meal, Muffy Catherine. Eight o'clock at your cabin, as long as all the paperwork gets done. Eleanor will drop off the hock at the big house for the turnip greens. Maude said she's fine with it. Try and have a pleasant day, Theresa Caputo. Don't go dying your hair and getting 12-inch fingernails just yet."

Hilarious. I had to walk around to the back to get into the building. Betty had locked me out again. The blue man group found the coffee pot and pound cake, but Brad Weasle did have the decency to wait to ram his fistful of carbs into his piehole after letting me in. Once settled, I cornered Betty. She already had a family waiting. "Betty, I am so sorry. With all the cars and commotion, I truly had no idea you had a family in here." Before I could finish my thought, Betty whispered, "Muffcat, why do you think I would be here this early in the morning without my eyebrows? Once they pick out a casket, we're gonna chat. You still have your old yearbooks?" Our chitchat was cut short by Melvin, who needed details on the Filson-Harvat arrangements. I went on to debrief the goon squad from hell about Tana's funeral and graveside details while Betty received the heart-wrenchingly miserable task of making funeral arrangements for a comatose five-year-old cancer patient.

It was only 7:10 a.m. by the time I'd made my way into the preparation room to embalm one of the stiffs that came in the night before. In hopes the monotony of counting bags of formaldehyde would squelch out the voices, I unenthusiastically opened the supply cabinet. Sally entered the room and tried to strike up a conversation. Even though I really like her, there is something strange about Sally but I cannot quite put my finger on it. A woman straight from Belize, in the middle of nowhere, with a license to practice mortuary services seemed peculiar to me. Sally never spoke of a spouse or a significant other, and confessed to not knowing a soul in the middle Tennessee area before deciding to uproot from paradise only to find a low-paying part-time position at Simon's. Without any family roots, Parrottville isn't the ideal destination for a woman to start over (especially seeing how she openly professes to abhor country music and prefers her Johnny Cakes to biscuits and gravy). Even more bizarre, my elderly grandfather hired Sally over a weekend. No one even knew we had a funeral director position open, much less could believe that Gran offered her a full benefits package for a thirty-hour work week. You do the math; something wasn't adding up.

Chapter VI

Thursday, July 19, 1984. 6:38 p.m. Highway I-65 near
Millersville, Tennessee.

As the spotless Oldsmobile purred down I-65, he played back the most miserable summer of his life. It was Steak and Ale night, the first time that season his father demanded he spiff up. He'd arrived over three weeks earlier, and this was the only meal that did not come from a can or McDonald's.

The mandatory visit had been dreadful. His calves were so white it made him uncomfortable to wear shorts. The baby was screeching in the back seat, again, but at least he had his Walkman back. "Synchronicity" blared from his headphones, but he was too busy trying to keep the flimsy plastic closed and obsessed with setting the numbers on his Walkman to enjoy the music. His mind wandered and raced, as usual, but he was talking to himself this time. It wasn't the others. The first year he'd come, Step-Monster claimed the Devil was in his DNA. Now with the testosterone coursing through his veins, there was no telling what would happen.

His favorite song, "Wrapped Around Your Finger" was playing as they sailed down the interstate. He'd been obsessed with The Police since Santa brought him the Walkman for Christmas. Music was the only thing that could calm him. It made the voices stop. The melodies and lyrics could soothe him in ways his mother's touch could not. She thought he was autistic; she was ready to give up. Dad didn't want him either. He was too much of a fuck-up.

He could feel callousness, cruelty, and spitefulness beginning to taking hold. His battle with good and evil was getting ready to explode. As he sang along, thoughts of his first crush began to unfold. *Devil and the deep blue sea behind me. Vanish in the air you'll never find me. I will turn your flesh to alabaster. Then you'll find your servant is your master.* She said he was too young, but then Shelia turned around and French kissed him. *Oh, you'll be wrapped around my finger. You'll be wrapped around my finger. You'll be wrapped around my finger.* He was supposedly grounded for sneaking out of the house, but Step-Monster would do anything to shuffle the malevolence away. She gave into his demands just to get him out of her hair, to get some relief.

Looking over to the window, he caught a glimpse of his reflection. Fortunately, he'd escaped wearing the stupid alligator shirt his mother packed for him for most of the summer, but he was now staring at himself in a pair of chinos and the Izod. *I like my camo pants the best. Ones from last year fit better, but Step-Monster threw them away when I fell in the creek. Stupid bitch. She said they were high waters anyway.* She had called father and told him he needed to change. He'd settled for dweeb wear but had her revenge planned before the car was in drive. So senseless, he thought. *Witch could have told me herself. I'll get her back. The stupid baby is all she cares about anyhow.*

He still did not understand why his parents had divorced, why his dad just up and moved forty-five minutes away to this stupid little town. This year was even worse than the last. His father was supposed to be free in the summertime when he took the job as a high school English teacher. Last year they hunted and fished almost every single day. But then he upped and took a part-time job with a heating and air company, leaving his son stuck in the house with his stupid half-sister and the dreaded Step-Monster for the better part of each day.

Today had been the worst.

That morning, Gremlin woke up screaming at 4:00 a.m. and Step-Monster didn't stir to prepare her bottle. He made the baby's bottle, too warm, on purpose. When Step-Monster finally appeared in the doorway, she went berserk. It all went downhill from there. The brat cried for over an hour before he HAD to shut her up again. It was only eight seconds. No big deal. He could hold his breath for 108. *She always just appears.* Then she called his father. Said it was her last straw; she wanted him tested. *What the hell would they test for? She's the stupid one.* Step-Monster set out the cheerios at 5:33 a.m., then bitched that he used too much of HER milk. When he skipped out the door, she loudly exhaled. He'd walked all the way to McDonalds before discovering he didn't have enough money for an Egg McMuffin. He settled on a small black coffee instead. It tasted like crap. There were WAY too many old people standing at the condiment station, so he walked over to EG's, looking to bum a smoke and something sweet instead. He never found the sugar. What he did find, however, changed his life. Forever.

*****

When Shelia got out of the eighteen-wheeler, she claimed to be a valley girl, but her makeup made her look more like a clown. She told him she was about his age, but looked every bit of twenty-one. Said she was on the run since the age of twelve, that a cheap motel was her latest home.

Man, that cheap hotel smelled filthy. *Stupid slut. Had to have some disgusting sex disease.* But she did let him watch. He had no idea people did such things.

6:22 a.m. and Stan was supposedly her last trick. He knocked on her door with his cock already in his hand. Sheila said the early birds pay more because they all have wives. He couldn't stop thinking about her slobber. Couldn't believe Stan let her tag along in his rig for the day. Forty dollars and she got a ride in the truck?

She said she would do him for only ten. That she'd be back by morning, after a quick trip up Interstate 65. He struggled to block her, to think about anything else to keep his pants from getting tight from his bulge, but the impulsive urges were getting harder for him to control.

As the Oldsmobile passed by the Highway 31 exit sign, his mind wandered, all his thoughts miserable. The hatred, loathing, animosity, bitterness, hostility, rancor, and resentment were suffocating. But now that Shelia made him hard as stone, there was an all new emotion scratching at the surface. It wasn't affection, devotedness, fondness, or passion. It wasn't longing either. The voices told him it was something greater than love. He had been hearing them since the days of *One Fish, Two Fish*. That cardinal virtue, the bright little beam of goodness that supposedly resides in all of us; those neurons never had a chance to fire. The waves of anger and pain building up inside him always blazed faster. It would only be a matter of time before evil would spring a shoot of the unscrupulous, giving rise to another monster. Mercy, not a spark of compassion, made it into his deck of cards.

He remembered pulling into the parking lot when the Devil commanded him to get Sissy out of her car seat. His torture was about ready to be unleashed on Gremlin. If he released the seat buckle just the right way, it would pinch her leg, and then Step-Monster would have to deal with the forty-five minutes of wailing. Just as he reached for it, his attention deficit kicked in, sparing the child the pain. He slipped his headphones down to hear the NPR news bulletin just before passing Gremlin to Step-Monster unscathed.

"At 3:59 p.m. yesterday, James Oliver Huberty entered a McDonald's in San Ysidro, on the outskirt of San Diego, California, and opened fire. He managed to get off 257 rounds of ammunition before he was fatally

shot by a SWAT team. On his person were a 9 mm Uzi semi-automatic, a Winchester pump-action 12-gauge shotgun, and a 9 mm Browning HP pistol; the massacre lasted 77 minutes. The victims were predominantly Mexican and Mexican-American, and ranged in age from 8 months to 74 years. The death toll has reached…"

His father cut the ignition before he could learn the final body count. He had to know the number. As Devil peered behind him, he knew it. No question, this kid was fucked. Three more weeks of trying to maintain any semblance of control was really gonna suck.

The fat hostess reeked of cigarettes. JJ inhaled her. She probably thought he was trying to smell her hair; that the kid seemed a little creepy. She complimented him on his green eyes as they made their way through the dimly lit dining room. His confidence surged recalling how Sheila told him that morning that his eyes looked like the caps on the waves down in the Gulf of Mexico. He scanned the tables for cash with a pep in his step. He had to collect that ten dollars before the night ended.

Before he could even unfold his napkin, Devil insisted that his obnoxious son fetch his wife a salad. He dared not let his feet step on the lines in the carpet as he made his way to the bustling salad bar. He had to almost hop and skip ahead in the pattern. His gate was awkward; people stared. *It's not my fault they made the pattern so damn big.* Step-Monster wanted a salad with cottage cheese and French dressing. The image in his head of watching her eat the slimy white ooze made him gag as he got in line. Only three plates left, but he couldn't take number three. It had to be an even number over his magic threshold of eight. He could let the others in front of him. Get Step-Monster's salad first. Another trip to the salad bar and he could maybe snag some tip money.

Five leaves of the lettuce were brown. He took his time collecting them. The stupid woman behind him was complaining that there was only one boiled egg left. He took it then acted as if he'd dropped it on the floor. He turned and smiled at her, his mouth full of yellow and white. The husband was not amused.

JJ had been labeled callous, unaware of others and rudely inconsiderate. Any bits of kindness were forever lost about the time he progressed to *Green Eggs and Ham.* Nobody knew what was really wrong. His IQ was more than average. He looked like a normal kid. His reading and writing were at a high school level, but he seemed to live inside his own head.

On his second trip from the salad bar, he noticed Monster had white wine and hoped it would distract her from realizing his plate was filled with croutons (twenty-eight). Taking the big steps had made him lose his balance en route back to the table. The fat hostess had laughed as the cubes of fried bread hit the floor. He had to count them out again. If he still had an even number, he would eat.

He found the perfect place to set down his plate. A tip sat waiting; four dollars, calling his name. *Take two, no one will notice. They'll just think the guy was a cheap bastard.* He shoved the wrinkled bills in his chinos as he counted out the croutons. An odd number; he'd go hungry. Back to the table empty handed. Devil shook his head and made him tell the truth. He kept his head down and the earphones on for the duration of the meal, devising his plan. He'd write Shelia a little poetry tonight, and take it to her at dawn. He would leave before Devil got up to go to work. He'd save his last few bites of steak for the Doberman, who would be his companion for the trek. He packed it up for the ride home in silence. He went straight to his room and stayed up for most of the night, writing in his notebook. His bulge grew harder than ever as he pried the codeine-laced cough syrup down the toddler's throat.

It was 4:58 a.m. by the time he packed his things. Gremlin didn't budge as he made his way to the garage. As he gathered his gun and hunting knife, he decided to take one last thing. A Polaroid camera. Sheila was going to love it; he could already see the expression on her face. After a quick pee, he brushed his teeth and collected his backpack. Shorts for the creek, one more hunting knife, a few pieces of meat for Claw, and his notebook full of poetry that was sure to seal the deal. The walk to the hotel was 2,398 steps. It would take fourteen minutes and twenty- eight seconds, but they'd take a shortcut this time. He'd have to cross through the neighbor's yard with the dog, but the gun could take care of their Yorkie if it gave him any crap. He thought his camo pants would impress her. She said she liked military men the best, and that Fort Campbell was her favorite place to ever work.

The leaves on the ground were crisp underneath his feet. He wished he'd brought a flashlight, even though the sun would be up soon. Unable to walk a straight line, he had to stop counting (temporarily), and instead recited his verses for Sheila. He decided to jump a toppled tree, but Claw took off ahead of him. He gave chase and was just a few feet from the decaying oak tree when an unpleasant odor pierced his nose. He bent down to check the clump of leaves as Claw starting bark madly. He looked back to the edge of the tree line for any lights flickering on. The lump was covered with dead leaves and branches, and a mass of something was rolled up in a black tarp. He pulled at the material before retrieving a stick. The horrid smell intensified as he poked at the plastic. He fiddled with the tape before taking out his knife and cutting at the fibers.

Sheila's eyes were open. It took ten minutes to get her body freed. Her mouth was still taped, and her makeup was almost perfect, but she smelled horrible. He tugged at the tape on her mouth to find smeared lipstick stuck to the metallic adhesive that was still halfway stuck to her lips. Her face was freezing, and she had marks on her neck. Her breath was rancid when he bent down to kiss her. He rocked her like a baby as he recited her poem, eight times. Then, he contemplated. He could always cover her back up, act like he never saw her.

The sun was beginning to pierce the treetops, and he needed to think fast. It wouldn't be long until the heat of the summer sun started to stifle in the wind and attract the other scavengers. So he wrapped the body back up and took a seat on the dead hickory tree. The voices started kicking in, instructing his next moves. "Lift her shirt just a little bit." Are they pink or brown?" Her nipples were so round. So perfect.

"Retrieve your knife, you stupid prick." He unrolled her body then made just a small cut to her left breast. Once he cut the left, he had to do the right. The first was deeper; more black goo squeezed out. As he evened them up, he started to get that feeling. There was a rock in his pants again.

"Just another peak, nobody will ever know. Look at her pussy, you fucking sissy." Her miniskirt had nothing under it. The hair was dark and shaved down there. It didn't match the bleached-out mess on her head. He cut one strand of her bangs and placed it on her pubic bone. "Touch her in-between the legs. Nobody will ever know." But he made the mistake of cumming on her breasts before snapping a Polaroid.

Chapter VII

Before noon hit, my day off was all but shot. The morning had turned into a discombobulated episode straight out of *Murder She Wrote*, scrambled with what can only be described as a madcap version of *CSI, Bumfuck Egypt*. While old classmates and church members congregated in the receiving line for the funeral of Tana Jade Filson-Harvat, strange dicks wearing cheap suits attempted to blend in. Outlandish rumors swirled amongst the casserole dishes and vegetable trays that concerned the recent homicide before the field reporters even had a chance to hunt down every toothless person in the crowd to interview. A fist fight broke out at the registry stand when Merle Mooneyhan broke the line, forcing the Fire Marshal to show up for the first time in over twenty years.

While Betty played the role of Jessica Fletcher, the rest of us had to practically form an assembly line in order to get the body count under control. On top of the three cadavers already in the supine anatomical position, Sally was on her way to retrieving two car crash fatalities from Skyline Medical Center. Then Hollis was dispatched to Vanderbilt Children's Hospital for the five-year-old cancer patient whose grief-stricken parents had made their kindergartener's pre-arrangements just hours beforehand. God-awful.

By the time they'd returned with the bodies, our parking lot was covered with media vans accompanied by talking heads that pounced on every local city councilman who was ready for a close-up. Betty and Officer McNabb were in deep conversation as the first of the mourners made their way to greet Tana's family. Melvin was not assigned to either of the homicide investigations, but you'd never know it from his boasting about crime scene details. I caught the tail end of his and Betty's conversation while delivering a bottle of water to Graham Harvat. Something about the HVAC units at both crime scenes being set at 90 degrees, and a manifesto that had turned up at the precinct. And Officer Melvin McNabb's pretty substantial suspect list. Hmmm. Food for thought.

Before the first mourner made it through the receiving line, hysteria ensued. The local senior citizens center decided to make a field trip out of the funeral. An elderly man, undoubtedly suffering from dementia, questioned a red-faced detective about his ear piece as soon as he exited the bus. I should have intervened, but was pleading with the Fire Marshall, who'd immobilized an angry mob of relatives, aggressively attempting to get back into the building.

As soon as the service got underway, there was no way to refrain from eavesdropping on the conversations taking place in the hallway. You know that everybody knew the killer or the motive, of course. *It has to be that man she dated from over in Selner County, Scott Byers. ... Well, I bet cha anything, it's that's son-of-a-bitch bouncer she met when she was desperate, Dallas Flippo. ... Earl always did say she could blow through ten grand faster than Charlie Sheen could an eight ball. ... When she gained all that weight, and she was seeing that guy, Billy. You seen her hair lately? June, over at Aunt B's, said that her last boyfriend was a mechanic. It has to be him. ... Everybody on Facebook knows it's this creepy guy from her work. ... I heard she dun gone and got her some rejuvenation and that pervert Doctor Horowitz. ... Activated these special chemicals. That man she plays Bingo with on Friday nights, Eddie Corley, has to be the killer. ... That wig salesman from over in West Moreland. ... Doris said she saw Tana and a man, 'bout a week ago in Walmart. ... I can't believe Graham went through with it. ... Always said she couldn't fry chicken like his momma.*

I just wanted to make it back to the prep room in order to dress Derek Kimbro, but even the flower delivery boy, sporting a pierced eyebrow, had a hunch as to the ID of the killer. Twenty minutes into the service, Sally made her way into the embalming room and relayed that the parlor was shoulder-to-shoulder. I exited to retrieve a Diet Coke, hopeful the coast would be clear. Scratch that; the place was still a zoo. And the animals were running wild. It was a hotbed of blather and hearsay, a small town in sheer fear of the possibility there was a killer amongst us, and maybe even within the crowd.

I noticed Sally and Hollis conversing with Gran, who forced his door closed after spotting me. I went back to the prep room and retrieved my mortician jacket. Hollis was quietly working on the five-year-old while I started on a seventy-eight-year-old ex-felon with peripheral artery disease. There were forty minutes of serenity before the service began to wrap up. Once the final hymn got underway, it was time to assist Betty with lining up the motorcade. A slew of relatives claimed they needed to get into position behind the hearse. As if they were reaching for an unclaimed winning lotto ticket, my stash of funeral flags were yanked out of my hands like Aunt Maude's hoecakes, and believe me, if you have never had her tiny fried mounds of cornmeal drenched in butter, let me tell you, they fly off our buffet line like condoms at a whorehouse. Sally was still prying information from the funeral-goers, in true Angela Lansbury fashion, as the last of the mourners exited the building. Every camera was on the hearse as it pulled out onto Main Street heading to the cemetery. After the caravan had departed, I returned to the embalming room eagerly anticipating some well-deserved tranquility. After getting new latex gloves snapped over my sleeves, my fingers moving up and down to get them comfortably fitted, the morose atmosphere was sure to compose me. It had been an uncanny day.

By 1:00 p.m., we still did not have a release time from the ME on Leighanna Petigro's body. Sally and Hollis were in the middle of a facial reconstruction procedure as I finished up my third stiff. We'd embalmed seven, an all-time, single-day record according to Gran, who was supervising my suturing techniques. The phone rang while I was in the middle of washing up my utensils. Gran announced Keith's plane was late getting into BNA. Which meant Betty could take the Petigro arrangement meeting now scheduled for 4:00 p.m. I know you're thinking this sounds insensitive, but when a funeral director has a suspicion about the willingness for a family to pay for a memorial service, we try and have them meet with someone they don't know personally. Not that he really left a real impression, but Keith Petigro was a few years older than me in high school. He moved away after his third attempt at starting a record label failed in the Music City. This would spare me the awkwardness of discussing his finances and being forced to hear about the West Coast rock-a-billy revolution he so desperately wanted to revive.

Gran headed out of the prep room for his afternoon nap in his chair. Mr. Kimbro was dressed. His face and hands touched up, the ex-felon looked peaceful in his casket. No one would ever be able to make out the racial slurs spewed across his knuckles under the full bottle of Avon spiced almond liquid foundation, but I strategically covered his hands with his black leather jacket sleeves anyhow. Sally and I wheeled the casket into the Rocky Top parlor. We rolled Mr. Kimbro's casket in-between two Harley Davidson Softail Rockers. Sally placed the half-spray of uncommon objects at the bottom end of the casket as I backed up to scrutinize the scene. The bottom half of the casket was adorned with twenty years' worth of panties he'd collected during his annual pilgrimage to Daytona's Biketoberfest. A picture of a very heavyset female riding bareback rested on the pillow beside his head. Sally uttered, "ebre pat gat e kibber." To that I added, "Yes Sally, you are right. Every pot does have a cover. But for the love of Jesus, could the widow not have found a better photograph?"

I stepped into my office to call the B&B. According to Tac, everything was on schedule with the food for the wedding. The duck breasts were being marinated for the groom's surf and turf; the redneck culinary duo was to include fried catfish as well. Go figure. Hey, what can I say, it's the South. The groom's culinary request was for the Sigma Chi's "covert" buffet going in the poker room. No bleeding armadillo cake here. $500.00 in wadded up twenties that smell like tequila still pays the bill. Next, I called the florist and the party rental store before phoning Eleanor. She had already dropped the ham hock off to Aunt Maude before heading downtown to film a segment for her new culinary talk show segment entitled "Gourmet Swine and Wine." This led me to assume Chief was expecting to get off at a decent hour.

I headed back to the prep room to start on my fourth stiff. Making my way to the storage closet for a new set of drainage tubes, the realization hit me that there was a huge possibility I might actually recognize the killer if I collected my old high school relics from Phillips Drive. My tormentor was singing that damn INXS song in my head again. *Here come the world, with the look in its eye. Future uncertain but certainly slight. Look at the faces. Listen to the bells. It's hard to believe we need a place called hell. Devil inside, Devil inside, every single one of us, the Devil inside.*

Chapter VIII

Even though I'd harbored no desire to mingle amongst my old classmates during the funeral, my curiosity was heightened by all the rumors about the murderer's manifesto. It was supposedly written in a 1988 Parrottville H.S. yearbook, but there was no telling if there was any truth to all the gossip. Fingers were pointing at every mechanic, butcher, and ex-boyfriend still living within a two hundred mile radius of our hometown. I, however, had a different take on the recent homicides.

I admit that my own surreal experience that morning left me more than a little convinced that the voice was somehow connected to Tana's killer. While injecting Sissy Tomlinson's carotid arteries with formaldehyde, and breaking up blood clots in Derek Kimbro's calves, I had another peculiar paranormal happening. Four or maybe five voices came to me all at once. Much like sitting in a loud, heavily crowded bar, it was hard to separate their words due to the white noise in the background, but these conversations were stuck in some sort of unremitting loop.

One of the familiar voices was that of the patriarch of the Tinnin family: Samuel Theodore. Sam-Tee, as we all know him, is the owner of the local Hee-Haw firework stand, a tourist destination that sells all sorts of humorous t-shirts as well as explosives from a ram-shackled old storefront that sits right off of I-65. Just as I reached for a 3/8" drainage tube, Sam-Tee came to me again. His booming voice was accompanied by an unmistakable nose whistle. "Pszzzzzz ... Lil' som' bitch is a twisted fuck. Run that demented bastard outta here." Then, what sounded like maybe a female jogger, could be half-marathon material, started in. Her breath was labored as she said, "Camo pants. Black t-shirt. (Pause) That's right, slit it from ear to ear. His dog chased me. Yes, sir. That is correct. There is something wrong with the kid." She kept calling her conversation partner "Sir." I picked up on a two-way radio or walkie-talkie with another voice calling for backup. The next was a mother; whose mother, I can't say. She had to be close to a body of water. Maybe at a pool or lake, because there was splashing in the background. She was discussing the same boy with one of our city's parks and recreations managers. "The sicko was pushing his penis into my daughter's back."

Trying to focus, I walked back over to my slab and started massaging the car crash victim's mouth into a peaceful line. If you don't get a cadaver's facial features in the correct positioning, the formaldehyde stiffens the tissue, making it impossible to manipulate the mouth into a natural stance. Sally kept eyeing me as I tried out a few different angles with the young female's lips. I must have been talking out loud to myself. The same voice that was singing the INXS song minutes beforehand was now jabbering over my shoulder. Sally's eyes wandered in my direction again. The young male was rambling to his dog again. Then the blare of gunfire caused me to curse. There was a brief pause for reloading before six more shots rang out. After the rapid shots, a different, but much more sinister voice roared. The tone and pitch were the same as the singer's, but this one was angry, much deeper. The spew of obscenities was belittling, calling out all sorts of wicked names, such as "pussy and wimp."

After the ominous voice ceased, more gunfire. Again, the INXS voice, then the sinister one. Over and over, in a maddening circle, the same words and phrases. The magazine chamber held fourteen rounds, which took me the better part of ten minutes to figure out. I felt terrifyingly short of breath. Sally edged her way up to my prep table. "Ghosts, di badda yo, Muffcat?" I didn't respond immediately. "Yo ansa, no?"

"When you're standing over an assembly line of dead people with what sounds like a firing squad going off in your head, Sal, it might seem like it, but no." I composed myself before ripping off my gloves. As I walked over to my cubbyhole to remove my mortician's jacket, Sally followed. I went ahead and answered her question, "Not ghosts, voices. They have been haunting me for years." Sally followed me out of the preparation room. Scavenging the refrigerator for a Diet Coke, she inquired, "weh taim yu gat?" I looked down to my wrist watch. "It's almost 1:30, Sal. Jesus Christ! I really need to get to the mansion." She brushed past me, unwrapping a paper towel to remove a dense pastry. The thud the johnny cake made hitting the counter gave the impression the meat pie had to weigh five pounds.

"No take lord's nayhn en vein, Muffcat. We se Cheese n' Rice en Belize." Sally placed the pastry on a paper plate before popping it in the microwave, and then retrieved her coconut milk from the refrigerator, offering me a cup of tea and half of her "janny kake." I declined, turning my purse inside out looking for change for the vending machine. Sally was watching my every move. "Blood tika dan wata but wata tase betta." I pressed the button for a Diet Coke with no idea as to what Sally was trying to tell me. In no mood to listen to yet another one of her proverbs, my interest was piqued when she pulled out a picture from the pocket of her mortician's jacket. She slid the photograph across the table towards me. It was an old photo of Sally, wearing a colorful dress. A young boy of no more than five or six was clinging to her leg. Next to them, an old man with long dreadlocks was leaning on a wooden stick.

"Who are the people with you in this picture, Sal?" As she doused her johnny cake with Marie Sharp's Beware Comatose Hot Sauce, she explained that the boy was her son and the old man her uncle. I reluctantly took a seat. Sally split her food down the middle and handed me half. She went on to tell me that her uncle was her village's most honorable Shaman, who practiced a form of magic she called "Obeah." She likened Obeah to the voodoo practiced down in New Orleans. A cross between a witch doctor and medicine man, her uncle was renowned for his ability to see into the future. Sally son's name was Raphel. He was the product of a brutal rape that she did not want to expand upon as she took a delicate nibble of her meat pie. She stayed on point. Seconds after that photograph was snapped, Raphel looked up to her with tears in his eyes. "Eena belli of tiga, gaut big-mout, Mumma." Not wanting Raphel exposed to the witchcraft of the Obeah, Sally claimed she never mentioned her son's prophecy to anyone, including her uncle. But throughout Raphel's childhood, Sally avowed that her son showed the ability to "noh tings" before they happened.

Sally couldn't look at me while recounting the details of Raphel's death. Through teary eyes, she described his seventeenth birthday. She had wanted to take him for his favorite meal of conch fritters, but her boy had already planned a scuba diving excursion with some friends. When he was killed by a rogue blacktip tiger shark while diving in the reef atolls off the coast of the Northern Cayes, Sally admitted she was riddled with guilt. It was gut-wrenching listening to the particulars of how his crushing loss drove her to question her faith. She spent years blaming herself for not seeking the spiritual guidance of her uncle, cursing God; she found her only solace at the bottom of a bottle.

It was easier than I expected, getting Sally to open up about the dreams and visions after she'd revealed her soul to me. She was transfixed by my reporting of the morning's play-by-play but confessed she was worried about me too. Claiming the voices were a bad omen, she begged me not to ignore my paranormal encounters and to seek either some psychological or spiritual counseling. By the time all of my ghosts were laid out on the table, and I had revealed my distaste for the field of psychology, Sally tried to encourage me to contact a religious studies professor she knew who had experience with exorcisms. I declined the offer of Sally's introduction, snatching my Nordstrom's jacket from the back of the chair. But she was right. There had to be some good explanation for my paranormal goings-on. With the death of yet another classmate so closely following my most recent hauntings, it was time for me to figure out, for myself, what the voices were trying to tell me, once and for all.

With all the talk about the manifesto being written in a PHS yearbook, the brisk walk to my brother's seemed like a reasonable place to start my exploration. Tommy had bought our old homestead from my mother a couple of years after Daddy died. Hoping the yearbooks would somehow help me identify the voices, I called Tommy's house to announce my otherwise unexpected visit. Anticipating that my sister-in-law, Keelie, would answer the phone, I was surprised when a thick, Hispanic accent shouted, "Mansker residence." The woman asked me my name a few times, in broken English, then hung up on me. I called Tommy at his law office. He told me that they'd hired a new cleaning service and that he would handle Amelia. Then, Amelia called me back, this time with a decidedly more enthusiastic tone. "Tommy say Muffcat OK." I had to laugh at this which felt good. It was the first exhale-worthy moment of the day.

When I arrived, an older, heavyset Hispanic woman, her hair pulled tightly back in a ponytail, answered the door. "Hablo español?" Within seconds of stepping into the foyer, Amelia had her fingers pressed to her lips as if she were harboring a terrible secret. I liked the fact that she had the sense to call my brother to verify my association before arriving, but man oh man did she ever overestimate my bilingual capabilities. I found myself furiously shaking my head and mimicking her facial expressions without a damn clue as to what Amelia was saying. Then, as if a switch had suddenly been flipped, she took on a look of panic. She kept pointing to the second floor with her as eyes big as Aunt Maude's pancakes. "Creo htere podría ser un fantasma en el ático." I caught something about a ghost in the attic. Shaking my head as Amelia rambled on, I stepped further into the hallway.

While I removed my coat, another cleaning attendant caught my attention. This rather masculine-looking woman seemed as if in her own little world. Amelia, pointing out at her colleague, made the universal symbol for crazy. She repeated "loco" with her pointer finger whirling around her temple a few times. The housekeeper had been looking up but glanced down to her cell phone as I made my way to the stairwell.

Amelia conversed about the ghost form at the bottom of the stairwell during my entire ascension. Just as I pulled on the attic's string, the vacuum cleaner went silent. The smell of tobacco hit me before making it past the third rung. Her eyes were on me; I could feel them. Something was not right. A flash of a praying woman underneath a portrait of the Devil made me bang my head on the ceiling. The blow threw me off-balance as the housekeeper's voice addressed me. My head was above the ceiling, but the housekeeper was persistent. "Hey, hey you! Hold on there for a minute." She spoke in a tone that was just above a whisper, yet the huskiness in her voice revealed she'd smoked most her life.

Once down from the ladder, the woman looked over her shoulder to see if she'd been followed by Amelia. "Hey, you Tommy's sister, right?" I shook my head up and down, cautiously, as she continued. "Just move down here from Bowling Green with my boyfriend 'bout a month ago. Overheard your brother last week say that you manage that B&B over by the campground. If you ever need someone to pick up any cleaning shifts, we have reliable transportation." The housekeeper handed me a folded piece of paper, then tried to smile while extending her left hand.

Her mannerisms were off-kilter. Speaking rapidly, she told me her name was Missy as we shook hands. She shoved her dirty hand into her pocket and then requested I not mention anything to her cleaning partner. I muttered "OK" then looked down and unfolded the paper. Realizing the name she'd given me did not match what she'd written, something told me not to mention my observation.

As Missy fidgeted with her greasy hair, another flash overcame my vision. As a wooden structure that we once used as our high school drinking cabin came into focus, a blindfolded woman was being led through the woods by two dark figures. Missy leaned up against the wall. One foot crossed over the other, she sized me up. I thanked her before looking up from the piece of paper. Missy's dark brown eyes jerked when meeting mine. "You, OK there." I nodded yes as yet another flash began to paralyze me. I had to reach for the walk to keep myself balanced. I saw the woman before me lying dead on a wooded trail. The flash caused me to gasp for breath. Missy ran her eyes down my body again, while I tried to pull myself together. Her pupils seemed distant, somehow haunted. They were just blank, had no soul, what Aunt Maude has always called "dead eyes." A huge part of me wanted to tell her about my premonition, but the awkward vibe she was sending out warned me to hold off. The woman before me was somehow associated with the killer. I had the feeling Missy could possibly lead me to him.

"I'm fine. Just bumped my head on the ceiling. Thanks for your information. We always are looking for cleaning attendants. I'll keep you in mind if we have a position come up. Thanks, again." The strange encounter finally came to an abrupt end when Amelia began to yell for "Helen." After another stroppy pause, Missy finally turned to depart. I had to wait for her to descend the stairwell before feeling comfortable enough to make my way back up the ladder. I climbed into the attic, confused as well as creeped out by the whole experience. It only took about two minutes to find the box Mother had labeled "Muffy Catherine/High School." After pushing the attic ladder back up, I tucked the box under my arm, then headed back to the main floor. Amelia did the crazy thing with her finger again before helping me with my coat.

*****

Hollis was resurrecting Mr. Corlew's mouth from fifty years of marital hell when I returned to Simon's with a six-inch Subway and my box of high school relics. After scarfing down the turkey on wheat in the employee breakroom, I returned to finish up the car crash fatality. My mortician's jacket wasn't yet buttoned up when Hollis joined me at the slab. He'd already completed the embalming procedure on the crash victim, so I started on the cosmetology touch- ups. Before getting the patient's face shaved, we heard what only can be described as a herd of buffalo come running down the hallway. Investigator Betty was all but out of breath and holding her heels in her left hand. She closed the door with her enormous right paw, and then hurriedly took a seat on my metal stool. "Muffcat, it has been nonstop since six a.m. Glad we got Sally." She then whispered under her breathe, "Hollis still does not want to interact with the living since that damn parrot died."

Hollis cleared his throat. "Please get my brows on properly. Can't believe I worked that service lookin' like this. After I consult with Keith, your Aunt Mila and I are meeting for drinks at the country club. Betty glared over at Hollis. The mere mention of Aunt Mila's name always made Hollis nervous. I had no idea why because Mila is a saint for putting up with my Uncle Vernon's antics for all these years.

Hollis grabbed the garden hose and began spraying down the floor. Even though I've known him for most of my life, Hollis Holsteader can only be described as an odd bird. He's never been married, lives upstairs in a tiny apartment over the funeral home, and has eaten cheese and crackers for two of his meals, every single day, for the past fifty years of his life. I've never had much of a conversation with Hollis, other than ones that involve some sort of clandestine embalming technique. But he is, hands freaking down, the best there is at postmortem facial reconstruction and tissue damage rejuvenation, so the industry says. Several country music stars that have died before their latest rhinoplasty or eyelift procedure could be completed have relied upon him. It is rumored his cards were passed out in the green room at the Grand Ole Opry by the Great Porter Wagner himself. Nevertheless, there was a story there about Hollis and my Aunt Mila, I just never worked up the nerve to ask the weird son-of-a-bitch.

I fidgeted for the brown eyeliner pencil in my mortician's jacket as Hollis scrubbed the floor drain with bleach. Betty took off her glasses, then breathed heavily straight into my face. I started on her eyebrows, wishing not to have to be so close to Betty for this conversation. Her breath always reeks of garlic and coffee mixed with Luden's cough drops. "Muffcat, you were too young to remember this. Back in the mid-eighties, we had a similar murder here in Parrottville. 1984 or 85, I think it was. Simon's did not get the body. The Jane Doe was an out of state runaway. Chief Shannon told my Hal it was the worst mutilation he had ever seen of a human being, and certainly the most horrific case of his career. Took over a month for the parents to identify the body because the damn ME we had in Davidson County at the time, that hot shot that moved up here from Miami-Dade, who turned out to be a pothead, miscalculated the poor child's age. Sandra told me today at Tana's funeral that Bill never did get over it. As a matter of fact, Sandra said she was glad Bill didn't have to live to see this type of horrific homicide happen in Parrottville again. She's talked to Melvin about the possibilities of the cases being related."

I was still holding my breath from the fumes, and about ready to pass out before turning to retrieve a Kleenex. I took a mouthful of air before responding. "So, was it your keen detective skills, Jessica Fletcher, or Melvin's profound dick work that has the mutilations tied to a high school classmate?"

Betty, not taking the bait, continued. "That is what I was just fixin' to tell you. Melvin said Leighanna and Tana were in you all's graduating class. Both girls had 'PHS' carved on their backsides. So he's pretty sure it's somebody from your alma mater." Betty snagged a mirror from the counter. "Melvin said the new guy from CID (that's the Criminal

Investigation Department) is a moron. With all this talk about the manifesto being written in a PHS annual, I can't believe Pammy assigned someone from California to be the lead on these cases."

I knew the new guy from CID was no idiot. The vodka the night before had left the details a little sketchy, however, Chief had mentioned something about having hand-selected the new detective for herself. Melvin was probably just resentful. Rumors were he'd been passed over for the new guy, and he was probably jealous.

There was something I needed to get off my chest. Granted, Angela Lansbury was not the safest person to discuss the matter with, but I had to know if Sally had ever opened up to Betty about her son. I whispered to Betty, who was sucking something out of her smelly teeth. "Betty, did you know that Sally had a son that died?"

Betty was holding her compact mirror two inches away from her face. Even with my six- inch Jimmy Choos on and Sally being seated, we were still eye to eye. "Umhum. She told me so her first day." Betty was only halfway paying attention but sat up straight as a stick after my next comment.

"I told her today about the voices, Betty. They're not like 9-11 when people were just shouting numbers at me. These voices are evil." She set the mirror down. "I really believe I'm hearing the voice of Tana's murderer. It's as if flashes from his past are coming to me in waves."

Betty put her glasses back on her nose. She then stared at me with a blank expression. I walked over to the storage closet. "I've got something I want to show you." After extracting my box of memories, I said, "Here's what's left of my annuals. Wanna show ya a picture. I keep seeing this portrait of Leighanna Petigro when I have these flashes." I had to press my glasses up on my face to find Page 56. Betty adjusted her leopard readers. "Look at this one first." I handed Betty over my senior yearbook. She studied the page from the Parrottville's annual art competition. She then thumbed through the pages. "I had a premonition about Tana before her death. Leighanna has come to me as well, but her encounters were postmortem."

Sally was watching Hollis. I turned around to find him on his hands and knees, snooping, while pretending to clean the floor's drain. Hollis rose then acted like he was washing his workstation. "I am almost certain my dreams are giving me some sort of insight into the killer's motive. Pretty sure this madman has been stalking Tana for years. And Leighanna had to have said something that really pissed this guy off."

Hollis dropped his scalpel on the floor. Betty motioned for him to leave the room. He strolled over to the storage closet instead. As Hollis randomly moved items around on the shelves, I continued with my story. The recount of Tana's dream made Betty shrink on the stool. "Betty, I keep seeing this other woman too. She is almost, like, mummified? The woman had a pentagram, or something to that effect, on the back of her neck. Her face is over a white prayer seat. Maybe a Catholic thing; I'm still not sure. That portrait, the one right there. It is above the woman's bowed head. I was deliberating whether or not she was Leighanna Petigro on my lunch break today, but after seeing this, I feel certain." Betty pulled the book in close to her face. "Skip back to Page 56. Leighanna had a wicked mane back in the day. At first, I thought the woman might be some sort of satanic devil worshiper because of the tattoo. Without her hair, it was almost impossible for me to identify her. But today, I realized it was Leighanna. In my flash, the woman's hands were bound in front of her. In some sort of way that made it look like Leighanna was praying to it. Praying to that portrait right here."

I pointed to the photograph of Leighanna Petigro's winning portrait of a devil sitting in a chair. The color was now all but drained from Betty's face. She stood up, then walked over and whispered something to Hollis. As soon as Hollis exited the room, Betty locked the door. "What are you doing?" I asked, getting worried. Betty was now pacing. "Muffcat, you talked to Larry Biggs? Anybody at the ME's office today?"

I was puzzled by her random questions. "Not anything other than checking for a release time on Leighanna earlier this morning. But that was before I came into work. Body was still at the crime scene," I replied, still confused. Betty reached for her phone. "Who are you calling?" Betty placed the phone to her ear. "Muffcat, what else did you see?" We both glanced over at the twenty-two-year-old with the broken jaw. The doorknob rattled. It was Sally. Betty cracked the door. "Call Sterner. Tell him that you were right." Betty handed Sally something through the cracked doorway. "Muffcat, you talk to Jimbo, Melvin, Brad, Detective Davenport? Anyone in law enforcement at the funeral today?" Betty knew I was in the middle of an embalming procedure during the funeral. "Who's Detective Davenport?" Betty let out a sigh. "Keep going. What else did you see?"

"There were all these cats. They were nipping at the legs of the praying woman. A four letter word was written on her forehead in all caps. With Leighanna's head bowed, it was hard to make out. But I think it said Nark or some such thing. That witch, devil thing-a-ma-gig that Leighanna had on was not on her skin when she was living up in New York. You'll see it when her body is released. It's some sort of religious symbol, I think. All black ink. Right on the nape of her neck." I pointed to the back of Betty's head. She was shaking and kept repeating the same thing. "There is no way. There is no way." I continued on about the flashes. "There were words scrawled on a mirror just a few feet away from the body. "You got to realize you're the Devil as much as you're God." I'm pretty sure it's another quote by Charles Manson."

It took us over an hour to go through all of the dreams and flashes. We never got to all the audible sensations I'd shared with Sally. Betty offered the occasional "Umhum. Keep going. Holly Shit. Tell me more." I felt like Bubba. When he and Forrest are cleaning their rifles, rattling off just about every conceivable shrimp recipe known to man. But, let's face it, this was some gruesome shit. "Betty, do you think it is possible I am channeling the murderer?" Betty's glasses came off again. "Look, Muffy Catherine, Dr. Biggs called while you were out. I have worked with him for over twelve years now. You know from experience, he is a need-to-know medical examiner. But these last two cases have him rattled. He reached out to me this morning. There is no doubt you just nailed the Petigro crime scene to a tee. You are definitely experiencing something that is out of the ordinary, but …"

Someone was rattling the door to the prep room again. It was Sally informing Betty that Keith had arrived. I really needed to get to the mansion, but decided to wait and finish up my conversation with Betty. Surprisingly, she was back in less than fifteen minutes.

Betty returned to the prep room with both our coats. "Pammy still coming over?" I shook my head while slipping on my jacket. "Look, Muffcat …" I cut Betty off, "was Leighanna mummified? Was her mouth sewn shut?" Betty grabbed me by my arm and led me out the back door. I'd forgotten my SUV was still out front. "Let me drive you around." Betty climbed into her tiny, red Mercedes convertible. Which has always perplexed me. Why an Amazon of a woman, a mortician only a year away from drawing social security, would drive such a small and flashy car.

As the red CLK-550 tore off around the building, Betty continued, "yes. Both homes, the ducts had been stuffed to direct hot air to the rooms where the bodies were found. Thermostats were set on overdrive. With the heat, Leighanna was pretty damn close to being mummified. Mouth sewn shut with dental floss, hair gone, that fucking demon portrait over her head. And that inscription on the mirror was spot-on, Muffcat." Betty stopped the car. "This homicidal maniac is not only provoking law enforcement; he is provoking God." Betty was parallel with my SUV and taking up half the road. An obvious undercover car was just down the block. The radio was on some random country station. Parrottville was mentioned three times before a horn honked.

I took off my glasses and rubbed my tired eyes. It was almost dark. "What the fuck is going on around here, Betty?" She shot a bird out her driver's side window. The car sped around us. "There's more." Betty parallel-parked behind my SUV, then flashed her lights to the car two blocks up. "Muffcat, Melvin told me in confidence that the murderer is using PHS yearbooks for his communication with law enforcement. That's no rumor. You need to find your missing yearbook." I turned and looked at Betty directly in the eyes. "Good God, Betty. My mother has the organizational skills of a schizophrenic. I once found my prom dress amongst the table clothes out in our storage barn. Don't be jumping to any conclusions about this. God, you really have to stop with all the gossiping."

Betty put the car in park. "This is no time to be making light of the situation, Muffcat. Find your missing yearbook, my dear. Otherwise, there is a chance you might be the next on the murderer's list."

Chapter IX

I'd just returned from ransacking the mansion, on a mission to locate my yearbook, when Eleanor shot me a text. She and Pammy were running late. Gavin and Dylan were playing in downtown Nashville at 3rd and Lindsey, so the girls would probably stay well into the witching hours.

Not sure what to make of the information Betty had shared, I poured a drink, then sat my tired ass down on the couch, alongside my 1989 annual. Leighanna's senior picture captivated me. She had wicked, long blond hair in the image; a mass of curls and frizz that made no sense. In the early years, I'd considered her edgy and quick-witted, but that was before we lost touch, and she disappeared from society. Local chatter alluded to her involvement with some strange religion associated with witchcraft or the occult, but I chalked the gossip mill up to people not understanding her creative awareness.

My mind wandered back to our last chance meeting, as I sucked down my first Cosmo. Regardless of her eccentricities and Goth clothing choices, Leighanna had serious talent back in the day. Amazingly, she lived in Alphabet City around the time Sonny and I were getting serious (small world and coincidence and all that). We bumped into her one night at our favorite deli. Sonny was instantly smitten with Leighanna's quirkiness and energy. She informed us she'd taken a set designer position for an Off-Broadway production company, but that her mystical dragon caricature series represented her true passion. Her out-of-the-way Soho gallery opening received some positive press. Sonny loved Dungeons and Dragons and insisted that we attend. After Leighanna's debut, we joined her for a midnight snack at Balthazar on Crosby Street. The ever hip and trendy eatery typically didn't seat new patrons after eleven p.m., but Sonny had finesse. And connections. After a three-tier seafood platter, four bottles of the finest wine, and a fabulous time had by all, I never saw Leighanna again. At first, I suffered some guilt about not staying in touch but had heard my old friend had become quite the hermit.

I was refreshing my cocktail when Aunt Maude appeared in the kitchen's doorway. She was pushing one of Uncle EG's shopping carts. Her famous turnip greens filled one Crock-Pot, her signature white bean soup another; her yummy hoecakes (cornbread to the rest of you) were tightly wrapped in aluminum foil. I turned the oven on low to keep the hoecakes warm, sliding Aunt Maude a rather heavy tip. She tucked the wad of twenties in her bra while making reference to the fact that my cabin was a little chilly. Tennessee's crazy weather had caused a thirty-degree drop in temperature in the last few hours alone.

Maude reminded me we might need to rent a few portable heaters for the wedding reception before we gathered some firewood from out back. I was just about ready to inquire if she knew where my junior yearbook was located when Mitch pulled up in my driveway. He offered to help us get the wood into the cabin in exchange for a gin and tonic. While Maude hit the liquor cabinet, I decided to attempt to get the fire going. Mitch assisted with the kindling while downing his drink. As soon as the fire was lit, Maude and Mitch headed out for their Friday night ritual. They were on their way up to Franklin, Kentucky, for a couple of wild rounds of Bingo before they'd end their night at Tac's playing poker.

Alone, I sighed and then plopped back down on my couch with my laptop. Just as I got comfortable, smoke started pouring from the ancient fireplace. I raced over to check things out; the fucking flue was closed. After fanning the air for a good ten minutes, I buried myself in the sofa.

Allison DuBois' website had been my latest obsession. I'd been following a cold case up in West Virginia, in which she was involved, for months. One of my favorite television dramas, *Medium*, was based on her book.

Getting comfy, I threw myself into searching for more, more, more about DuBois, I learned that several police departments (surprise, surprise) didn't portray a favorable image of her psychic abilities. I moved between Wikipedia and AllisonDubois.com; the contradictions and different versions of the same story were mind-boggling. According to Wiki, several of the crimes she'd boasted about solving looked to be retracted. One of the cases she claimed credit for solving was flat-out denied by the Texas Rangers. The Glendale Arizona Police Department blatantly declared her a flake. I hit the print command then retrieved the documents as they shot out, the paper still warm. Headlights pinged in my kitchen window pane. I was surprised to see Chief's patrol car pulling up. I stepped out back to greet my girlfriends. Eleanor was the first through my door with a case of beer under each arm. "Holy shit, Muffcat! I am a menopausal lesbian with enough testosterone to bench press your ass! Good God! It is hotter than holy hell in here!" Pammy was still in her patrol car on her cell phone, so I reentered the cabin with Eleanor. She ran to the refrigerator, placed the beer inside, and then put her entire head in the freezer. With two beers in hand and newly chilled, she joined me on the couch and started flipping through my 1989 yearbook. "Pammy will be in shortly. She was chewing someone's ass out 'bout the current investigation."

I glanced over at my best friend's lover. To tell you the truth, Eleanor is not a bad looking woman. It's her attire that distracts most everyone from her natural beauty. She's almost always wearing men's blue jeans and t-shirts which proclaim her sexual orientation. Today's rainbow shirt announced "Everybody Loves a Lesbian." Eleanor is twelve years older than Pammy (which puts her in her mid-fifties). Her short, auburn hair (which is cut into a boy's crew) normally has a little gray at the temples. Darryl's Barber Shop plops some color on it every once in a while; come to think of it, it did seem a little redder than the night before. Eleanor is a little overweight and stands around five-foot-nine; she's forever wearing these ugly sandals accompanied by black socks.

Despite her mani-pack obsession and lack of makeup, Eleanor has a flair for all things domestic. After moving to Parrottville from Jackson, Tennessee, and establishing her epicurean swine farm, she hit the culinary lottery. Her gourmet sausages were featured on an episode of Guy Fieri's, *Diner's, Drive-ins, and Dives*. Shortly afterwards, her Lipstick Pale Ale Microbrewery became a cult sensation; she won a Ninkasi Award. Eleanor was asked to be a reoccurring guest correspondent for a local t.v. station as a culinary expert. Word has it took three grown men to hold her down to get her lipstick on for her first appearance.

Pammy still hadn't made it into the cabin by the time Eleanor pounded down two Lipstick Pale Ales. I could hear her discussion through the cracked doorway. Melvin McNabb has had a booming voice ever since he grew his mustache in the sixth grade.

Standing at the door to gauge how much longer she was going to be, Chief's piercing aquamarine eyes caught the light of the kennel as she paced back and forth in front of her patrol car. Her slim frame was just as athletic as it had been in high school. Her long, blond hair (which is usually slung into a low ponytail) now obscured her face. She walked out of earshot then signaled for me to give her another minute. Her voice roared, "keep your goddamn mouth shut, McNabb. No more leaks to the media or Betty. You got two strikes on you. Don't think for a fucking second that I will not put you on unpaid leave. ... Fine. You can call the goddamn union. ... Now get your shit together." Chief slapped her phone back on the clip of her belt then took a swig of Pale Ale. I had not ever seen Pammy have a beer in hand before crossing my door's threshold, and Chief was in civilian clothing tonight. But Pammy was never without a weapon, and customarily carried two.

I placed my arm around my friend's shoulder as we slipped inside the cabin to find Eleanor frantically turning the pages of my yearbook. Eleanor erupted into a full belly laugh. "How in the hell did this get-up not give you away, Pammy?" Eleanor held up a picture of Chief in her senior superlative picture as Parrottville's "Most School Spirit." The comment did not sit well with Chief, who ignored her life partner. Eleanor began eating beans straight out of the Crock-Pot. I regained my seat on the couch and let Pammy scarf down a few bites.

Eleanor and I were cracking up over a prom picture of Pammy in a hoop skirt. She was in a pale blue dress with a white, fake flower obscuring one of her eyes. Blaine Patton, her date for the evening, was smiling from ear to ear in a pale, blue tuxedo. Chief ran over and grabbed the book from my hand. She slammed it on the coffee table then plopped down next to me. Chief eyed my now idol laptop. She scrolled the touch-pad until the computer sputtered back to life.

"Muffcat, on a serious note, David Davenport, my new detective from CID, is assigned to these homicide investigations. Not sure how much you remember from the conversation last night, but he's the one that followed me here from West Tennessee. Big D wants to speak to you about Shelley's homicide. Told him you had a huge event at the house this weekend, but I would really appreciate you meeting with him the first part of the week. Be forewarned, he is damaged goods. Also, he's not much on psychic assistance, so you might want to keep that bullshit on the down-low." Chief pointed to my laptop, then took a swig of beer. The damaged good comment seemed strange, knowing what I did about Pammy's past. I decided to let it go. For the time being.

We wandered into the kitchen to make our plates. I already had the mixed match bowls down from my cupboard. We were all excited about digging into our favorite meal. Aunt Maude's white bean soup is made with the hock that Eleanor smokes herself in what we all call "the pig palace" that sits behind the couple's home. Aunt Maude's recipe is a magical combination of homemade chicken stock that's infused with the smoked hock, chicken bones, water, sautéed onions, celery, and carrots. Her pre-soaked beans are drained then seasoned with coriander, allspice, and a few secret ingredients before Aunt Maude adds the stock. She usually zings the soup up with a few dashes of tobacco after the Crock-Pot simmers for several hours. My bowl gets about ten more dashes, but I've always been told I could eat lightning.

Then there are Maude's turnip greens, which are a religious experience. They are our second most beloved green vegetable, right after the fried okra we call our Southern popcorn. Chief was now cutting up my last summer tomato and a yellow onion to add to her greens. Eleanor retrieved the hoecakes from the oven and the vinegar from the cabinet.

I couldn't stop obsessing about why Pammy would refer to anyone as "damaged goods." She was a normal kid up until the ninth grade. Jumped from one boy to the next up until she just disappeared into the woods. Took up hunting and fishing with the boys we call the "Bubbas." Skipped school and four-wheeled while dipping tobacco and listening to Bocephus with the ole rednecks. It was after we graduated from high school that she finally confessed her reason for skipping out on all the shopping, parties and dances: Pammy was being sexually molested by her own stepbrother. It felt, to me, like one of my most epic fails in friendship. Not picking up on her abuse that is.

But it was yours truly who went with her when she informed her parents she was a lesbian. She came home from her first semester of college at the local community college and came out to me. I encouraged her to be proud of who she was; she claims she's never forgotten that support. The next summer, Pammy escaped Parrottville and fled to Knoxville. She studied at the University of Tennessee under the famous Body Farm forensic anthropologist; her career in law enforcement ensued. After graduating from the police academy, Pammy was accepted onto the force over in Jackson, Tennessee. She spent ten years climbing the ladder, CID to Sargent, then to Assistant Captain. She wanted to be a part of a bigger force, and could have gone over to Memphis homicide. Even got an offer down in New Orleans that she reluctantly passed up when her mother fell ill with cancer the first time. But then her mother received a really bad report: the cancer was back and had spread to her bones. With a little help from my Uncle Vernon, the town mayor, Pammy begrudgingly moved back to Parrottville to take the position as Chief of Police; she had Eleanor in tow.

Now, her harsh remark about another person being "damaged goods" seemed so hypocritical. I knew there had to be a good reason for her judgmental sentiment. Whatever Mr. CID's issues were, they had to be pretty freaking horrendous to deserve the criticism.

Sitting with our feet folded into our thighs in front of the almost flameless fire, our conversation took an unexpected turn. Pammy was discussing her new detective, David Davenport, when she slipped and mentioned his physical attractiveness. It was shocking, her confession that her new homicide detective was a hunk. Eleanor surprisingly had a good laugh about it before her cell phone rang. She jumped up then went into the kitchen to take the call. Pammy took her last slurp of soup. Clanked the spoon around the bowl a few times, and then whispered, "So, more please about these voices Betty told Melvin about this afternoon. I'd like to hear about it before we both get lit up like Christmas trees." Pammy always has eaten faster than me, but this was a record. She went in like a starved animal. Given the events of the night before, this was probably the first food since then that had not come out of a vending machine. Pammy slid close to me, realizing Eleanor was still in deep conversation about pig parts. "I did not want to say anything in front of Eleanor. Your damn dreams have scared the shit out of her."

Pammy and I decided to act as if we were going to retrieve more firewood in order to continue our conversation. It was freezing outside. Pammy tucked her hands into her jeans then eyed my ax. She picked up the ancient metal apparatus and took a swing. "AGHHHH…..Tell me about the voices, Muffcat." I hastily recounted most of the latest manifestations, sipping my cocktail at every pause. After taking another few good swipes at the stump, Pammy got very quiet then set down the ax. Her breathing was labored. "And you are sure you seem to know this guy?" She had stopped drinking but took a swig from my cup.

We'd been outside for a good twenty minutes before Pammy decided to open up. "Look, Muffcat. We have no goddamn idea who this perp is yet. The twisted freak left nothing behind besides the messages on the bodies. Fucking psychopath has an obsession with Charles Manson. Only got one detective that is worth a shit. Even with a freaking sicko preying on women, the city commissioners are worried about budget reports. Two mutilated hometown classmates gruesomely and horribly raped with objects, probably subjected to hours of torture, and the mayor wants me to make time for interviews with local reporters? You have no idea the pressure I am under." Pammy picked up the ax. "TBI are gonna have a field day with my force. Gotta get this department cleaned up. Otherwise, my ass is gone."

Chief looked thin. She was agitated. Pammy took another swing at the massacred log then asked me for a favor. "Muffcat, need something from ya. I need you to lay off my force. We all know they are a bunch of backwards assholes, but Melvin has Big D convinced you are a complete nut job." I shook my head and muttered, "Okay," feeling guilty for the defiance. My eyes were watering from the cold, but there was a little fury mixed in as well. Betty Simon and Melvin McNabb had both just made it onto my shit list. If there were any truth to the rumor about the yearbook manifesto, Pammy would have surely told me by now.

Eleanor cracked open the doorway. Pammy set the ax down and whispered, "Big D got burned by a damn psychic. Bout cost him his career. Just stick to the Danderson details for now. He knows what he is doing. Trust me. I know what you see and hear is real to you but, hell, hon, the shit you were rambling off last night really is not what my detectives are accustomed to dealing with. We use professionally trained profilers. Assigned some out of Metro for these cases. Maybe there is a way for you to refine your skills? Please. Just don't freak him out. Need Big D at the top of his game while I get the force back into shape."

Pammy took one last swing, leaving the ax head in the wood, before heading back towards my cabin. I reluctantly followed, feeling like a child who had just been scolded. The bird dogs howled from their cedar lined homes as we gathered around the now flameless fireplace. Pammy stoked the fire then added three new logs. I was trying desperately to bring some sense of normality back to our weekend routine. Was hopeful a round of Scattergories might ease the tension in the air.

*****

"Girls, you know I never do deliveries on Saturdays. But Lovelace Café just called. Got a last minute order for a Jack Daniels Distillery tour group tomorrow. Seven busloads of tourists, all want my ham! Saw me on *Talk of the Town*."

Pammy and I looked at each other. Pammy was the closest to being sober, but Eleanor and I were all but blind-running naked at this point. I contemplated letting Eleanor take my SUV, but, A) she was drunk, and B) it was filled to the brim with crap collected for one of our upcoming Halloween events at the mansion. We decided to all leave together, with Pammy our designated driver. It was still hot and a little smoky in the cabin, so we left a few windows cracked in our mad dash to hand-slice some gourmet swine.

As we approached Pammy's house, I announced my need to use the restroom. Chief stopped the car in her driveway, letting me out at the main house. The old, single-level ranch had been her mother's residence. The homestead sits on the outskirts of town and is not geographically desirable, but they'd made the best of the five acres. I extracted the key from underneath the planter of succulents then unlocked the door. The patrol car continued on to the barn area. The headlights pinged and illuminated the massive, pink structure that reigned in the back yard. I was impressed. For a dumpy dresser, Eleanor is a kick-ass, damn near impeccable interior designer. Their furnishings reminded me of West Elm meets bordello, modern and kitschy, in a *Birdcage* kinda way.

I headed down the hallway of the reinvented ranch. After using the facilities, I found Pammy's yearbooks in a coat closet. I made my way back to the kitchen to pour a few drinks, 1988 yearbook in hand. Eleanor breached the doorway. She was screaming frantically, "holy shit! Muffcat! Hit the floor! Bullets are flying!"

Eleanor's voice shrieked. She proceeded to tackle my intoxicated ass then forcefully push me backwards across the concrete floor. We ended our rendition of "the worm" right in front of their metal fireplace. I must have let out a whimper that sounded like one of my bitches in the middle of laboring out a litter after Eleanor's linebacker tackle.

"What the hell?" She rubbed my head. It had bounced a few times during her clobber. "Holly shit! Muff, two of the bullets went through one of my damn hams! Pammy drew her gun then tore off on one of our four-wheelers."

Laughter was the only sound I could muster. Eleanor's despair over her prize-winning hams. Not one ounce of concern for Pammy's life. We were warped. Drunk as hell and morally corrupt. I was still lying in a fetal position, head resting on the rainbow of Eleanor's shirt. Sirens wooshed, and gravel was being thrown. Blue lights blazed as several police cars flew past the house. Not realizing one of the patrol cars had stopped at the main house, I about bit Eleanor's rainbow-covered titty off when Brad Weasle's voice roared, "Eleanor! Open up! Open the damn door!" The door was kicked in. Eleanor and I laughed hysterically, clutching each other like mischievous little girls.

Brad jetted in with his gun drawn. He rushed over to what only could have looked like a girl-on-girl porno gone way wrong. Sergeant had to think we were nuts. "Chief called. Wanted me to make sure you girls are OK. Caught a runner. Has him hog-tied just down the street."

Holy shit. *This really is Mayberry BFE*, I thought to myself. Worse than the damn funeral earlier today, when the senior citizens made a field trip of the funeral. This had to be on film. Some camera man was sure to pop out of the cupboard. We were staring up at Barney Fife on steroids, a Glock now pointed down at our heads. And we just kept on laughing. Like there was nothing out of the ordinary about the situation. Two females. One, the local, crazy mortician in Jimmy Choos. The other, a hog farmer with a fanny pack, keys hanging from a belt loop, and brown sandals lying on top of each other in the middle of the floor in the home of the Chief of Police. Bullets blazing like the Wild West in a backyard that has a pink pig barn containing bullet-riddled gourmet swine.

"Are you sure you girls are alone in here? Chief wants me to check out the rest of the house. Eleanor, come with me. See if anything is out of place."

Eleanor jumped up then set off with the out-of-shape officer. He was practically heaving to catch his breath. The panting sounded as if he were having sex. I have to admit, even snockered and cloudy, the thought made me cringe. I hit the liquor cabinet, but there was no vodka. The freezer. Surely they had to have some vodka in the freezer. The duo appeared back in the hallway before my heart could restart. "Well?" I proceeded to swig the vodka straight from the bottle. Eleanor escorted Brad to the hallway's half bath. "Everything still here?" Eleanor gave me a disapproving look as she pointed to the still open freezer. She shook her head. "Nothing seems out of place." She walked over and whispered, "tone it down." Eleanor was in the fridge grabbing something for herself. The bathroom water never ran. Brad exited the restroom. "You gonna wash those sausages before you shovel some more doughnuts in your piehole?" That made Eleanor spit her beer out in the sink. She swatted at my head. Weasle walked over, bent down, and then opened up the cover of the yearbook that was still on the floor.

"You prim and proper debutantes need to stay inside. Might want to be sure you got your copy of this one, Muffcat. Gonna go check on Chief." Brad looked up at me, adjusting his buckle then sauntered towards the doorway. There was more to the story. Eleanor obviously could not share it now. Chief barreled through the broken doorway, soaking wet and pissed as hell. "Brad, take Blaine Patton down to the station. Call Davenport. Melvin is not on this one."

As Chief tore off to her bedroom, Brad set out to the yard. Other officers gathered in the light underneath the massive window. Chief was in uniform in less than three minutes. Not one word as she finished buttoning the blue shirt over her bulletproof vest in the den. She barreled out the broken doorway. Once her lights faded down the driveway, we made our way out to the pig palace. Eleanor could not drive, and I did not have a car. We were stuck. Stupid me. No transportation. Our conversation went on until the wee hours of the morning as we listened to Bocephus and carved up the ham.

After the sixth rendition of "Whiskey Bent and Hell Bound", Eleanor told me her worst nightmares were coming true. She thought middle Tennessee would be a safe place for her to live openly with her partner. And now, someone had taken a shot at her girlfriend's head in their own backyard. A no-good moonshiner, a one time a friend, was now seeking revenge for his stills being decimated.

We were sobering up. The night had turned out to be a crappy one. Eleanor explained how Pammy had been working on an internal investigation for months. From the sound of it, there had been a lot of pissed off renegade shiners harassing her, and a lot of threats on her life. A majority of her force was under suspicion for aiding and abetting. Not knowing if one of the corrupt cops was now familiar with the layout of their home, we tried to patch the door around 1:30 a.m., but the entire doorframe was shattered. Two of the worst homicides in the history of the city taking place on Pammy's watch, and we couldn't even lock her door.

Eleanor was not aware of the fact that my yearbook was missing, so I went ahead and filled her in. "You have to be kidding me? And the one from 1988 was not in the attic with the others?" In the middle of explaining the details, my phone started ringing compulsively from somewhere in the living room. We went and found it slung under one of the couches in the den. I had six voicemails and thirteen texts. Before I could retrieve the messages, the house phone started ringing off the hook. Eleanor's face went white after she answered it.

"This night is the gift that keeps on giving. More lovely news, Muffcat. Your house was burglarized."

Chapter X

Pammy asked us to walk to the bottom of the driveway to meet the patrol car. I don't mind saying we both looked like hell. I smelled like Hogzilla. An unmarked car came to a stop; the detective exited his vehicle with the engine still running. Holy hell. Chief was not lying. This man was massive. While apologizing for the bad news, he eased a crooked grin at the lesbian quote on Eleanor's shirt. A short, witty banter ensued between them.

The detective then turned to me and explained what the dispatched officer had discovered. Mr. Claude Mansker, aka Gran, had called the home invasion in to 911 shortly after midnight when he was awakened by the bird dogs. Eleanor explained how my phone wound up underneath the couch, which caused the detective, who had yet to introduce himself, to roar with laughter. When he finally did get back to being professional, he told us about a string of robberies in Parrottville, kids pawning small electronics and jewelry. It was obvious Eleanor was already aware of everything he was sharing, but I found the whole scene kind of strange. I couldn't figure out why Chief would send her best detective, in the middle of a homicide investigation, to handle my somewhat trivial break-in. Something wasn't adding up.

Detective David Davenport (yes, he saw his way to identifying himself) opened the passenger's side door then stuck out his hand out in order to shuffle me into his vehicle. The ham juice wafting off my shirt made the back seat my best option. Ever the drama queen with a flair for stretching the truth, I played it off like I'd never ridden in the back of a patrol car before. That was a lie.

The vibe in the police car was confusing and intense. It was damn near impossible not to stare at the handsome detective from the rear view mirror, as he proceeded with his idle chatter. Speculation about his demons preoccupied me. I caught the glare back around Lucinda Avenue. Back and forth, we both taxied for glimpses of rear view mirror eye contact as we shot the shit about nothing at all. Man, his angular jawline was strong. His blue eyes were nice, and probably dreamy, when not bloodshot. He kept pushing his dark brown, unkempt hair out of his eyes. This big boy needed a haircut.

He told me to call him Big D. A fitting moniker for a man with such an enormous and intimidating physique. He had to be six foot six; weightwise, I'd give him two-fifty. No fat, mind you. He'd obviously been hitting a gym when he wasn't chasing serial killers or picking up women that smelled like barbeque. There was definitely a curiosity coming from both of us, but there was no telling what he'd heard about me down at the precinct. Oh boy.

As we turned down Long Hollow Pike, my English setter was running from the KOA campground back towards the cabin. Smokey had either escaped his cage during the break-in or had been deliberately set free. We pulled over, and the detective took a call while leaning on his unmarked patrol car. It took me ten minutes to get Smokey back into his pen. When I returned to the patrol car, Big D was just clipping his phone back onto his belt. He was silent upon our approach towards the open front doorway. He yawned then apologized.

The detective bent down to pick up an envelope thrown into the bushes. "So you *are* the infamous Muffcat Mansker?"

The house was in disarray when we entered. "Depends on what you mean by infamous."

Every kitchen cabinet door was open. Dishes were broken; papers were scattered. My bedroom door was ajar. There were drawers on the floor, my bras and panties strewn. "Here, you might want something to write on. List out any electronics, jewelry, or valuables that are missing. Makes it easier for your insurance report if you keep a count as you go." He handed me a clipboard and a pen, then started to dust the door frame for prints.

The whole place was ransacked. Big D and I had several uncomfortable passes in the hallway as he processed every surface conceivable. It took about an hour to go through everything to be sure; oddly, not much seemed to be missing. I headed into my bedroom to double-check my bathroom and changing area. All of my heirloom jewelry, expensive rings, chains, and watches were untouched. There was a set of rosary beads, which were not mine, placed on a metal hook in my jewelry box. Strange. Very, very strange, and more than a bit creepy.

Over five hundred dollars in emergency cash was still in my tampon box. My toiletries were scattered on the floor. I gazed over to my vanity. A white porcelain Virgin Mary statue had been placed amongst my displayed perfume bottles on the only surface that had not been vandalized. The plot thickened, as goose bumps erupted on my forearms. I collected the items with tissue paper then took them to the detective. He questioned me about where they were found before I made my way up to the boys' loft. I yelled down to him, "beads were in my jewelry box; Mary was on my vanity. These rooms seem untouched. iPads and Bluerays are all still here."

More eye contact without words as I made my way back down into the kitchen area. Another twenty minutes of uncomfortable silence passed before Big D abruptly asked me to take a seat. He spoke in a slow, deep voice, "so, you are sure your laptop is the only thing missing?" I shook my head, "yes," then looked down at the beads and statue now on my coffee table. The hangover was kicking in, and I needed a few good hours of sleep or I was not going to be worth a shit at the wedding.

"I got to admit, I'm baffled by the religious paraphernalia. But I need to warn you, the same items were left at the home of our victims." He began to question me about my faith and association with the Church and went down a list of men that attended the First Baptist Church as if he had the entire congregation memorized. Aside from naming just about every deacon and Sunday school teacher, he seemed particularly interested in our music minister, Ken Akers, who also happens to be the youth minister. After a good thirty minutes of enlightening the detective as to why everyone on the list could not be the killer, I took over the questioning. "Since we are on the topic of religion, detective, how many cuts did Leighanna have below her sternum? I'll explain the relevance." Big D looked up from his notepad. "Not sure, Muffcat. Twenty-something, maybe." I shifted in my seat. "Want some coffee?" The detective answered "Black." I got up to try and find two saucers that had not been smashed to pieces while starting a pot of Pete's Bali Kintamani. Big D flipped through his notepad then joined me at the kitchen bar. He washed his hands. "What do you know about the Feast of Assumption, detective? Are you a religious man?" He looked for a place to dry his hands. I grabbed a tea towel and handed it to him. "This guy clearly has some conflicting ideologies in regards to religion, but I don't know much about the Feast of Assumption; nor has there been any reference to it in any of his communication. We have several priests and a criminologist working on the religious aspects of the case. The intelligence our profilers have gathered is mystifying. Good versus evil seems to be a theme, however, there is just as much sappy poetry mixed in with quotes from Charles Manson as there are Bible references. It appears our murderer cannot figure out which side he's on. The communication we received …

hey, don't you have a big wedding today to prepare for?"

Big D redirected the conversation while rummaging through my cupboard. "Chief talk to you about coming down to the precinct?" The giant was doing a sideways smirk with his upper lip. The gesture seemed awkward and kept me from immediately responding. "Umhum, she has, but not at four o'clock in the morning. I need to get some rest, detective. Seven o'clock wedding with over eight hundred guests."

Big D bit his bottom lip and tilted his head as if he was waiting for me to change my mind. "Let me get one cup of coffee in me before we leave, damn it." He gave a wide, toothy, sideways grin and then thanked me. I pointed to my good China at the very top of the cupboard. Big D pulled down two tiny cups.

Upon reentering the patrol car, our conversation turned one-sided. Credibility establishment was first. Big D was originally from San Diego, and Parrottville was the smallest town he had ever lived in; this was definitely the smallest force he'd ever served on. The detective and his father both had military backgrounds. He'd been in CID for over ten years and had overseen dozens of homicide cases in his career, which included the investigation of a convicted serial killer, Derrick Todd Lee, over in Memphis. Big D had been specially trained in interrogation techniques before his deployment to the Gulf War and had a ninety-five percent conviction rate on his homicide cases. This guy was clearly one bad-ass motherfucker, and he was now wanting my assistance on a cold case that was over a decade old. I knew a lot about Shelley Danderson's case because, at one point, Duke and I had been questioned about her disappearance. It was one of the darkest times in my life, right after the death of Sonny and my father, and I was not sure if dredging up the sensitive topic was such a good idea. Especially on so little sleep, with a buzz still on, and no legal counsel present.

We coasted into our City Hall at 4:22 a.m. The red brick building with a green metal roof houses the Chamber of Commerce as well as the police precinct, which resides in the back. Chief was a few steps in front of us when we exited the patrol car. Pammy tapped a code into the door's keypad without as much as a greeting. Once inside, Chief walked straight for a closed door, entered, and then slammed it back closed. Big D offered coffee then disappeared around the corner. The place was buzzing with unfamiliar law enforcement agents all wearing suits. While waiting for Big D to return, Chief popped her head out into the hallway, her phone glued to her ear. She waved for me to come inside. A small conference table displayed a dozen folders on top of the fake wood grain. Chief signaled for me to take a seat. Detective Davenport entered, set a cup in front of me, and then one in front of Pammy. The stream rose and danced in the flicker of the dimly lit room as the smells of Chinese food and hand sanitizer mingled with the Folgers classic roast. Hey, I know my food and beverage aromas, even when they're stale.

Photocopied pieces of paper were taped up all around the room. The pictures of the crime scene were hard to stomach but impossible to ignore. Detective Davenport apologized for the boxes that were piled next to my chair as we waited on Chief to end her call. Messages written on sticky notes covered his three-ring binder's cheap plastic cover. A bag full of trash was tied tight, yet still in the can. Big D took his gun off and laid it on the table. He then went over to pull a screen down. It probably led to an observing room, although I wasn't sure. My guess came from binging on *Law & Order*; I'd never been in those rooms before tonight.

My eyes followed Big D's every move as he collected a few files before attempting to regain his seat. Chief glared at me while tying up her call. It sounded like she could have possibly been talking to another law enforcement officer. Pammy pointed to her coffee. Big D looked baffled but stood to retrieve another cup. Chief slammed her phone down on the table. "Keep your damn mouth shut, Muffcat, about your damn dreams. Stick to the facts. And get the fucking drool off your chin." Chief grimaced. She snapped gloves on, and then bent over to one of the boxes. Detective Dreamy rejoined us with a box under his right arm and Chief's coffee in the other. He began his conversation just as his phone vibrated from his hip. He shot me another spectacular grin, apologized, and then exited the room again.

"That call you heard me on? Bowling Green cold case detective. Big D's working with them. He knows about the affair, Muffcat. It was in Shelley's files."

Great. Just freaking wonderful. Big D's first impression of me was sliding downhill fast. I was wearing a ridiculous shirt and still drunk when he picked me up, and there was no telling what the backwards fucks had shared with him at the precinct. Muffcat Homewrecker. Muffcat Mansteater. Big D had seen his fair share of my dirty laundry in less than two hours, and now he was aware of the fact that I am a known Jezebel as well.

Big D returned and took his seat. He handed me an article from the *Tennessean*, then started the interview out by asking questions about the men in Shelley's life. It was awkward. Talking about my dead lover's wife. "She was a spoiled rotten only child. Lived in the area we called the golden triangle. Her parents divorced when we were ten. Rich daddy with a garage full of Mercedes-Benzes."

We moved on to guys she dated in high school, her marriage, the affair. Big D asked if I was aware of any lovers on her part. "It wasn't like that." I stuck to the facts, but it was awkward trying to paint Shelley as a good person. Telling this story was making my stomach clench. Especially how the fact of my refusing to stop sleeping with her husband after he was diagnosed with terminal cancer was what sent her over the edge. How her drug problem started with just a little Wild Turkey and a few pills, then quickly progressed when Duke moved out of their house and into my B&B. He took her only child away from her when she refused rehab. Dylan spent more time at my cabin than he did at the mansion, and it was difficult for her to deal with the betrayal and the loss at the same time. Then, right before Duke died, she just disappeared. Duke was under suspicion, with a colostomy bag and feeding tube rammed through his nostrils and down his throat. I was questioned. Guilty for all that I'd taken from her, but innocent of all the cynical rumors.

The boys and I searched for Shelley relentlessly. A year later, the *Tennessean* article about a Jane Doe was published and was accompanied by a composite sketch. A woman that they thought to be a homeless drifter or possible prostitute was found behind a truck stop up in Kentucky. The detective wanted to know how I recognized her. "Actually, the composite sketch was off. She had been a curvaceous bombshell. The crank whittled her down to nothing. But I got to stare at her picture every morning while waking Dylan up for school. A necklace mentioned in the article helped. It had been found in her vagina."

The conversation continued for a good hour. Possible suspects, places where we'd find Shelley when she was shooting up or on a crank binger. It was difficult, but if it could help save one person, solve these homicides, the humiliation was worth it. Hell, I'd faced worse. At 8:30 a.m., Big D handed me a pair of latex gloves. My hangover was brutal, and the twelve cups of coffee were not helping my heart rate. Big D extracted a book from an evidence bin. The Duran-Duran sticker on the cover gave it away before he could set it down. "Page 39, Muffcat." I opened up Leighanna Petigro's yearbook. The first word of the manifesto started on her face. That was sobering. The inscription was written out in all capital letters. I pushed my glasses up onto the bridge of my nose. The message was cryptic and read like the voices in the embalming room. "It talks about revenge, lack of self-control. Birds on a wire are easy prey, but mine all have names. He is picking them off. Hunting them like animals. Payback for emotional pain, maybe? He seems to be well-educated and articulate. Nothing like the "Bubbas" Pammy mudded with back in the day."

Chief cleared her throat and got up from her chair. "I got to take a break." I had to flip to Page seventy-something before the communication ended. It was signed J∞f. Big D handed over another Ziplock bag. "This note here is from the Filson-Harvat case. Notice the handwriting."

Big D set two pieces of evidence down in front of me. He pointed to one with Tana's name. An unfamiliar series of letters and numbers labeled the translucent bag. The epistle was on a page torn from a yearbook page entitled "Guess who?" Smiling babies covered the page, and the answers were written upside down in small type. The random poetry, scrawled in the same bold lettering, reminded me of Shakespeare. Words we rarely use in daily conversation were spread throughout. Words like hath, thou, thee, doth, maketh, were all there, multiple times. The last word of the murderer's handwritten poem ended on Tana's face. "This took some time. Not to mention, it's creepy as hell." Both notes only had four lines, unlike the rambling manifesto, which was thousands of words long. Their structure was the same: the first line rhymed with the third, the second with the forth, and so on. I read each letter twice before Big D began to ask me more questions.

"Handwriting look familiar?" It did not. I turned the plastic over to see a page from Shelley Danderson's yearbook. "Camille Carr's handwriting is on the reverse side, but I haven't seen the capped handwriting before except on Tana's body."

We went back to the manifesto. After we got through four or five pages, Big D had more questions. Chief was back from her restroom break; her eyes were bloodshot. Big D continued, "do you know the difference between a psychopath and being psychotic?" I played it dumb. Wanted to see what the detective would say. "Richard Ramires, the Night Stalker, said it the best. Serial killers have a dead conscience. No morals, no scruples. What you have in front of you came from a psychopath. Psychotics are delusional, mentally incapable of telling right from wrong. This screwball is rational and has a damn good grip on morality and sin. He knows what he's doing is wrong, even cries out for repentance on Page 69 after discussing his infatuation with women's hair."

Big D took the book and turned to Page 69. Pammy chimed in, "he probably seems normal to most. Keep that in mind. Average job. Probably a mechanic, but more intelligent and could have worked in a more demanding job. He probably likes the monotony of simple tasks and works independently, in a body shop, plumber, electrician, HVAC guy. Might have lived on a farm at some point; he keeps talking about his flock. He's definitely a hunter. Might have a cabin or place he goes on the weekends."

It seemed strange for Pammy not to mention the religious suggestions in the writing, but then, religion had never been her thing. We bantered back and forth over the fact that the flock was probably a reference to his followers; however, there was so much going in the manifesto there was no need to argue about one simple passage. Pammy finally broke. "The religious aspect to his writing is plain bullshit, Muffcat. The guy goes from thinking he is God to portraying himself as the antichrist. I think he's just trying to throw us off." I argued back, "but he is obviously well-versed in multiple idealisms, with regard to religion. I think you need to speak with the local ministers and priests in the area. He has some weird infatuation with religion and Charlie Manson, from the looks of it."

Chief slapped the book closed. "Muffcat, we did not bring you here to give us advice on how to do our jobs. We brought you here to see if you recognized the handwriting and to find out what you knew about Shelley's past."

Hey, I am just being realistic. If he is confused about religion, he might have tried to reach out to someone …" Chief cut me off, "Big D, please take Miss Mansker home."

Big D could sense the tension in the room. "Would you two stop it? Let's at least ask her about the poetry. You're the one that said she was in AP English, Chief." Big D pointed to one of the poems. I looked over the four lines while he skimmed over the passage with his immense pointer finger. "Here, he goes from talking about a fucking gremlin to flying a damn kite. Look here." Big D pointed to the last line of the poem on Leighanna's crime scene note: BOYS FLYING KITES ARE THE ONLY ONES THAT WIN.

I adjusted my glasses then read all four lines out loud. "Big D, he is speaking figuratively here. It's partially a sonnet by Will Carleton, famous American poet. 1881 First Settler's Story, pretty sure. Goes like this. Boys flying kites haul in their white-winged birds, you can't do that when you're flying words. Thoughts unexpressed sometimes fall back dead, but God himself can't kill them once they're said." I set the notes side by side.

"Look, both his sonnets have the same poetic line as Carlton's. Their structure is the same line length, speed, rhythm. He's studied Carlton and is making a reference to not being able to take back what you say once you say it."

"This is Leighanna's right?" I turned the Ziplock bag over to confirm. "Leighanna must have said or done something that pissed him off. Maybe the portrait left at the crime scene is a representation of her killer?" Big D and Chief stared at each other. "Look, I know you won't believe me, but I am pretty damn sure Leighanna knew this man from the park, back when we were kids. I think she witnessed him kill someone's pet. I know you do not want me to talk about it Pammy, however, I feel certain that without a shadow of a doubt this guy lived here at some point in his life. Only time I sense him here is in the summer." Pammy scoffed, "Muffcat, shut it." I reached down to the box on the floor. "Do you have a 1989 yearbook in here?" Pammy grabbed for my wrist. She then kicked the box under the table. Big D walked over to a filing cabinet and extracted another yearbook. Pammy glared at me. "Keep this to a minimum, Muffcat. Remember what we discussed." Big D handed me a yearbook. I flipped to the art competition page. "You cannot sit here and tell me this was not at the crime scene." I pointed to the portrait. "Leighanna was bound in a position that made her look like she was praying to the man, don't lie to me. And look, look, here at this part of the manifesto." I flipped through Leighanna's 1988 yearbook. "Why would he talk about a witness to sins committeth by the Devil? And here he talks about the Devil hath been in me from the beginning on Page 42." I turned to the page and pointed. "Just an observation, but as I said, Leighanna was more than likely a witness to a slaying by your suspect when the murderer was still a teen. I think it was a dog. Maybe over at the Toss-Knight Park, and there was a report by a female runner. This portrait is her interpretation of the killer."

Big D was taking notes. Chief grilled him, "did we recover the portrait from the crime scene?" Big D glanced up. "We printed it at the scene. It was clean. Hector got over a dozen pictures." They conversed amongst themselves. I, of course, interjected. "And the gremlin comment. It is a reference to children. Not the eighties character from the movie. I observed burns on Tana's inner thighs and around the pubic bone region during her embalming procedure. This is not the first time your suspect has sexual assaulted Tana. Was there something found in her vagina like Shelley? Maybe an artifact religious in nature?" Pammy shuffled in her seat. She still was not comfortable with my observations. I was trying to relate my comments back to the autopsy room to keep my credibility, even though my dreams were the true reason for my annotations. "Rosary beads. We recovered rosary beads. Go ahead, Muffcat. Tell Big D your thoughts." I stood up and walked over to the crime scene pictures lining the walls.

There was a knock on the door. Big D handed a piece of paper over to a female in a black suit without an introduction. It was clear to me that their manhunt now included representatives from several different agencies. "Big D, show me the pictures of Leighanna's crime scene. I really think I might have an idea as to why the killer leaves the 365 postmortem cuts on his victims." Big D looked over at Chief. She nodded her head. He stood up. "Over here."

The photographs were just as my dream had portrayed her; a hairless woman hunched over a toilet bowl. I took the time to analyze each picture before making the request. "May I make a call? I want to get a hold of Biggs if you don't mind." Big D pointed to a landline and told me to dial nine. The ME was not available, but one of the lab techs confirmed my suspicions. "ME's office confirms twenty-five cuts below the sternum of Leighanna. She was killed the night before Tana." Big D looked over at Chief. "Do enlighten us, Muffcat." Pammy's tone of voice was beginning to really piss me off. "Look, Pammy, I voluntarily came down here. Pretty sure you don't want Big D to hear how I really know, so let me get all scientific for you." I walked over to the wall where Tana's crime scene photos hung. "Theokotos is the Greek title for Mary, the mother of Jesus. Either of you heathens know that?"

Big D took a seat and stretched his massive arms behind his head. They both shook their heads no, but Pammy still had a pompous look on her face. She scoffed "The word was written on the floor at Tana's house where the body was found." I pointed to the picture. "Twenty-four of Tana's cuts were below her sternum; I know that from the embalming procedure. The ME's office just confirmed Leighanna's sternum had twenty-five cuts. The Feast of Assumption takes place on September the fifteenth. Twenty-four days before Tana was murdered. Twenty-five days prior to Leighanna's death, so you now have a better time frame on the abductions. Or at least their time of death. Look, I heard rumors up at Simon's the air ducts had been tampered with at Tana's residence. The hot air obviously sped up the decomposition, and there was very little blood left in Tana's veins by the time she made it to my embalming table. But I think Leighanna was killed the day before Tana. The other cuts around the outskirts of their torso could possibly represent the number of days the women have to wait before the next feast of assumption when Mary can possibly save their souls from Purgatory."

Chief stopped with her smirking and grabbed for a file. "According to the beliefs of the Roman Catholic Church, this is the day Mary, the mother of Jesus, died. Some believe she returns every year on the anniversary of her death, as an act of mercy, and frees souls from Purgatory. The ones who believe in her immaculate conception are chosen to ascend back to heaven with her, pretty sure of it. The Catholics defined it as infallible dogma, but the Catholic Church only recently recognized the day of her assumption into heaven, and many think the story stops there. In 1950, Pope Pius the XII, I think, finally recognized the day, but variations of the story have circulated since at least the 4th century. To him, it might be his final act of mercy. Who knows? The statues, the rosary beads, just a theory."

Big D grilled me, "so why would a serial killer care about the souls of women he so brutally tortured?" I was not sure on this but offered up my only explanation that did not involve detailing my experience with Fredrick and the "Wind Whispers." "Maybe out of guilt. In hopes that Mary might return for them. Look, I am dangerous at best with my knowledge of the Bible. And the whole Roman Catholic beliefs around dogma is over my little old Southern Baptist head. It's just something to think about. You might want to check with some of the local Catholic priests in downtown. He could have possibly been a member of their congregation."

Chief stood up, then departed with one of the nameless agents waiting for her in the doorway. Big D took some notes on my observations. I announced that I had to get to the mansion. Just as Big D proceeded to give me a lecture about my personal safety, another Parrottville officer breached the doorway. Big D stood as Jimbo Filson entered the room. "Chief needs you ASAP. Has a possible eyewitness on the line." Jimbo Filson and Big D discussed my transportation options. It was decided that Jimbo was going to be the one to drive me back to my cabin for a Wonder Woman clothes changing session. I collected my phone and purse while they finished their conversation. Big D walked back over to the table where I was now standing. He towered over me. "Again, thank you for your assistance. Here's my card and your report number. The pleasure has been all mine."

I was going to have to wring my panties out in the sink thinking about his pleasure. Was fantasizing face-fucking him, but not in a Hogzilla shirt.

Chapter XI

His legs were not as white this year. He'd grown six inches since last summer, and his voice was two octaves deeper. He rolled out of bed while reaching for the magazine on his dresser. Flipping to the picture of the white 1982 Camaro with black stripes down the hood made him grin. And got him thinking about the hours he was putting in. Up at 5:00 a.m. every day to ride alongside his father in his company-issued work van. Long days servicing air conditioners made for a pretty boring summer, but at least he got to wear shorts and was learning how to drive. His father offered up a deal: stay out of trouble this year and he'd contribute five hundred dollars toward the purchase of his first set of wheels.

It seemed like something to look forward to, but, in reality, that deal would never close. He'd be stuck at his Catholic reform school for two and a half more years, on somebody else's dime. He had few, if any, real friends to call his own in the dormitory. Fewer, if it were possible, could be found while hauling Freon in the sticky heat. Truth be told, his visceral anger, hostility, and social awkwardness conspired to keep him from finding anyone to even talk to at the pool today as well. Yes, it would be fair to say that by the end of the day, a fucking shitty one to be certain, Jonah Wayne Johnson would have one person left in this world apart from the imaginary variety; the friend he'd conjured and named Big Horn.

He waited for his raging hard-on to go down before heading for the bathroom, where he counted the seconds it took to push out his pee. 116 was an all-time record, and one he was rather proud of. Upon his entrance into the kitchen, Step-Monster didn't offer any of the bacon drippings from the paper plate. He poured a glass of milk then took the last strip from the opened microwave. "That is *not* for you. Why don't you find somewhere to go today? Cliff was called in for some overtime hours."

Grabbing a stale donut, he mumbled through its dense pastiness. "Where are the beach towels?" He knew she kept the nice towels on the shelf above the dryer, and also that those were not for him. She exhaled a seemingly annoyed sigh and pointed to the garage. "Use the one out there.

And don't even think about bringing it back covered in blood and guts this time. I am not your maid."

Heading back down the hallway, he turned, then shot the bird to the back of her miserable head. He didn't bother to brush his teeth but did reach for the Listerine. Though the liquid burned the hell out of the back of his throat, he had to hold it in for 108 seconds before expelling it from his mouth. After a quick wash of his face, he ran a brush through his hair eight times. First on the left side, then on the right. It was imperative to reach the same place on the nape of his neck before switching hands.

While trying to pop an unsightly pimple on his chin, he went over his plans for the day. Pleasant Green swimming pool from ten to two. That would give him enough time to check out the babes before meeting Blaine at their treehouse, their favorite place in the world to hang out. Where they could safely and privately skin animals alive then watch as the worms and other lowly scavengers did their business. For Blaine, it was just a childhood curiosity, or so he said. For him, it was anything but. It was basic training, preparation for the next phase of his compulsive debauchery.

He gathered his Walkman, eight tapes, and sunscreen, then threw his wallet and hunting knife into his backpack. He sniffed the blue towel on the hook in the garage, which smelled worse than the deer carcass they'd gutted a few nights earlier. After sneaking back into the laundry room to retrieve a fresh towel, he gathered his last two cigarettes from beneath Claw's water bowl. He missed his pet; the Doberman had been dead for three weeks now, rotting in a shallow grave underneath their hallowed hangout.

There was one last thing he needed to do before heading out the side door of the garage. Unzipping his backpack, he pulled out the eight-inch blade from its leather case and poked a small hole in the driver's rear tire. All while replaying the comment about the witch his father married not being his maid.

Don't think twice about it, Little Horn commanded. *The stupid bitch deserves it. Don't forget the change in her ashtray.* When he first heard the voice, he didn't talk back, couldn't believe it could possibly be real. He knew nobody else could hear him, but had grown grateful for the company. He welcomed having someone he could respect calling the shots.

Once at the end of the driveway, he began to count each step while simultaneously reciting his newest poem to Big Horn. A police car began tailing him around Lucinda Drive. As nervousness and palpitations set in, Big Horn talked him out of the panic attack. *You are above the law. Do not look back; I got this.* He reminded himself that he never wanted to be under interrogation again. If not for the Polaroid and semen, the lawyer told him, he would never have been caught. But that power-mongering, asshole cop was relentless with his questioning and finally got a confession out of him after Blaine Patton's dad showed up at the precinct. The mutilation of a corpse charges were eventually dropped, but the idea still scared the shit out of him. He couldn't, ever, experience the likes of that again. He'd resigned himself to walking a tight line; if he made it to his eighteenth birthday, the charges would be expunged. After 762 steps, when the patrol vehicle finally turned the corner, he let out a deep breath.

He paid the five dollars at the gate then looked for a spot to lay his towel. As he searched for the best place to scope out the neon bikinis, Big Horn started back up. *Concrete in-between the concessions stand and the girl's restroom will give you the best vantage point. It's time for you to find a real girlfriend. Two more weeks before the summer is shot. You need to get laid.*

Before he could extract his clean towel from his backpack, the lifeguard's whistle blasted. JJ headed to the deep end of the pool, neither interested enough to look nor in any way acknowledging that a kid was drowning. As he climbed the ladder to the high dive, he surveyed the landscape for the nearly naked girls. Three compliments about his eyes by temperature-tormented females in one week had boosted his self-esteem. *Why wouldn't they notice you? You're good looking.* Big Horn regularly told him he was handsome, that is, when he wasn't calling him a worthless prick.

He paused at the end of the board before taking a lung full of air. *You little fucking sissy! You don't have the balls to dive!* He let his body fall forward, shutting his eyes as he plunged head- first into the depths. Laughter had erupted by the time his head broke the surface. He coughed up a fountain of water. *Should have plugged your nose, dumb ass!*

His face flushed, and his fury sparked as the boy in the plaid shorts trash-talked him from the edge of the pool. "Nice belly flop! That was the worst dive I have ever seen!"

Once on dry ground, JJ wasted no time pushing the bastard in. The big boobs in the red one- piece screeched her whistle. The thirty-minute break was gonna suck. While he was facedown for the duration of his punishment, Big Horn lit into him. *You freak; you impulsive piece of shit.*

Never in public. You should have waited and caught up with him in the bathroom. We have to tame your temper, you moronic twit.

Red one-piece blew her whistle, yet again. She was looking straight at him and pointing to her watch. His mandatory time-out was over. Plaid shorts was now in the concessions line. JJ got close; only three girls separated him from his tormentor. He tried to concentrate on something else to keep his anger from exploding. *Yellow with side braid has a big butt. Green is too cheerful; she would get on your nerves with her bouncing. Orange has nice legs. Hair is really pretty.* When orange bathing suit turned around and smiled at him, he was at a loss, couldn't muster even a lousy hello. He scanned her up and down while struggling to find the words. She was really hot; he liked her eyes. She seemed so innocent.

Nervously, he opened his wallet and started to fidget with the Velcro. Big Horn screamed, lambasting him for being a pussy. *Cat got your tongue, you dweeb? Is that the best that you can do, you little coward?* He rubbed the Velcro, first with his right hand, and then with his left. Three, four, five, six, seven times before finishing on his right hand. Fearing his mounting excitement, he peered up to the menu overhead. It would be either an ice cream cone or a box of popcorn.

He had to scan her silhouette one more time. He stared at the back of her leg, at the birthmark low on her calf, just above her right ankle. It wasn't attractive, but her ass and legs were damn near perfect. As he continued to walk his eyes up the back of Orange's thighs, that feeling returned. Fiddling with the waistband of his bathing suit only made the bulge more obvious. Big Horn weighed in with encouragement. *Do not give! I bet her hair smells like strawberries. Go ahead, give it a whiff.*

JJ's eyes moved to the wet hair stuck against her back. All he could smell was chlorine, but that was okay; he liked being close to her. *Rub up against her before she steps out of the line.* Orange bathing suit ordered a Bombpop, oblivious to the evil lurking behind her. *Wouldn't you love to lie on top of her and feel yourself in-between her thighs?*

The lifeguard blew her whistle, calling for thirty minutes of adult swim. It was just a matter of seconds before the line would begin to swell. He took advantage of the surge, pushing hard up against her back. He took too long to pull away. Orange screamed and yelled, calling out for help. Plaid took no time to point out the hardness of his dick. The adults began to gather before the manager could make his way over to the commotion. JJ peered down at his bare feet as the mother pried answers out of her preteen daughter. When Orange turned and began to speak, he noticed the cross around her neck. "Who are you and where are your parents," the manager demanded. He lifted his eyes to meet the frightened girl's then calmly replied, "Lucifer. You will find my father in hell."

While being dragged, he broke the manager's grip, snatched his backpack from the concrete, and hopped the fence. Just as the sirens were sounding in the parking lot, he found a hiding spot behind a rusted out barrel in the clump of trees. Before making a break for it, he scanned the lot for the girl. She was standing next to a Black Mercedes-Benz with the officer and her mother. The mother pointed to the tree line, her arms flailing. As the officer made his way in JJ's direction, he scampered on his hands and knees for a better place to hide. He knew if they caught him, it was off to juvenile detention. He waited out the officer for forty-five minutes before running like hell. As if his life depended upon getting away. Blaine was waiting at the treehouse, a new demon in his hand. They finished off the jar of white lightning, making Big Horn very happy.

Sexually frustrated, alcohol dependent, cruel to animals, elusive and defiant, Jonah Wayne Johnson entered manhood.

Chapter XII

There was barely enough time for a whore bath once I made it home from the precinct. A quick exchange with Gav and Dyl revealed one of the bird dogs was still missing. The cabin was still in ruins, but the boys vowed to pitch in.

A little lip liner and some gloss were applied, before darting over to the big house to meet Lana Coombs, the mother of the bride. As my heels dug into wet grass, I searched for the weather app on my iPhone. With only one bar left, it had just enough juice to load before the low battery warning flashed. The Doppler radar showed the rain was on top of us. It was predicted to cease later in the afternoon. Shit on toast; the yard was going to be a big problem. We needed to roll out the weatherproof carpeting in-between the tent and the barn, otherwise, the wedding party would track mud all over the place.

I slipped into the barn to find Wookiee. It was no surprise to see him carrying an armload of ten folding chairs in one hand. The folklore about Wookiee's past is more captivating than any George Lucas script. His parents were migrant farmhands, who'd hitched a ride from Birmingham, Alabama, in the spring of 1959. They had high hopes of finding work harvesting strawberries around the Portland, Tennessee area. According to the news archives, they were just three exits from their destination when the accident occurred.

It was just around midnight on the eve of March the 18th, when the trucker hit a patch of black ice at the SR-174 Goodlettsville exit. Wookiee's mother was thrown through the windshield; her body ripped in half during the collision that ensued. An off-duty nurse found the eleven pound Jesus Amante sticking out of what was left of his mother's lower torso. He was later adopted by a local farmer, and it was rumored he grew to weigh over three hundred pounds, and stand seven feet something or other by the age of fifteen. Sadly, the "Midnight Miracle" never learned to speak. He was diagnosed with Dysarthria, resulting from his neurological injury, and though you would think his future would be bleak, I'm here to tell you there has never been a misconception farther from the truth.

Our paths crossed in the winter of '77, in the lobby of the Bank of Parrottville. Daddy said it took six suckers to pry me out of the arms of the hairy giant. By the time they did, Jesus Amante had a nickname that the whole town quickly embraced. Wookiee might look like a Mexican Sasquatch, but my behemoth bodyguard is actually as gentle as a lamb. Wookeneese is our own language, a series of grunts and hand gestures we've developed over the years. Everybody knows that Wookiee would take a bullet for me and that I'd do the same for him.

Before I could even retrieve the Banquet Event Order off the wall, seven employees were yapping in my face. Apparently, my grandmother, Nanny, had fallen in the yard. Now, Nanny is a rather large woman, and she's crazier than a loon. I, of course, mean that in the most affectionate way. According to Tac, she'd hijacked the flatbed delivery cart after realizing her rear end was too large for the wheelchair. She'd demanded one of our dishwashers, Pan Aak, push her around the mansion while she barked orders through a megaphone. It seemed an employee strike was inevitable if we could not get her under control.

Nanny was not hard to find (after broadcasting she needed some pie) when her wheels got stuck in the mud behind the old slave quarter we call the speakeasy. Employee mutiny was held at bay after enticing her down from her throne, with the aid of a lemon meringue. After I got a handle on the situation, I realized, to my horror, that Nanny's right ankle was the size of an oil barrel. So we commandeered the flatbed over to the mansion for a better evaluation. Upon further inspection, there was no doubt that the bone was broken. I called 9-11, knowing an employee conquest would be certain by the time the ambulance breached the drive. Wookiee stayed behind to help the paramedics get Nanny in the ambulance. I was running on zero hours of sleep and was going to be thirty minutes late (best case scenario) to my meeting with Lana, so I gave my grandma a peck on the cheek and headed towards the big house.

*****

The mother of the bride was in the tearoom with a plate full of Aunt Maude's chicken salad heaping over the sides of a croissant. I apologized for my tardiness before making my way to the table. "The Dark Lord of Wedding Coordination," aka, Camille Rainey Carr-Glass, was tapping her fingers. Leg swinging furiously, she was sobbing into her phone. My arch-nemesis, ever since I found her stuck to my fitted sheet (long story), Camille is my first husband's second wife.

It was obvious there was something terribly wrong. I whispered a greeting to Lana, who was wearing a face of crocodile tears. *Surely the wedding hadn't been called off? For God's sake, not with four hundred pounds of*

90

Kobe beef flown in from Hyogo on a private Leer and caviar from the Caspian Sea sitting in the cooler. Wookiee penetrated the doorway, then, sounding agitated, growled. I glanced up to see what he wanted. His presence disturbed the "Dark Lord." "What's going on, Camille? Lana? Tell me now?" "Dark Lord" was curt. "Get him out of here, Muffcat."

Adding theatrics to her conversation, Camille rose and looked towards the bar. Aunt Maude started pointing to a variety of liquor bottles lined up on the antique maple countertop. With her cell phone firmly pressed to her perfectly chiseled chin, Camille reached for the ultra premium Ciroc and poured a shot. I could hear my ex-husband trying to console the "Dark Lord" through her muffled cries. "I was just up there Johnny. The church doors were unlocked, and the name tents were on her desk, but Chandra was nowhere to be found."

Camille threw back a shot of the Ciroc then shook her glass at Maude as if to say "Get me some damn ice." Maude complied, then added another shot to her glass, placing a delicately carved lime wedge on a napkin beside her trembling hand. We were all waiting with baited breath, while the Dark Lord went on and on about how scared she was, with not one ounce of empathy for the true victim of this horrendous crime. Wookiee had not budged from the edge of the doorway. Camille placed her hand over the speaker then shouted, "I said to get him out of here, Muffcat. Now!" I reluctantly motioned for Wookiee to give us some privacy. It was Camille who informed me. Chandra Sue Worsham, our First Baptist Church Secretary, the wedding calligraphist, one of my best friends since Miss Rizor's first grade class, had been found dead in the Baptismal. The entire table was in shock. It took five minutes before anyone could muster a word. The news about another homicide was sure to impact the highbrow event. The wedding party had some serious decisions to make, so I went into my disaster recovery mode.

Aunt Maude dialed the ancient rotary phone from behind the bar. Three groomsmen made it down to sit on the decision panel. Non-refundable dance floor already installed, casino games being hauled into the barn, ice carver with chainsaw in hand; the men were leaning towards going ahead with the ceremony. The maid of honor (whose head was still in rollers) sided with the still intoxicated groomsmen. The father of the bride entered the room and demanded a Scotch on the rocks. The bride was not two steps behind him and asked for "your signature drink." Aunt Maude cleared the untouched plates before heading back to the bar. After taking the rest of the drink orders, I joined her, still reeling from the news.

She whispered, "Wookiee needsa tell you sumpin." I stepped in the hallway to find him anxiously waiting. He seemed frantic while signing a random string of words: dream/ barn/ church/ van/ murder.

I presented the bride with my muddled blueberry, lemon, mint, and Jack Daniels concoction. The wedding was a go, however, it was imperative that I leave the property for a few hours. Handing the keys to the bar over to Aunt Maude, Wookiee and I headed out to my SUV. He had just revealed to me there was a huge possibility he'd seen the murderer earlier that morning, during his hour-long trek into work, driving the church van. I knew the place where he was taking me. The barn that sits off of Old Shackle Island Road has been a part of my reality and dreams for years.

We set out on the back roads of the country abyss for an impromptu sleuthing adventure. "Wookiee, are you sure the place where you saw the church van is the same barn from my dreams? The dream about Boy?"

Wookiee shook his head emphatically, and as he pointed his meaty finger in the direction of Selner County, my mind wandered way back to that dream.

Chapter XIII

Daddy tossed his twenty-gauge Browning into the back of our yellow GMC truck as we headed out into the country abyss with Uncle Vernon in the front seat. I had on a red cape over my camouflage overalls; my hair was braided into pigtails. Corn mazes and smoldering tobacco barns sprinkled the landscape as Will the Circle be Unbroken infiltrated the cab.

I was in the second-row seat; the back window to the cab was open. The original Smokey and a few more shit eaters panted in their cabin as we stopped to gas up. Vernon ran in to get Uncle E.G., as well as a fried bologna sandwich for the ride. Uncle E.G. was smoking unfiltered Camels, which made my nose burn.

Daddy designated me the official bird cleaner as we set up shop under a tree line overlooking the half-bare corn stalks. We sat and waited. The shit eaters ran back and forth amongst the corn rows, scaring up birds that were scavenging for their last supper.

E.G.'s smoke signal wasn't enough warning on that particular day; we were on the right side of the firing squad, and our execution was coming along splendidly. Daddy knelt behind me, his arms around me like a cocoon. "Muffy, Muffy, incoming! Pull the trigger, honey!"

I complied, and then proceeded to my kill. While I scampered through the corn stalks to retrieve the wounded dove, it took flight. Barely making it off the ground, it hopped about a foot in the air and landed just out of my reach. I bent down and reached out, attempting to wring its neck. Just as my fingers grazed the bird, it ascended again, moving deeper into the stalks, and out of the sight of Daddy. The ground gave out underneath me; the earth ate me up.

I fell hard and fast. Paralyzed with fear, lying facedown in a pool of cool water, I slowly rolled over. It was pitch black, with only tiny beams of light penetrating my uncertainty. As I gazed at the very small opening fifteen feet above my head, Boy appeared. Pale, with long, thick white hair all the way down his back, his eyes were as blue as the ocean. Extending his hand, he jerked me to an erect position.

With Boy leading the way, we traveled parallel to the underwater creek, down a very long, musty rock corridor. Majestic stalactites hovered like flawless statues above our heads. I wasn't scared, but Daddy, who was calling my name from up above, was in a panic.

My new friend clutched my arm and quickened our pace, but then slowed to a creep as we took a sharp left into a well-lit limestone room. As the smell of burning tobacco pierced my nostrils, I had a fleeting expectation that E.G. was the culprit, but he wasn't in the room. The cavity was a hundred feet high; a large fire lit the space, revealing flowstones, stalactites, stalagmites, helictites, and soda straws that had leached for millions of years.

Things grew more intense when my new family eagerly greeted me as I sat beside the fire. All with tobacco pipes in hand, one by one, each new relative stepped forward, then bowed. In war paint and feather headdresses, the men seem nervous as they puffed their pipes and spoke amongst themselves. Dad was still pacing the corn field, but his voice was fading. Chitto, Ahuli, Istaqa, Chapowits, Enapay, and his father, Kuckunniwi stood council while others introduced themselves and expressed awe at the sight of my tanned, brown skin. I saw children being put down for naps in the crevices of the limestone walls that were covered with red, yellow, and green, tightly woven blankets.

Kuckunniwi recalled how it was before they were driven underground by cohorts of Old Hickory when they were free to hunt buffalo and worship the sun. He spoke about the tribe. Pale and discontent, they refused to march and decided to hide, only coming out on the blackest of nights, when the moon was covered by storm clouds and thunder masked the whoosh of their arrows. They missed the sun and their horses, but still, they were grateful to be alive.

They stole corn, hens, the occasional cow, but mainly tobacco during their short stints out into the darkness. Their positioning under the barn kept locals from growing suspicious about the smoke from their pipes and the torches that lined their home. They laughed while he disclosed why you always seem to smell tobacco burning when you come upon a country barn. It was the tallest of tales, and they were the tribe behind the deception and legend.

Boy gathered charcoaled remains from a partially burned log. He addressed me as "Girl from Rock," as the elders joined me around the fire. My father went on calling out my name from the cornfield above our heads.

*****

It took us twenty minutes to reach our destination. Luckily, the rain held off. We spotted the van while passing by the weather worn structure.

I was more than a little nervous after witnessing the owner exiting his residence, so we continued past the barn. Merle Mooneyhan was not what you'd call an upstanding citizen. Oh no, no, no. That man was a legendary moonshiner with a wicked temper, a reputation for cruelty, and a huge distaste for organized religion.

I thought Wookiee might be on to something as we looked for a place to park the SUV. It was true; Merle did make for a perfect suspect. We drove down the country lane about three hundred yards before pulling off the side of the road. Once we came to a halt behind a huge oak tree, my vehicle was barely visible from the country lane.

Just then, a beat-up royal blue El Camino backed out of the Mooneyhan's driveway and crossed over to the barn. A boy of no more than ten or eleven jumped out the back of the car and entered the structure. The El Camino tore off in the opposite direction, towards town. I had no particular plan in mind but definitely intended to get a closer inspection of the property.

We made our way through the defeated-looking corn field, and up to the front of the house. Wookiee crossed the street and headed to the barn, so I approached the shack to see what could be found. While I navigated through the carcasses of cars, hungry dogs, and weathered junk sitting on the front lawn, the door to the Mooneyhan residence flung open. A petite, redheaded girl of maybe nine or ten stepped out and introduced herself as Lucy Anabelle Mooneyhan. Lucy told me that she and her brother were home alone, and revealed that her daddy and his friend were on their way to the hardware store for some supplies. When pressed, I had no good explanation for what we were doing there or the nature of our visit. Heading back, I concocted an admittedly asinine plan to gain entry into the residence, but hey, I can't *always* dazzle, and the pressure was on. With a fake smile plastered across my face, I handed over a fake spider and a pile of candy and told Lucy her family had won the mayor's Halloween home invasion contest. I was shocked that my crazy lie did the trick; the child actually invited me in.

The odors of stale tobacco and alcohol hit me like a sledgehammer before I even crossed the threshold of the door. I looked around to find a baby in a makeshift swing, covered in food. Ball jars cluttered every surface of the main living area; dishes were piled up two feet high in a filthy sink. There was not a toy or book anywhere in sight.

While I explored the space, Lucy devoured the miniature boxes of Nerds I'd tucked into her tiny hand. A peculiar noise echoed from a cluttered hallway. "Lucy, are you sure you are alone in here? Can you show me your room?" She picked up her fake spider then took off down the well-worn carpet. May it be duly noted that Muffcat Mansker has smelled just about every conceivable body odor that can come from a human being. That being said, there was something even fouler than death permeating the air.

"You wanna see my granny?" My eyes peered into a bedroom where a dog was lying on a filthy bedspread. "Sure, Lucy. Where is she?" Lucy opened the closet doorway. Confused and scared eyes locked onto mine as the thing tried to grab for my feet. "Oh my god! Lucy, who is this?" Crumpled on the floor, in a fetal position, Charlene Busby-Mooneyhan gurgled. The emaciated woman, who supposedly had been dead for over a decade, was in dire need of immediate medical care.

"Where's your telephone, Lucy?" The six-year-old led me back into the kitchen to a rotary phone. I dialed 911 while hunting for anything that contained an address. Fumbling through the pile of seemingly ignored mail, my hands were shaking as the bills scattered across the counter. I lifted a postcard to my face, searching for something. The handwriting from the precinct shuffled into focus. Every ounce of empathy told me to stay, make sure the emergency responders got to the scene and DCS was called, but Wookiee charged into the shack. He practically cattle-prodded me out of the door as blood dripped from his hands and forehead.

Once in the SUV, it was obvious Wookiee was shaken up. Blood was pouring from his right hand, and he had a gash over his left eye. I handed him a stack of napkins from my console, then told him to hold on as my wheels spun up onto the blacktop. We were out of sight before the paramedics could cross the county line. Back at the big house, we got his head cleaned up and his hand bandaged.

While sitting at the bar, I handed him a piece of paper. "Here, Wook. Take your time. Tell me what happened." It took a good ten minutes for him to write down what had transpired at the barn, what with the bandages around his dominant hand. When he finished, I read the note carefully, out loud. "Make cave under barn/ bury seven metal drums/ man from church with red hair/ he hurt boy in bad way/ break nose and two teeth."

I was still prying information out of Wookiee when he started to go berserk. He let out a meaty growl, just as someone yanked my entire body from the barstool. It was my Uncle Vernon, the hot-headed and controversial town mayor. My Uncle Vernon practically yanked me off my bar stool. He yelled for Wookiee to stay the hell back, and then dragged me out the door. His green eyes were full of fury as he led me from the mansion and over to the building we call the speakeasy. While fidgeting with the key, he began to roar in my face. "Fill me in now, Muffy Catherine! No bullshit. You are fucking with my political career!"

Once inside the ancient cabin, he slammed the door behind us and then continued to unleash his rage as his hand firmly gripped my bicep. "Merle said you were trespassing. Thinking about filing charges. What the hell were you doing over in Selner County?" I refused to answer him. His grip got firmer. "You are lucky, child, I am in this position! You better start talking, if you want me to get you out of this hornets' nest." Vernon was inches from my face with his black cowboy hat touching my forehead. When I again refused to answer him, he let out a string of obscenities, turned on the lights, and made his way over to the kitchen area in his charcoal, hand-finished wool suit.

Vernon reached into a small cupboard over the sink, got down some Wild Turkey and a highball glass, and then started messing with his cell phone. He was pacing and asking random questions about what I had witnessed at the Mooneyhans'. He received and read a text message, drinking while staring at the phone's screen. "You know Aunt Mila is gonna smell that on you, Vernon. And no, I did not see any men at the house. Just two kids left alone in degradation and squalor."

I took a seat at the poker table and buried my head in my hands. When looking up for a response, my uncle just glared at me. "Uncle Vernon, please hear me out. These murders are personal to me. Two mutilated classmates, brutally tortured and murdered. Had the pleasure of making another trip to the ME's for a deceased church secretary with a bullet between her eyes; she grew up three doors down from me in the golden triangle. We have a serial killer preying on women of our community. Stop worrying about those goddamn shiners!"

Vernon was relentless. I was not going to escape the conversation without telling him the entirety of what we had witnessed. He lowered his voice and asked me once again, "what did you see, Muffcat?" I reluctantly responded this time, "a lot of shit. Charlene is alive, for one. Being held against her will in a drug-induced state. The young girl claims Merle is her and the baby's father. He was on a trip to the hardware store probably for supplies for his moonshine operation with one of his buddies. Wookiee discovered seven drums being buried underneath the barn. Ken Akers is involved. He had the church van there. Pretty sure he is somehow connected to these murders. Most shocking, however, Wookiee walked in on him and a young boy. He was sexually molesting the poor kid. Broke the stupid bastard's face up pretty bad from the looks of Wookiee's hands." Vernon was now seated at the poker table and gripping his highball glass with both hands. His head was hung low. "Shit, Muffcat. Please do not tell me that Mexican freak accosted our youth minister? The deacons have all known Akers was light in his loafers for years. The church does not need any more scandal right now." Vernon banged his fists on the poker table, causing his highball glass to flipping it over. He jumped up and wiped his forehead. "Who else have you told about the van being over at Merle's barn?" I proceeded to tell him about the 911 call and the letter. How the handwriting matched the manifesto, and my suspicions that either Merle or one of his redneck renegade associates were behind the murders.

Vernon slammed his hands down on the poker table again, repeatedly, cussing every other word. The highball glass rolled then shattered on the ground. Vernon leaned into me, got as close to my face as humanly possible, then stared me directly in my eyes. "Stop your bullshit investigation, Muffcat. I will get you out of the legal situation, but your fucking meddling is done this very minute! You have no idea what evil you are dealing with." He lifted his phone from the table then lit into me again. He went so far as to say that if I told the authorities about any of the illegal activities, or about Charlene, he would see to it that Merle's charges stood. Then suggested that I get sort of mental evaluation. He'd caught wind of my premonitions and thought I was losing it.

I continued to plead my case, to urge him to contact the authorities about the note. All to no avail. After some more very heated words, Vernon stood up to make his exit. I began yelling to his back; what was said next, stopped Vernon in his tracks.

"One more thing, Uncle Vernon. Wookiee is on the other side of that door." Vernon's spun around and scowled at me. He rushed back over to the poker table, grabbing me up by my arm. We were looking at each other, eye to eye. As if he were examining my soul, he glared into my pupils and snarled. Then Vernon got as close to my ear as he possibly could and whispered, "Muffcat, seems the emotional toll of your job has caused you to lose your mind, yet again. I'm going to ask that your little visit to the Mooneyhan's be swept under the rug if you shut your goddamn mouth. Stop this bullshit little private eye investigation Melvin told me about. Or else. I *will* go public with what the doctors told us about you when you were five, you crazy, embarrassing bitch. Stay out of the precinct, stay away from that new detective, and get the fucking giant to back down."

Dear old Uncle Vernon let go of my arm, then waited for me to call off Wookiee before making his exit.

Chapter XIV

Wednesday, November 14, 1988, 9:42 am. Office of the Headmaster, Baylor School, Chattanooga, Tennessee.

As the chaplain threw him down onto the bench outside the headmaster's door, JJ laughed at the ridiculousness of his situation. His tormentor, Sterner Hammond, the ordained Christian minister, who also happened to be his religious studies teacher, yanked him up all 232 steps by his ear. Hammond's pastoral governance, he made crystal clear, led him to believe Jonah Wayne Johnson had bigger issues other than being flogged in the middle of the night as he lay in his dormitory bed. He announced that this would be the last time Mr. Johnson would turn his classroom into a babbling and twisted platform for his unconventional ideals about religious conviction.

Headmaster's voice was now overpowering the chaplain. "He's just seeking attention, Sterner. Surely the boy does not believe the Devil is inside him. It is a foolish, but understandable mistake for a child who has been raised by an agnostic father and a schizophrenic mother to blame one's imprudent decisions on someone else. At least this shows us that he does recognize the depravity of his actions. I agree that he is compulsive and desensitized, but I still believe the child can be reformed. We have invested way too many resources to just give up on him now." The chaplain bellowed back, "this is over my head, Thomas. Last month, the janitorial staff uncovered an ancient manuscript detailing the six pillars of Iman in his dorm room. All 105 key points of creed were highlighted. Even though his professed belief in the prophet Allah undermines the teachings of this university, it was at least a step in the right direction. And then, just as we made accommodations for his five daily prayers, Agnes discovered Mary Pride's *The Way Home* in his backpack in the library. His explanation? He'd accepted the Quiverfull philosophy and lifestyle. Listen, after today's antics, I was the one who uncovered a copy of *Helter Skelter* and *Satanic Bible* in his dorm room." With that, the chaplain spanked the books in question down onto the headmaster's desk.

After a few beats, to seemingly create a dramatic impact, the chaplain continued, "He feels he belongs on the dark side, Thomas. By his own confession, Satan choked out any of the voices that would have been beneficial to our cause. It's time we cut our losses and selected a new recruit. Have you gained any headway with Claude or Clyde?"

Headmaster wasted no time before answering. "The girl's abilities have gone cold, Sterner. Her own father professed she's a loose cannon. Dax cannot take any chances on our next recruit. There is too much at stake with our Washington funding."

To which, Sterner roared back, "She was the most accurate out of the seventy-six tested, Thomas! She would have never pulled a stunt like her cousin did today." Headmaster quizzed Sterner, "and what, exactly, was the stunt?"

Sterner's voice lowered to a whisper, "JJ proclaimed that Charles Manson is the true Messiah. When he stood in front of the classroom to read his thesis, it was riddled with babbling references to the crazed, cold-blooded killer being Jesus Christ. He is making a mockery out of me, Thomas. Replicating my accent, my dialect; he went so far as to tuck his tie into his shirt as I do in the cafeteria. He is claiming Big Horn, Lucifer himself, speaks to him. He compared his bullying by his classmates to the suffering and pain Jesus endured by the Romans. Then he went on some wild rant about assembling a harem of women he called his flock. Talked about the time he spent at the Spahn Movie Ranch with Manson as if it were heaven on Earth. He actually thinks he can carry the women with him into the afterlife. He's even conceived of a ritual to perform in exchange for what he called the ultimate sacrifice. Do you know what he considers the ultimate sacrifice?"

Which was followed by no audible reply from the headmaster.

"Their lives. Their lives, Thomas." And the ritual?" After a long silence, the headmaster inquired, "is he using the ancient manuscript, *Transitus Mariae*?" Sterner's voice quivered "yes, yes... it was sandwiched in back of *Helter Skelter* as if it were a postscript ... but, there's more."

The headmaster got up to shut the door. JJ began to rock in his seat, as he rubbed the worn fabric on the top of his knees. Their voices were now muffled, but he was still able to make out most of what the chaplain was divulging to Headmaster.

"Marla intercepted an encrypted letter headed to Corcoran State Prison just a few days ago. Once we found the key in his pillowcase, poor Agnes spent the better part of the morning deciphering the text. He's somehow intercepted our communication with Clyde Mansker, Thomas.

You need to read this. It's Agnes' ciphered version of the letter he attempted to send to Charles Manson. The child confesses he's harbored fantasies about killing humans even before hitting puberty, God help us."

Twenty minutes of prickling silence made the clock's ticking sound like the roar of a tornado in JJ's head. His damn tie was too tight, and the pants that his mother sent him were annoyingly snug around his waist.

As his fate sank into an almost inaudible mumble, JJ read the words written in Latin from above the archway. "Honesty, Respect, Spirituality, Leadership, Academics, Character, Individuality." Seven was his ticket out. He was almost free.

"Sterner, this is blasphemy. I know your intentions were admirable, taking the child in, but you are right. We cannot allow him to compromise the morality of the other students in this project. Regretful as I am about Mansker's predicament, the efforts of Giavanna haven't been fruitful."

"Vernon wants nothing to do with the boy. With Castle Heights closing, should we look into Riverside Military Academy down in Gainesville?" Sterner asked. Headmaster replied, "It'll be impossible to transfer him there. They're thorough with their psychological assessments. Look into The Ranch over in Nunnelly, Tennessee. They can provide the mental health support the child needs. You were right Sterner; we should have lobbied harder for the Mansker girl."

As the men discussed their next guinea pig, JJ became lost in his thoughts. After reading the letter one final time, he extracted a lighter from his pocket. Vernon Mansker might not want him as a son, but he was going to put him into business. There was not going to be a senior year. No freaking reform school in Nunnelly either. As the letter began to burn, JJ threw it in the nearest trash receptacle, and then pulled the plastic container directly underneath the smoke detector. He was sure to be expelled. The years' worth of spared tuition was all he wanted. Little Horn Heating and Air did have a good ring to it. The blackmail money would be enough to purchase a used van and a good set of tools.

*****

Jonah Wayne Johnson would not let his feet step on the lines in the concrete as he made his way to the Olympic-sized swimming pool, which meant he had to almost hop and skip to stay on point. He knew his gate was awkward; his classmates stared. It wasn't his fault they made the pattern so damn big. There was nothing in this world he wanted more than to jump in the water, to cleanse himself from this chapter of his life. As he stripped his clothing from his body, JJ lit a cigarette, and then screamed at the top of his lungs, "repent and be baptized every one of you! In the name of Charles Manson for the forgiveness of your sins, receive the gift of the Holy Spirit!"

Chapter XV

I could not remember the last time anyone had called and left a message on our home answering machine, but damn if we didn't have five voicemails waiting for us when we returned to the cabin after the wedding. Gavin was at his girlfriend's, so Dylan and I were alone. Drop dead gorgeous, Dylan Michael Danderson looks just like his mother. He has blond hair with olive skin that gets gloriously tan in the summertime, and one feature that is undeniably his father's; he has Duke's eyes. They kill me. They have the same passion that drew me to Dylan's father. Not light brown, but amber. With just a hint of ginger that reminds me of fire; they're mysterious and profound. One of them, however, was now black.

The wedding reception had gotten off to a rocky start, to say the very least, when Dylan was cornered by one of the groomsmen's fathers right before the toasts were about to begin. With his mother's death now relevant news, questions and rumors about her homicide had been tormenting Dylan for days.

One of the deacons of our church, Chris Dickens, cornered Dylan and made a flat-out insensitive remark. The crass comment was something to the effect of "It is a real shame that a Christian woman as God-fearing as Chandra Sue Worsham-Carter will be forever be tied to the death of two whores and a voodoo witch." With a Dickel and water still in hand, the deacon, who wasn't yet finished, weighed in with an outlandish remark about my lifestyle. Dylan told me how the holy man (yeah, right) alluded to the fact that my hedonism was as much to blame for Shelley Danderson's murder as her own lack of self-control over her personal demons. I did not see the tray of Armand de Brignac Rose get dropped over the retired school teacher's head, but did, however, enjoy the great pleasure of breaking up the fistfight that ensued. I am pretty sure it was Dylan who threw the first punch. Nonetheless, by the time the brawl was over, Wookiee had to pull me off the deacon, whose head somehow wound up underneath the wedding party's table. My heel stuck in his thigh (oh yes, it was a keeper).

While looking for a frozen bag of anything for Dylan to put on his formerly dreamy eye, I hesitantly pushed play on the answering machine. The first message was Chris Dickens' attorney, dropping hints about a lawsuit. The second voicemail was from my mother. She'd already heard about the brawl from my sister and was on her way in from Florida. Not exactly the news I needed at the moment, if you know what I mean, but the worst was yet to come. The third delightful message was from Randolph Danderson, Dylan's fraternal grandfather, who was screaming about cutting off his grandson's trust fund, his third such threat since the moment Dylan had dropped out of college to pursue a career in music. This time, though, the retired county prosecutor turned judge included a pretty strong warning about *my* obnoxious behavior as well. Dylan hit pause when Randolph went into a tirade and demanded that he move out of my cabin.

"You want me to play the last two, Momcat?" By then, it was 2:00 a.m. I handed Dyl a bag of lima beans while kicking off my stilettos. Then I hit the play button for myself. According to the robotic voice, the fourth message had been received just minutes before. It seemed strange getting this many voicemails after midnight. Queenie's voice stopped me and Dylan dead in our tracks. She was shrieking about Carligene Byron-Byrd's SUV; then there was something about another abduction. She reported that Carligene was last seen by her grandfather around 5:30 p.m. when she stopped by her grandfather's fireworks stand to pick up her check. When she was not home in time to depart for the wedding, her husband tried to file a missing person's report. It was not until her SUV was found at a local boat dock, with massive amounts of blood in the cab, that the police took the situation seriously. They issued an all-points bulletin for a boat, of all things. Just hours before the wedding, Troy McNease (Queenie's husband) had reported his twenty-five-foot cabin cruiser missing. It was now alleged the kidnappers were armed and dangerous, and heading somewhere up Old Hickory Lake. I grabbed the phone off the receiver just as the robot announced we had another message. I stood there listening, in stunned disbelief. "Dylan, you need to hear this. Now. "

I rewound the message then handed the receiver over to Dylan. His face turned white as a ghost as the eerie message, which he put back on speaker, filled the air. "Remember the former things of old, for I am God, and there is no other. Dylan Michal Danderson, your mother, was the best whore ever." There were screams in the background of the message, and then the line went dead. Dylan was now pacing and trying to recollect the voice. He played the recording back a few times while I called the police from my cell phone. We both just stared at the machine while waiting for dispatch to pick up.

Dylan was visibly shaken. He turned to me, struggling to get his words out. "Mom moommm moomcat… cat, I… I… I nu… nu… know that voice. Ba-ba-back whe-whe when I was nine, may… maybe ten. Mu-mu-mum was taking me to Pleasant Green pool for a birthday party. We stopped by EG's for a few sandwiches and some…"

I interjected, "who is he? Why is he taunting you, Dyl?"

The dispatch operator answered on the fourth ring. I held my hand up as soon as the female on the other end of the line asked if it was an emergency. After a brief explanation, I rewound the message and held my iPhone up to the machine. The dispatch officer repeated my address twice. 'Yes, the same house that was broken into Friday night." Dylan did not waste a second before picking the story back up.

"I… I… I don't think she ever told me his nu-nu-name. I… I do remember everything that happened that day, though." I had not heard him stutter this badly in a long time. "Calm down Dylan. Slow down, son."

He took a breath and went on. "After she spotted him, Mom told me the man had killed her childhood pet. Sh-sh-she was scared. Said we needed to wa-wa-wait for him to leave before going into the store. We sat without the air conditioning for whha… waaa… what felt like a fucking eternity. When he disappeared around the corner, she told me to stay it the car until she could come around to my door. Mom yanked my arm almost out of the socket as we ran inside. I… I… remember her bathing suit cover-up. It was see-through. Da-Dad always told her it was too revealing. She kept pulling it down as we rushed through the aisles. Wa-wa-we were in checkout when the man entered E.G's. Mom thrust the cart to a bagboy, grabbed me by my neck, then pushed me out the door."

Recounting all this was obviously agonizing for Dyl. He'd not been this rattled since his mother disappeared.

"I… I remember having a Payday bar in hand. The bagboy yelled at us to come and pay for it, but we never looked back. The man followed us to the car. Then he demanded that Mom roll down her window. His eyes were wild, green, bloodshot, filled with rage. She started honking the horn at the bagboy, but he turned and ran away after seeing the guy. I was scared shitless as Mom fumbled to get the key in the ignition. She reached over to make sure my door was locked.

The man was disheveled. I never will forget the look in his eyes. Mom told me that she knew him. Told me not to even glance his way. She kept referring to him as the fucking devil, told me he'd been the one to kill her dog. He was rambling in riddles, asking her if she had fallen from heaven; then he started to spew obscenities. Mom was trying to cover my ears. Then, just as if a light had flipped, the weird son-of-a-bitch started reciting a poem. When she didn't respond, he started beating on her driver's side window as we pulled away. He chased us for a good fifty yards, all the while pounding on the trunk. Mom drove to the country club instead of the public pool. She was still upset. Dad met us for lunch. He told her she was getting a restraining order this time." I ran through my mental Rolodex of men with green eyes. Nobody fitting the description was rising to the surface. My cell phone rang, making us jump. It was Big D.

"Momcat, I have something I want you to listen to." I held up my hand then proceeded to take the call. "Yes, Big D, I am sure the message has something to do with the disappearance. You can hear a woman screaming in the background. Yes, the message is cryptic. No, I did not recognize the number. No, we did not try to call God back. Yes, yes, that is what he said." I repeated the number back to the detective, who sounded like he was in motion. I could hear engines roaring in the background. After I finished the call, Dylan handed me his iPad. He had Nashville Public Radio's website pulled up.

I used the restroom then poured a cup of coffee before sitting down to study the website. "Big D is sending a federal agent over here, Dyl." We sat back down at the kitchen counter, and I adjusted my glasses. "You'll have to listen to the entire podcast, Momcat. It will better explain it." Dyl eyes appeared dejected as he shared his thoughts. "Momcat, I truly believe my mother knew her murderer. I think this sick bastard might have tormented her for years."

Chapter XVI

I think it would be fair to admit that it's been some time since I studied anatomy at the John A. Gupton Mortuary College. Yes; it's all very glamorous, I know. But there are some things that get foggy over time.

After listening to the podcast for a few minutes, I had to restart it. The criminologist had a thick British accent, one of those that seems tinged with Scottish that can feel like another language altogether. But, I digress.

Most of the terminology this expert was using was difficult to follow. And yet, for some strange reason I can't really explain, I had the strongest sense that I knew the doctor. The interview started out in a very precise and detailed fashion; there was a research study on anti-social individuals, all of whom had experienced some sort of medical phenomenon with one of the lobes of their brains. There was also something going on with their hypothalamus and mirror neurons. "Good Lord." I needed to back up. "What in the hell is a mirror neuron? This doc sounds like a pompous ass, Dyl. And I swear I'm not just saying that because I don't have any idea what he's talking about." I put the podcast on pause, pulled up a diagram of the brain, and then quickly studied the components and their functions. Before I could press play again, the doorbell rang.

Ah, good times. We now had not one, but two FBI agents in the cabin drinking coffee around our kitchen table. After we discussed our whereabouts for the evening and played the recording, the female agent said she wanted to know more about the Danderson case. J-Laz, as she introduced herself, was working with Big D on the current homicide investigations, and was aware of my connection to Shelley and her husband. After a short synopsis of my part in solving the missing person's case, we started to discuss the possibility that Dylan's run-in with the crazy guy in the parking lot of E.G.'s could somehow be tied to it all.

J-Laz, who, truth be told, was rather attractive, was familiar with the study from the NPR podcast. Dyl questioned her with interest. She engaged him. "Yes, Dylan, the study took place in Russia, with a large population of the young subjects starting when they were only toddlers. Scientists documented their childhood and maturing behaviors for decades, and then all the participants willingly received brain scans in their mid-thirties. Of those who turned out to be violent criminal offenders, the majority displayed the same brain abnormalities. As a part of our profiler training, we both work closely with Dr. Dax Tansley, who oversaw the brain scans. Dax and one of our very own FBI agents, John Douglas, were instrumental in developing the behavioral science method of law enforcement we all now use in our profiling efforts."

Dylan was hungrily hanging on every word the perky agent was serving up. "So, J-Laz, tell me. Do you believe people can be prewired to murder? I mean, this guy obviously already had issues when he killed Mom's Cocker Spaniel."

The older, male agent, who didn't give his name, spoke directly to Dylan as he pointed to the diagram of the brain that was still up on the iPad screen. "The short answer, in my opinion, is yes. To break it down for you, the frontal lobe of the brain controls reasoning, planning, parts of speech, movement, emotions, and problem solving. In the violent criminal population, Dax discovered lower brain weight. Contained in this same lobe is the orbitofrontal cortex. When functioning correctly, it allows normal people to manage emotional impulses in socially appropriate ways. Sociopaths have a hard time with productive behaviors like empathy, altruism, and forgiveness. So they're more likely to lash out when faced with situations that summon feelings of anger, resentment, and other volatile reactions linked with emotional pain."

Without coming up for air, the agent continued with the chilling lesson. "In violent offenders, the orbital cortex doesn't suppress behaviors like rage and violence, or the compulsion to eat or have sex excessively. Or, as in your mother's case, the impulse to murder. Those behaviors are caused by lower activity levels in this area."

Man, I felt like I was in the middle of some surreal, middle of the night science-fiction class, as the no-name pointed out the various components of the brain. But, sure as shit, I was intrigued. I had to give it to him; the man knew his stuff, and the information was bubbling out of his mouth like a geyser. I got up to retrieve the pot of coffee as he went on. "The brain scans picked up on the amount of carbon monoxide being put off by the cells while they are active. The scans display the saturation rates in the form of various colors. The less oxygen, the less carbon monoxide they are putting off, thus less activity in that part of the brain. The blue color indicates lower levels of activity. Look here."

The agent pulled up a website while J-Laz saw her opportunity and took the conversation back. "More research led the doctor to discover what they call the Warrior Gene. Now, this part is fascinating, because this gene contributes to the regulating of the serotonin in the brain. Serotonin controls mood. The more you have, the calmer you become. Dax's studies have linked those who have the Warrior Gene to increased risk-taking and retaliatory behavior. Almost all serial killers who've been tested have the gene. Even as young children, future male serial killers, especially, are more likely to respond aggressively to perceived conflict." She turned to Dyl. "I'm thinking your encounter with this guy could be something for us to look into, given what you shared about your mother's pet."

I jumped in, "so what is your take on all the religious aspects of these cases, J-Laz?" The other agent received a text on his Blackberry and excused himself before walking over towards the kitchen. J-Laz looked over to her partner. "Funny she should ask, huh?" She gave him a disconcerting look. "We are still working on that, Muffcat. His correspondence seems to bounce around from believing he is God to insisting he is being controlled by the Devil. But for now, all I can say is that we are leaning more towards the religious artifacts being associated with a time in his life where spirituality was forced upon him."

No-name chimed in from across the room. "It's like he has created his own philosophies on good and evil, but oftentimes these sickos are just trying to string us along and tie up our resources. He's probably more infatuated with Charles Manson than any religion. In my opinion, the religious crap is his way of setting up his own insanity plea. We saw the same modis operandi up in Seattle a few years ago. A priest that denounced Catholicism then turned around and killed six women living at the homeless shelter the church ran across the street. He claimed he was an offspring from some species mentioned in the Bible. What were the children of the fallen called, J-Laz, Nephilim?" J-Laz shook her head "Yes." Then she added, "His case was actually the first to use Dr. Tansley's research against the prosecution. The prewired murderer defense actually exploded in our faces."

No-name walked over to his partner and put his hand on the back of her chair. "J-Laz, I think we've shared enough here. Mrs. Mansker, Dylan, thank you so much for your time this morning." J-Laz took Dylan's contact information, then handed him her card. She mentioned that there might possibly be a police report or restraining order stemming from the incident, before asking if Dylan would be willing to review some mug shots. She gathered the answering machine and said it would be a few days before they would be able to get the recorder back to us.

It was four o'clock in the morning by the time the agents departed. I reached for a sticky note and a pen, just as Dylan started to ascend the ladder to his loft. "Dyl, you're really on to something. Remember the voices I told you I heard in the embalming room? The female runner who was reporting some sort of attack over at the Toss-Knight Park? I want you to get ahold of Joey Philpot tomorrow. His mother's name is Barbara. She was an avid runner, back in the eighties. I think she moved to Phoenix after she remarried. Her son has a title company in town over by Tommy's office. Ask him to get you in touch with Barb. See if she can recall filing a report about a dog being killed down by the jogging trails back then. I wrote the name of the title company and told Dylan I'd left the sticky note for him on the counter. "Uh, yeah, okay, Momcat." My stomach clenched. Dyl's voice seemed weary.

I plopped back onto the couch with Dylan's iPad, in order to listen to the rest of the podcast. I probably wasn't ten minutes in before I started nodding off. Next thing I knew, my dreams were taking me back to a place I'd held dear to my heart for most of my life: the Hee-Haw Firework and T-Shirt Shack. This time, however, I was not there as an embodied participant. Watching from above the checkout counter, I saw women covering the buffet line with homemade pies and Crock-Pots full of barbeque, wieners in grape jelly, and baked beans. Setting up the buffet was normally my job for the Independence Day festivities at the roadside, ramshackle fireworks stand.

Unable to move from my positioning about three feet above everyone's heads, my soul felt stuck. Holy shit, it was the strangest sensation. Like scuba diving without flippers, weights, or a regulator to offset buoyancy, I just hung in the air. I couldn't control my movement with my own muscles; the sensation was frustrating.

As my spirit floated from place to place, I wound up outside the building. A city commissioner, one who had been dead for years, greeted the old-timers as they lined the red benches on the front porch. Tommy's baseball team welcomed the patrons as they collected donations for their summer tournament. My brother was amongst the sea of ball caps, yet he was thinner, younger, and his voice was still high-pitched. Random I-65 travelers and local folk bustled in-and-out of the building, yet no one noticed me looming in the air over their heads. Granted, I had no shape, no form, and there was no mass to my being. I felt so weird, both somehow omnipotent and powerless over my own destiny. One second I was floating over the parking lot, and then an unsystematic current of air would blow me back inside the building.

Back to hovering over the cash register for what felt like an eternity, I finally let out my breath. Even my huffing and puffing just inches from the patrons and salespeople's faces produced no purchase. My invisibility was really beginning to piss me off. Speech seemed impossible, at first, but, in due course, I was able to produce the faintest of noises. The sounds pouring from my mouth were nothing like my booming and husky voice. I had the essence of a house cat or small child. But, the more frustrated I became, the stronger the projections of my voice. Then, after what felt like my thousandth attempt to scream, Carligene glimpsed up in my direction.

Checking out customer after customer, Carligene was monitoring the flow of homemade hooch from behind the cash register. Tilly Jean Sanders left with her bag of sparklers in one hand and a moonshine punch in the other. Again, I tried to get my voice to billow in the sticky air. This time Carligene looked up and asked, "who is that?" Just as Sam-Tee, the family patriarch, retrieves a record from an old credenza, our connection was broken. Just like that. Damn it! When the 45 was placed on the decrepit old record player, well, let's just say my voice cannot compete with the likes of Hank Williams.

As soon as the song began to saturate the air, the raven-haired maidens lined up in front of the bank of cash registers, then proceeded to line dance in perfect synchronicity. Glenda, Carligene's mother, took her rightful place as the choreographer. As she placed each woman into position and assumed the lead, the sales force gathered around and proceeded to howl and clap along to the rhythm. Carligene was, as always, in perfect tempo. In an old pair of boots and cut-off blue jeans, she began to twirl on her heels. My existence was easily overshadowed by the clamor of the tapping cowboy boots and slapping of hands. A huge mother of an industrial fan made the raven-haired beauties' tresses flutter in the wind. The shutter of the blades rapidly pushed me farther and farther away from the festivities. And just like that, my spirit was on the move again.

The voyage ended with my spirit becoming immobile just above an exit sign at the back of the building. I felt like a tightly wound ball. Instead of viewing a wide area of space, my senses were now focused on just one tiny spot; maybe a three-foot radius of space. A bizarre figure entered through the door below me. A demon, with horns and wide-set eyes, hastily shoved a small child into a display of Sexy Riders, and then pushed a cart into an elderly gentleman's thigh. His bare feet were touching the cheap, dirty titles as he lurked around the corner of one of the displays. The beast continued to prowl towards the line of women, as his figure took on a loftier form. He looked to be over seven or eight feet tall; his size forced him to squat down to home in on the women's faces. He walked up and down the line of beautiful women, bending almost in half to glare into their eyes. All of a sudden, the shadow of the beast, which did not seem to be connected to its body, started mimicking the dancers' every move. As the demon ranted and wailed in the dancers' faces, he threw his head back and tilted it up towards the sky. As my fear took over, using emotions as my leverage, I knew I had to try to get someone to notice me.

I approached Sam-Tee first. Like he was sensing a gnat, he swatted at me. As the needle on the vinyl skipped into silence, Sam-Tee hastily made his way back to the record player. Only stopping for Sam-Tee to change out the 45, the gussied up ladies again started twirling on their heels.

Sam-Tee now sensed something, but it sure wasn't me. The Devil was lurking, getting closer, and studying the face of Carligene. I tried to distract him, but the beast and the shadow had detached, and the female silhouette was snarling at me. The demon recklessly tried to dance with Carligene, but silhouette jumped in-between. A confrontation ensued. Sam-Tee chased off the beast, but the female shadow stayed put. Still unaware of the danger she was in, Carligene kept on dancing. The silhouette moved behind her and started caressing Carligene's breasts; the form rubbed its hands up and down the length of her body. Afterwards, the female shadow howled in the wind before following the ghastly creature out of the building.

Chapter XVII

Saturday, July 3' 1991, 4:02 pm. Interstate 65, just south of the Kentucky border.

JJ hadn't been this fired up in a long time. Granted, he had blown through the twenty-five thousand in hush money on pot, hookers, and that failed attempt at building a commune out of his deceased mother's house. And yet, somehow he'd never imagined his biological father would completely cut him off financially.

He'd been stuck working for Angus Hellman for the last three and a half years and was sick of the long hours and the anonymity. If he didn't get the cash to start his own company soon, he might just let the cat out of the bag. Who gave a fuck that he had signed some legal documents back in 1988? All it would take would be telling one person about the affair, and like magic — poof! — his father's political aspirations and marriage would be over.

JJ decided to turn the van around. His on-call shift didn't start for another two hours. He had just enough time to make it back Parrottville, and then he could be in Bowling Green in time to work the late shift. Of course, if he wasn't back by six o'clock, he'd lose his shitty job. Even though he was the only NATE certified technician in the entire company, his boss would not think twice about firing him if he missed one more service call. Those two speeding tickets he'd racked up, not to mention the fight with Jose in the shop, hadn't helped his situation either. But he knew full well the real reason: Angus Hellman was suspicious of the 1,200 unexplained miles he'd put on Truck 8.

JJ looked down at the temperature gauge before exiting the SR 52 Portland/Orlinda ramp. With the temperature still at 91 degrees, it was going to be one really long, miserable fucking night. As he barreled towards the on-ramp, he had a pretty good idea where his biological father could be found. The Hee-Haw fireworks stand near the Millersville's exit was the most probable destination. He'd check there first before driving over to the B&B, where Vernon had been earlier in the day.

JJ wasted no time picking up speed once he'd ascended the southbound ramp while singing along to every lyric pouring from the radio. *Michael Hutchence's voice hides so much pain*, he thought. He remembered the time he'd spent in Parrottville and wondered what tactics, exactly, his father had used to shut Cliff Johnson up. The DNA analysis Step-Monster had seethed about for all those years had opened up a can of worms for Cliff. Right after discovering JJ was not his son, he'd been thrown in the county jail for supposedly molesting the Gremlin. JJ couldn't help but wonder what the stupid little shit looked like as she entered her teens. Thinking about the chubby little toddler made the bile in the back of his throat rise.

After pulling off of the interstate, he made a quick stop at the store where he had met Shelia. The thought of her was like conjuring an old ghost. He sat in the van for a good ten minutes, reciting the poetry he'd written for the runaway those many years ago. He could still see the kinky blond hair lying on her pubic bone; could almost taste her rancid breath. The excitement coursing through his veins at the vision of her in that helpless position turned his dick hard as stone. Seconds before he could undo his belt buckle, a small-framed girl with long, wavy, dark hair snagged his attention. She was conversing with the owner of the store, next to one of the gas pumps. He knew her. As a matter of fact, he knew her quite well. She was the girl from the skating rink. The girl that he told his best friend about seeing down at the park. He had lacked the courage to introduce himself then, realizing the crazy-haired bitch walking next to her knew about the Cocker Spaniel. But she was the one he'd asked to slow skate the summer before he was sent away. The one that caused the big blow up with Blaine Patton. He put the van in drive, then drove over and parked next to the gas pump on the other side of her maroon Grand Am.

He took a deep breath and zipped his pants back up before killing the ignition. The owner took a hard look at him and then spun back to talk to the girl. JJ turned towards the van as the gas meter began to climb. "Yes, Uncle E.G. I am really doing it! Gavin and I are moving to New York. She forked over the proceeds to start her own fashion line. We're heading out Monday morning!"

JJ peered over his shoulder. He liked her spunk. She had beautiful brown eyes and really perky tits. He continued to eavesdrop on the conversation until the handle of the gas pump snapped into the idle position. The girl followed the elderly owner into the building, while JJ twisted the gas cap, closed the door, and then grabbed his keys from the ignition.

As he made his way to the beer, he scanned the tiny storefront for the girl. She was at the meat counter. He stopped short of the cooler in order to get a better look. Yeah; she looked good enough to eat. Her legs were tight and muscular, and he liked the bracelet she wore around her ankle.

"Excuse me, buddy, you mind if I reach in here for a second?" JJ stepped out the way of a middle-aged man, just as she turned her head in his direction. He stared down at his work boots while the guy tried to strike up an empty conversation about his favorite brand of beer. JJ hated that the stupid fat-ass was so aware of him. The abductions always went smoother when nobody noticed. JJ had decided a long time ago not to shit where he ate. Even though he'd not lived in the God-forsaken place in years, he couldn't take any chances on anyone identifying him at the scene.

He reluctantly grabbed for a twelve pack of Milwaukee's Best and headed towards the cash register. The girl passed by him without even paying for her sandwich. He fidgeted with his belt buckle while waiting for the annoying loudmouth to pay for his beer. JJ watched the girl get into her car, taking note of the direction she was heading. The same way as the Hee-Haw. He placed his beer up on the counter then motioned to the lady behind him. "Forgot something. You can go ahead."

JJ did not let his feet hit the lines in the tiles as he made his way to the meat counter. He snagged a numbered slip, waited to be called, and placed his order. "Ham with American and mayonnaise." "White or wheat there, Sonny?" the owner asked, looking him up and down. JJ tried not to make eye contact as he requested the white bread. "That girl just in here. She go to PHS by any chance?" JJ's eyes never left the newspaper. "You mean Muffcat? Yup; she sure did. Graduated in 89, I think. She's my great-niece. Heading up to New York City with her son. Can't believe she finally left Johnny. You know the cheatin' som'bitch, Johnny Glass? Daddy owns that Oldsmobile lot over yonder."

JJ didn't answer. He'd put two and two together with astonishing speed. The acid rose in the back of his throat, again, while waiting for his food. The thought of not getting a dime from Vernon earlier in the day made his palms perspire. He grabbed for the ham and cheese, paid for it and the beer, then threw the sandwich away in the first trash receptacle he passed.

Truck 8 barreled out of the parking lot in the opposite direction of the Hee-Haw. He downed three beers in the short jaunt to the mansion. Placing the van in park, he jolted through the doorway and into the restaurant. A disgustingly fat, old woman greeted him. "How many you got with you today, you little whippersnapper?" JJ grabbed for the woman's face. He brought his head to her ear. "Maude, fetch me the petty cash from the safe."

JJ never took his eyes off the nappy-headed nigger until she strolled out of sight. Once she reappeared, he didn't utter a single peep as his grandmother counted out the six hundred dollars and begged him to keep his promise. He was back on the interstate in less than five minutes. Six large was nothing to write home about. But then, he really did not have a place to call home. And his three out-of-state attempts to find a female companion had turned out really badly.

By the time he made it past the state line, he still had an hour until his shift started. He had time to pop into his favorite hangout and watch the 38DD's spin headfirst down the stripper pole. The good news was he'd get one good jerk in before his he had to leave for work; on the other hand, the anger, pain, and humiliation of living as an outcast was really starting to ruffle him. It wasn't like he needed to be doted on, or even wanted to have a relationship with any of his biological relatives. He was more pissed off about the perks he was missing out on. The mansion they all grew up in was huge. If he could prance into the house and walk away with six hundred dollars, there was no telling how much cash they would send his cousin when she got to New York City.

His mind wandered back to the girl with the weird name. Why in the hell would anyone name their child Muffcat? He had to admit, she did have some pretty spectacular boobs, though. And she seemed to know it too, the way she showed them off. He homed in on her physical features. It wasn't her spunk that preoccupied the rest of the drive; it was her rejection of him that spawned his fantasy. He imagined torturing her, then cutting off all of her hair. By the time he hit the state line, the scenario playing out in his head was murderous.

He was expert at memorizing every detail of their physiques, and summoning the sensation of being between their thighs. He could almost smell what her mouth would taste like once she
was dead. His photographic memory, heartlessness (so he'd been told), and compulsive nature cooked up many varieties of his wicked contemplations and desires. He rolled each deliciously deplorable and sadistic action over and over in his mind as the van coasted into the parking lot of Uncle Sam's Exotic Girls Club.

He took the farthest spot from the road, closest to the alleyway, then reached for his bag and pipe. Just as he let out his first lung full of air, Marvelous Missy ejected out the back door with a familiar face. She proceeded to hump Wayne's leg as he threw his head back against the wall. Just as Marvelous Missy went down on Wayne, JJ's company cell phone rang. *What the fuck?* He still had another twenty-two minutes until his shift. As Vickie's voice purred into the phone, JJ rubbed at the bulge in his cheap boxers.

"Street address, Vickie?"

"423 Tyree Springs Road."

"I shall taketh the call."

Before he could put the van into drive, a sweaty bouncer barged out the back door. Marvelous Missy and Wayne were busted. Taking the last pull from his pipe, JJ watched Wayne shove his hard, slimy dick back into his pants, then follow the horse-faced stripper back into the club. JJ took a deep breath and headed out for the call. It only took five minutes to figure out 423 was low on Freon. He went back to the truck for the thirty-pound cylinder of refrigerant. Once the interdynamics A/C manifold gauges were connected, he watched the gauge as it released into the two-ton American Standard's compressor. He could not get the image of Marvelous Missy and Wayne out of his head as he waited for the refrigerant to expel. Before he could get the cylinder back in the van, his thoughts were once again interrupted, as his phone blared.

"Still diagnosing the unit on Tyree," JJ lied. Vickie was out of options. Truck 8 and Truck 12 were the only two vans left on the road. "Give me the address, Vickie. Tell them it might be eight before I can get there." Once he heard the address, his heart skipped a beat. It was the home of an old classmate: Tardi Triva. Stupid chick was dumber than a box of rocks, but she had some great, juicy tits. Even better, her husband, Wayne, was more than a little preoccupied at the moment. Things might be looking up. "I shall taketh the call."

*****

Trivia answered the door with a baby on her hip. His greens eyes gawked, and then her gaze went completely blank. She seemed unable to get enough spit collected in her mouth to even swallow. When she did gulp, her face contorted as if she were in the presence of the Devil. "You've been a bad apple ever since kindergarten. We don't need you here, JJ. Please leave. Now!" She slammed the door.

JJ went back to his service van for his gloves and tool belt. He'd find Tardi's unit on his own. Meanwhile, she seemed to have wasted no time jetting out the back door once it became clear he was not planning on leaving anytime soon. "Get out of here! Wayne is on his way home! Leave or I will call the police!" It took less time without the gloves, but the unit would never be fixed. "Get off my property! Hey asshole, can you hear me? You fucker? You stupid motherfucker! Stop!" JJ did not comply. He never touched the bolts as he smiled at Tardi half-heartedly from his crouched position.

"Stop with that, JJ! Look, you creep, we will not pay you a fucking dime! Stop wasting your time. I swear my husband is on his way home!" JJ knew that they both knew he was not. He hoped she knew the Devil would not stop. That time under the bleachers, there was no stopping him. He wanted her to know he would do it again. Act as if he didn't hear her, and then smile the entire way through his brutality. He dared her to run or stand her ground. But then, she was never a quick decision maker.

She obviously wanted to call his bluff again, as she yelled obscenities and promised her husband would be pulling up, any second now. This was the cue he needed. JJ could smell her fear. He took the wrench from his tool belt then charged at her. Trivia couldn't scream as he wrestled with his belt buckle; she was fading fast. Just as he got his hard dick into his hands, a gremlin wailed from the open doorway. The distraction gave her a few seconds to react. Pulling her way across the aggregate concrete, sliding on her stomach, her fingernails became bloodied from the rocks. JJ watched as her bra swung out from underneath her cheap shirt. He stepped down hard on the retard's head, rolled her over, and then lifted the dime store sleeveless shirt. She had on a nursing bra. He yanked on the snap as her erect nipple poured out milk. His preoccupation with the nursing bra almost gave her one more shot. She gasped then kicked at the air, aiming straight for his crotch. He was not deterred. He had strong hands and fast reflexes; she was not the first to try *that* move.

Zipper undone, erection tearing into the unforgiving boxer's cheap cotton blend, he followed her as she scampered towards the baby. Hand then knee, the crippled desperado attempted to crawl up the three steps leading to the gremlin. Just one more blow with the wrench and she quit whimpering. Not the baby, though. He jumped over her, then grasped for the child's neck as she sat helpless in the highchair. Once the spawn went limp, he took a hard hit to the side of his head. He reached for the phone cord, winding it tightly around Trivia's neck. The cord was slick with the gloves on, making it impossible to grip. He bit the right one off, then the left. Tighter, tighter.

The next twenty minutes were a blur. When he was finished with the useless mother, JJ collected the phone cord and the pot, not recollecting the mutilation that lay in a heap on the floor beneath him. He wiped his blade on a hand towel. JJ went back for his gas can; time to plot his alibi. "Vickie. Truck 8. Need to send Truck 12 to Littleton. Got a flat on Tyree Springs. Need a jack."

He went back into the house and proceeded to pour gasoline over the body. Drove the truck back to Tyree Springs, and then took out his crowbar and beat on his back tire till the rubber started to hiss. He dialed dispatch once again as he rubbed at the ring on the chain around his neck.

"Vickie, who's in truck 12?"

"Jose Rose."

"At the corner of Piedmont and Tyree. Don't forget to remind Jose about the jack."

Chapter XVIII

Big D did not even get out of his car when he pulled under the front awning of Simon's. He just rolled down the window and shouted, "I need to speak to you, Miss Mansker. In my car, NOW!"

I pointed the elderly couple down the road then made a hasty retreat over to Big D's car. Upon entering the patrol car, I found the handsome detective gripping the steering wheel with both hands. So tightly, in fact, his long fingers looked ghostly white, as if all the blood had been drained from them.

There was no small talk or eye contact between us. "Where's your Audi?" he inquired, still not looking at me. Before I had a chance to answer, his car began to roll. "Out back, why?" Big D punched the gas, pulled around back, and then parked his sedan next to my SUV. He demanded my keys. I had to run inside to retrieve them. When I approached the back door, it became apparent the detective's vehicle was no longer where it had been parked. I looked in every direction through the glass window before stepping outside. Just as the door eased back closed, someone grabbed me from behind. Hot breath to my ear. "Go on inside. I'll have it back by three."

Big D reached around me, quickly extracted the car key from my hand, and then slowly placed the rest of the keys in the front pocket of my pants. The forcefulness that he used to pull me into him was disturbing, yet, I don't mind telling you, very arousing. He spun me so we were looking at each other. I should have been in a frantic haze of suspicion, but his gaze, those eyes, made me feel completely calm. Big D came in close, that heated breath mixed with whiskers that were three days old. He whispered, "We apparently need to talk about personal safety again. Just what the hell do you think you were doing over in Selner County yesterday? And don't bother lying to me, Muffcat."

I just froze, then murmured, "nothing." Sultry eyes and whiskers spoke again. "Next time, you might not be so lucky, pretty lady. The Mooneyhans run with a rough crowd." Big D did not give me a chance to respond before jetting to my SUV. His hand was on the door before he finished our conversation. He looked back at me. "Did you really think we wouldn't find out about your little trip over to Selner County? We had an

APB out for the church van the second we secured the crime scene. Chief is pissed as hell at you. She'd just talked Chris Dickens out of not filing an assault charge when McNabb got the call from Merle. You are going to have to stay out of these investigations, Muffcat. I know we pulled you in to assist with the manifesto, but there's a lot about these cases that you don't know. Give us a chance. This is not my first rodeo. And, by the way, stop stabbing people with your stiletto, for God's sake." The detective, done with his tirade, tore out of the parking lot. He was gone in the proverbial flash.

I returned to my office, feeling like a big old fool. My impulsiveness was something I'd been working on for years, but it was obviously still getting me in trouble. I needed to be preparing for the 1:00 p.m. arrangement meeting with Chandra's family but decided to look over my notes regarding the homicides instead. Pulling my notebook out of my desk, I looked over the names written earlier that morning: Shelley/Leighanna/Tana/Chandra/Carligene/Muffcat. Below each I'd written down every conceivable suspect; there were old boyfriends, husbands, local mechanics, pest control technicians, car dealers, bosses, coworkers, mailmen, bartenders, friends, enemies, and even our doctors and dentists. There were only a handful of men that we all had in common. These were quickly eliminated with a few phone calls. Trying to figure out how the voices were connected to the murders, I moved my focus to my paranormal experiences.

A new voice had manifested while I was in the shower earlier that morning. It came from an obviously terrified female. Before hearing her voice, a series of precise flashes, in threes, occurred; they were not accompanied by sound. In the first flash, I saw myself at EG's ordering another bologna sandwich. I made an observation about the length of my miniskirt and the anklet that I was wearing with my sandals. Given my attire in the flash, it had to have taken place in the sweltering heat of summer, sometime after Gavin was born, perhaps in the early nineties. The same man from the series of dreams involving Tana was present. He had on a Sex Pistols or INXS concert t-shirt this time. As well as a work shirt, clunky boots, and a very distinguishable hat. I could make out "Hellman's Heating and Air" just above the brim. He was thin-framed with a twelve-pack of beer under his arm. He watched my every move. When not staring at me, he was glancing down at his work boots or a copy of *The Tennessean* as he interacted with the people in the storefront.

In the next flash, the same man was standing in a doorway. A woman with a baby on her hip answered the door. At first, her voice was firm and confident. She plainly stated, "We don't need you, and then slammed the door.

The final flash was of the same man on the very same day. Perspiring, he was crouching next to an air conditioning unit. He was mumbling in the hot, sticky air as the woman reappeared, this time without the baby. She called the service technician's bluff before unleashing a stream of obscenity-laced threats. Despite her anger and aggression, I could tell she was terrified. And that she knew the man.

After twenty minutes of scanning the names in my notes, I'd come up empty-handed. To my knowledge, not one of the men listed had ever had been an HVAC guy. I Googled "Hellman's Heating and Air," and found an article about an unsolved homicide up in Bowling Green. A Hellman's service technician was a suspect in a gruesome 1991 homicide. I read that Angus Hellman sold his business to a competitor in 1994. Next, I Googled the 1991 murder of Trivia Sanders-McMurtry, the homicide victim. She was found on her kitchen floor; her infant daughter was discovered sitting in her high chair, just feet from her mother's corpse. Both had been strangled, and there had been postmortem mutilation to the mother. Two service techs with Hellman's company were questioned. Their main suspect, Jose Rose, committed suicide before his trial made it into the court system. The small photo accompanying the article of the deceased suspect told me Jose Rose was not the man from my flashes.

I wondered if these voices were even connected to the cases. I concentrated on the one from the embalming room, which came from the upset mother, who described a sexual assault. I'd already determined that the woman's conversation partner was the former manager of Pleasant Green swimming pool: Kyle Frey. I was almost positive he'd made a reference to a "Tuck" in the conversation. That was Shelley's father's nickname. If it had been Nancy Phillips' voice, it would explain Shelley's panic when she witnessed her stalker in the parking lot. Maybe the fact that she was in a bathing suit during the encounter had drawn her stalker back to her.

I moved on to the voice of the female runner. Barb Philpot was describing someone slitting the throat of a pet. My first assumption, given what Dylan had shared with the FBI about the Cocker Spaniel, was that this voice belonged under Shelley's name as well. Nevertheless, after looking over the postmortem pictures of Leighanna at the crime scene at the precinct, I'd already formulated another theory. Given the fact that

Leighanna's mouth had been sewn shut, and her body had been posed to look as if she was praying to a portrait of the Devil, there was a huge possibility Leighanna had witnessed the same incident at the park as the jogger, and then confronted the person responsible for the attack. Could Leighanna have conceivably confronted her killer years ago?

I flashed back to a peculiar encounter. Leighanna and I were walking on the trails over at the Toss-Knight Park close to the soccer fields. A boy approached us from the opposite direction, a big dog by his side. Leighanna stopped then swiftly grabbed me by the arm. After she changed had our direction, she quickened our pace. She told me that the kid was the "fucking devil," but I chalked it up to the fact that the kid had a menacing looking Doberman pinscher with him. I hadn't given it another thought. Until now, that is. I made a note for Dylan to ask Barb if she recounted seeing Leighanna during the attack, then moved on to Chandra.

Peering down at the list of distinguishing accomplishments of my now former best friend left a ginormous lump in my throat. Church secretary/Sunday School teacher/President of the PTA/ no enemies/ no mutilation. Chandra's murder was the only homicide not accompanied by a premonition or a dream. The fact that she was not disfigured like the other girls made her death seem more spontaneous. I narrowed her murder down to two scenarios: the moonshine ring was trying to silence her about their use of the church van, or her assassin had reached out for spiritual guidance and something set him off during the encounter.

I moved on to the dream about Tana and the editorial meetings. Looking down at the evidence, a few things stood out. Played bingo/frequented bars/brutal rape/dating websites/burns to her thighs/hair removed. Tana's murder felt more personal than the others. Her body received more postmortem mutilation. I wondered why the inside of her thighs were scalded, and why her eyes were doused in chemicals. The series of dreams involving Tana led me to the conclusion that the murderer had been living in Parrottville around the time we had all hit puberty. I thought back to the meeting with Big D and Chief. And how Tana's manifesto was written on a page that contained baby pictures.

Leighanna's note talked about gremlins, but it was referencing Tana's death. I thought she had to have been raped by this guy. The baby from my dreams was his. She had an abortion. A clear psychological profile of the murderer was starting to form in my head. The progression of violence, sexual deviance, and misguided anger were all signs of a serial killer in the making.

Was it possible that the voices were granting me insight to the events that led up into this guy becoming a serial killer? The frizzy-headed girl in my first dream involving Tana and the boy kept me preoccupied for a good ten minutes. I questioned whether the runaway Betty mentioned in the embalming room might possibly be the murderer's first victim. Sally walked past my office just as I murmured the question I thought was in my head, aloud.

"Wen dah tree ben yu can't straiten ah." I glanced up from my notes. "Sorry, Sally. Just thinking out loud." She lingered in the doorway. I completely understood what Sally was trying to tell me, but I really did not feel like a ten-minute conversation, loaded with every freaking detail of yet another one of her Belizean Kriol old wives' tales. "Just getting ready for the Carter arrangement meeting. Would you mind closing my door? Please?" Sally complied.

Alone again, I returned to my notes. I felt pretty damn certain that I had a front row seat into the making of a madman. And, don't forget, we still had a missing woman out there who could become his next victim.

Of course, there was nothing my premonitions could do for Shelley, Tana, Leighanna, or Chandra, but there was a slight chance Carligene could be saved if she was still alive. I thought back to the image of the female shadow lurking around the dancing women at the Hee-Haw, and a light bulb went on over my crowded head. Tommy's housekeeper said she had just moved here from Bowling Green. Could she possibly be this guy's sidekick? As sickening as it was to even think about, I wondered if our murderer could be traveling with another sociopath. I had to call Big D to see if the authorities suspected the homicides could possibly involve more than one suspect.

While I fumbled in my purse for my iPhone, Sally knocked on the door and announced that Steven Carter had just arrived. I hid the notebook in my top drawer and then headed out to greet Chandra's widower in the lobby.

As we made our way to the conference room, Steven seemed surprisingly composed. Experience told me that his shock would soon be replaced with anger, inconsolable sorrow, guilt, and loneliness; then, perhaps it would all move back to anger again. Steven was by himself, which seemed bizarre, seeing how Chandra had many relatives. I asked him how he was doing. (Make a mental note of this. This is the last question any funeral director needs to ask someone whose wife was just gunned down in a Baptismal. Man, I'm fucking good, huh?) As appropriate, before my backside could hit the chair, the sudden widower went into a full-fledged rant. He explained that in the last 24 hours he'd been interrogated by detectives, had his personal computer and phone confiscated. The Cub Scouts had put him on probation until the BSA's Youth Protection policies could be reviewed, and then DCS had removed the twins from his home, pending the outcome of the investigation. Steven was forced to hire an attorney to represent him. The lawyer advised him not to go back to work until his name had been cleared. To add insult to injury, Chandra's disengaged father was called to the ME's office in order to identify her body.

You would assume a faithful husband with a solid alibi would easily be cleared of murder charges, but that was not the case. Steven's next statement threw me for a loop. "Muffcat, McNabb stopped me in the parking lot just a few minutes ago. Did you know that the Pammy is in a sexual relationship with the lead detective in charge of Chandra's case?" Oh boy. Thinking on my incredibly quick feet, I diverted the conversation back to the memorial arrangements. We decided to push Chandra's visitation off to Tuesday afternoon, hoping another day would give the lawyer ample time to clear Steven's name.

The next topic was the most personal and difficult one for me to handle, the service details. "The family wants the funeral at the church, Muffcat." Sometimes there is no rationalization to a brokenhearted psyche, I had to keep reminding myself. Steven knew it was difficult for me to comprehend my best friend's final life tribute being held in the same place she was so callously gunned down, but I kept my comments to a minimum. Just as we started to discuss the musical arrangements, Steven brought up Ken Akers' name. Come to find out, the deacons, as well as the TBI, were all looking for Ken.

I kept the disturbing details about my trip over to the Mooneyhan's to myself. It was sickening to think about someone from our church being a child molester, much less a serial killer, but it was an angle that needed consideration. As Steven rambled on about the similarities of Ken's situation to the BTK killer, I could not help but wonder if I'd been barking up the wrong tree. Maybe this guy was not a former classmate.

Steven continued with his theory. "Did you know Dennis Raider was elected President of his church's Congregation Council just weeks before confessing to killing his ten victims?" I nodded my head then tried to get our discussion back on track, but Steven kept interjecting. "Chandra was on to Akers, Muffcat. She knew about the church van being used to haul and sell moonshine. She knew Ken was involved." Steven rammed his hand into his blue jeans. "Can you believe, the freaking detectives actually made me take a polygraph?"

Emotional outbursts are not uncommon in arrangement meetings. Steven stayed steady on his profanity-laced rampage about the polygraph test. It sounded as if the investigators were more interested in Ken Akers as a suspect than they were Steven, even though they were taking their sweet ass time on clearing his name.

After a thirty-minute sidebar conversation about Ken Akers and his moonlighting for the shiners, I wanted to ask Steven more questions about his interrogation at the precinct. I needed to validate if any of the voices could possibly be associated with Ken, but decided to just sit back and listen to my best friend's grieving husband.

Steven handed me a folded note as he exited the funeral home. "Muffcat, there was only one thing Chandra ever mentioned wanting at her own funeral. Said she wanted it Tina Turner style or she will come back to haunt you."

I opened the note as Steven strolled off to his car. "The Old Rugged Cross"-George Jones, "I'll Fly Away"-Alison Kraus, and "Proud Mary"-MM and the Gang. I yelled to Steven, who was halfway across the parking lot, "I'll make it happen."

But the thought of pumping tane down in New Orleans in the First Baptist Church, well, let's just say, in all honesty, it made me fearful of a lightning strike.

Chapter XVIIII

After Steven departed, I couldn't stop thinking about the comment he'd made about Pammy and Big D. Given the fact that everyone knew about Pammy's girlfriend, it was amazing how much gossip one disgruntled police officer could stir up.

Now, as I viewed the forty-four-year-old heart attack victim, whose fat was overhanging the table in front of me, and contemplating what to do about lunch, I started to think about Big D. *God help me*, I thought. Old classmates dropping like flies over here, my adopted son being taunted by a serial killer over there. I'd made it onto the Mooneyhan's hit list, our very own music minister was being hunted by the FBI, and let's not forget the legal troubles that lay before me after I'd assaulted Chris Dickens with my stiletto. Yet, here I was, horny old Muffcat, having sexual fantasies about a man I'd only known for a few days. All while viewing a dead body and fancying salad greens. You get the picture. I took multitasking to a whole new, troubling level.

Still considering whether or not to embalm the corpse before me, I made an executive decision. I drove the hearse to Applebee's instead, and after a Fiesta Chicken Chopped Salad and two Bloody Marys, I was ready for action. My mortician's jacket awaited my return.

Realizing Gran was in the prep room, I reached for a mint out of my purse. Even though the eighty-five-year-old hung up his own mortician's jacket in 2006, Claude Mansker still came into Simon's for a few hours every day. I knew he'd be pissed as hell at me if he even suspected I was drinking on the job.

"Muffy Catherine, this here is the finest man that ever lived. I'm paying my respects to Colonel Crim. He was the most excellent commandant at Castle Heights Military Academy. Was your daddy's headmaster in the Sixties. Cannot believe I outlived him. Just checked his chart. His right carotid is blocked, and he had peripheral artery disease. I'd use the left carotid, cut injection." Taking only a single beat for a quick breath, Gran continued "listen, I'm proud of you, Muffcat. Hard sometimes, when they are good apples."

Gran pulled the sheet back over the Colonel's face, grabbed his hat, and then shuffled out the door. I scrubbed up then snapped on gloves in order to inspect the Colonel's veins for myself. Once the formaldehyde was injected, the embalming and interstitial fluids expelled fairly easily out of his right femoral vein. Betty breached the doorway. "Muffcat, your granddaddy needs you. We have some guests." I extracted my gloves and made my way to the hallway.

"Muffcat, this here is Madame Movina and Roberta." Gran turned crimson as Roberta's overabundant cleavage greeted me before she did. "It is actually Rosemurta," she said, "named after the Celtic Goddess of Abundance. My friend here has been contacted with Tiaret from her afterlife. We're here to arrange her life's celebration."

Rosemurta's skintight dress was not nearly as revealing as her ancient Wiccan tattoos. I chimed on in, "Gran, I have this. Well, it is nice to meet you, Rosemurta, is it? I don't know if you've noticed, but this is a funeral home. We have dead bodies that need attending to, in order for them to make it to their afterlife. What can I do for you today?" I gagged at the befuddled odors wafting off the pagan deity. "Wiccan Tits'" home-brewed perfume and the stench of clove cigarettes were worse than Betty's breath. Believe you me, that's saying a whole lot.

"Agh, Muffcat, I have been aware of your overindulgence since Tiaret told me about your midnight dinner following her Magic Dragon exhibit. You need some willow bark tea. Luckily I just happen to have some in the cab. It's a natural Tylenol; I will get a knob of ginger to assist with your digestive woes." With that, whatever that actually was, Wiccan Tits was off, and I was left to ponder whether or not the funeral home was a bigger nuthouse than the B&B.

"Red Turban" followed me into the family room just as the "Goddess of Abundant Boobies" reappeared. "Cover it with a plate or saucer to keep the heat in, and then steep for two minutes. Now I need to freshen up. Where is your lavatory?"

Rosemurta had obviously hotboxed a clove. I'd have done anything to get her out of my personal body space, or else I'd start dry-heaving again. Gran reappeared and escorted the pagan Elvira deity to the restroom. I turned my attention to "Red Turban," who was pouring hot water over something that looked like tree bark. "Movina, I am sorry, but what exactly is your connection to Leighanna?" Movina's eyebrows were painted on, and her red lipstick covered more space on her teeth than her lips. "I worked for Sister Tiaret for over a decade. Been her number one graveyard shift clairvoyant for eight years running, bless her." Just before I could ask what the hell she was talking about, Rosemurta reappeared and abruptly hijacked the conversation. "As you know her, Leighanna Shiane Petigro, our departed sister, was my roommate in New York in the mid-Nineties. From the day she answered my ad in the *Village Voice*, her gorgeous locks reminded me of a lion's mane. Tiaret, to our African sisterhood, means lioness. It cannot come close to describing the visual beauty her hair beheld."

Okay, now I knew Leighanna was a little freaky in high school, but I was starting to believe her bohemian lifestyle must have cartwheeled out of control. "Look, ladies, as much as I would like to chat, it's against the funeral home's privacy policy to discuss arrangement details with anyone besides first of kin or legal conservators."

Rosemurta smiled as she grasped for her knapsack. "Look, Muffcat is it? We have been on a Greyhound bus for almost 24 hours from the Port Authority. I am the executress of her will." Rosemurta pulled out a folded document. I unfolded it and placed it next to the tea Movina had set at the table. After adjusting my reading glasses, I turned to the last page. The attorney's name and the date of execution of the will were surprising. The will was executed by a lawyer in Salem, Massachusetts, and had been signed only six weeks prior to Leighanna's death. "This document seems to be in solemn form, Betty. The testator, Leighanna Shane Petigro, declared that the document revokes all previous wills and codicils."

Now, "Red Turban" piped up. "A legal consent for cremation is on page four." This was a relief, seeing how Betty had already executed Leighanna's cremation. I fingered through the sheets; on the sixth page, an executory bequest caught my attention. Leighanna's personal artwork, including a collection by Tiaret Akie currently on display at MoMA, was to be bequeathed to Rosemurta. The gifting would take place only if the testator's memorial wishes were executed. The last few pages detailed her memorial ceremony.

"These service details are insane. We'll have to verify the document for authenticity and speak to the family." I continued reading. The amount of artwork in the collection was astonishing. "Wow, I never knew she had her work in MoMA. I take it she exhibited under Tiaret Akie?" Rosemurta verified my assumption.

Betty made a motion with her head. "Excuse us for a moment, ladies, will you?" Once outside the door, Betty whispered, "we need to discuss our legal obligations with Tommy." I shook my head, and whispered back, "if Rosemurta had access to Leighanna's famous artwork, she might have an idea as to the identity of the man in the portrait." Betty took the lead back into the family room. "Ladies, we need to verify this with the attorney up in Salem and contact our attorney before we can discuss her arrangements any further."

Against my best judgment, I called the B&B and had a room reserved for the pagan deities. The ladies (*surprise, surprise*) were thrilled to have a free place to stay for the night. I suggested that we might have an answer around six o'clock, then proposed that we meet at the tearoom. As the cabbie (who looked exactly like Flea from the Red Hot Chili Peppers) tore off with the women down Main Street, Betty shrieked, "get back in here! Muffcat, hurry!" Betty ran back into the breakroom in her bare feet.

Holly Thompson was breaking to a live video feed. Everyone rushed to the small TV to see what was going on. Holly fed the story to a female field reporter, who was in front of our town hall. Pammy cleared her throat from a podium in front of a sea of microphones "Test. Testing." The reporter had missed her cue. She just smiled, uncomfortably, then fidgeted with her hair. The camera cut back to Holly. "We will bring you that live news conference in a few minutes." After some updates on local politics, the camera cut back to the female field reporter. The wind had picked up so much, it obstructed her face. She started her correspondence on cue this time, as the camera panned in on Pammy, who'd yet to start the news conference.

"It seems a lot of attention has been focused on the small town of Parrottville, Tennessee. Police now suspect the homicides we have reported on over the last couple of days are possibly connected to a serial killer. The most recent victim is the local secretary from the First Baptist Church." The reporter pointed to the church, but the camera never moved. Nice work, guys. Awkward much?

Looking embarrassed, the reporter went on, "according to local authorities, Chandra Carter was shot at point blank range yesterday morning at approximately 9:20 a.m. Now authorities tell us another local woman, Carligene Byrd, has been reported missing." As she continued her coverage of the abduction, my sixth sense started to kick in. It was a blinding feeling, and it rocked me. "The murderer has left two manifestos. The latest correspondence actually details the names of those authorities here feel might be his next victims."

Chapter XX

The entire room went dark as I grabbed for the back of the folding chair. The broadcast was still audible, but two new voices overpowered the field correspondent.

"Goddammit! I spotted her first!" A Pet Shop Boys song was playing in the background, as two men argued. "You've already knocked up the blond chick, JJ. It's just one song."

The voices were encircling me, poking me, on my breasts, my hair, the side of my face. Round and round the ominous apparitions taunted me. The experience was so rapid and disorienting. When Wookiee entered the breakroom, he let out an intense series of grunts. A cold sweat broke out on my chest and the back of my neck as I crumpled into the chair. While I let out a lungful of air, Betty went for the sink. It was obvious to everyone some sort of medical emergency was underway. Wookiee fumbled to lower the volume on the TV and accidently changed the channel in the process. "You need us to call 911, Muffcat?"

Betty placed a wet rag on my head just as another voice became audible. This voice was that of an infuriated female. "She is your cousin, for God's sake. Why do you want to waste a camera on her, you idiot? We need to keep our eye on the church."

I looked up at Betty while trying to collect enough spit to speak. "No emergency. Just a hot flash. Go ahead with the debrief without me."

I glanced back up at the monitor. One reporter was now broadcasting from Simon's parking lot, while another, on the split screen, was standing in front of the Hee-Haw. It was on; we were about to be bombarded. My balance was still off as I tried to stand. I had to hold onto the back of the chair while I made an announcement. "Look, everyone, Betty needs to speak to you all about the undercover police and security details for the upcoming services. It seems serial killers and dead church secretaries are big news for the Music City." I went to close the door and must have turned white as a ghost. Steven's mother-in-law was just a few feet away with one of my and Chandra's mutual friends, Julie Maddox. Ugh! They'd overheard my insensitive remark. I refreshed Betty on the security details then stepped into the hallway.

Julie is a local pharmacist, who graduated PHS in 1989. She was just a few steps behind Mrs. Worsham, with a plastic hang-up bag in hand. Julie took a seat while I greeted Jana Worsham. "Jana, forgive me. I am so sorry if you overheard that unacceptable remark. Didn't mean it the way it came out. CID told us to expect some plainclothes officers, and all the media attention has everyone around here on edge. But there's no excuse for my behavior, and I do hope you'll accept my apology." Clumsy silence ensued for a few beats. I cleared my throat and went on like the smooth pro I was. "Um, so, we will have the large parlor in the front set up for you to receive mourners Tuesday. Let me take the clothing."

As I made my way to Julie, the grieving mother stopped me with her hand. "Do you really think a serial killer is behind this, Muffcat? The ME said she was not cut up like the others." Her voice broke. "The extra security is welcomed, but I just cannot believe this is happening."

Jana began to weep uncontrollably. I reached for the Kleenex on the credenza before she fully lost her composure. "No, Jana. Steven was just up here. Unfortunately, the investigation team seems to be focusing in on Ken Akers. I know the shock of it all is impossible to comprehend. In this type of situation, many people will show up to Chandra's service just out of curiosity. We want to make sure the family…"

Jana was not hearing a word of what I was saying. I motioned for Betty, who crammed her size elevens into her leopard skin heels, then slid out of the breakroom and offered to escort Jana to a private area. Once they made their way down the hallway, Julie stood up. "Muffcat, a slew of reports were at Chandra's house wanting an exclusive with Steven. You have to understand how hard this is for Jana. We had to call the police to get those media pricks off the front lawn. The vultures are heading out to 31-W as we speak."

I knew exactly where the media circus was going, The Hee-Haw firework stand, from where the NBC affiliate had run the exclusive story. They'd done their homework. Nothing screams "Hillbilly town has a serial killer on the loose" as clearly as reporters standing in front of a half-backwards donkey, jabbering on about a missing local woman whose name made it into a serial killer's manifesto.

*****

A crowd was starting to gather for the visitation of the five-year-old cancer patient. I grabbed the clothes out of Julie's arms then pulled her into the prep room. Once the door was closed, I hung up the clothing bag on a hook by my mortician's jacket. "Julie, I have a confession to make." Julie did not react to me. She just began to churn her immense, cerulean eyes around the room. "You remember the experience I had in New York after 9-11?" Julie shook her head, "yes," while peering over at Mr. Crim's body. "How in the hell do you do this, Muffcat?" she asked.

I unzipped the garment bag and continued, "The voices are back, Julie." Julie stopped glaring at the dead body then just stared straight at me. "Look, there is too much to explain at the moment. I need for you to call Eleanor. She can fill you in. Have that friend of hers from the biker bar with the PI firm investigate Ken Akers then meet me at my house tonight at eight. I need to know everything about his past. Find out if he has any aliases. See if he maybe owned a Doberman pinscher in the late Eighties. Have her determine if he spent any time in Parrottville or Bowling Green before taking the position over at the church. Check into his previous occupations as well."

Julie peered underneath Mr. Crim's sheet. "Good God, Muffcat. Why don't you just ask Pammy? The cops have had a warrant out for him ever since yesterday afternoon."

I went ahead and told Julie everything. It took a good hour, but it was better than relying on Eleanor. Just as we finished up our conversation, Melvin McNabb started calling my name from the hallway.

The minute Julie exited the room, Melvin McNabb was in my grill. I looked around to see if there was anyone watching us. Big D was peering from behind my office doorway with his finger up to his lips as if to say "Don't tell him I am here."

"What can I do for you, Officer?" Melvin looked to be sweating profusely. Eyes bloodshot and darting around irrationally, he was lurching a little too close for comfort into my face. "You're lucky Mooneyhan did not file those trespassing charges." I wanted to laugh in his face. "Ugh, I think you might want to turn THAT badge in, you stupid asswipe." I poked at the shine on his shirt. Big D was all but silently screaming with his body language for me to stop. "Since when is rescuing two kids and an abused wife from squalor a crime?"

Melvin pushed me back into the embalming room, slamming the door behind him. His breath wreaked of pure grain alcohol as he threw me up against the wall. His nasty stomach in my personal space, Melvin's meaty hands were now on my throat. "Huh. You are playing with fire here, you crazy bitch. You've been a mental case ever since preschool. What is this I hear about your little paranormal investigations?"

Melvin pushed harder on my throat when I refused to answer him. "Know whose name turned up at the precinct today? Birds on a wire are easy prey, but mine all have names." Melvin made a gun with the hand not pressing on my neck then placed it to my forehead. "BAM! Yours, bitch!" He proceeded to ram his hand in-between my legs while licking the side of my face. He then threw me hard against the wall once more before departing. Grasping for air and sickened to my core, I made my way to the hallway. Big D waited for the officer to pass him by before grabbing me by the arm and yanking me back into the embalming room.

"What the fuck was that?" Big D glanced over to the embalming room door that leads to the outside parking lot. He pulled me toward the storage closet and shoved me in. His arms were now firmly around my waist. His hard pecks pressed into my glasses (hey, I was upset and shaken, but not dead) as I burst out in tears.

"I heard everything, Muffcat. Don't worry. Chief will investigate." The detective was now rubbing my hair. God, it felt so wonderful. But, wait. Was I just staring into the eyes of a serial killer?

"Do you suspect him?" The detective let go of my waist. "No. He's caught up in that moonshine ring, Muffcat. But he was the one that had the tracking device placed on your car." The closet was pitch black.

"So, I guess you think I'm nuts?" Big D yanked me into him and whispered, "Well, the jury is still out on that one." We both had a good laugh. And then, it happened. Slow tongue, dark room, let's just say my glasses came off.

The tension between us had been building since the hogzilla shirt. Once we decided to exit the closet, Big D became serious again. He walked to the door to peer out over the parking lot. "Look, this killer is in a manic phase, but your name was not mentioned in the manifesto, Muffcat. I will need to take a statement from you regarding the incident with Melvin."

With three employees staring at us, we headed over to my office. After Big D had taken my statement, I decided to call it a day. Tommy was meeting me at the Big House at 5:30 and I really wanted to get a quick workout in before dealing with Movina and Rosemurta. If I didn't settle my nerves and find a way to healthfully get rid of my crazed energy, I worried I might do something crazy. Hard to imagine, right?

Chapter XXI

Once suiting up in yoga pants and a hooded sweatshirt, I grabbed for my iPhone and a bottled water. At 138 pounds and only five-foot-five, my size 8 jeans were getting snug. I headed out for a brisk walk over at the KOA campground at 4:37 pm. A lone camper, who was stoking his fire at his campsite, watched me loop for almost an hour. Near the end of my last round, a vehicle caught my attention. An older model van with black plastic taped on the sides slowed as it passed the mansion. The vehicle stopped in the middle of the street, then backed up to the barn, where a slim-framed silhouette exited the passenger side. The figure opened up the back doors, then placed several milk jugs next to the van. My two calls to the B&B's went to voicemail. I made my way towards the trespassers while trying to get ahold of Tommy.

Just as I got my brother's voicemail, a Parrottville police car pulled in behind the van. When the grotesque blob wearing black got out, it took me only a few seconds to realize it was Melvin McNabb. He placed something in the palm of the driver's hand, which was extended out of the window. I tried to get close enough to make out the license plate but was busted when the passenger pointed me out to Melvin.

I walked over to a wooden structure and threw my leg up on the restroom wall to act like I was stretching. Melvin's patrol lights sputtered to life within seconds of his spotting me. I walked behind the wooden fence constructed to obscure the restroom's entryway. Hunkered down behind it, I made my way into the furthest stall just as Melvin's patrol siren started up. My initial instinct was to wait him out; to pull my feet up and make absolutely no noise whatsoever, but the rattle of the door told me that luck was not on my side. The sirens quit howling only after a good five minutes of me standing on the toilet bowl. I tiptoed to the door to make a break for it but wound up bouncing off the officer's waistband instead.

I thought to myself, play dumb. Apologize for the collision. The look on the officer's face, however, told me my situation was more serious than at first blush. Melvin looked like a bull in a rodeo. Steam poured from his opened mouth as he began to speak. "Muffcat, Chief just called. You file a report on me with your fucking boyfriend?"

Melvin wiped his disgusting brow with his forearm. His eyes looked about ready to pop from his head. I slowly backed up, but he had me cornered, and he was enjoying it. He swayed his considerable flab from side to side in the partition's entryway. Realizing there was nowhere to run except back in, I backed up towards the stalls. "You're NOT going anywhere, bitch! Turn me in for sexual assault? I'll show you assault, you fucking cunt!"

I tried to talk Melvin down from his rampage by playing dumb. "What are you talking about, Melvin?" Well (surprise, surprise) that routine backfired quickly. The officer grabbed for my waist. "I strongly suggest whatever you think you saw stays in that pretty little head, you psycho whore." With that, I was drug back into the building. Melvin locked the door behind us, and then rammed me against the bank of sinks in front of the mirror. My screams were being muffled by his stocky fingers, as he flipped me around, then ripped at my yoga pants. He was holding my hands behind my back as he attempted to extract his belt from his waistband. But I was prepared for this. Always told myself if rape were ever a possibility, death would be a better option. And I meant it.

Before attempting to head-butt the bastard, I kicked, bit, and then proceeded to spit in the officer's face. Nothing was stopping him. Blue neon danced underneath the cheap structure's door. I thought about my options; I had to distract him long enough to make a break for it. The only thing in my sweatshirt pocket was my iPhone. I stopped fighting Melvin and slowly pulled my phone free as he wrestled with his belt buckle. "You're going to enjoy this, you crazy bitch."

Once Melvin's picture was snapped in the mirror, he became even more enraged. His belt was set free in one fail swoop. Ripping into the flesh on my now exposed legs and backside, the fat-ass tightly gripped the fabric of my sweatshirt as he rammed me harder against the sink with his knee. Just as I let out a hallowing scream, Melvin's gun flew across the floor from the ferocity of his lashes. As he went for his weapon, I scampered to the door with my pants around my ankles. I did not even unlock the door, just pulled with enough force to thrash the flimsy door open. I dislodged my tennis shoes and ran like hell.

By the time my hand was on the gearshift, Melvin had already unloaded his gun. With no idea where to go, the tires squealed out of the parking lot onto the main road. The police station was my only option, but there was no way of explaining this. Upon exiting the vehicle, my lack of pants was not my biggest concern. Seconds after the patrol car crashed into the doorframe, Big D jumped over the top of the vehicle to reach me. As the other officers tried to push the patrol car out of the doorway, I fell into the detective's arms sobbing like a schoolgirl. Realizing underwear hadn't been a consistent part of my wardrobe in the last twenty years, the earth needed to swallow me whole. Blood was everywhere. But even with a bullet in my bicep, all I could think about was the last time I'd shaved my private parts.

Once the other officers moved the vehicle, Big D picked me up and carried me into the station. He kept asking, "Where are you hit?" The handsome detective carried me straight into the interrogation room and set me in a chair. The amount of blood that covered my sweatshirt was shocking. Little pings of light crept into my peripheral vision as Big D exited the room and another officer rushed in. "Muffcat, stay calm! You're gonna be okay. But wait. In the name of Jesus, how did you wind up in McNabb's car half-naked? Uh, I'll be right back."

Chief breached the doorway before the fireman did. "Move back. Greg will take over until the medics get here." Pammy knelt down beside me. I was starting to lose consciousness. The fireman cut my sweatshirt up the front with a pair of scissors. As he surveyed the wound, the other officers were in a heated discussion. Nothing in life can ever prepare you for lying in a precinct floor, in nothing but your sports bra, while a bunch of pigs discuss your mental stability.

Chapter XXII

Tuesday, September 30, 2003, 8:23 pm. Love's Truck Stop, Horse Cave, Kentucky

As the radiator poured vapor over the hood, the Little Devil Heating and Air van coasted off Exit 58, and into Love's Truck Stop. The years he'd spent in Truck 8 had spoiled him. Then life became a little rough after he took a shit where he ate. He had to quick claim the deed to his mother's house over to his step-dad in order to get the money he needed to start his own company. But the last ten years weren't exactly on point. Even when the cash wasn't going to strippers, marijuana, his girlfriend's bail, or alcohol, it surely wasn't going to any marketing efforts. The business-sized ad in the Yellowbook did summon the occasional customer, however, after his old company sold to a competitor, they had the entire mid-south Kentucky market locked up. The 1994 GMC van could barely make it to the rural calls without overheating, but that was all that he got.

JJ counted out the change in his pocket before reaching for his baggie of marijuana. Since the temperature had dropped nearly twenty degrees, it wouldn't take too long for the radiator to cool, but it still really sucked. He killed the ignition, packed his pipe, and then took a quick toke. As the smoke flowed from his lips, JJ began to rock in his seat. The voices always seemed to quiet down once the cannabis hit his brain.

After gathering the change in the ashtray, he took the notebook containing the letter Missy had written him from the Kentucky Women's Correctional Institute, and shoved it into his notebook.

He rubbed the ring that hung around his neck before exiting the van. JJ had long since forgotten the name of the big, fat hooker it belonged to, no matter, it was his old lucky charm. When Jose was arrested for the murder of the retard and her gremlin, JJ had sworn the ring had some mystical powers. As he scanned the parking lot, a skinny chick wearing a pair of shorts and a gray t-shirt jumped to the pavement, a backpack dangling from her arm. Legs so thin, you could drive a truck through them, the skank had to be freezing.

JJ popped the hood of his van then headed into the store. He grabbed for a Styrofoam cup; the creamer and sugar would be his only calories for the day. It was a ritual. The not eating thing. A form of self-punishment he'd practiced for a long time.

The scraggy woman approached him as he began to pour his coffee. "Got any change to spare?" JJ scanned up to meet the emaciated woman's eyes, reckoning she was trolling for a john. Truth was, she could have any story to tell. Maybe she'd just woken up after a five-day binger. Maybe she had crashed, then found herself at the Army Surplus Store on West Main Street in Louisville, Kentucky before hitching a ride south. Maybe, because of her deteriorated state and utter exhaustion, she had two weeks left. Whatever the details, they didn't matter all that much. If he had his way, she'd be dead before the end of the night.

Their gaze only lasted a second before JJ murmured, "Nope," then strolled over to the counter to pay. He moseyed over to the restaurant to find a place to light up. A heavyset employee eyed JJ's coffee from behind the counter, shaking her head. JJ placed his notebook on the table, then began to reread Missy's letter. Her decade-long pattern of jail stints for prostitution and drug-related charges was really getting old. But still, Missy was the only one that understood his impulsive urges, the only soul on this earth who knew about his heartless desires. She was well aware of his fixation, had even participated in a few of the abductions when she was in the mood for a threesome, but she left the postmortem endeavors to her paramour. Her lips were sealed as long JJ continued to bail her out. And while he appreciated the devotion, it was getting harder and harder to live with the separation, or so he told himself. Being real, he knew Missy wasn't ever likely to be as sugary sweet when she wasn't wearing orange.

JJ took his pen from the spiral binding then tapped the phenolic resin twenty-eight times against his cheek. The repetitive movement calmed him. Just as the retractable ballpoint reached the page, the skeletal chick exited the restroom. He scanned the parking lot for the rig she had arrived in, noticing it was gone. As she seemed to come to the realization that she had been stranded, the woman began to visibly panic. She rushed past him for the doorway, begging Jesus for "Fatdaddy" to still be in the parking lot. Once outside, she crumpled into a ball on the filthy blacktop and pulled her knees into her miniscule chest. JJ watched, fully engrossed, as she swayed like a mourner in front of a tombstone. As he took the first swig of his coffee, he peered back down to the blank page, contemplating his first expression. Just as his pen made contact, the woman stood up on her feet. Glancing over, he noticed the birthmark on the back of her calf.

He had to do a double-take.

He placed Missy's letter back in the envelope, then bent it precisely into three perfect folds. He headed over to refresh his coffee while keeping his eyes peeled on the woman as she made her way over to the fleet of rigs parked to the side of the gas pumps. JJ gathered his notebook from the counter then sprinted to his van. After placing his coffee inside the cab, he pulled out his last container of antifreeze. Luckily, the weather had spared him a good fifteen minutes of wait time, but he still needed to act fast. As he filled the translucent, plastic tank with the glycol-based formula, JJ began to reminisce. Before closing the hood, he was already getting that feeling. Recounting the very first day he'd smell Shelley's hair made his growing bulge began to rise. From the looks of it, he doubted it smelled like strawberries or chlorine any longer, but it was a chance he was more than willing to take.

After placing the gearshift in drive, he rolled down his window. Shelley was in deep conversation with a trucker as he idled up to the rig. After their quick exchange, Shelley swiftly marched around towards the passenger side of the Tyson's Foods truck, before stopping dead in her tracks. JJ called out her name. The passenger's side door was open. He was afraid it might be too late. Shelley quickened her pace and sped around the front of the white cab before he could eject himself out of his seat.

JJ swiftly motioned for the trucker to roll down his window. He had to step up onto the running board to get close enough to murmur his lies. As JJ swirled his pointer finger around his temple, the trucker rapidly scooted over, slamming the passenger's door closed. Before he climbed down from the running board, Shelley began to run. He meandered back to his van while giving the trucker a heroic wave. He knew his "wife" would not get very far in her wasted and emaciated state. Once her no-so-promising head start to the insane asylum began, JJ put the gearshift back into drive. Just before the onramp, he rolled down the passenger's side window then held up his stash. Anthony Kiedis' voice filled the cab with despair. *"I don't ever want to feel, like I did that day. Take me to the place I love, take me all the way... ayyyy... ayyyy... ayeeyeha..."* Shelley stopped dead in her tracks as the tires shrieked to a stop. *"It's hard to believe. That there's nobody out there. It's hard to believe that I'm all alone."*

JJ killed the volume. Man, how he hated when he had to talk to them. And he utterly despised having to manipulate the ones that knew him. As he conjured every ounce of charm that lay hidden beneath his disconnected soul, Shelley rubbed her hands through her smarmy hair. He'd become fairly good at the foreplay that proceeded the brutality. Learned the vital verses to swoon those with offspring. It made the bile rise in his throat to talk about their children, but it worked. *Gremlin love has to be the greatest love of all, he thought to himself,* as he probed her about the tow-headed boy that once cowered by her side. Shelley's lips were almost blue as she tried to answer him. He held up the coffee and cooed. "Got one for you, come on now. Let's get you all warmed up. Then, I'll take you back. Gotta stop off and feed the dog, but I'll take you all the way. Don't you worry."

As the van gained speed on the 65 southbound ramp, Shelley's trembling hands reached past the coffee to the pipe lying on the dashboard. There was no small talk between them now, not until the van veered off the KY 234 exit. Before he could make it to Lover's Lane, she struggled to open her door. This brought on a backhanded slap to the side of her temple. She didn't budge again until noticing the van careening towards Cemetery Road. Peering through her obvious pain, she began to plead. "Just let me off here, JJ. I am fine. I swear. I can just find another ride. Please just let me off here."

He pulled into Kerieakes Park with a grip on the bitch's hair as his mind wandered back to the last time she had tried to circumvent him. The cannabis wasn't potent enough to keep the voices at bay this time. Big Horn did not speak to him this time; no, Big Horn was thundering. "You're gonna let this little fucking bitch get away with it again? She's already rejected you a thousand times, you good-for-nothing loser! Your little girlfriend cannot suck your dick through those bars! Go ahead, take her from behind. She owes you one, you senseless idiot!"

As they made it past the tennis courts, JJ began to belittle Shelley for the condition that she was in. "Stupid slut. Look at yourself? No man is ever gonna want a cunt that smells as bad as yours. You are lucky to have me. Go ahead, admit it. Tell me how much you want me." She slipped a book out of her backpack and hurled it at JJ's head. He quickly realized fucking her while she was alive was not going to be an option. As her hand grasped for the backpack that was now in the floorboard, he reached inside his doorwell. She looked up to him. He hoped the rage, fury, and emptiness in his eyes was her last vision of this world. He wound his fist full of her hair, tighter, tighter, even tighter while pulling the unconscious whore to the floorboard. After anally penetrating her six times over the course of two hours, he decided to transport her filthy, useless body back to his trailer. It was there that her tiny corpse would receive the most vicious punishment he could muster. The thought got him smiling.

By the third day, even the Doberman Pincher would not come into the sordid, prefabricated single-wide. Which gave JJ all the time he needed to ponder the book that was tossed at his head. He questioned the lifeless woman about every one of his tormentors. By the fifth day, he'd written Missy eight letters, detailing each and every one of them. He'd promised to be good while she was away, but Missy really understood this one. She knew how to read through the encryption of his viciousness. They had developed their own language through their times of separation. It wasn't what you would call elevated enlightenment.

On the sixth day, he performed the ritual to set the soul free. He felt a little touch of remorse for the 350 days she would have to wait but went ahead anyhow with the fifteen cuts to her upper torso. With all that seepage, her body really was not useful to him any longer. But the sensation he got performing the postmortem violence took his climax to a whole new level.

After his last delicious act of sexual gratification was completed, he removed the necklace from around Shelley's neck. He could barely contain himself as the cross pierced her cervix.

Chapter XXIII

My parents learned the hard way that morphine turns Muffcat right into a mental patient. Clearly, the attending ER doctor had no idea what he was in for.

It all started with a haze of narcotic glory. Mother came into focus while imaginary people danced on the ceiling, and Lionel Richie tunes sprang from my lips. When Big D and Chief showed up to take my statement, Mother left the room to take a mental break from my catastrophic karaoke performance. Pammy brushed my dark brown hair from my eyes then proceeded to wave her hand in front of my face. As I peered over, I noticed Big D was acting strange. He was all official now. Not the charismatic, hot-headed sexpot I'd anticipated would be taking my statement. As Pammy began to question me about the incident at the KOA campground, the tension in the air was thick. Oh boy, you couldn't winch it up, not even with the aid of a forklift.

Big D was reserved as he took Mother's now empty chair. He let Chief do the talking. "Muffcat, it has been an unprecedented few days. We need to fill you in on what Melvin is claiming happened at the KOA." As Pammy relayed the details of Melvin's sworn confession, I can tell you that no words ever sobered me up faster. Hearing that I had lured fat-ass Melvin McNabb into the bathroom stall for a mutual sexual rendezvous, well now, that just blew my mind. He was claiming that I flagged him down while jogging. The six jugs of white lightning? Are you ready for this bullshit? I was selling moonshine out of a restroom stall at the KOA campground. According to the incarcerated asswipe, a fight had ensued when he tried to confiscate the contraband. His alibi? I know you are about to burst. Okay, if you insist. It was the toothless fire-stoker.

It was obvious to everyone that Big D's confrontation of Melvin about the incident at the funeral home was behind the attack; there was no need to explain the truth to Chief. She knew my hair would have to have been on fire in order for Muffcat Mansker to run, but they did find moonshine at my speakeasy. Sexpot was red in the face and kept gazing down at his boots. He was probably in enough trouble with the way he handled the situation, confronting one of his fellow officers instead of following protocol. The look on his face told me Big D already had a knot yanked in his ass by Chief. Surely she wouldn't be that rough on him. He was, as a matter of fact, simply defending my honor.

After my side of the story had been shared, Big D spoke up. "Muffy Catherine, Greg found your phone in your sweatshirt. We had our cyber forensics guy download the picture of the assault. Here you go." The detective stood up to hand it over, his breath smelling of orange Tic-Tacs. Big D reached for my hand. I looked up to meet his eyes. Damn it if they weren't as blue as Boy's, from my childhood dreams. And his dimple was in the same spot as my daddy's. I tried not to let the detective's physical attractiveness distract me as he continued to recite the charges they were planning to file on Melvin, but, come on now, I'm only a human, hot-blooded American female. His fucking side smile was killing me.

Good God and holy hell; sweet tobacco and well-worn leather had defended my honor. "On top of the aggregated assault and attempted rape charges, attempted murder is warranted here. Chief, don't you agree?" Big D looked over at Pammy, who nodded. There was a knock at the door. The attending physician was making his rounds. Both visitors were asked to leave the room. Chief glared at her subordinate, then motioned for him to step outside.

After going over wound care, scar prevention, and being prescribed a standard antibiotic and some pain meds, I was discharged, but not from the conversation with Chief. Her official dialogue was finished, but my girlfriend's chat was just getting heated up, and man oh man, was this conversation promising to be a doozie. "Muffcat, goddamnit! You cannot do this to me. Look, Big D's damaged goods happen to be yours truly." *Um, somebody, is anybody out there? I'm gonna need to get me some additional morphine for this conversation.*

"Why are you telling me this, Pammy?" It would be impossible for me to watch another episode of *The Andy Griffith Show*, EVER AGAIN. Because Mayberry BFE had just turned pornographic in my head. Chief proceeded, however, I wasn't sure if I really wanted to hear the details. "I truly do love Eleanor, Muffcat. But it is time you know the truth. When you asked Vernon to contact me about the position, I kinda lied to you. Granted, Momma was sick, but I needed to get the hell out of Jackson. The affair with Big D and his wife is the real reason I took this job. Ugh, this is hard for me to share. Look, I swear on our friendship, NOTHING has happened since Big D moved here. I'm not envious or upset he's interested in you. You have to believe that. Y'all would be quite an impressive pairing, to tell ya the truth. But, I must have him completely focused on these investigations right now."

Okay, so, it was now crystal clear why Big D was fifty shades of chartreuse. But Chief needed to rewind the part about the affair. The part about Big D *and* his wife. Hey, I wasn't too stoned to have missed that little ditty.

"He's my best homicide detective. *Both* of our reputations are on the line here. But damn, girl, you are in for such a pleasant ride." Pammy's voice lowered on the last sentence. Her aquamarine eyes were so piercing it was crazy, but tears were now welling up in them, which left me concerned as well as confounded. *She did say AND wife, right. I know you heard that.*

Chief tried to compose herself as she took a seat. I thought to myself. *That must be some damn good dick for Pammy to be crying over it.* "Look, Muffcat, David is really a fabulous guy. That being said, his past taste in woman, wasn't exactly remarkable." Chief shuffled in her seat. *There was more coming, holy hell. Well, bring it on then. Might as well know all the juicy details about my once gay and suddenly bisexual best friend and the man who had just face-fucked me.*

"Big D was new in CID. It was kind of a joke he was going through deevorce number four. I had no idea his soon to be ex-wife was my personal trainer." She waited for me to say something. Of course, I kept my damn mouth closed for once, just laid there, completely and utterly speechless. "Mercedes was just a fling. A one-night stand over in Memphis, well before I ever even met Eleanor. I ran into Mercedes at my gym about eight years ago and hired her on the spot to train me. She'd just moved to Jackson after her house had finally sold, and she claimed she needed some extra income. Even though I knew she was married, I never put two and two together about Big D being her husband. Then, one day, out of the blue, my new detective showed me a picture of his wife.

And then, he couldn't figure out why his partner was so cold, so distant. I was the one who had to break the news to him that his spouse was a closet lesbian. God! This is so embarrassing! Well, we wound up having some fun together, all three of us. It lasted for less than six months. Just casual and occasional sex for him. Hell, he didn't care if he had to have another woman in his bed in order to sleep with his own wife, but Mercedes got jealous. Thought we were doing it without her. We never did; I swear to you about that. But they never could work it out. Tried for almost five years. She finally sought revenge. I was drug up onto the witness stand to testify. That all happened a *long* time ago, and I'm not proud of it. Don't get me wrong. I'm not saying it wasn't any good. It was great actually, it's just not who I really am." Pammy stood. "Muffcat, I know my sexuality must confuse the hell out of you, but I do truly love Eleanor. If she found out, it would only upset her. She'd leave me. And I need Big D to be focused on these investigations right now."

A nurse came to the door with a wheelchair. Mother's eyes were as big as Aunt Maude's pancakes once the door swung open. She'd obviously been snooping. "Muffcat, honey, it is raining cats and dogs," she managed to choke out. "I need to get you home. Chief, good to see you again, I think."

*****

I woke up the next morning to Gavin smacking my cheeks. The odors of broccoli, mayonnaise, and Cheese Whiz wafting in the air about made me puke. "You look like shit, Mother. How many of those pain pills did you choke down last night?"

Alrighty then. I rolled over to look at the clock. It was 9:45 and the cabin was freezing. "Gavin Clyde Mansker-Glass, why aren't you in your classroom?" Gavin went over to collect the tray of food he'd placed on the dresser. "No thanks, Gav. It's amazing what Southerners can do with a little mayonnaise and a can of Cream of Crap, but I need to get some caffeine and one of my pain pills into me first."

Gavin handed me the coffee and my pill bottle, then grabbed for the remote on my side table. "Okay, but you have to see this first. You're never gonna believe what's going on around here. Selner County schools are closed due to the pending manhunt, for starters." He tried to flip through the channels.

"What's going on, Gav? Did they find Carligene?" Gavin was standing too to close the armoire to get the channel to change. He backed up a few feet and tried again. "No. But Movina predicted that the authorities would pin the murders on Ken and Merle Mooneyhan last night. Well, she didn't know their names; she just referred to them as the child molester and moonshiner. But she senses neither are tied to the recent homicides."

I adjusted my glasses. "You met Movina and Rosemurta?" WSMV was airing a commercial. Gavin's father, Johnny Glass, was standing in front of a used car screaming into the camera. "Uh, Dad's put on a few pounds, don't you think?" I had to agree. "We all assumed you got tied up at Simon's yesterday afternoon. Rosemurta and Movina asked Dyl to drive them over to the U-Haul rental place in Hendersonville before receiving the news about you being involved in the shooting over at the KOA. Dyl claimed Movina knew you were somehow involved even before they released your name to the media. And then you were out of surgery by the time Tommy called us. After a rendition of "Stuck on You", you'd already invited the entire waiting room to our cabin."

Thankfully, I had no recollection of any conversations or performances, with the exception of Pammy's little chat. The image of her in the middle of a threesome with Big D and his wife would require some sort of psychological therapy; I was sure of it. "You don't remember a flippin' thing about last night, do you, Mother?"

I looked down to the *Little House on the Prairie* gown my ex-husband had long ago given me as an anniversary present. "Who the hell dressed me last night, Gav?" With his pointer finger pressed to his lips, he made the universal "Shush" sign. "Now, watch this," he said. Holly Thompson was setting up a news segment. The "Breaking News" graphic flashed across the screen. "We have this just in from Parrottville, Tennessee this morning..."

As the talking head began to discuss the recent homicide investigations, the image of the no-name FBI agent from my cabin appeared to the right of Holly's head. He was being interviewed by the same field reporter that had missed her cue in front of City Hall. After Holly had detailed the events leading up to Carligene's abduction, the broadcast cut to the interview. "In our experience, the amount of blood loss the victim endured during the kidnapping is not survivable; we've gone from search and rescue to recovery mode at this point in our investigation. We suspect two people are behind the recent kidnapping and want to question both of them in regards to the string of homicides that have transpired over the ..." As a picture of our music minister and Merle Mooneyhan flashed across the bottom corner of the screen, the FBI agent repeated the license plate number of the royal blue El Camino, and the make and model of the church van.

"They have it all wrong. Merle's not involved. The letter I found at his place wasn't the killer's handwriting. The note was addressed to Merle. It was a recipe for blueberry hooch. And the language used in the message on our answering machine was waaaayyyy too polished to be either one of those assholes."

The field reporter took the interview back over. "Does your agency believe the recent shooting of the mortician by the Parrottville police officer is in any way related to these current investigations?" The no-name agent was now Marlowe Cho, according to the caption on the lower third of the screen. Agent Cho took a deep breath then danced around the question. The next query from the sprightly reporter about sent shock waves through the room. "Why would a person who has been diagnosed with schizophrenia be asked to aid in these investigations? Can you verify the claim by her uncle, Vernon Mansker, the Mayor of Parrotville, about Muffcat Mansker's mental instability?"

Ugh! Just as a video of me (looking hungover and being rammed into Mother's SUV) flashed onto the screen, Agent Cho choked out a lie. I was fuming at this point. Gavin clicked the TV off. "We have a potential PR crisis on our hands, Mother." My bird dogs started to bark like mad while I struggled to swallow the bitterness wafting up from my gullet.

Gavin went over to peer out the window. "They're here." He closed the curtain. "Who's here, Gav?" He stopped in the doorway. "That group from last night. You might want to get dressed. Between Aunt Maude's DUI's, your legal troubles, and this hot mess, Tommy feels you need to contact that PR firm we used when Maude ran over the preacher's foot."

Not anticipating the weakness of my knees, I face-planted onto the floor while attempting to get up out of bed. Gavin hastily assisted me back into a sitting position just as the doorbell rang. "Gav, the thought of receiving company right now is about as pleasant as having diarrhea during a two-hour Sunday sermon. No way; I'm just not up to it."

I lay down, face-first, then buried my aching head in my pillow.

Chapter XXIV

Rolling over just in time to witness Aunt Maude's slim frame making it through the doorway, I let out a groan. She had a copy of the *Parrottville Press* in hand; my attempted murder article was circled, boldly, with a red ink pen. I noticed it had only made page six of the local news. Hmmm.

Aunt Maude proceeded to light into me. "Child, we've all dun and tolds you about messin' with them po-po. When you gonna learn, my baby gurl? Vernon's pissed as hell which chu."

Mom dashed in from the living room, about knocking Movina down while trying to get around her in the doorway. "Move over, Maude. I'll deal with Vernon. No reason to upset Muffy Catherine any further with all the gossip swirling around this God-forsaken rumor mill of a town. Now, Muffy Catherine, what can Aunt Maude fix ya for breakfast, sweetie?" I pointed to the food Gavin had placed on my dresser. Mother grabbed for the bamboo tray then shrieked, "Mary Love Francis' casserole is not fit for those shit eaters out there, much less appropriate for human consumption!" Momma glanced back over to the muumuu in the doorway. "We call it Baptist Blasphemy. It's made with that processed cheese that comes from an aerosol can and Hellman's salad dressing. All good Southerners know that Duke's is the only mayonnaise suitable for casserole preparation." Mother walked over and handed the tray to Aunt Maude. "Maude, go fix Muffy Catherine a proper breakfast."

Good Lord, I was in hell. My mother was ordering the woman who actually raised me around like a servant in front of my company. Ugh! Maude, meanwhile, headed towards the door with an "eat shit" look on her face. "And call that damn heating and air company over in Hendersonville while you are at it. We cannot have Muffy Catherine freeze to death with her hair such a mess." Delightful, I know.

Eleanor approached my bedside, sporting a shirt proclaiming "I came out of the closet to kick your ass." She took her cell phone out from her baggy Levi's then took a seat. "Muffcat, Pammy would kill me if she knew what we did last night after leaving your cabin, however, Ken Akers had nothing to do with these homicides. Wait until you all get a load of this."

Eleanor made a few adjustments to her Samsung Note then handed over the clunky electronic device. I put on my glasses, only to find a blindfolded man, naked from the waist down. When Denise and Eleanor started their drunken rendition of "He Arose a Victor to the Dark Domain," well, uh, let's just say the crowd gathered around me erupted into laughter, even before Denise's whip made it onto the screen. By the sixth rerun of Ken's tiny manhood being risen with the aid of "a mighty whip o'er his foes," Aunt Maude had already carried a tray of Bloody Marys into the room.

Movina and Rosemurta waited patiently for the commotion to calm down before Rosemurta made her way over to me; she brushed my right leg with her tattooed covered hand. "Movina recognized you had the gift from the second you accepted the tea. We're here to teach you how to hone your abilities, my dear sister." I looked over at Movina. Her face was bloated, and without her red turban, it was obvious she was undergoing some sort of medical treatment. With some assistance from Eleanor, she slowly sauntered over to my side in her colorful dress. "Pardon me, dear one. I usually wear my chemo cap." She touched her head, seeming self-conscious. "Now, then," she continued, "We have the portrait. The one you inquired about yesterday at the funeral home."

Knowing full well I'd never asked Movina about the portrait, Wookiee breached the doorway with a massive canvas under his arm. The PI from the biker bar, Denise, slipped into the room sporting a red doo-rag. Julie, Queenie, and another one of my old classmates, Aimee Monroe, were two steps behind her. Aimee helped Wookiee place the gigantic portrait on my dresser; then she walked back over to the doorway.

"Hi, Muffcat. I flew in for Leighanna and Chandra's memorial services. So sorry about your accident." She gave me a wave like I had some sort of dreaded disease, then mumbled, "Hope you do not mind if I join in on the séance."

I looked up to Rosemurta. "Séance? What the hell is she talking about? I am in no condition to conjure any ghosts today." Rosemurta extracted a metal bowl from her knapsack, along with something that looked like a leather drumstick. "You are the one that wanted to learn the truth, dear sister. Now, we must purge the air of the evil spirits before we begin."

Movina asked Eleanor to hit the lights. She then pulled something from her muumuu that looked like a bunch of dried herbs and lit it. As

Rosemurta swirled the leather stick around the bowl, the smell of burning sage and the ringing coming from the bowl made it seem as if we were preparing for a Thanksgiving meal in a Tibetan Monastery. Movina's eyes rolled back into a shark-like attack position. With no eyelashes, eyebrows, or turban, the psychic began to chant. "Seven spirits of the coven, carriers of the powers of the seventh star, seven witches who guard the door to the eternal afterlife, whose names will always remain unspoken, I entreat you, in the silence of your seven names, to grant me the wholeness of my request for protection. It is in your care we lay our trust that you will allow Tariet's soul to transport one of us to the aid of our sister in kinship, Carligene. Give us the powers to uncover the true identities of her kidnappers. By the powers of…"

Looking around, I noticed that everyone's eyes were snugly closed. Once the ritual that was surefire certain to transport one of the lunatics in the room to Carligene's aid began, our sleuthing adventure supervened with full awareness that my friendship circle consisted of a motley crew of misfits.

Once the room was cleansed, Aimee was the one to make the first observation about the portrait. "It used to look like Picasso's 'Seated Women with a Wrist Watch,' but the image was of a male when Leighanna originally painted it. This canvas has been altered." Rosemurta expanded. "Tariet mastered her cubism techniques early in her career. She had such talent with her color blocking. I am surprised about the crudeness of the breasts and must agree with you, Sister Monroe."

We all continued to stare at the portrait. It really did look like the one from my flash, with the exception of the fluorescent green lopsided breasts that had obviously been added after the art competition. Finally, Movina broke the silence. "Do any of you know about our dear sister's series of male genitalia on display at MoMA?" She was seated at the foot of my bed on a leopard settee and was still breathing heavily from her chanting. "I bet none of you ever knew Rue Paul and Bono made their way into Parrottville for nude photo sessions with Tariet, did you?"

Aimee went over for a closer inspection of the portrait as Rosemurta took the conversation back over. "Tariet had an infatuation with separating one's sexuality from their soul. But her latest series was to be focused on real people from her hometown. We believe someone from her past has returned and is her killer. Movina accepts as truth that the defamation of this canvas portrays the murderer's lover. The coven has confirmed it."

Aimee reached up to rub her hand over one of the uneven breasts. I weighed in, "I have the same feeling, Rosemurta. I keep hearing this angry female in my head." Something kept drawing Aimee to the canvas. "Gav, you got a flashlight?" Gavin pulled his keys from his pocket and walked over to the portrait. He placed his keychain behind the massive image. As the LED light hit the backside of the image, Aimee scrutinized the back of the canvas. She then removed it from the dresser and placed it on the ground for further inspection. "There seems to be some sort of message written in white paint or maybe wax on the back of this canvas." Movina called out to Rosemurta, "we must quicken our pace, Rosemurta. The Hasbeens are waiting for us to review their performance for Tariet's life celebration. Wookiee, pull up a chair." He had apparently been clued into his part into the upcoming séance but seemed nervous. "We must get started," Movina ordered.

Wookiee gave me a disconcerting look, but then followed Movina's instruction. She extracted a triangular plastic disc she called a planchette from her muumuu and placed it on the Ouija board. I crawled to the foot of my bed in order to get a better view of the activities transpiring on my settee. Movina coached Wookiee on the correct finger positioning before her eyes rolled back into her head again. She cried out, in a low, monotone. "Is anyone here?" The planchette took no time to glide erratically from side to side. Once she began to chant, it stopping on the word "yes." I had to sojourn the ceremony for an instant.

"Look, Movina, our most pressing issue right now is the whereabouts of Carligene. Sad as it is, she's the only woman we might be able to assist at this point." Movina nodded, then called out, "who is here with us? Make your presence known." The plastic disc paused briefly, then began to glide over the letters on the board. We all began to call out those letters. T-A-R-I-E. Aunt Maude started hysterically wailing as the last letter was called. The planchette went motionless. While everyone tried to calm Maude, my vision began to tunnel; the room went completely black. Touch, smell, hearing; all of my other senses were on overdrive, yet I was unable to see a damn thing. It seemed as if something was suffocating my face. The space I was in became excruciatingly cold. My hands felt as heavy as a sack full of rocks, and they were now twisted up behind my back. An overwhelming sense of depression crept into my brain, which made me start sobbing. The experience was nauseating, disorienting; I'll call it what it was, fucking scary as hell.

As the others started to scream around me, my gut began to gurgle. I had no control over the movement of my body. Now crouching on the top of my bed and trying in desperation to shout, a horrid female body odor was coming from me, and mixing with the familiar stench of gasoline. A booming voice bounced off the walls and echoed like gunshots across a cannon. The voice was female, and she was pissed as hell at someone. "You stupid slut. Why do you refuse to see the splendor that lies before you?"

Hands started groping at my breasts as my pants were being pulled off. Something around my right ankle made it impossible for the fabric to completely dislodge. Another voice began taunting me as the tape was ripped from my lips. He was belittling me for my body odor and the sagginess of my breasts. Someone crawled on top of me. The smell of pure grain alcohol and cigarettes was making me sick as cold, slimy lips met mine. I was being waterboarded with a stinging liquid; hands continued to grope and tug at my privates. The molestation suddenly ceased when the second voice yelled out. "Wash her." After what felt like ice washing over me, my mouth was retaped, and we were alone again. As the couple's argument faded into the roar of an engine, I thought the worst was over.

My legs felt weak, and my right foot was contorted behind my knee, but at least we were no longer being taunted. I could hear the rattle of a chain, but was not sure where the sound was coming from. As soon as the cold metal dug into my ankle, we began to stand. With my wrists tightly bound behind my back, the act of walking was taxing; damn near impossible, but we were now vertical on the bed. The binding around my wrists was so tight my fingers were going numb. As we proceeded to elevate to the tips of our toes, the unsteadiness of our movement led me to believe we had been drugged. Once getting our footing, my face was being rubbed up against what felt like logs. They had been stripped of their bark, not square like my cabin, but smooth and worn. The wind did not penetrate the crevices in-between the log's butting. We were in a well-constructed log cabin, I was sure of it. I yearned to take control back over my own movement. I struggled, but the act threw us off balance. As my face ran up the side of the logs, a piercing sensation suddenly penetrated right below my left eye. It unsettled me. The cold metal was flat on top, yet sharp at the same time. The sensation of warm liquid pouring down my cheek made me gasp for breath. My face was being rubbed against the sharp, metal object; the experience was excruciating. Tugging, pulling, swaying in-between each miniscule rip; the struggle went on for what felt like a good, long ten minutes. After what seemed like hundreds of jerks, tiny beams of light danced like diminutive fireflies in beams of brilliant white before me. Whoever she was, she was clever. Rubbing her face and cheek furiously against the nail head had dislodged the tape over our eyes. The process was uncomfortable, but we now had a new perspective, that of sight.

My vision was still limited, but I could see a workbench that sat on the opposite side of the room. A long chain attached to the leg of the bench flounced across the dirt floor. The blood that covered my face made it hard to see much else. The body that I was in then knelt down on the dirt floor and used its knee to wipe the gore from our faces. The horrid smell was more intense, reminding me of a ladies restroom with one of those tampon disposals, one that had not been emptied for weeks. The pain in what felt like my own gut was more intense than any hunger pains. The piercing throbs in my stomach told me something more serious was wrong. It was the sensation of labor pain, but with no respite separating the contractions. Our wrists, which were still behind our backs, were our next mission. The contortionist positioning shot pain through my shoulder blades as she slid our hands up the wall. The stretching only intensified the pain in my gut. The cramping made it difficult to fully stand.

Slowly, meticulously, painfully, the metal nail head tore into my right wrist. As she shook her hands furiously onto the log that held the nail, the tape began to rip. Next came pins and needles so intense, the sensation was like frostbite when you finally get to a warm space. After our hands had been freed from the tape, we knelt back down. A 70-grade chain with a simple combination lock was the only thing separating us from our freedom. A small tattoo of butterflies on our ankles came into focus as the tape was ripped from our mouths. I was trapped in the body of Carligene.

Suddenly, there were more rattles coming from behind us. My head felt to be strapped to a merry-go-round as it spun from one place to another, looking to find the culprit of the noise. There, in the corner of the room, sitting on the dirt floor, was a filthy, bald silhouette, a coward with its hands around pale, soiled knees.

And just like crossing into a parallel universe, Gavin's fearful eyes came into focus; he was just inches from my face. My positioning made me feel like I'd been through an exorcism: head thrust back against the headboard, my limbs were in no position that was humanly possible. Mother handed Maude a cold rag. They both were in tears. Dyl was now in the room, and he was terrified, clawing at the fabric that had bunched up around my waist. Wookiee had to leave the room, according to Denise. I could hear his meaty growls in the den. Some of the others were trying to reassure him. Eleanor lifted the Bloody Mary to my lips. "Tell us everything, Muffcat." The next few minutes were a flurry of brainstorming and psychic interfering by Movina. We had established that Carligene was alive, nonetheless, I knew from our experience it was just a matter of time before she would be sexually assaulted or succumb to the unforgivingly frigid air.

At this point, my fear was gone. I had every detail of my surroundings memorized. The lack of traffic told me they were in a sparsely populated area. In a cabin, with smooth logs. No heat. A dirt floor. There was hickory smoke burning in the air. She was with a man and a twisted female, but they were staying in another location. I could hear them quarreling as they got into a vehicle and drove away. They were out of money. The frustration and tension between them was mounting. I knew I needed to act fast. Carligene was in no condition to survive much longer.

Gavin pulled up a map of Selner County on his iPad. Within minutes, my cabin was completely empty, with the exception of Aunt Maude and two very stiff Bloody Marys.

Chapter XXV

Now, you haven't lived until you and your drunken girlfriends have ridden in the back of a U-Haul filled with portraits of winged severed penises.

Even with the low deck, all three grown men had to assist Movina into the trailer. Rosemurta's confession of only keeping a driver's license for identification purposes made Gavin a better choice as designated driver. Dylan and Wookiee were his co-pilots. Julie, Aimee, Eleanor, Denise (minus her doo-rag), Movina, Aunt Maude, Rosemurta, Mother, Queenie and I crammed into the back of the U-Haul like a can of talkative sardines conferring about the placement of airborne genitalia.

Furrowed in the floor and staring up at phallic freedom flyers, Movina questioned me. "So, my little free-floater. Was today your first out of body experience?" The trailer went silent. Eyes darted around the U-Haul as I recounted the hijacking of my soul. With the exception of Movina and Rosemurta, it was obvious none of the others believed me.

It was brought to my attention that during their afternoon sleuthing adventure, the U-Haul was pulled over by Brad Weasle. It seems the owners of one of the cabins over in Selner County called in an attempted break-in as they tried to find Carligene. Eleanor was emphatic that the cops were tailing them, but there was no way of proving it. She relayed to me that Dyl took the heat for the lock-picking incident then spent the better part of the afternoon detained at the Parrottville precinct. It was there he discovered a volunteer recovered one of Carligene's tennis shoes on the banks of the lake, two miles north of the boat dock. According to Queenie, when the search and rescue dogs picked up on the scent of death, the search was called off. They were in the process of dragging the waterways before a thunderstorm halted their recovery efforts.

Movina tried to explain to the group that what I had experienced was real, but most of them were stuck and standing, intractably, on the side of science. Hell, I was used to it. Mother went ahead and told us that an FBI press conference revealed they'd captured Merle Mooneyhan and were closing in on Ken. My insistence that a different perpetrator was behind the abductions and murders was becoming little more than a broken record. And as far as the soul-jacking incident was concerned, the majority felt pretty confident that the experience was a side effect of the stress of the shooting.

Leave it to Mother, who did her bid to apply salt to my wounds. "A little therapy might be helpful, Muffy Catherine. It is nothing to be ashamed of, my dear. Your father went in about every five years for a little downtime." While the U-Haul inhabitants debated the best destination for my "unplanned vacation," Movina grasped for my arm. "The child molester has departed this world, Muffcat. Someone else's life is in danger now. Someone who is here, with us, in this trailer." I surveyed the group (they were still in a heated debate about my mental stability) and then whispered to Movina, "which one of us?" When she didn't answer me, I peered over and noticed she was in some sort of trance. She sat motionless with her eyes rolled back into her head for what felt like an eternity before breaking into song. "Happiness is... two kinds of ice cream... finding your skate key... telling the time..." The entire cab joined in for an impromptu A cappella before the U-Haul came to an abrupt stop, throwing us around like rag dolls amongst a sea of penises.

After we crawled out of the back of the rental truck, like a congregate of clowns preparing to entertain a parade, I sensed something was not right. The parking lot lights were set on a timer, but Hollis was well aware of the midnight service and should have already overridden the device. A bus stopped at the curb before the boys could get Movina out of the trailer. Rosemurta walked over to greet passengers as they began to assemble in the dark parking lot. An idol van, at the very back of the parking lot, flashed its lights. Upon my approach, someone hopped in the passenger side of the van then swiftly tore out of the lot. I yelled for Gavin to get a plate number then hurriedly unlocked the door to the embalming room. Gavin busted into the room, out of breath, with Wookiee two steps behind him. Their attempt to retrieve the license plate number had not been fruitful. Of course, I was hesitant to contact the police after learning of Dyl's arrest, but went ahead and dialed Big D's cell phone anyway. Wookiee was making hand gestures for "female," and howling uncontrollably. Big D demanded that I put Wookiee on the phone before even offering a greeting. His voice was booming through the phone. "Fucking make her keep a low profile goddamn it! I'll be there in less than ten, Wook."

Hollis unlocked the back door for the caravan of mourners while Wook and I proceeded towards my office. Before we could get two steps into the parlor, a six-foot transvestite with a three-foot beehive named

Kent Fuckthis professed she *had* to rehearse. I asked my mortified mother to escort her to the parlor's podium just as Eleanor and Denise approached. They needed some instruction as to where to place the portrait of the four-foot black slong, covered in over 34,000 chocolate-hued Swarovski Crystals, I might add.

While I was busy playing ringmaster to the "Most Unhallowed Show on Earth," a behemoth silhouette appeared at the front doorway. I walked across the foyer to unlock the door. Big D had on a suit. This was no Five-O, cheap diddy either. "Muffcat, goddamn it! I need you to tell me the direction but didn't I tell Wookiee to keep you in your office?" Oh boy. I didn't know whether to give him the finger (I don't take well to displays of male domination) or shudder from his fabulously masculine display (because, sometimes I do). I know; I'm screwed up. No need to point out the obvious. That's just cruel.

I swiftly made my way to the covered portico with Wookiee tailing me, then pointed Big D down the street. The fine detective hauled ass down the sidewalk and yelled back, "got three TBI on their way. Get back in your office, woman! This time, Wookiee, do not let her out of your sight!" The detective collided into Keith Petigro and never even slowed down. I did as told, heading to my office, with Keith bitching a mile a minute in my ear.

Wookiee was standing at the door like a bouncer at a Las Vegas nightclub as Keith attempted to pry his estranged sister's net worth out of my mouth. By the time he started in on his failing record label, thankfully, Betty had penetrated the doorway. "Keith, you are going to have to excuse us. We have a minor emergency."

Keith thrust himself from my wingback then headed out to the parlor. Betty's eyebrows were attempting to be resurrected from their Botox paralysis while she shuffled a bunch of old newspaper clippings across my desk. "Wait until you get a load of the parlor. Lord, Muffcat. I haven't seen this many freaks since wearing my teddy to see the *Rocky Horror Picture Show* in the Seventies." Betty pointed to one of the clippings. "Got these from the library. Canita needs them back, but you gotta see all this." I picked them up and skimmed through a few of the articles. They scanned over a decade of activity on the Parrottville homicide that had happened in the mid-Eighties.

"So, I gather the victim is the out-of-state runaway, the one later identified as Sheila Lynn Byers. Did they ever name the boys who found her body?" Betty shuffled a later article to the top of the heap. The mug shot captured looked nothing like the man in my dreams. He was old, stout, and had coal-black eyes.

"This guy was charged with her murder, but her case never went to trial." I searched for a photo of his victim and found a shot of an innocent looking preteen, with wildly over-processed hair. "I heard the murderer the other day, Betty. While waiting on Aunt Maude. This INXS song was stuck in my head. *Devil Inside, Devil Inside, every single one of us the Devil Inside.* After the chorus, I distinctly heard him say, "Her face is so cold. There are marks on her neck. She was so beautiful, Claw!"

I held up the clip of the convicted trucker. 'Unh uh. This is not our murderer." Betty set down opposite my desk. "I believe you, Muffcat. Maude told me about your experience. And Stanley Wayne Mullinax is currently on death row over at the Riverbend Maximum Security Institution anyhow. He was stopped during a routine traffic violation, and the authorities found a dead body in his rig. He admitted to the Byers' murder but later retracted his confession when he was hit with the mutilation of a corpse charges."

I flipped through the remaining articles but felt compelled to go back to the picture of the girl. The image of Shelia Lynn Byers transfixed me. "This is definitely the same girl from my dreams, Betty. But how she's connected to the recent homicides is still a mystery." Betty slouched in her seat. "Sally told me about the voices you are experiencing. You should have said something to me about them sooner, Muffcat. Since when do we keep secrets?" I shuffled the papers in my hand. "Betty, do you think it's possible that one of the boys mentioned in the article is our killer?" She stood too close my door then walked over to stand behind me. "You have a gift, Muffcat. Your father was aware of it when you were just a small child, and your instincts have been spot-on for most of your life. That is when you are not jumping to conclusions and spouting off at the mouth."

Betty placed her hands on my shoulders. I turned around to meet her gaze. "Betty, I cannot help but feel Vernon is somehow associated with the murderer. I can't explain it. But the boy I keep seeing in my dreams has his eyes. They're light emerald green, with these dark lashes. When Nanny fell the other day, I saw the rage in them. Do you think it could be that…"

Movina entered the room before I had the chance to finish my thought. "Aye, Muffcat. You have discovered the root of his evil. His lust for the flesh of the dead has been festering for three decades. I saw the boy last night in my dreams." Movina was breathing heavily. Betty pulled up a chair for the heavyset clairvoyant. "Please take a seat." Movina reached for my hand, and then tightly closed her eyes. "He will come to you again, my dear one. He wants you to understand the reasoning behind his personal demons. He is well aware of yours. The truth will be a bitter pill to swallow; nonetheless, the self-discovery will be excellent training for your next career endeavor."

Betty gathered the clippings then swiftly put an end to our conversation. "I'm sorry, but we need Muffcat focused on her recovery right now, Movina. There's work to be done. Now, let's get this service underway."

Chapter XXVI

As I exited my office, the hair on the back of my neck fluttered with static energy. Betty was telling the truth; dead bodies do not scare me. Not even being alone with a stiff with what sounds like a firing squad going off in my head gives me any serious creeps. Having said that, however, the sight of dozens of alternative-lifestyle mourners draped in black tunics, capes, surcoats, and hooded robes was an altogether different story. Now, we're talking downright frightful.

It was impossible to make out who was who in the sea of black hoodies, but a few gentlemen were recognizable. They were the undercover TBI agents from Tana's memorial service.

Movina walked us over to a bank of tables; the half-dozen silk-clad tablecloths were covered with crystal balls. Movina introduced Betty to her palm reading partner as Vlad the Inhaler. I leaned over towards Betty. "Good Lord, the night is going to be crazy." I searched the room for Gavin and Dylan. My friends had already taken their seats, but the boys were nowhere to be seen. Huddled in the back row next to my mother, Aunt Maude pulled a flask out of her sock and passed it. Mother took a swig. I honestly contemplated doing so myself but needed to find Dyl and Gav before the service began.

Dylan was in deep conversation with Big D while rounding the stairwell. The detective had obviously not caught up with the van. "I need to speak to you both, in private. Now. Where's Gavin?" We only had twenty minutes until the service was to begin. I motioned for Wookiee to find Gav. "Look, Detective, I need to be assisting Betty. Can't this wait?"

Big D grabbed us both by our arms, then forcefully led me and Dyl to the conference room. As soon as the door slammed, Big D started roaring in my face. "For God's sake, what the fuck are you trying to accomplish? Getting yourself killed? The last thing I need is for my officers to have to keep tabs on your renegade whereabouts." I did not let more than a second pass before going back at him. "If you were doing your job right, you would know that there is a terrified woman out there who is still alive and in dire need of medical assistance." The detective huffed. Ran his hand through his messy hair and looked away. "You have no proof of that. Now sit your ass down."

Dyl asked if he needed to leave just as Big D forced me into the chair. Big D lowered his voice as he took his seat. "Look, we know who this guy is now. Tennessee, Indiana, Alabama, Kentucky, and West Virginia, all have victims. All previously unsolved cases." Dyl took a seat. "TBI agent Isaac Lewis out there, just reopened a cold case. He was with the Bowling Green force when a woman and her baby turned up dead in' 91. Baby was suffocated, and the mother took 365 cuts to her upper torso. Lewis just had a witness come forward. Goddammit! I am not supposed to share this."

Big D beat on the table with such strength, it was startling. "Eighty years of combined experience stands on the other side of that door, Muffy Catherine, and what do you do? Send your friends and your own flesh and blood to hunt a serial killer, all because of some séance?" Big D was pointing his finger toward the doorway. I knew it was the flesh and blood comment that made Dyl hang his head. I wanted to ask him if the suspect was a former employee of Hellman Heating and Air, but Big D changed the direction of the conversation.

"Look, Muffcat. You are about to ruin the career of your best friend, and if I cannot get your psychic investigation under control, Vernon will go after my job as well. The threat has been made. Read my lips: No more fucking séances."

I was confused. I had not spoken to anyone about my out of body experience, with the exception of the people who were at my cabin, that is. Big D took a deep breath, exhaled, and continued. "Muffcat, we found the postcard at Merle Mooneyhan's during the arrest. Just when were you going to share this little tidbit of information with us? I thought we had built up some rapport."

According to the now red-faced detective, if they'd known about the letter sooner, it would have saved them forty-eight hours of hunting down the wrong suspect. "Merle's taken a polygraph test and passed. Has a solid alibi for the time during Chandra's murder. We have him on camera at the hardware store over at Rivergate during the attack."

I felt horrible about the deception, but the worst was yet to come. Big D filled us in on the backstory. Apparently, the Mayor and the Chief of Police each had the other by the tail. Vernon had been in touch with Jackson. Allegedly, if Pammy tried to uncover Vernon's association with the shiners, he would expose Pammy and Big D's affair. If Chief didn't turn a blind eye to his funding of the moonshine operation, Pammy's relationship with Eleanor and her career were on the line. Big D had three dead Parrottvillians and no break in a homicide investigation that was tarnishing the whole town's reputation. Sam's and Best Buy were pulling out of development plans. That was a fact. Tax dollars were bleeding out on Uncle Vernon's watch. Vernon wanted this guy caught as badly as the rest of us but did not want his name drug through the mud in the process.

I glanced over to Big D. His eyes told me he was still hiding something, and his story sure as shit wasn't making any sense. "How can Vernon hold Pammy's sexuality over her head? This is 2012, Detective." Big D unleashed what sounded like a monumental lie. I urged him to tell me the truth; he insisted he was. A disagreement arose. Big D called me stubborn and irrational. I called him a horrible liar and a hothead. He said I was a loon but had pretty eyes. I told him he had on a nice suit. Our banter was cut short by Rosemurta, who needed instructions for the podium's microphone. Dylan stayed behind with the detective while Wookiee escorted me to the parlor.

Three transvestites and Magenta joined "Madame of Abundant Cleavage" at the podium. Their costumes were absurd, to say the least, but everyone was in awe of Dr. Frank-n-Furter's legs. Rosemurta introduced the group as "The Hasbeens." They were a local theater group Leighanna had specifically requested perform at her service. They'd been contracted to execute a theatrical interpretation from Sylvia Plath's 1965 Ariel Series. Magenta would be reciting a monologue of the poem entitled "Daddy". As the bustier-clad thespian took a test drive on the mic, the other gender-benders rolled around on the floor. "You do not do, you do not do, anymore, black shoe, in which I have lived like a foot, for thirty years, poor and white, barely daring to breathe or Achoo. Daddy, I have had to kill you. You died before I had time. Marble-heavy, a bag full of God, Ghastly statue with one gray toe, big as a Frisco seal."

I returned to the conference room to find Dylan in deep conversation with Big D. He was sharing his and Shelley's experience in the parking lot of Uncle EG's. Dylan began relentlessly begging the detective to reveal the identity of the killer, but Big D was keeping the identity close to his vest. His unwillingness to share the name of the murderer was maddening.

"Big D, seriously. The early onset cruelty to animals? Stalking his prey? Uncontrolled anger and outbursts? Can you at least let Dylan see a picture of your suspect so he will know if it's the same guy? His mother was a victim, remember." Nope; Big D was not budging. 'I really need to be surveying the crowd, Muffcat." He claimed he could not share any more than he already had with us as the authorities had not formally announced their findings.

Betty entered the conference room. "You need to see these, detective." Big D ran his hand through his hair before extracting the clippings from Betty's hand. "Muffcat has been hearing the murderer's voice. She seems to believe that one of the unnamed boys mentioned here is somehow involved." Betty pointed to the article. "If she is right about it, this case might explain the psychological reasoning behind his sickness. You need to have the case file of Sheila Lynn Byers exhumed."

Big D shuffled the articles in his hands. "I'll get the case file exhumed, but Kentucky authorities are on their way to the residence of our suspect as we speak. Honestly, I am not sure a thirty-year-old case will have top priority until we have him in custody."

Wookiee was now pointing to a copy of the partial manifesto that was leaked by the *Parrottville Press*. He grunted three times and made the hand gesture for female. I knew what he wanted me to share. "Big D, I really think this guy is traveling with a female companion. In my dreams, the killer has two personas. One is a male demon and the other seems to be a bisexual female." The detective looked as if he were going to wiggle out of his chair. He mumbled. "There is not a male around that would have a problem with a bisexual female, Muff."

I gave him the truncated version of the dream that took place at the Hee-Haw. As I started in on the peculiarity of Tommy's housekeeper, Big D's body language screeched that his wheels were turning. When I got to the part about Missy's giving me a fake name, the blood had all but drained out of the detective's face. He then looked down and sent a rapid text. "I have to go." Big D shot up within seconds of sending the message. Just as he placed his hand on the door knob, I served up the one last detail I had to share with the detective. "Just minutes before the hit on Chandra, Camille Carr-Glass was at the church." Big D nodded then darted into the hallway. "The Dark Lord of Wedding Coordination" and my ex-husband were gonna shit when TBI showed up at their door.

We exited the conference room just as the ceremony was getting underway. Everyone was seated. Betty closed the doors as Rosemurta took the mic. "We are here today, a few weeks shy of our Wiccan Sabbat, Samhain, to celebrate the life of Tiaret Akie, otherwise known as mortals as Leighanna Shiane Petigro. We must take the time to recharge our spiritual batteries, align ourselves with the Earth's shifting energies, and celebrate the loving witch-sister who has crossed before us."

Man, though I hated to admit it, Rosemurta and Movina's unexpected introduction into my life was turning out to be an engaging and enlightening experience. At 2:00 a.m., Wookiee corralled the last of the trannies to the parking lot, where we all clamored back into the U-haul. All that was missing was the *Twilight Zone* theme. (do-do-do-do)

Chapter XXVII

The visitation of Chandra Sue Worsham-Carter was interesting, to say the very least. First, Hollis called to inform me that the parking lot was a madhouse. Now, the event was scheduled to get underway at 6:00 p.m., but, by 4:30, utter mayhem had erupted. Once again (it seemed to be becoming a regular thing) the shit had hit the fan; Hollis was in dire need of assistance.

I threw a black jacket over my war wound and hauled ass up to the funeral home. Three police cars were on my tail before I entered the roundabout in the heart of town square. The patrol vehicles raced around my SUV but then flew ahead of the chaos in the parking lot of Simon's. Four locally-syndicated media vans were already there, cluttering the curbs.

While attempting to part the sea of bodies in the parking lot, I noticed Parrottville had a new sightseer; CNN had arrived. They had a communication hub set up across the street, with a satellite the size of a kiddy pool. I turned on my radio, but the local stations weren't airing any news about the tumult. Before it was possible to even park, my SUV was surrounded by a media frenzy. My iPhone pinged with a message from Betty: "Side door. Embalm." Microphones and cameras were being thrust into my face as I attempted to exit my vehicle. A helicopter made it difficult to understand what the reporters were trying to probe from me. It seemed it was not the residing funeral director's point of view the gang of media was seeking. Everyone wanted an exclusive with "that woman from the video."

"Mrs. Mansker, can you explain how your face wound up in the video leaked by the serial killer?... How do you know Jonah Wayne Johnson?... Why did a serial killer have a tracking device on your vehicle?... How does it feel to be possessed?... Mrs. Mansker, is it true you have been conducting your own investigation into the recent homicides?... How is your brother's family handling this?... Why do you think the serial killer is portraying YOU as the Devil?"

I had never in my life, and I do mean not ever, experienced anything so dizzying and daunting. Betty shoved her way through the mayhem and shrieked, "Keep your damn mouth closed, Muffcat!" It was almost impossible to get the door open due to the thrusting of the vultures. Betty reached her man-like hand into the doorway, then jerked us both inside while swatting at the microphones being pushed at us. A TBI agent donning aviator shades led me out of view of the glass window and into the hallway, stopping short of the threshold of the conference room. "Stay here. Don't make a peep." Betty locked all of the remaining doors in order to contain the madness. I knew my mind was not as sharp as it needed to be. I was not sure if it was the pain meds or disorientation from the questions being thrown at me like I was a Kardashian. I knew one thing for sure: nothing was making any sense.

Hollis set off into the parking lot with an officer to locate the family. I attempted to follow him, but a TBI agent had me by my jacket. I was getting pissed. "Can somebody *please* tell me what the *hell* is going on?" The lanky agent was on his cell, but firmly demanded that I "hold on; stay calm!" When Big D approached, the smug-faced agent sprinted for the parking lot and told me to lock the door behind him. Big D raced past me in the hallway, his phone glued to his ear. I followed but was left standing alone in the hallway with my jaw thumping the carpet.

Big D shouted into the receiver. "I have Mansker. We're going to need a full sweep of the building. Get them dispatched ASAP, Chief." The detective then proceeded to ransack the conference room. Every picture was taken off the wall; then, he flipped over a couch. I tried to interject but might as well have been yapping my questions into the wind. He yanked an armchair from the now overturned table and jerked it over towards the bookcase. "What the hell are you doing?" I tried. Still nothing. He searched through every knickknack on the shelves before taking the vent cover off the wall. Big D stuck something in his pocket then jumped down from the chair. "Come with me." I did not argue, just ran as fast as humanly possible in my six-inch stilettos.

More reporters were in my face as we exited the building. Big D was not exactly polite as he all but machete-hacked us through the crowd. The cruiser was in drive before my door could shut. Police as well as TBI cars were fleeing the parking lot as if it were on fire. 'Where the hell are we going?" I cried out. Still nil from the dick. Okay now, c'mon, really? I was going in. "Big D, I need to be in attendance at the visitation of my best friend. Please tell me what the fuck is going on around here. Now would be great." He handed over what he'd pulled out of the air duct and mumbled. "2.4 gigahertz wireless Spy Cam Ultra-Mini. Killer made a video of us. It went viral. Fingerprints on your vehicle matched the serial killer." I took the device in my hands as I realized we were not heading in the same direction as the rest of the parade of blue lights. Traveling over eighty miles per hour down Main Street, we were heading in the opposite direction from the rest of the emergency responders. I let out a cry.

Once we turned onto Long Hollow Pike, a roadblock was visible up ahead just before the I-65 Northbound entrance ramp. The Tennessee Highway Patrol had both on-ramps blocked off. Overhead, a good quarter mile in each direction, several others patrol cars had I-65 completely shut down. There were a dozen or so civilian vehicles in front of us. Two County police cars rested sideways underneath the bridge, blocking both directions of Long Hollow Pike. The detective slowed then made his way up onto the center partition. The Selner Sherriff waved us through. We rapidly picked up speed after weaving through a dozen or so idle vehicles. An APB was issued for an older model black Lincoln town car. Big D's phone was glued to his ear. He was giving directions to the athletic facility located behind Gavin's school.

We hit my driveway with enough rapidity to throw me into the passenger side door. Dispatch was going haywire. My arm and head were throbbing. Big D did not even turn the engine off. I yelled out my half-opened door. "Shit! Big D, my keys are at the funeral home. I'll have to get the spare from the big house." The officer did not ease up on his warpath toward my cabin. I headed for the B&B but turned around after not receiving a response from the detective. He ripped his jacket off, wrapped the fabric around his right hand around a few times, and then punched. My one hundred-year-old hand-blown glass windowpane was shattered.

The detective was like a wild animal scavenging his last meal. In no time flat, he was in my bedroom grabbing artwork off the walls. Big D ignored my pleas for some insight into the insanity. The detective just yelled for me to keep quiet. I plopped down on the settee at the foot of my bed and waited for the hunt to subside. My iPhone was going off like a strobe light, with a slew of unrecognizable numbers. A scarf placed on my pillow seized my attention. I went over to pick it up, but the detective barked for me leave it and to exit the room.

Once I made it to the kitchen, my brother's name popped up on my iPhone. The panic in his voice was unmistakable. "Where are you, Sis?" I trudged outside to take the call. "Currently having my home ransacked by the police. Are you OK?" Tommy did not waste a breath. He was alright, but there was bad news. His home had been burglarized. The intruders invaded at around 4:00 p.m. while he was still at his office. They tied our mother, Keelie (his wife), and their kids up with duct tape, then made off with thousands of dollars' worth of weapons and ammo, as well as laptops, cell phones, and jewelry. A neighbor called 911 after witnessing a man and a woman exiting their home, in broad daylight, brandishing shotguns. The neighbor had already identified the female intruder as their housekeeper. Keelie and the kids were en route with our mother to the hospital. Even though they had not been physically harmed, the FBI was adamant about psychological assessments for Tommy's children.

My big brother then turned his attention to my situation. He was concerned for my safety. He wanted to make sure the boys had protection as well. Tommy was unbending on one demand. "Do NOT speak to anyone in law enforcement without me being present, Muffcat. You have no filter, Sis. You really need to work on that." *Okay, thanks, Bro. I'll put that on my to-do list, just as soon as things settle down.* Not saying he wasn't right about me being a loose cannon and all that. When God was handing out filters … well, you get the idea.

Tommy proceeded to reveal more bad news. A video had been sent via my personal Gmail account around the same time as the home invasion. He went on to explain that it was sent as a hyperlink from a Youtube account; there were four words in the subject line of the email: "We are all monsters." The video showed images of our dead youth minister. He'd been shot at point blank range in a bathtub. Tommy said there were also clips of me, in my own bed, during the séance. According to my brother, there were even close-ups of Dyl at the conference table at Simon's. Images of Carligene and the three recent homicide victims were also weaved into the cryptic imagery, but there was some good news. Carligene was still alive. Some images apparently portrayed me as the Devil. There was also a scrolling feed at the bottom of the video that Tommy needed more time to review. When I pressed for specifics on the content, he just whispered, "It's disturbing, Sis." I charged back into the cabin.

"Okay, spill it! Right now, David Davenport!" The detective was standing on my antique dresser. His pounce down to the floor made the entire cabin shake. This time, my bad arm received the fury. The scream of a thousand banshees did not deter the detective from his firm grip. He led me out of the open doorway; we did not stop until he'd marched me two hundred yards away from the cabin. We finally came to a rest just feet from a traveling CSX train. The detective was close but still had to scream for me to be able to hear him. "We have TBI agents en route to Gavin's school; two should be arriving at the B&B any second. You were right. Our suspect is traveling with Tommy's housekeeper and her young son, who they kidnapped a few weeks ago. Hijacked a car at a gas station after evading Tommy's residence. They're armed and dangerous. Had a live video feed streaming from your bedroom."

The detective handed over another camera that looked exactly like the one he'd removed from the funeral home's air duct. "We are going to have to sweep the entire property. Figure out why they are targeting you." I fell to my knees. In less than twenty minutes, my world had come crashing down around me. Not only was my life in peril, my son's and brother's lives had now been mixed up in the absurdity as well. It was surreal; it was devastating. It was too much to take in and process.

Big D knelt down and tried to snatch me up from my crouched position, but I was not going anywhere. "Muffcat, come on, now. You have to regain your composure. Please, we do not have a lot of time." The detective's voice was beginning to soften, but shit, my mental breakdown was just getting underway. He put his entire body around mine. Big D just held me and let me sob in a crumpled heap on the ground. "Hon, you were right about Carligene. You can break down on me later. Right now, you are our best shot at ending this rampage."

I tried to push myself up on my hands and knees. My arm was throbbing from his firm grip. I fell back to the sod. The detective grabbed me underneath my armpits and lifted me up. By the time my heels hit the grass, there were blue lights everywhere. An unhappy-looking Dylan was being led out of the kitchen door by a man in a suit. Unaware of what had transpired at Tommy's, I surmised he'd figure he was being detained for the trespassing charge again. Once Big D got involved and calmed Dyl down, he explained the situation and escorted us back to his patrol car.

There was silence in the car as we rolled into the precinct. What we were witnessing was unprecedented. It was apparent the entire town of Parrottville had been put on lockdown. The interstate was no longer blocked overhead, but Long Hollow Pike was littered with patrol cars, and the North and South bound exit ramps remained obstructed. As we entered the roundabout, the funeral home's parking lot appeared to be packed. Bizarre, given that the town was deserted. Our car was the only one on the road. The reporters had been pushed down the street several blocks, but otherwise there was not another soul anywhere to be seen. Once back at the precinct, Big D exited the patrol car and tapped a code into the keypad. His tone sober, he instructed us, "don't even think about moving a muscle."

Chapter XXVIII

"Momcat, you cold?" Dyl asked, with a worried look on his face. I might have been shaking like a crack whore in church, but my fear had long since turned to fury. Chief stepped into the hallway, making no eye contact. She yelled to a plainclothes officer, "Set up a news conference, ASAP. We need to get their photographs circulating, along with the car tag, make, and model. Be sure the media knows these guys are armed and dangerous."

I could see Eleanor through the cracked doorway. She was seated at a table with an unfamiliar man in a suit. "Good God! Is Eleanor under interrogation?" There was no answer from Chief. She had Denise in handcuffs and was leading her across the hall. Another suit entered the room with Eleanor and closed the door. Another two were with Big D when he returned. Big D made the introduction to Agent Isaac Lewis, who was with the TBI. We already knew J-Laz from the night at our cabin; she stated her name and shook Dylan's hand before escorting him into a separate opened doorway. Isaac Lewis asked me to follow him. Once seated, Big D offered coffee or water; Agent Lewis and I both declined. Big D slipped out of the room anyway.

Agent Lewis stood up, took off his coat, and placed it on the back of his chair. His eyes were bloodshot, but Isaac Lewis had a sincere face. Tommy told me not to speak to anyone; I had complied, thus far. The plainclothes agent was the only one doing any of the talking. He retook his seat. "Our madman is a guy by the name of Jonah Wayne Johnson. Goes by JJ. Has a female companion with him named Jennifer Melissa Jenkins, also known by her johns as Marvelous Missy. JJ is originally from Bowling Green but has ties here in Parrottville; we're still trying to figure out his complicated family situation. We know he was a suspect in a 1991 homicide investigation while I was on the force up north. Not a good omen to have your first homicide investigation go unprosecuted."

Agent Lewis grinned, as if halfheartedly. His deep voice had a raspy quality, reminding me of a jazz singer you might hear on Beale's Street. Big D reentered the room with a laptop, a manila file, and Tommy in tow. It was my laptop that had been stolen from the cabin during the break-in.

173

My brother and Agent Lewis exchanged cards and some legal mumbo jumbo. Then Agent Lewis continued. "After the stories about Parrottville hit the airwaves last week, we got a call from a woman by the name of Vickie Lambert, an HVAC dispatcher who provided Johnson with an alibi back in '91. A resident called in about a broken AC unit after hours. She originally dispatched our suspect, but JJ claimed he had a flat. When a twenty-two-year-old mother and her baby turned up dead, our focus was on the second technician Vickie dispatched. She was under the impression JJ never made it to the residence. Had him logged six miles from the crime scene. An eyewitness collaborated JJ's story about the flat. Both technicians were brought in for questioning. We had them printed and took DNA samples, but there was not much forensic evidence to go on. Female victim had been doused in gasoline. Only a few fibers from the kid's nose and throat were in evidence. Our focus was on a technician by the name of Jose Rose, whose work boots were covered in the victim's blood. His criminal record included sexual assault; the phone cord used to strangle the mother was later found in the trunk of Rose's personal vehicle. After Vickie's call, JJ's prints were the ones that turned up on your SUV, Muffcat.

Big D interjected, "along with McNabb's prints on the tracking device." Agent Lewis continued, "we've had a half-dozen agents on you ever since. We need to find out how you know this guy. The reason for him stalking you." I glared at Big D. He had been holding back. The fucking detective had lied through his damn teeth. Granted, they were some spectacular teeth, but I digress. He'd known about me being targeted by the serial killer for quite some time, sounded like. His insistence for me to stop my investigations was not because of the feud between Pammy and Uncle Vernon. Hell no. How could I have been so stupid? Big D and the FBI were using me as bait.

Agent Lewis slid some pictures under my nose. Missy's photographs were all mug shots. JJ's looked to be an ID work badge, perhaps an advertisement from a Web site for Little Devil Heating and Air. "It sounds as if you could have caught this sicko years ago," Tommy said. I glanced over to my attorney and whispered, "Can I ask a question?" Tommy articulated for me to relay the inquiry to him. "Agent Lewis, my client wants to know about the female." What the agent told us was not surprising. "Well, Marvelous Missy has a long criminal record. Goes all the way back to 1987. A drifter/prostitute who spent some time in Bowling Green in-between her numerous arrests. Married four times, before giving birth to a son at the Greenview Regional Hospital that she later put up for adoption. A few months after the kid's birth, she served over eight years in PeWee Valley Correctional Institute for aggravated assault and attempted murder on a police officer, committed during a prostitution sting operation. She was later diagnosed with bipolar disorder and Crohn's diseases while behind bars. We are still working to establish her whereabouts during the earlier homicides through her criminal records but have evidence to indicate that Marvelous Missy and JJ have murdered together before. The day Missy was last paroled, we suspect she skipped town with JJ. Her eleven-year-old son was abducted from his school within weeks of her parole. Kid has fetal alcohol syndrome and some special needs. We have the kid in protective custody, but he's not saying much.

I whispered to Tommy, who spoke for me again. "My client wants to know if Missy was ever a stripper, and also the date of her release." Big D adjusted himself in his seat. He did not seem comfortable with my inquiry. Agent Lewis flipped through his paperwork while Big D proceeded to hang his head. "Release was August 15th. Stripping would not be out of the question, but not probable in the last decade. Marvelous Missy ain't so marvelous anymore."

We all had a good, nervous laugh. Agent Lewis' came from way down in his belly. He went on with Missy's background. "Once we put two and two together last night, about the possibility of the couple traveling together, the local authorities raided JJ's trailer park up in Horse Cave. Found out from the neighbors that he had not been seen for almost a month. Our agents found over a thousand hand-written notes the couple exchanged during Jennifer's numerous incarcerations. She had JJ convinced the kid was his, but we're skeptical. It'll take several days for our specialist to comb through the evidence and to get the DNA analysis back from the lab. The place is a hoarder's paradise." Big D gave me a wink. It seems detailing my experience with Tommy's housekeeper had given him his big break in the case. Tommy looked over at me and inquired if there was something he needed to know. "Being a loose cannon has its perks, Bro."

Now, Big D spoke directly to me. "We're having a hard time communicating with Wookiee. Hoping he'll be able to ID the kid. We think he's the same boy from the incident at the Mooneyhans' barn, Muffcat." I glared over at Big D. Somehow, the detective knew everything about my trip into Selner, County. The only person besides

Wookiee who was aware of the sexual assault on the boy was my uncle Vernon. I was beginning to feel a little guilty for what I'd shared with Betty, that suspicion about Uncle Vernon being somehow connected to the serial killer. Big D turned my laptop around, avoiding my eye contact. I got the message. The less shared about Vernon's involvement in the moonshine operation, the better. "Before we get started on the video, let me just preface that it is rather disturbing." Big D pecked at the keyboard. "You need a better password, Muffcat. The clip I want to warn you about is at the 4:14 mark. It shows the castration of your music minister. I'll give you a few seconds warning, but just to forewarn you, Ken did not make it."

A remix of the INXS' 1988 hit, "Devil Inside," video started blaring from my speakers as Big D struggled to turn the volume down. I wondered how an ex-felon, straight out of the pen, and a mechanic could have pulled off making the video as the images began to roll. There was rudimentary editing, but the opening scene was clearly my face with a big set of devil's horns on top of my ears. As I lay in my own bed in the contortionist position after the séance, the scarlet letter "A" began to hover over my forehead; then my eyes blazed red. Quotes from what Big D claimed was some random pornographic movie scrolled across the bottom of the screen. A long series of numbers were spread in-between the vulgar text. Pre- and postmortem images of Tana, Leighanna, and Chandra were scattered throughout the streaming video, superimposed onto the screen in revolting sexual poses. All of the postmortem clips had been shot up at Simon's; all of them were dressed in the same black lingerie. How this tidbit of information had not leaked to the press was beyond me.

Witnessing Chandra floating in the baptismal was horrifying to watch. But, by far, the most repulsive images were of Carligene and Missy. Carligene was pictured lying on a filthy dirt floor, half nude, chained to the very same workbench I'd observed during the séance. Missy was fondling her breasts. Carligene could barely hold her head up as Missy rammed what looked to be a flashlight inside her. Missy then smiled at JJ, who was standing off camera. JJ's voice had been altered to sound demonic; he coached and cheered Missy on. Big D gave us a few seconds to decide if we wanted to see the footage of Ken. Tommy looked over at me. "Go ahead with it."

Watching the hedge trimmers clamp down on Ken's scrotum was gut-wrenching. After a few more excerpts of me and Dylan with the detective up at Simon's, the video cut back to Ken. Lying in a pool of crimson water, a pillow over his head, the word "sodomite" was sprayed onto the white linen. The song ended. JJ leaned into the camera and blurted, "If you're going to do something, do it well. And leave something witchy." He then turned and made out with Missy. Ken's body was still visible in the background. Detective Lewis expounded, "His corpse was discovered at a motel off of Dickerson Road, notorious for prostitution over in Madison. The water and the pillow were used to muffle the single gunshot to the head. Pretty sure the kid was the cameraman. Cleaning lady found the body this afternoon. Madison Homicide is placing time of death sometime in the early morning hours. Biggs hasn't confirmed it. He just got to the crime scene about ten minutes ago."

I turned the laptop's screen towards me. "Uh, it actually happened at 10:30 p.m. last night, Agent Lewis." Big D looked up from his notebook. "Don't ask, Isaac." Big D opened the manila folder then slid a photo across the table. "Is this the van you saw last night at Simon's?" I only had to take a quick glance. "That's it. It's the same vehicle McNabb purchased the hooch from before I was attacked as well." I peered back over to the computer screen. "We have that software at the funeral home. Got a part-time guy that does our photo montages for the memorial services, Chad Bridges." Agent Lewis asked for the employee's name and a phone number. I retrieved his number from my contacts on my iPhone, then jotted down Chad's cell for the agent.

Agent Lewis dialed the phone sitting on the table, without picking up the receiver. "Send in Stanley and someone who can arrange a pick up from Parrottville." A young man with crazy hair appeared in the doorway with Jimbo Filson. Agent Lewis handed over the information to the local officer. "Let's bring Chad Bridges in. Muffcat, you got a home address?" I shot a text to Betty. She responded immediately, but with a question. I texted back that it was urgent. She blasted me Chad's address then demanded I call her back. I did not respond.

While waiting for Agent Lewis and Jimbo's exchange to conclude, Tommy questioned Big D. "Is there any way we can get screen shots of the scrolling feed? As fast as the words are moving, it's hard to make out the text." "Cyber is printing the screen shots off frame by frame as we speak." Lewis shifted back to Tommy once Stanley and Jimbo departed. "Been doing this for a long time, Davenport. The couple's brazenness with their camera reminds me of the Paul Bernardo and Karla Homolka homicides. Been a while since we've seen a case of lust and perversion so twisted. Too bad the kid had to be exposed to it." Big D agreed with

Lewis then changed gears. "We need the words to the original song. There might be hidden messages that correlate to the lyrics. Should I get someone to download the original video?" I grabbed for my laptop. "No need. It's on Youtube. We can get the lyrics from the Lyricsfreak website as well."

As my fingernails jabbed at the keyboard, another agent entered the room. He did not give an introduction, but I knew him from the WSMV interview. The suit addressed Isaac. "Kid's not saying much. But he was able to lead us to where they were squatting. No sign of the Byrd woman. Patterson is taking the kid to Vanderbilt for observation. We'll coordinate the ID with Summers."

"Agent Cho, the cabin where they were squatting, it belongs to a retired Army Lieutenant, correct? Goes by the nickname Duck, and his last name is Cologne, right?" Cho ignored me. I turned to Isaac. "Place sits up on the ridge overlooking Anchor High marina." Agent Lewis looked up at Cho, who just shrugged his shoulders. I leaned into Lewis, and whispered, "She is being kept in a different location. Smaller cabin. Round logs. Gasoline is stored in the space. There is a recent campfire at the site that's burning hickory wood. Just trust me on this. Carligene had to be on her menstrual cycle at the time of her abduction. You can verify with her husband, but it has to be the only reason she is still alive. Now that they know you are on to them, they will leave Carligene to starve to death."

I closed my eyes and took a deep breath as the flash hit me. "There is another woman at the location. They have another victim." Everyone looked around the room at each other. It was obvious they were concealing something from us. The subject was swiftly changed.

Big D grilled Cho, "any forensics back on the scarf?" The smug-faced agent looked down at me. Isaac snapped at him. "Go ahead, Cho." "Human hair; likely from multiple individuals. Forensics is still separating the strands." There was no way I could hold my tongue. "So I guess you don't see me sitting here right now, Cho?" Tommy snatched for my arm. Cho's eyes narrowed into thin lines. His mouth drew up at the corners. He was clearly restraining himself from saying what his face already told me he was thinking. Cho addressed Big D, "we're going to have a psychologist work with the kid. Looks like he was with them when they shot the video of the molestation. Stanley claims the way the camera panned; they were not using a tripod. But I need to speak with you all… um, in private. Found something you need to see."

I didn't wait for Tommy to filter me. "There's no time for that. Carligene's had a cyst rupture in her right ovary, and I strongly sense they have another hostage. Please. Stop acting as if you are not hearing what I am trying to tell you." Just then, J-Laz bolted into the room with an armload of paperwork. "Got the scrolling feed data. It's going to take us a while to weed through all this fucking shit. Take them across the hall, Cho," she instructed. "That would be my pleasure, J-Laz." Cho made a sideways movement with his head. "Why don't *you two* follow me?"

Chapter IXXX

As she pulled her last pay stub from her top drawer, Tana Harvat had to beam; passing her PHR certification the summer beforehand had really paid off. Twelve years as a human resources generalist did not leave much left over at the end of the month to send to Henry, who was in his second semester at the university. Now that she was promoted to the compensation & benefits manager position, Tana knew exactly how she was going to spend the extra income. After her second marriage had failed, she'd promised herself that she would hire a cleaning service to come at least every two weeks to perform the heavy housework duties. While she didn't mind giving Earl Busby his last name back, she sure did miss the big house and the disposable income that came along with his racehorse siring empire.

Tana proudly transferred three hundred dollars into her son's checking account (for his fraternity dues) then shot her only child a text. Her life, as uncomplicated as it was now, was finally looking up. She reached for the card in her purse that Melvin McNabb had given her just a few short days earlier. Surely a reference from a police officer meant this woman could be trusted. Tana shut down her Dell desktop, collected her fuchsia trimmed Coach purse, and then hurried past the cubicles that lined the hallway leading to the elevator. It would be the first time she'd see the parking lot before 5:30 since getting the promotion, and didn't at all feel the need to justify her early departure to her colleagues. But as luck would have it, her boss, L.J. Elliott, was standing by the security shack as she tried to breeze by his idle conversation with Mac Templeton, the security officer who took his job way too earnestly. "You're heading out early, Ms. Harvat. Got another SHRM event?" Tana did not waste a breath as she lied through her tobacco-stained teeth. "Sure do, Mac. We have a committee meeting to go over sponsorship opportunities for the upcoming golf tournament taking place next spring." It was not a complete lie. She did have plans to meet Lynn Hutson, the local SHRM vice-president, later on that evening for a few cocktails. The topic would undoubtedly come up.

As Tana pulled into her driveway, she noticed a beat-up white work van parked at the curb in front of her modest two-story saltbox. A lanky woman with thinning hair and a young boy were waiting on her front porch steps as her Barcelona Red Met Camry came to a halt in front of the taupe plastic garage door. Tana rolled down her window while waiting for the door to winch up. "Glad to see you found it OK. Let me get my car in the garage, then I'll let ya'll in." Tana bounced up the three steps leading to her spotless kitchen, pondering why she felt the need to clean before interviewing for a housekeeper. She wasn't thrilled about the boy being with her prospective cleaning lady, but it was probably just a one-time occurrence, she reassured herself, while placing her car keys and purse on the deep, elderberry-hued Corian countertop. She seized the list of chores off of the refrigerator then promenaded towards the main living area feeling rather regal. As she attempted to unlock the dead bolt, a sudden and monstrous pain shot through the left side of her skull. Before she had time to react, Tana was on the ground; someone was sitting on her back. She tried to scream, but with every attempt, Tana sucked in plastic. As her concealed face was shoved hard against the snowy, marble tiles that normally greeted visitors in the entryway, her life, as they say, flashed before her eyes.

Warm blood puddled in her left ear, as her hands were hastily bound behind her back. She strained, but with the panic and anxiety welling up inside, her ability to reason was overwhelmed. "What took you so long to unlock the door, you moron?"

While her feet were being bound, Tana recognized the sound of her garage door beginning to roll up. She was conscious but felt as if in some outlandish dream as the rumbling muffler idled in the garage. While the invaders rummaged through her home, Tana thought it best if she played dead, at the very least, incapacitated. Memorizing every conversation, hoping one of them would slip up and bellow a name or at the very least a clue as to their true identities, Tana fought to remain calm. Her head was throbbing so intensely that even with her eyes opened she was witnessing bizarre geometric shapes, which bounced around the creases in the plastic in which her head was encased. She was going to have some very harsh words for Melvin when the burglary was over; she was already planning her scathing phone call about the deceitful reference he'd so haphazardly given her.

As the female's raspy voice faded down the hallway, Tana felt a hand on her back. This touch was not brutal. It was not stabbing or rough. It was the faintest of pats, right to the top of her shoulder blade. This voice was merciful, caring, and full of compassion. "You OK. You be OK. Me sorry. You be OK." Seconds after the tenderness, rage and fury as harsh as a sonic boom thundered through the room. "Wyatt, No! Stay away from her! She's a very bad woman. She kills little babies. Now, sit on the couch and Mommy will give you a treat."

Tana pulled her knees up to her rib cage as *Spongebob Squarepants* blared to life. The front door was just feet away. She wouldn't have to get far. If she could just make it to her front porch steps, surely the elderly couple next door would hear her urgent screams for help. Gambling on whether or not she could find a way to stand, Tana thought through her next move. With the tape so tightly binding her ankles, and her hands tied behind her back, she would have to hop, then turn, and then pray her hands would reach the door knob before her movement was detected by the intruders.

Lying perfectly still, she waited for the adrenaline to kick in, along with the right moment to make a break for it. But just as she got the courage to attempt the seemingly impossible feat, Tana felt as if she were going to be sick. Her labored breath only complicated her dire situation. The plastic bag was bound tight around her neck, and the oxygen didn't seem to be as potent with her mind racing.

Working to get her breathing under control, Tana heard the burglars in the garage. The couple was bickering over who was going to wipe up Wyatt's fingerprints. They were meticulously reviewing every surface that had been touched by the boy. Someone eating something crunchy was on Tana's leather coach. So, she seized her opportunity and took a chance. She whispered, "Wyatt, please help me." The boy did not respond, but the loud masticating ceased. There was a desultory tug at the tape that constricted her wrists. The jerks then became more determined as the arguing got brasher from the kitchen. Just when the tape was loose enough for her to feel her fingers again, the jerking ceased. The adults were back in the room. And from the sound of it, they'd found her emergency cash in the freezer. "Get on a nice dress. I found enough for a fun night." As soon as the female's voice passed by and then faded back down the hall, Tana's panic began to swell. She knew what this was all about now. The man's voice was deeper, but she'd recognized the nasal tenor that had once convinced her to make the worst decision of her life.

JJ was mumbling to himself as he entered the room. The pop of his beer tab caused Tana to flinch. She was sucking in plastic again. Determined to try something, anything, she struggled with all of her might to wiggle to the door. Tana took a kick to the ribs, followed by a hard stomp on her cranium. "Just where do you think you're going? We're just getting started."

Tana tried not to make eye contact as her tormentor rolled her over and ripped the bag from her face. Though she wasn't surprised it was him, the rage and anxiety in his eyes told her this was way more than just a simple robbery. JJ knelt down beside her, brushing her dull brown hair from her eyes. "You're not in wonderland anymore, Alice. Such a pity you must die to join my flock."

Her screams were short-lived as the tape wrapped around her head eight times. JJ grabbed Tana up by her hair, forcing her to her feet. There was no way for her to walk with the bindings. As she began to sway uncontrollably from the disorientation of the blows to her head, JJ slung her petite body over the top of the couch. She landed on the terrified boy before bouncing down onto the area rug. Tana tried not to show any fear as the boy began to wail. Jonah Wayne Johnson grabbed her up by her underarms then flung her down onto the mocha colored leather. Wrath, fury, and profanity spewed from his mouth. He was just inches from her face when he held up the piece of white paper. "Baby Killer" was written in all caps, in red ink. "You're the one who caused this, you worthless slut. Once a whore, always a whore. You revolting, ruthless baby killer."

JJ pointed down the hallway. His breath wreaked of marijuana and alcohol. Clothing soiled, JJ smelled like Tana's second husband when he returned from a hunt: musty, with an underlying stench of dried blood and gun residue. Oscillating as he spewed on the back of the paper in front of his face, JJ peered over the top of the single rule, his eyes as wide as, it seemed, the cannabis would allow them to open. "Even with a looming prison sentence that woman had the decency to see her pregnancy through. She is the saint. You are the sinner. And you will die knowing the pain my gremlin felt as they sucked out his brains."

Tana sat on her hands, trying not to let her secret from so long ago fissure her unemotional reaction. But the tears fell anyway. Not for the life her father convinced her to terminate during her fourteenth week. No; it had more to do with the fact that she was only fifteen when her innocence was stripped from her. With her mother deceased, there wasn't anyone to talk to about her period, much less what to do about an unwanted pregnancy. The isolation, shame, and humiliation that came with the burden of her decision were more than she or her father could manage; it forever tore them apart. Oh, how the birth of Henry unleashed the spirits of her worthlessness. The postpartum depression had destroyed her first marriage and led her down a path of reckless relationships. Those left her feeling even more devoid of value after the hedonistic sex romps, whose purpose was to keep the thrill in her short-lived relationships alive.

"Are you ready for a fashion show, my king?" Jonah Wayne Johnson was back in the kitchen again. He returned with a Coors Light and Tana's cell phone in his hand. "You bet your sweet ass I am, Miss Marvelous." JJ extracted a staple gun from the back of his waistband and placed it beside Tana on the sofa. He looked at the phone's screen. "See you are still hanging out with Lynn. I'll let her know you're tied up at the moment." JJ lit a cigarette before plopping down in-between Tana and the boy. Wyatt instantaneously jumped up and moved over to the Lazyboy, never taking his eyes from the monitor over the fireplace. JJ returned the text with a wayward smirk that twisted up the sides of his cheeks.

Music blared from her bedroom television set. "Hurry up and put it on 428; it's your favorite." Sting's voice echoed down the hall. JJ stood then jerked the remote out of Wyatt's hands. He fumbled through the channels and then, The Police poured from the surround sound overhead. *"I have stood here before in the pouring rain, with the world turning circles running 'round my brain. I guess I'm always hoping that you'll end this reign, but it's my destiny to be the king of pain..."* Beer in hand, JJ crooned along, resting his head on the leather sofa with his eyes halfway closed, flailing his cigarette in the air as if he were the conductor of a grandiose orchestra. His frail accomplice slung her leg around the doorframe. She was wearing Tana's strapless, white terrycloth bathing suit cover up, and her childhood roller skates, with their little pink balls of fuzz at the toe. There was something in-between her teeth as her body glided towards them. After a few suggestive dance moves, the woman got down on her hands and knees. She began to crawl towards the sofa, making lurid growls through her clenched, grey teeth, which were encircled with Revlon Unapologetic Colorburst. JJ slid his right hand into the top of his filthy blue jeans as she continued to glide her face up his leg. Finally, she released a plastic card onto his crotch: Tana's Kentucky Down's player's card.

"Take me there tonight, JJ. It's much nicer than the place we went last week." He pulled the card up to his face as he let out a lungful of smoke. JJ shook the beer and must have decided there was too much liquid to use the can as an ashtray. The woman lowered the top of the terrycloth garment, exposing her enormous breasts. JJ went in for a nibble at her erect, left nipple. As he pulled back, he transferred the cigarette from his right hand to his left, shoving the lit end inches from Tana's trembling thigh and into her leather sofa. With her bare chest exposed, JJ handed the staple gun to his partner, who started massaging his cock. "Go ahead; I want to see you do it."

Tana hastily shut her eyes. She wanted to yell for Wyatt to turn his head, but with her mouth bound, the warning was impossible. The thump was surprisingly not as painful as she'd anticipated. There was no blood, but her sight was now limited. The hallowing cries from the boy were more than Tana could bear. The couple laughed uncontrollably at their entertainment. Though clearly meant to amplify her humiliation and pain, this nightmare only proved what Tana had known for a very, very long time. Jonah Wayne Johnson was a heartless bastard. There was not one single ounce of empathy in the man she had willingly shared her most valuable womanly possession with behind the skating rink those thirty years ago.

JJ recited a poem to his grubby lover before she heaved him off the couch and dragged him out of the room. Wyatt was on the ground, crumpled into a ball. He was rocking back and forth, banging his head against the hardwood and making noises way too young for his age. Meanwhile, the couple planned out their last hurrah from her kitchen table.

Tana gazed at her cell phone out of the corner of her right eye; it was still on the sofa beside her. She nodded her head at Wyatt, hoping he would understand what the sideways jerk to her lifeline meant, wholly confused about why the obviously petrified disabled preteen was gaping at her forehead. The phone was quickly snatched up by the female, who seemed eager to get on the road. Tana could see tan streaks on the woman's legs. "Don't worry; your last night will not be spent alone."

The woman had on latex gloves. She wiped down Tana's cell phone with a dishtowel before the sheet plotted back down on the bridge of Tana's nose. "One of your pathetic friends, we call her Nark, will be your company for the evening, though I doubt the fat bitch will be able to chat much, Baby Killer."

Chapter XXX

Agent Stanley Fessmire was calling out longitude and latitude coordinates to the Smyrna Army National Guard's chopper pilot with the aid of his fellow cyber specialist, Reece Woosley. Which was throwing my already pushed-to-the-limit sensory system into overdrive. We'd been relinquished to the waiting room, still officially in custody, but now wallflowers. All we could do was sit and wait.

Agent Fessmire was exactly what you'd expect from a relatively young cyber goon. He had a snout covered with white dots of pustules. Disobedient ocher tresses his neurotic hair products couldn't tame framed his black horned-rimmed glasses, which made his gray eyes appear three times their actual size. Agent Woosley's clammy paws were smoking on the keyboard, breaking only for gulps of coffee he professed to be weak as preacher's piss. Reece was a little easier on the eyes, I had to admit, but had a blanket of Mackerel Tabby covering his wrinkled point collar, off-the-rack slim shirt.

The space wasn't what you'd customarily picture an FBI command center resembling. I'd always envisioned some colossal warehouse rammed full of IBM industrial-sized computer storage towers that could only be accessed by a rack and pinion elevator, staunchly defended by ogre-faced men in polarized wraparound sunglasses. Crammed into the minuscule waiting room, right beside the lone coffee pot, were two folding tables covered in discombobulated wiring. Tommy was forced to incorporate his nervous pacing into unremitting circles as he clamored on to one of his partners at Bone, Pigg, and Mansker about the Fourth Amendment's definition of "reasonable scope" regarding search and seizures. My enraged but elegantly attired attorney, with his Winsor knot in his Armani Collezioni woven silk tie, pressed me to pillage my Gucci purse for a pain pill. Luckily, I always carried a fresh supply. Hey, you never know. A woman's got to be prepared. You can probably already guess that I'm not a big proponent of toughing out pain.

Bored and trying to calm my nerves, I'd counted seven Jos. A. Banks buy-one-get-two-free suits by the time Marlowe Cho reentered the confined space. Elongated and bony, with a hard-bitten temperament that forced the folds in corner of his eyelids to spider web almost to his ears,

Marlowe Cho's chalk-like skin indicated he was in desperate need of a vacation. Gavin and Dyl stood at attention, as if a drill sergeant had entered the room, when Cho bellowed my entire given name: Muffy Catherine Tennessee Lucinda Mansker. Tommy did not terminate his profanity-laced debate regarding extenuating criteria that circumvents probable cause. Instead, he put superfluous emphasis on the words "affidavit" and "search warrant," before clipping his phone back onto his $3,100 Anderson & Sheppard trousers. The men exchanged some heated words about the "back-handed slap to our constitutional right to privacy," before Tommy and I were escorted back over to the space where Big D and Chief had first questioned me about the Shelley Danderson case.

The door thumped behind us. Hand sanitizer and rancid Chinese food tortured my nostrils. A whiteboard had been rolled in front of the crime scene photos, and someone had removed the trashcan liner that had been bursting at the seams with Kung Pow. We were marched to the interrogation table, which had a box of extra-large Kimberly-Clark Professional Purple Nitrile* Exam Gloves placed next to a half empty bottle of water. A box sat on the floor next to where Cho was standing. He punched a button on the Polycom's SoundStation 2, which had replaced the black Panasonic that had been in the room during the get-together with Chief and Big D. Cho bent down before Tommy announced, "somebody better start sharing with me why in the hell you have detained my client. And you better pray to God you got a search warrant to invade her private property." The spew of intimidations didn't fodder Cho's bluff. "Take a seat, Mr. Mansker, Muffcat. I'll answer all of your questions in due time."

Cho pulled out my chair. My attorney slapped his phone down and flung his seat out from underneath the table. He flipped the plastic folding chair around before plopping down with his strapping legs straddling the seat. "Pray tell." Cho murmured, "Let's get acquainted," and sat down on the opposite side of the table. The men exchanged business cards. Tommy's attention never left the flimsy white stock as Cho described his role with The National Center for the Analysis of Violent Crime, NCAVC for short, as a behavioral-based investigative resource to the TBI, FBI, and local law enforcement. I glimpsed over to Cho's card that was being firmly clenched in Tommy's fist. Cho's official title was "profiling coordinator," which just did not sound as high-ranking as his petulant disposition made him appear.

"Why the maiden name, Miss Mansker?" The rather personal question caught me off guard. I peered over at my brother as if to ask, "Do

I really need to answer this?" He got the drift. "Go ahead, Sis." Fully aware the question was meant to be a long overdue icebreaker, I said, "After my first marriage failed, I went back to my maiden name. My second husband was not hung up on matrimonial formalities. I was in the process of launching my own clothing line at the time we eloped. Muffcat Mansker had a better ring to it than Muffcat Felterbush."

For the first time since being introduced to Agent Cho, the man cracked a sinewy smile. "You could have given Victoria's Secret a run for their money if you'd branched out in the lingerie world." Tommy was preoccupied arranging his double Gancini cuff links next to his perfectly folded Armani Collezioni while I devised a retort. "Pardon the observation Cho, but why do they call you by your last name while the gamers out there are Stanley and Reece?" Cho flicked the corner of Tommy's business card with his middle finger. "Do this as long as I have and, you're lucky not to get stuck with an undignified nickname. Last names are our badge of honor, I suppose, if you can hang on for long enough."

A door slammed that snapped Cho back into character. "Let's have a little heart to heart about the reason we've brought you here." My iPhone was vibrating on the table. The irritating tremors ceased before Tommy's *Kill Bill* whistle ringtone pricked the dead air. My brother's masculine hands fumbled to turn his cell phone off. "Cho, I have five traumatized children, a really pissed off wife, and our mother in FBI protective custody all at the hospital. Can you please cut the bullshit now?"

"Fair enough. Tell me about your encounter with Jennifer Melissa Jenkins, Miss Mansker."

"What do you want to know?"

"Everything you can remember."

"It was a very brief encounter, Cho. Happened last Friday during the Harvat graveside ceremony, after walking over to Tommy's home. Missy is how she introduced herself before inquiring about some part-time housekeeping work at my family's B&B. Claimed she overheard my brother mention that I was the current owner. But the name she'd written down did not match the name she verbally stated."

"Helen Sammons? Was that the name she gave you?" I shifted in my seat. "Uh, yeah, pretty sure that was it."

"Fake identity. The real Helen Sammons was a customer of the Little Devil Heating and Air. Jonah Wayne Johnson opened up the one-man show after being fired from a commercial HVAC gig. Husband verified his wife's identity was stolen around the same time our female suspect was paroled on the aggravated assault charges. Fifty-six-year-old with dementia. Didn't even know what year it was." Agent Cho did not have a notebook. The pen he was carrying was a cheap, BIC Round Stic ballpoint, which was penetrating out of his deep olive jacket pocket.

"Let's not concentrate on the dialogue. How did Jennifer Melissa Jenkins make you feel?"

"First impression was that she reminded me of a classic pickpocket. Someone you'd see working the subway for an easy wallet snag. Greasy hair; smelled heavily of tobacco. Her hands were dirty. Missy seemed nervous while she kept sizing me up. Her eyes jumped around a lot." The recollection was the truth, but the paranormal visions that had transpired during the encounter overshadowed most of our conversation.

Cho nodded for me to continue. "I suppose you could say she made me feel... uncomfortable. Her gaze was more like, umm, I don't know... like she was trying to pick me up?"

"Like she was attracted to you?" The question forced me to ruminate. "I suppose. There was a lot going on around us. I was in the process of climbing a ladder that lead to Tommy's attic and had just bumped my head on the ceiling. But Helen... I mean Missy, I suppose she is called, was persistent. She definitely had a peculiarity about her." I cleared my throat. "It was her stare. It was blank... like she had no soul. And her gaze might have lingered a little too long on my breasts."

Cho extracted his pen, placing it on the table before reaching for a file inside an orderly box that set next to his feet. Tommy looked as if he was ready to wiggle out of his seat. "Had no idea we were harboring a fugitive, Cho. The cleaning service provided Keelie with credible references." Cho never lifted his head from the box. "You're not under suspicion of any crimes, Tommy. I'm simply trying to expand my psychological profile of our suspects." Cho's bony left hand scratched at the table as he dug in the box. "Most serial killers work alone. It's relatively uncommon to have a couple cut a swath of murder through a small town like this. Little is known about the chemistry between two people that sparks a killing rampage of this magnitude."

Cho's head popped back up above the table. "Now, Muffcat, are you certain you never encountered Jennifer Melissa Jenkins before last Friday?" My first thought was to elaborate on the image of Missy's body lying lifeless on the wooded trail. But Cho had broadcast to the entire WSMV viewing audience, and I do mean verbatim... "That mortician involved in the police shooting has never been connected with the FBI's current homicide investigations, nor is there any credible evidence to verify Miss Mansker's claims that she's a psychic detective." The only real reason I was opening up to Cho was my hope that Carligene would not become the couple's next victim. Still uneasy with the situation, and skeptical about Cho's choice of words, which excluded my name from "under suspicion of any crime", I said "Pretty sure it was my first and only encounter with the female, Agent. But I've had some paranormal experiences with the couple that I can share with you."

Cho took a deep breath and then spoke directly to Tommy. "What we are looking for from your client are hardcore facts. The FBI does not currently, nor have we ever sought the assistance of any psychic, medium, or paranormal ghost chaser. Whatever your client reads on the Internet is just plain bullshit." Tommy glared over at me. "Let's just stick to the facts, Sis." Cho opened his file. He tapped his pen upside down on the fake wood grain, not taking his eyes from mine. They'd found my notepad in my desk drawer. Either that or Stanley or Reece had obtained my temporary Internet cookies off my laptop.

"We're fairly certain the female, Marvelous Missy, as her former johns called her, is in it for the sexual fulfillment." Cho was still tapping his pen. And observing me for any rapid eye movement or signs of incongruence; I was sure of it. The vibe he was putting off gave me the sense that whatever he was trying to accomplish, well, let's just say, some sort of setup was involved. Tap… tap… tap…"But that does not explain how or why the couple chose their victims or the reason behind the postmortem mutilation." Cho continued to observe me for a few beats before making some notes in his file. "Any idea how you know Jonah Wayne Johnson, Miss Mansker?" I shook my head "No," debating whether or not Cho would pick up on the dishonesty, or if his definition of "knowing someone" was more straightforward than my characterization, which included having my stream of conscience hijacked.

"Can you think of any reason Jonah Wayne Johnson would have surveillance in your residence and workplace?" Tommy interrupted Cho, "did any of the other victims have hidden cameras on them, Cho?" I was starting to wonder if Tommy, who spends the better part of his day tied up in civil litigation cases, needed to be seated beside me. Not anticipating Cho's answer, I was amazed by what the agent offered up. "Not by the time the local authorities discovered their bodies. But we're pretty certain the cleaning business was used to lure at least two of the women. Tana

Harvat's purse contained a business card with Helen Sammons' name and cell phone number scrawled on the back. So we're not certain how long the couple had access to their homes." Cho then made a statement that sounded as though he were thinking out loud. "Then again, it is feasible they could have removed the cameras after staging the bodies."

"Staging the bodies?" Tommy quizzed. "Yep. The Harvat and Petigro women were both kidnapped then held in an undetermined location, kept alive for a few days before their bodies were moved." Cho had been directing his attention toward Tommy, which was a first. But when he mentioned both girls had been kept alive for some time, I abruptly recalled the waxy residue on the back of the altered canvas. Cho directed his attention to me again. "Two of the women were subjected to hours, if not days, of torment. All three women had disparaging inscriptions stapled to their foreheads. You might be disappointed to learn, Miss Mansker, the church secretary was not tortured before being slain."

This is a game. Cho is goading me. The way he worded that last sentence was his attempt to fluster me. Stick to the medical facts. "That would explain the prick marks we observed on Tana's forehead during her embalming procedure." Tommy had yet to realize Cho had some cheese set in his mousetrap. I was trying to hold Cho's gaze but had to peer over at Tommy when he took Cho's bait.

"What were the inscriptions, Cho?" Cho was tapping his pen again. Clearly trying to determine how much he wanted to offer up. After another awkward pause, he stated, "Your client has quite a history with these women. But to answer your question, Tommy, the HR executive had 'baby killer' stapled to her forehead with her own Stanley Sharpshooter. The gifted artist was labeled Nark. Let your client tell you about the unfortunate church secretary."

Cho's eyes were fixated on mine; then, he glanced over my head to the whiteboard, strategically placed next to the two-way mirror that the other "Jos. A. Banks" were probably clamoring behind. Cho had deliberately not used the women's names. Nonetheless, he was humanizing them. Trying to tug on my heartstrings in order to drill into me that these women were real people, with admirable professions at one point in their lives, before they were slain. He narrowed his eyes before reaching for the container of gloves, then bent back down to his box, snapping the purple glove over his right hand. He removed a yellow notepad, and placed two gloves on the top of it, then slid it over towards Tommy. "Glove up. Your client's copious notes might explain where I'm going with this."

My attorney gave me a hard look before picking up the gloves. Tommy patted down his shirt with his purple latex hands, not realizing he'd left his readers across the hall in his jacket. I shrugged my shoulders at Tommy's arched eyebrows before handing over my Matsuda titanium frames. Tommy scrutinized the evidence and then placed my yellow legal pad back down on the table. "I don't see anything incriminating here if that's what you're getting at Cho. Just some notes detailing the slain women's connections and maybe some possible suspects." Tommy slid my titanium frames onto the top of his head. "Just what are you trying to imply here, Agent?"

Cho narrowed his eyes then ducked back below the table's edge. This time, his bony gloved hand emerged with an orange and white yearbook. There were three turquoise sticky notes waving past the pages. He cracked the spine of my 1988 PHS yearbook, gloved his free hand, and put two more gloves on the yearbook's opened page. This time, Cho thrust the evidence in my direction. "Glove up, buttercup. Then, why don't you read the comments out loud, Miss Mansker?"

"Hold on a minute, Sis." Tommy grasped my hands, tossing my gloves down to the table. He slid the yearbook underneath his nose, before asking Cho if he could retrieve his glasses from the waiting area. Cho snapped his loose-fitting latex down next to the tripod-shaped speaker phone. My cell vibrated the fake wood grain again. "Yo Reece. Bring me Mr. Mansker's Anderson and Sheppard jacket that he had custom-tailored on Old Burlington Street last month." Cho uncrossed his legs, grunting as he shoved his chair away from the table's edge. Tommy used the brief interlude to whisper through his clenched jaw, "what the fuck is this about?" I whispered back, "not really sure."

"Did the ME share Chandra's inscription with you?"

"Hollis retrieved her body from the morgue. Nothing was on her forehead except a bullet hole. But Chandra's label is probably religious in nature."

"For real, Sis, or ESP?"

"ESP."

"It's in your best interest to not know."

"Roger that."

Cho had his entire right arm extended into the hallway. He turned with Tommy's jacket neatly laid over his arm. Cho extracted Tommy's readers then walked around the table. He handed him his gunmetal Porsche frames, which matched his vintage Carrera. Cho observed Tommy's backwards chair and then placed Tommy's jacket down on the table. He reached for my iPhone. "You mind if we turn this off, Miss Mansker?"

"Go right ahead."

Cho regained his seat. His scrawny ankle bumped the bottom of the table as he recrossed his lanky legs. "Okay, where were we?" I snapped on the gloves before Tommy handed my glasses back. "I guess you want me to read what Chandra wrote back in 1988?" Cho nodded. Four raised fingerprints were circled on the page. I cleared my throat. "Muffcat, I can't believe we survived another year! Smiley face. You should have been in detention for a week after that breakdance performance during the FCA's talent show. Exclamation point. Another smiley face, then endless exclamation points. I pray you do not get into any more trouble over the summer. It would be a shame if you were grounded during our youth ministry camping adventures. Exclamation point. Smiley face, heart, heart, cross." I cleared my throat. "Do you want me to describe the sketch, Cho?" The Federal Agent said, 'that will be enough. Flip to the second tab labeled Nark."

I took off my glasses. "Cho, I know what Leighanna wrote in here. I assume you are making reference to the fact that both Tana and I were suspended after Leighanna testified in the Aqua Net incident?" Cho had gathered more items from his box during my "reading." This time, he flung the pages across the table, forcing the evidence to scatter. Tommy picked up one of the glossy laser photo sheets; he was still straddling his seat. He stood up, flipping his chair around before regaining his seat, scooting up to the interrogation. Tommy observed, "This must be the Carter woman. Bigot is her label, I assume. And what is the relevance of the rosary beads pictured?" Tommy looked up from the evidence at Cho before continuing his thought. "I assume those were discovered at the crime scene?" Cho smirked. "They're not just any ordinary rosary beads, Tommy. Your sister's partial fingerprint was lifted off that wooden cross dangling from the end."

Cho waited a few seconds for a reaction from me before continuing. "Detective Davenport had the gumption to lift her prints off that coffee cup labeled as evidence." Cho pointed to the top of the filing cabinet. A white coffee cup was atop the cabinet, tucked neatly inside a clear Ziplock. My face was burning as Tommy mustered an "Ummmhum. I think I see where you are going with this." Tommy was still flipping through the pictures as Cho stood up then smacked a plastic bag in front of Tommy. "I believe your client was instrumental in assisting the cold case detectives with this 2003 murder case up in Bowling Green."

And there we had it Cho had done his homework. *The Parrottville Press* had interviewed me after Shelley Danderson's body was positively identified. It was front page news back then, unlike my attempted murder, which was buried on Page six, with a little political manipulation from dear old Uncle Vernon.

Cho held my gaze. "Bigot was the same caption used in '89 up in Alma, West Virginia. Young female camper on a church retreat was discovered with 365 postmortem cuts and her own Bible rammed in her anus." I let out a horrified sigh. Cho seemed to drink in my reaction. He was now twirling his pen in his fingers, leaning back in his seat. My attorney made an observation, unaware he was fanning the fire. "Weren't those rosary beads left at your house after the break-in?" Cho looked down at Tommy's tie. He reached up, loosening his own half-Windsor knot, thankfully setting his baton down in the process.

Cho was changing gears, attempting to make us comfortable. Dangling crime scene details in front of our faces, waiting to scrutinize my body language. The unloosing of his tie was meant to subliminally let us know that Cho felt he had all the time in the world. Dozens of turquoise 3x3 sticky notes were neatly fanning out from the edge of Cho's four inches of paperwork. He picked the pen back up, opening the manila file with the head of the point. "We've deciphered some subliminal messages in the manifestos that someone mailed to the precinct. An offender's method of perpetrating a crime shows his or her degree or lack of planning. Some highly systematized serial killers leave a personal stamp that can reveal specific fantasy-driven rituals based on their own needs or personal compulsions. It's what profilers call the serial killer's signature. But never in my career have I encountered such an orderly, over-controlled, socially competent, intelligent serial killer who uses a signature to retaliate for somebody else's socially immature desires. The PHS carved on these former classmates of your client's detail her own emotional pain, humiliation, and suffering she perceives enduring at the hands of four women who had to pay for Miss Mansker's apparent emotional trauma with their very lives."

Cho made the quote, unquote sign with his bony fingers when he said, "emotional trauma." His voice elevated during his crescendoing tirade. Cho knew Tommy was clueless. He focused on my hands as he continued. "We've determined this guy is relatively intelligent. I'd go so far as to say Jonah Wayne Johnson is actually one of the more articulate serial killers that we've encountered. And I've got thirty years of criminal profiling under my belt."

Cho was putting all his cards out on the table, displaying his authority like a peacock fanning its tail feathers. I was waiting for his, "But then again." He went on, "even Ted Kaczynski's manuscript contains instances of irregular spelling and hyphenation. Not this bloke. Jonah Wayne Johnson is calculated, has the gift of poetic thought, shrewd enough to incorporate numerical algorithms into his manifestos. This guy is educated. Spent several years at an exorbitantly priced boarding school over in East Tennessee." Cho paused again. There was no, "On the other hand," as I'd anticipated. He was stopping short of insinuating that I had perpetrated the crimes, but he was surely crafty in his delivery. I could tell he assumed that I had somehow sparked the killing rampage out of some sort of vigilante high-school payback, and I was not so sure Cho wasn't convinced that I had written the manifestos. "So where does a man with a bankrupt company, living on the lam with an ex-felon and her kidnapped son, get the money to afford a 2010 Acura MDX?" OK. The whole scenario had rapidly cascaded into some bizarre nightmare. Tommy had finally caught on. "So, Cho, are you insinuating my client conspired with this madman? You really believe *my sister* paid this guy to murder?" Cho retorted, with his hand on Tommy's business card, "You tell me, Mr. Three-Hundred-Fifty-Bucks-An-Hour civil litigation attorney."

Tommy removed his gloves, then stood and moved his hands into his trouser pockets. My brother was pacing again, as he shouted, "Are you really moving forward with your asinine theory that this God-fearing women sitting in front of you orchestrated the kidnapping, rape, torture, and murders of three of her high-school friends?" Cho's boney arms were stretched behind his head. He replied "Four" before tapping his chair back down to the tile floor. Cho smirked as Tommy ensued. "You are seriously going to sit there and imply *my sister* has joined forces with a serial killer for some late-in-life attempt at branching out into the psychic PI world, all because of some comments made after she bumped and grinded our high-school principal during a karaoke performance of "Darlin' Nikki" during a 1988 Fellowship of Christian Athletes talent show?" Tommy looked down at me. "Sorry, Sis. It was horrendously risqué." Cho uncrossed his legs. He took a sip from his bottle but didn't bother to screw the cap back on before responding. "We found some documents up at Simon's that prove her involvement in these crimes." Cho pulled a partially charred article from the file then flung it. Tommy stepped back to the table, adjusting his glasses, and hovered over the document with his sweaty palms firmly pressed down on the tabletop. Cho expounded, "That document right there led us to a very large wire transfer. My agents found it in the incinerator during our sweep of Simon's." Tommy glanced down at me before responding to Cho. "You found this in the morgue's crematory?" Cho had his pen out again. He was feverously flipping through his turquoise sticky notes. "Your client is lying to us, Tommy. She knows Jonah Wayne Johnson. And we have proof she was aiding and abetting him in his attempt to leave the country."

Tommy looked flustered. He murmured, "Is this a bank authorization form?" Cho never took his eyes from mine as he ripped another document apart from a staple. "Over $55,000 was transferred by one Maudine Abigail Edgefield with TTW Enterprises into an account belonging to Hollis M. Holstetter Monday afternoon." Tommy regained his seat, grappling for yet another document. "Johnny Glass with the local car dealership on Main Street contacted the precinct this afternoon. Your client's ex-husband just came clean about a man matching Jonah Wayne Johnson's description making a cash purchase on one used 2010 Acura MDX." Another document was flung. "That's a copy of your sister's passport. It was recovered from the Acura, along with your passport. After we put an APB out on the Acura, they carjacked an elderly couple at the Piggly Wiggly." Tommy was tapping his shirt for his readers again, not realizing his glasses were sitting on the top of his head. I pointed to them then exclaimed, "Tommy, Maude's never been authorized on TTW Enterprises bank account. But $55,000 is the exact amount Lana Coombs paid me after the wedding. I deposited their down payment months ago but haven't had time to deposit their final payment what with all that has been going on. I was there when Davenport bagged the beads in my cabin. I used a tissue to pick them up. They were in evidence; I watched Davenport bagged the beads myself."

Cho cleared his throat. Tommy was furiously turning the evidence over and over in his hands. A commotion broke out across the hallway. Cho crooked his gaunt head. Tommy peered over at me with his eyebrows standing at attention then bit his bottom lip. "I need to confer with my client, Cho. In private." Cho was already standing. He closed his file and walked over to the doorway, examining the tumult through the elongated pane that ran down the side of the doorframe. "You can do that after she's been read her rights." Cho tapped a code into the metal door then exited the room. Tommy's eyebrows were still frozen into bends.

"Tommy, none of this makes any sense. You know I would never funnel money to a mass murderer who has slain three, excuse me, four of my classmates. They were all my friends. This is a setup. Isn't that obvious? This whole goddamn interrogation is bullshit, Tommy." He still had the fragment of charred paper in his hand. "Well, this form right here tells me you authorized Maude on the B&B account." I pushed my glasses up on the bridge of my nose, shaking as Tommy held out the form. "I don't know what to tell you. It sure looks like my signature, but Aunt Maude is the last person I'd authorize on the TTW Enterprises. Hell, she doesn't even know the combination to the petty cash vault. After that robbery in the early Nineties, she claimed she did not want the responsibility, so we had the combination changed on the safe. You have to believe me. My house was burglarized. Those beads were on my dresser, but I swear to you there is no way that my prints are on that cross. My passport must have been stolen during the robbery, but I did not realize it at the time. Hell, they invaded your home and stole weapons, Tommy. They are targeting us, Tommy. They are targeting our family. And now they are trying to frame me for these murders."

Tommy rubbed his face. 'They can say you staged the robbery, Muffcat." He rounded my shoulders towards his as he regained his seat. We were looking at each other eye to eye. I peered down to the box on the other side of the table. "God. That scarf was on my pillow today when you called. Wonder how many more murders they are going to be pinning on me after they arrest me? Are they gonna claim I lured Fat-Ass Melvin McNabb in the KOA restroom to blow him for crime scene details so I could take credit for solving these homicides? Why would Maude and Hollis do this to me?"

Tommy stared at me, with crazy intensity. "Don't say a word after they read you your rights. Their evidence has been compromised. Cho is really stretching on this."

Pammy breached the doorway. She looked to have been in a fist fight with a briar patch. Cockleburs were stuck to her uniform and dangling from the wisps of hair that had fallen from her ponytail; her face and hands were all red and scratched. "Tommy, you are needed out here." I went to stand but was forced back down to my seat by my brother. I was alone and scared out of my fucking mind. Was this my worst nightmare, I wondered, or were things about to get even worse?

Chapter XXXI

An overhead halogen light popped and then flickered upon Tommy's departure, as a heated conversation leaked through the walls. I glanced down to the charred sheet in my trembling hands before setting the authorization form back on the table. I couldn't recall most of the conversations that had taken place at the cabin the night I was released from the E.R. And, truth be told, I was more than fairly out of it on Monday, from the pain meds and anesthesia hangover during the séance.

Maude had mixed up a gigantic pitcher of Bloody Marys after the others left to search for Carligene, but this was seriously ridiculous. Why in the world would Aunt Maude want to steal from me only to turn around and hand my hard-earned profits over to a known serial killer?

Cho's file was still on the table. I looked back to the two-way mirror behind me. From the sound of it, everyone was gathered in the hall, and embroiled in one hellacious argument. Of course, I just had to see what else was in Cho's stash of documents. Plucking my Gucci purse from the back of my chair, I placed it in front of me then reached for my iPhone. After turning my cell on, the Apple icon appeared. Once my apps were up, I noticed my voicemail was full; I had loads of messages, not to mention more than 70 posts to my Facebook page. But it was the dozen texts that dominated my attention. They were from an unrecognizable number with a 917 area code. I scrolled through a few of them before realizing they were from Movina. A few of her most recent ones included pictures. I expanded my screen to see a Mardi Gras purple background; some sort of ponderous manuscript was displayed in irregularly formed letters. It was a cryptic message. I scrolled down four or five screens to Movina's type. "My dearie, it seems the RIT dye was the best method. It took some creative thinking to melt the wax in order to read Tariet's message. I believe you will find your beloved sister at a small hunting cabin off of the John Claude Garrett Highway. On the northwest corner of a farm that looks to be owned by the Fesmire or possibly Fesmore family. Poor Tariet was tortured and starved for days before being forced to paint under deplorable conditions. No need to call. I already know the outcome. Good luck with your new career endeavors; I am really sorry about your uncle. Mila will be fine. She's had her eye on Sam-Tee's brother for years."

A flurry of police uniforms rushed past the window. The commotion had now reached a fevered pitch. Profanity bangs, a chair hit the door. Its metal leg shattered the window pane. My initial reaction was to rush out to the hallway. But then, I realized this was the perfect, most tailor-made time to snoop. Wasting nary a second, I rapidly slid Cho's file directly in front of my chest. The first tab that grabbed my interest was labeled "Mansker." I jumped in, only to find a document labeled "Top Secret." The file had the FBI logo embossed on the bottom, right-hand corner. The words "Stargate Project Findings" were in bold lettering and followed by a possible FBI report number. Professor Jessica Utts' name was under the bold type. The University of California, Irvine's address was underneath the professor's name.

I flipped through the first few pages, pondering why the report was filed under my maiden name. Twenty-something pages in, I saw my father's name, Clyde Mansker, was highlighted in yellow, with some notes scrawled in the margin. Somebody pulled the chair from the doorframe. I snapped a quick picture of the page containing Daddy's name, then stood, shoving the file back across the desk. Hoping the distraction and the angle had worked in my favor, I rushed over to the door, surprised to find the handle frozen. I reached outside and easily turned the knob from the other side.

A flurry of suits had Tommy and Gavin pinned against the wall. Gavin's well-built arms were around Tommy's sturdy chest as he hurled a profanity-laced rant in Cho's grill. Tommy's right hand was firmly grasping Hollis' mortician's jacket. The weasel was struggling out of the white coat, and crying out for someone to save him, his handcuffs held up and protecting his face. Chief inched in-between Hollis and my attorney's frenzied brawl, goddamning everyone in her warpath. Dylan had the chair over his head. Big D hastily snatched it, throwing Dylan back into the waiting room, where Aunt Maude was trying to wiggle out of her own handcuffs.

"What the fuck is going on, Tommy, Dyl!" Someone grabbed me by the collar of my jacket. J-Laz spun me around, then thrust me back in. The force she used to hurl me was disorienting; she had the strength of three grown men and could no doubt have taken down Tommy if she felt the need or desire to do so. I drew back my hand, only to discover blood. My right hoop earring had been ripped straight through my earlobe. Turning to reach for the cylindrical lockset, J-Laz boomed. "Take your seat,

Muffcat. Now."

J-Laz was not what you'd expect from a FBI agent. In her better moments, she was slim, attractive, and rather polished. At this juncture, however, her black eyeliner was smeared halfway down her cheeks, and her untucked periwinkle silk blouse had a dribble of my blood on the lapel. She snatched my phone out of my hand.

"I'm bleeding."

"Don't make me ask you again, Miss Mansker. Sit!" J-Laz walked over to the filing cabinet after snapping gloves over her perfectly manicured hands. Objecting to her demand was not my intention, but my head was not as clear as it needed to be. I was still trying to refasten my earring, but the fact that it was still hooked when it landed in my palm indicated my earlobe had clearly been ripped in two. I hoped for a clean slice. Ya know; I like everything pretty.

"Oh, I'll take a seat alright, but not without my lawyer." J-Laz slammed the filing cabinet closed with a bump of her hip. "Your attorney is having his rights read to him at the moment." She murmured as she released her armload of evidence onto the table and huffed when she noticed my bloody palm. "Let me get you something to stop the bleeding." J-Laz extracted her gloved hand from her tailored black blazer, then handed me a tiny container of Kleenex. The agent then removed her coat, placing it over the back of Cho's chair, and backed up. Not taking her eyes from mine, she put me on notice, "Assaulting a federal agent is a federal offense." Her tone caught me off guard. "Gary Pigg is his partner. He's representing Steven Carter, Chandra's husband. I assume you were in the middle of that bullshit investigation."

J-Laz had been standing. We were about the same height, but she was now slumped over, focusing her attention on a computer screen, a Dell Inspiron One 20. It was a new addition to the bank of computers that sat idle against the wall. I had seen Reece deliver the monitor to the room while we were waiting in the lobby. J-Laz walked over to it and punched the speaker-phone. "Any luck with the hybrid positioning system, Reece?"

Reece was snapping chewing gum. "GPS was directly obtained from satellites. The service provider's network gave us the active Google Latitude standing. The phone was ditched on the side of the road. Carlos is on his way back with it. There's a video. But we've been busy trying to break up this goddammed fight."

"Recent?"

"Yep. Substantiates your theory. The kidnapping happened after the carjacking in the Piggly Wiggly parking lot. Husband just confirmed his wife's SUV and two all-terrain vehicles are missing. They've got another hostage. One Leisa Anne McNeece. Forty-two-year-old local resident. Her husband is the contractor whose boat was recovered after the Byrd abduction."

J-Laz cut Reece off without so much as an adieu.

"They've got Queenie?" I asked, positively stunned.

J-Laz did not answer my question. She glared at me, took a deep breath, and reached for her handcuffs. "Miss Mansker, you have the right to remain silent…"

Chapter XXXII

Sitting there all alone, electrical tape on my hemorrhaging earlobe, my life started flashing before my eyes. I'd just been read my rights and booked on conspiracy to commit felony murder charges. Additional obstruction of justice, accessory to commit murder, aiding and abetting a felon, and federal money laundering charges were still being deliberated while the FBI and what sounded like the entire state police force hunted down a serial killer and his child-abducting ex-felon girlfriend. Short and sweet: surreal.

I sat in what now was officially an interrogation room for what felt like an eternity before the door cracked. Tommy was led in by Brad Weasle. My attorney was handcuffed. Just great. Dylan and Gavin were two steps behind Weasle's Stetson; the boys were feverishly chitchatting with J-Laz. The agent who had ripped my earlobe in two was holding a white first aid kit like a briefcase. Her Blackberry buzzed on her hip.

My attorney crumpled into a chair. I had never seen my brother as ruffled. His shirt's delicate Egyptian cotton was wadded and twisted, his mouth warped up into a snarl. He placed his handcuffed fists on his knees. If not for my earlobe ordeal, I had no doubt in my mind J-Laz would have cuffed me as well. Tommy lurched towards me. "Tommy? What's wrong?" He leaned in my direction and whispered, "Nanny overdosed. Mitch found her during the illegal search of the mansion, facedown in a pan of bourbon balls."

Brad Weasle cleared his throat. The portly officer took off his hat and then extended his condolences. The gesture left a momentary lump in my throat. He expounded, "I do apologize for what's happened, Tommy, Muffcat. Mrs. Catherine insisted on me a-wheelin' her into the kitchen for a snack. Had no cotton pickin' idea she planned on polishing off the rest of her Methadone as well as a bottle of Wild Turkey. Greg, over at the fire hall, said the medics are pumping her stomach as we speak. Believe they got to her in the nick of time."

The boys were not in handcuffs. Gavin pleaded with J-Laz to allow Weasle to drive them to the hospital. J-Laz set the first aid kit down in front of me before instructing Weasle to "escort" my boys to Skyline Medical Center. Dyl rushed over to the table and placed his cell phone in the palm of my hand. "Here, Momcat. One of us will call you as soon as we know something." J-Laz snatched the cracked iPhone from my hand, and dropped it into her jacket pocket.

Big D appeared at the doorway. I could not even look at that hotheaded asshole while he escorted Aunt Maude and Hollis into the interrogation room in handcuffs. Big D heaved out two chairs opposite my seat then gave me a hard look before pulling out his own chair. Agent Isaac Lewis was the next one through the door. Isaac's hands were in his pockets. He took his time observing the pane of glass that had been shattered as he held the door open for Weasle and my boys to depart. Isaac was still standing by the cracked up window pane when he greeted Gary Pigg. Tommy's partner was caring a tattered briefcase; his bald head glowed with perspiration. Gary pulled out the chair separating me from my attorney. He and Tommy exchanged some words about the charges brought against us while I gave Big D the stink eye from across the table.

J-Laz strode towards the filing cabinet, holding her cell phone to her ear with her shoulder, her tussling deep mahogany tresses obscuring her attractive face. She was instructing one of her field agents to relocate some mobile equipment as she snapped on some medical gloves. The woman was really striking; I had to give her that. I guessed her age to be around late thirties or early forties. Her heavily pancaked makeup was a telltale sign of a desperate woman overcompensating for her femininity. The business card she'd given Dylan at the cabin told us she was with the FBI, and based out of Washington D.C. Her real name: Jackie D. Lazenby. She was some sort of behavioral analysis specialist with a doctoral degree behind her name.

After several hours of observing her, one thing was clear to me, J-Laz was the one calling the shots. Even the grittier looking "Jos. A. Banks" jumped when she entered a room. But I couldn't help but wonder why such a high-ranking female federal agent would only be afforded a partial last name. Even with a freshly split tract of skin forging down my earlobe, and these ridiculous circumstances in which I found myself, I afforded her some pity. I couldn't fathom her having a man or woman in her life, much less any children to brag about. Her luggage tucked behind the coat rack in the waiting room told me she was a government vagabond. She'd probably not eaten a morsel or slept in a few days because J-Laz was now in complete raging-bitch-mode as she tugged at my earlobe. "She's probably going to need some plastic surgery for this to heal properly. I'll see what I can do; we've got very little time to pull this off." She snapped her Blackberry back on her waistband, before ripping the tape off of my ear without so much as a warning.

Isaac remained calm as J-Laz pillaged the first aid kit. She shouted to him to "Get the video up first" before placing a needle in between her lips. "Davenport, make yourself useful and pull that table over here." Big D obeyed J-Laz's command while Isaac shouted across the hallway. Reece and Stanley raced into the room with wires trailing behind them. Reece heaved the Dell monitor from the bank of computers, as Big D scooted a small desk to the head of our table. Reece left the room while Stanley ran an extension cord across the floor.

Cho observed J-Laz as he entered the room. His tie was off and his phone was rammed onto the side of his gaunt cheek. "The offsite facility did not have steady enough Wifi, Doc. We had to make due. RCFL is stationed down the block. SWAT's deployed about twelve miles north at a state park, where we suspect they've taken cover... Yep, we're pretty much in the middle of nowhere... From Teterboro to John C Toon?... In the Cessna Citation? Yes, I'd say that is accurate doctor... No, none of the algorithms have worked... Yes, two confirmed hostages but we caught a break on the Byrd woman... Call when you land." Cho set his phone down on the desk beside the monitor. Isaac's hands were still in his pockets when he chimed in, "But even with all this technology that sounds like something out of *Star Wars*, no one predicted the keen minds of two sociopaths". He pulled out the chair to the left of Aunt Maude. Isaac's temperament was not nearly as high strung as J-Laz or Cho's. It seemed as if there were some contrariety going on between Cho and Isaac as the agent took his seat. Isaac peered behind the table where Aunt Maude was struggling with her handcuffs. We'd learned during the booking process the scratches on Chief's hands and face occurred during Maude's arrest. Her wiry hair was sticking out in every direction as Isaac leaned over then lambasted Cho. "Cho, get someone to loosen these." Aunt Maude gave him a giddy grin as Isaac scooted up to the table.

Hollis' head was hung. His right eye was almost a slit as he choked out, "My attorney should be here momentarily. I'm evoking my rights." Cho killed the halogen light that was still flickering overhead, before ordering Detective Davenport to loosen Maude's cuffs. When Pammy opened the door, I could see a man in a camel-colored trench coat, examining the reader board behind Chief. The board held pictures of the ribbon cutting ceremony from the grand opening of City Hall. Hollis cranked his head. 'Thank God." Sally was standing with Hollis' lawyer.

She reeled her head towards the reader board after noticing my gaze. "Come with me Hollis," Pammy insisted, never looking in my direction. Big D bent down to loosen Aunt Maude's handcuffs. The detective stood then looked back to Chief. Pammy nodded as if to say "Go ahead and release Hollis." Hollis stood and turned his back to Big D, who unfastened his restraints. Hollis rubbed his wrists as Chief escorted him out of the room; he adjusted the collar of his blood-stained mortician's jacket before taking one last glance through the window at me.

Cho placed his hands behind his emaciated rear end, pacing at the head of our table. "I believe you all are fully aware of why you have been detained. Now, I want you to witness the brutality of the man you've been aiding and abetting." J-Laz did not bother to look up at the monitor while threading a needle. I slid my chair back to allow for Tommy and Gary to have a better view of the monitor, forcing J-Laz to miss the eye.

The video jumped around in the beginning before the image of JJ pulling Queenie's head down to the console of her own Mercedes SUV came into focus. JJ questioned, "You getting this, Missy?" before the SUV was put into drive. A barn and barren cornfield were visible over the hood. Trees whooshed by within a matter of seconds of his foot hitting the gas pedal. "That's the Mooneyhans' farm," I cried out before Queenie's high-pitched voice, begging for her life, gave me the chills. Missy leaned up from the back seat and closed up on Queenie's face. My dear friend was crying and pleading as JJ coached her, his fist full of her hair. "Muffcat, please just go through with it; God, please if you see this, please do not leave me with these people!"

JJ's knee was strategically positioned on the bottom of the steering wheel as Missy handed him a joint. He took a long pull before unzipping his pants, his grip breaking long enough for Queenie to attempt sitting up. Queenie's blond bob, stained with blood oozing from her temple, was thrust back down by Missy's grimy hand. JJ resumed his grip on Queenie's hair and then heaved her head over the console and into his lap. Missy was snickering when she panned the camera in for another close-up, her free hand groping at Queenie's crotch. The camera moved back to the driver, he shot a grin over his shoulder before spouting, "Make it seem real, or Queenie is a goner." Queenie could be heard screaming, "No, no… no… God… no, please she will do it. I swear to God, she will do it. Don't make me do this. My children… please… I have three children." Just then, a tennis shoe landed on the bridge of Queenie's nose. Maniacal laughter penetrated the air, competing, eerily, for center stage, with the horrifyingly haunted screams of my terrorized friend.

My chest clenched. I could practically hear the thunderous palpation of my heart, as nausea ripped from my stomach and pulsated up into my lurching throat.

Chapter XXXIII

The room's deathly silence was interrupted by Aunt Maude's screeching. "Lawd ha' murcy! Dats the man who shown up wif Vernon da other de to fix da heat. Vernon knows him reeeal gooudt. Had me sign da receipt befor' realizin' Muffcat was asleep in da bedroom."

Tommy's cuffs clanked down on the conference table. Gary Pigg leaned over, then whispered something to Tommy, who did not lower his voice when he addressed Aunt Maude. "Did you get a copy of the service ticket, Maude?" She looked directly at Tommy. "No, but I seen dat fool 'round the mansion befo'. Axe Vernon. He knows him fo' sho. Come to git those Benjamins from yo grandmudda. Lef widda wad da cash the utter day. Not da first time, edda." With that, Maude looked directly at J-Laz, who was about ready to penetrate my earlobe with a needle. "You crakas better get your bitch asses out of my way when deese damn cuffs come off." To that, J-Laz responded by letting out a chuckle. Tommy was just about to say something when I interrupted him, "I don't remember signing anything, Tommy." Aunt Maude weighed in, "I ain't never in my life stolen a dime from you, Muffcat. You know dat don't you, Tommy? Dat man is evil. Has been fo' years."

All business and no bullshit, J-Laz gave no warning before jabbing me and barking out orders. "You can sort out your human resource issues another day, Mrs. Edgefield. Davenport, take Mrs. Edgefield across the hall."

There were so many questions flying around in my brain, but Aunt Maude's trustworthiness was not one of them. I did not dare take my eyes off the monitor as the pig led my childhood nanny and best employee out of the room.

Clenching my fists as the white thread moved through my earlobe for the third time, my watering eyes were focused on Cho, who was intently scrutinizing the reeling video. "Davenport, do any of these landmarks look familiar?" Big D had barely penetrated the doorway. "That's Selner County, Cho. Let me get Jimbo Filson in here. Jimbo's an avid hunter, grew up over in Selner."

After knotting the thread behind my ear and cutting the string with a pair of scissors, J-Laz instructed, "Cho, let Isaac explain our proposal to

Miss Mansker." She shut the first aid kit, looked down at me, and grimaced. "My suturing techniques are battlefield worthy at best. You might want to see a plastic surgeon when we're through with you. If you cooperate, we'll give you a lift." The thought of living with a jacked up earlobe was not exactly cheering me up, but it almost sounded as if J-Laz was trying to compromise. I'd take any tidbit of promise I could get.

Isaac, his hands folded in front of him, took a deep breath before catching a file Cho had launched down the table. I waited for their stare-down to subside before speaking. "Isaac, before you get started, there is something you all need to know about Carligene." Gary Pigg craned his portly neck in my direction. "Let me confer with Miss Mansker." I whispered to Gary the particulars about the images Movina had sent to my cell phone. "Can you use this as leverage on the conspiracy charges?" Pigg turned to Tommy before looking back at me. 'We'll try it." Gary cleared his throat. "My client has some information regarding the whereabouts of Carligene Byrd, which might aid in your investigation, agents. We are looking for leniency on the charges you've filed against her, in exchange for her cooperation."

Isaac's grin was deceiving. Even though he was the most personable of the agents, the TBI behind his name led me to assume this was not his rodeo. "If you are talking about the pictures Stanley just downloaded from your client's cell phone, we deployed a SWAT team twenty minutes ago. You will be pleased to learn, Muffcat, that Carligene was recovered. Alive. She's being airlifted to Vanderbilt and has a long road ahead of her, but I suspect she'll recover."

Isaac banged the edge of the file down on the table and opened it. "What we need from you now, Miss Mansker, is far more personal." Isaac looked over to Cho, who was talking vociferously with Jimbo. He cut in, "JJ has made contact with us. Tommy, Gary, now what our suspect is demanding is highly unusual, and frankly, rather bizarre." Cho interjected, "Get to the point, Isaac. We don't have all night." Undeterred, Isaac did not change his slow, methodical parlance. "What Leisa Anne McNeese is referring to doing in the video is a game for Jonah Wayne Johnson. He knows that we are closing in on him. Tommy, you and your oldest son's passports were found along with Miss Mansker's in the SUV the couple abandoned at the Piggy Wiggly. The GPS was set for Brownsville, Texas, a little hole-in-the-wall biker bar close to the border."

It was obvious Cho was not happy with Isaac and what he was sharing with us. He interjected, "Jonah Wayne Johnson and Jennifer Melissa

Jenkins know their party is over. We got the Bledsoe Creek State Park surrounded. Over fifty- seven campsites and six miles of hiking trails are in the process of being combed." Isaac threw his hands up. After an uncomfortable pause, Cho turned back to Jimbo. "So let me just preface our negotiation with this. SWAT will find them. It's only a matter of time." Isaac hesitated long enough, it seemed, to let it all sink in. Everyone was dead silent as Isaac looked all three of us dead in the eyes. "Either Muffcat complies with some rather demeaning demands or Leisa Anne McNeese's execution will be uploaded to a YouTube account."

Tommy was about ready to jump out of his seat. "Their community guidelines will never allow that. Predatory behavior, stalking, threats, harassment, intimidation, invading privacy, committing violent acts; it will all be blocked." Gary Pigg pushed down on Tommy's shoulder. Isaac's eyes left mine; he was now looking directly towards Gary. "You can see from the video that they're not in any condition to know that. What we are trying to avoid here is that poor woman's execution." Isaac pointed to J-Laz. "We've been in contact with Susan Wojcicki's team at YouTube. They take terrorist threats very seriously, Mr. Mansker." Isaac slid a document across the table. Gary and Tommy both tried to scoop it up. After another pregnant pause, I grabbed my chance to be heard. "Gary, Tommy. Don't bother. This is Queenie's life we are talking about. Whatever it is, I'll do it."

Pigg tapped down on my hand. "Not so fast. This performance is sexual in nature; it references a script... Just what exactly are we talking about, Agent Lewis?" J-Laz dropped the script over my shoulder then pointed. "The self-erotic pleasuring comes after the roller derby erotic. We plan to tape the more intimate portion in a private area. If the video goes viral, Stanley and Reece will do everything in their power to take it down."

Holy shit. My face burned red as the scrolling feed from the video came into focus. Isaac assured, "Remember we have them surrounded." Tommy's cuffed hands lurched for the script. "Goddammit! Are these things really necessary? Let me see that, Sis."

Gary's fat neck was really starting to irritate me. Stubble was poking out from underneath his waddle as he grappled with his collar. "Why my client? Have any of you figured that one out yet?" Big D and Jimbo left the room, thank God, and then Cho rejoined us at the table. "We've recovered three, maybe four dozen letters referencing Miss Mansker. The sick fuck has been stalking your client for years." Cho's bony hip leaned into the table. "Look, the ball is in your court, Miss Mansker. Stop wasting precious time." J-Laz was still standing over me. "Cho, cut the bullshit." Isaac slid another handful of papers towards Pigg. "It looks worse on paper. J-Laz and Reece will be doing the filming. Stanley will monitor every file-sharing Web site conceivable from a specially equipped van that will be onsite." Gary piped up. "And if my client goes through with this, these charges will be dropped?"

This time, I turned to Gary. "I'm going to do this, regardless of the charges. But I have a question I want answered first." Isaac did not so much as flinch as he addressed me. "I'm not sure if I can answer it, but I'll try. What do you want to know?" I had to stand up. The whelps from Melvin's lashes were sticking to the seat of my trousers. "What's the Stargate Project?" Pigg shot me a seemingly bewildered glance. For the first time during the interrogation, Isaac asked Cho for his assistance. Cho did not make eye contact; his bony ass cheek was now propped on the table. J-Laz cleared her throat. She walked over to Cho with her arms folded, then whispered to the agent. Cho pressed himself up from the fake wood grain and walked over towards the two-way mirror, forcing us to turn in his direction. "The Stargate Project is the umbrella code name of for a series of research projects originally established by the CIA and DIA back in the early Seventies. Their hopes were to substantiate psychic phenomena with potential military and domestic applications, but the subprojects got bounced around from agency to agency. The CIA shut down Stargate in 1995. The project landed in my lap a couple of years ago."

J-Laz was pacing. Her frustration clearly mounting, she knelt down beside my chair. "Look. Both you and JJ were preliminary candidates for one of the projects, way back before Doctor Dax Tanley appointed me to lead the remote viewing lab at Stanford. Your father contacted Dax back in 1976 about your gift. We've had one of our agents surveilling you for a couple of months. You were one of our most hopeful contenders, Muffcat, though we never anticipated a serial homicide was going to supersede our research."

Well, now. Okay, time for a deep breath. Exhale. I can tell you this was the first honest and heartfelt statement that had come out of Jackie Lazenby's mouth since Big D drug me down to the precinct. Her penetrating focus only intensified as she rounded my shoulders towards hers. "I hate that you are caught up in the middle of this, but you have the ability to save one terrified woman from being executed. One who was a bridesmaid in your first wedding. One that has three terrified children and a really desperate husband counting on us to rescue her."

J-Laz released my shoulders and reached across the table, pressing the speaker phone with the tip of her gelled fingertip. "Stanley, please have Agent Magaña step into the conference room." For once, Gary Pigg and Tommy were speechless as Sally walked in. As the agent introduced herself, reality was beginning to settle into my being. The mortician who had helped me embalm a dozen bodies over the last several months was not Sally.

As Dr. Giovanna Magaña placed her hand on my shoulder, I had to pull away. "Noh mek dehn get weh." Tommy inquired, "What the hell does that mean?" I peered over to my brother. "She said, 'don't let them get away.' Hell no. Not gonna happen."

Chapter XXXIV

Sometimes, there's just not enough vodka. As I stood in the detonation of a thousand strobe lights in nothing but a black teddy, a thick hand passed a vodka tonic from the bowling alley's bar my way. While agents lingered between the arcade games and chattered amongst themselves from behind the carpeted railing, I did not even bother squeezing the lime. Hair slung into a side ponytail that made me look like I just stepped off the set of a *Napoleon Dynamite* sequel; I realized a kid of no more than seventeen was strapping pink fuzz to my feet. Big D handed over the humiliating script. Eyes bloodshot, flannel shirt untucked, he leaned into me. "Pretty sure I'm gonna lose my job over the botched evidence, Muffcat." Downing my drink, I shot back, "And you think I give two shits?"

I peered over to J-Laz. With my confiscated iPhone in hand, she stripped off her jacket, going down to her stained, silk blouse; she passed it to Giovanna, who was standing underneath the strobe light. The Fun Center's manager was working to get the requested songs programmed to play in the correct sequence from the DJ's booth. Journey's "Faithfully" blared overhead, causing J-Laz to wobble on her skates.

Ignoring Big D, I waved the glass over my head, all while trying to memorize JJ's pathetic attempt at Roller Derby erotica. My pantyhose were making the whelps from Melvin's lashes stick to the unforgiving nylon. I was a nervous wreck, who looked increasingly like a Cyndi Lauper video extra. Brad Weasle entered the arcade. The county sheriff and a few of his deputies were two steps behind him with some British gentleman, who sported a plaid jacket and bow tie. Davenport was invading my personal space. "You're a real sport for doing this, Muffcat. You've earned my respect." I sucked on an ice cube, spit it back into the glass, and said, "What the fuck do you know about respect, Detective?"

Big D gave me the side smirk again. Flannel shirt untucked, hair a discombobulating tuft of sex, there was no way he was going to regain my admiration, even with that fabulous grin.

The kid clamoring at my feet popped up and darted across the waxy floor to the DJ's booth. "All of the evidence in these case has been tampered with, Muffcat. I am sure you know by whom, but it was my evidence, my cases." Big D sounded bitter. My concentration was focused on the script. He plucked the pages from my sweaty palms, and then placing the paperwork on the railing, the detective took my hands. He pulled me into him with no regard for the assembly of "Jos .A. Banks" whispering around us. I looked up to meet his gaze. "I've got enough respect to know I need to make myself scarce." Big D grabbed me tighter, and I relented, giving into the embrace, and burying my head in his chest. "You know they have nothing on you, right?" The detective's brazenness was shocking. Big D rubbed the back of my shoulders. "They still have a laundry list of charges pending against me." His arms were now around my waist; not once did he acknowledge the scene he was creating. "I mean it, Muffcat. Cho's never once suspected you. You do know that, right?"

Though J-Laz was moving in our direction, Big D pulled me in closer. "I'm turning in my badge after the FBI debriefs me on these cases." I hesitantly pulled away. "What is that supposed to mean?" I insisted. He ran his hand through his thick clump of hair; the dark brown pieces cascading into his eyes. "My credibility has been questioned." Big D moved his hand to my cheek, as his big toothy grin receded into a straight line. He seemed to be waiting for a response while stroking my face. "I'm gonna take the fall for this, to protect Pammy," he said, sounding resigned. "You can't take the fall for this. Hell, they've got Melvin in custody for felony attempted murder; pin it on him. Pammy will never accept this anyway." Big D's lips softened. He broke our connection seconds before J-Laz crashed into the carpeted railing, shouting, "we've gotta move on this. Let's get the more intimate portion over with first. Reece can slice it together once we're done." J-Laz had to have been watching my eyes follow Big D swagger towards the exit. Hands in his pockets, the detective looked back and gave a quick wink. "I'll be waiting for you outside."

As I rolled the edge of the railing, Brad Weasle emerged with the bow-tied clad gentleman a good twenty paces behind him. The man had the wildest blond hair I had ever seen. J-Laz skated over to me. "That's Doctor Dax Tansley. He was one of the original researchers assigned to formulate the set of protocols used to gauge the statistical accuracy of the clairvoyance test group before he branched out into criminal profiling. Forty years later, and he still looks like a rock star." J-Laz reached for my hand. "Dax can drink me under the table and has one perverse sense of humor. You two will hit it off. We have to make the introduction quick."

J-Laz reminded the doctor of our time constraint before I had a chance to stick out my hand. The doctor made a rather colorful introduction. His tendency to say "bloody" and "fuck" every other word reminded me of Chef Ramsey. But the wrinkles in his forehead and the blank expression that was now on his rather striking face made his contemplations impossible to construe. J-Laz interrupted us. "Muffcat, it's show time. Follow me. Let's find a private space." I skated past the "Jos. A. Banks" in utter disbelief at my situation. What the fuck? Seriously.

The overhead halogen lights made the skating rink's storage closet seem rather clinical. J-Laz plopped down on a chair then tugged at the laces of her skates. I could tell the eye-catching TBI agent had freshened up. She extracted some lipstick from the pocket of her perfectly tailored, black slacks, then rimmed her heart-shaped lips. "Stick to the script. I'm going to get some close-ups, but remember, nobody but JJ and Missy will get the pleasure of viewing this." After J-Laz adjusted the tongue of her skate, she peered up and handed over her tube of lipstick. "All I can say is, fake it. It will be impossible to climax given the circumstances." I peered down at the crumpled script, wincing.

We experienced a few technical difficulties during the masturbation scene, but at least the worst was over. J-Laz looked exhausted. She was now trying to skate backwards while I practiced the script under the disco ball in the center of the rink. John Waite's "Missing You" thumped overhead. *"There's a message in the wire. And I'm sending you this signal tonight. You don't know how desperate I've become. And it looks like I'm losing this fight. In your world I have no meaning. Though I'm trying hard to understand. And it's my heart that's breaking down this long-distance line tonight. I ain't missing you at all. Since you've been gone away. I ain't missing you, No matter what my friends say."*

As I tried my damndest to recite my lines with a straight face, the DJ started the song over again. "Action." JJ's name, spread heavily throughout the script, was hard for me to muster. Conjuring the requested enthusiasm proved rather emotionally tormenting. "Make it seem real, or Queenie is a goner" kept lingering in my head as we encircled the rink. We made it through a good portion of the suggestive dialect without faltering, with just minutes to spare. Just as the song went into the chorus, something began to happen in my head.

As I precipitously followed the sensation of being in someone else's body, an overwhelming sense of emotional instability took over my mood. I felt love-struck, giddy, yet so utterly chagrined with myself. It was as if I had the whole world to share with someone. Someone, that is, who meant everything to me but was unaware of my existence. There was a terrible dread harboring in my gut that told me I was not good enough; that I was unclean and unworthy of love or affection. Something so awful and wretched about my past; the thought of sharing it was unbearable. The longing of a thousand years was heavy on my heart. Beams of light danced to the floor making waves break across the hardwood.

As we continued to glide in circles, only the blues and greens of the strobe lights were obtainable by my vision. All of a sudden, grand white caps appeared, trundling across the hardwood. Flashes of a beautiful mermaid pinged in the light ahead of me as I followed the senseless script. The majestic creature had long, blond hair, with dark roots in her part, flowing as she hurdled through the waves. I came to an abrupt halt, causing J-Laz to crash. Now waiting at the ocean's edge with my arms spread wide to receive the beast, my heart raced and felt like it would leap from my chest as the words of another script dispensed from my mouth.

There I was, transforming, turning into something that was not human. Mythical powers of thousands of generations of poets, artists, dictators, and the most sophisticated of intellects of the universe, their voices raged in-between my ears. The closer the beautiful creature got to the ocean's edge, the loftier my shadow became in the perfectly waxed hardwood. I looked down to notice my head sprouting horns that felt to be pugnaciously cracking through my skull. The longing and waiting, ready to break with the tide of the sea, danced with brilliant illumination in my soul and at my feet. Just as the creature disappeared under a whitecap, the script was replaced with a sonnet that felt natural and somehow a part of me.

J-Laz peered up from my iPhone. "Script, Muffcat; stick to the script. We're almost through here." Just as the water was disappearing, and the last wave broke at the pink balls strapped to my feet, the mystical beast landed in a crumpled ball, forced against the carpeted railing. I broke away from J-Laz then rolled up to the mass that was disappearing and fading into a fine mist before my eyes. The horrific smell of death surrounded us. Peering up with the gaze of a cadaver, I knew her. Her eyes were open, yet the naked girl was now gray, lifeless, dead. She was the adolescent from Betty's newspaper clipping, the girl from my visions. Just as I reached down to try and grasp what was left of her vanishing image, the mermaid's face began to contort. Black goo oozed from her lips, as the image of petrified woman flashed over her decaying face like a hologram. The creature flapped her rotting tail, then pulled the lower end of her body towards her chest. She looked back up at me while the goo unremittingly seeped from her lips. Then she faded into the pattern of the carpeted railing.

I was on my knees weeping for her soul when Cho approached. Dax was just steps behind, a martini glass in his hand. They were clearly aware of the fact that something paranormal had happened, yet I was still not able to communicate. J-Laz was on her knees beside me when she handed my phone to Reece. Three agents surrounded Reece as he raced to the parking lot. Cho was hurling unremitting questions at me. Someone flung a blazer over my shoulders. J-Laz stood then rolled me over to the wall lined with an elongated bench. Cho was practically running after us as we plopped down in synchronicity. "Now's not the time, Cho. Let her catch her breath."

Dax was a few steps behind Cho, calmly drinking from his stemmed glass. "Did you just have a visualization of Jonah Wayne Johnson's victims?" Cho questioned. I was still huffing when Dax handed me his drink. I took the last gulp before responding. "Yes, every single one of them. And Missy was his latest casualty." J-Laz pulled the "Jos. A. Banks" over my shoulders. "You've got what you wanted from her, Cho. Let's let Muffcat get some rest." Cho placed his hands in his pockets, cursing under his breath before spinning on his heels. After getting only a few steps away, he turned and grimaced. "You might want to let her know that Jonah Wayne Johnson is her cousin."

All I could do was draw my hand to my mouth. J-Laz tore after Cho, profanity-laced threats jumping from her trucker's lips. Dax stepped up from the perfectly waxed hardwood, extracting the martini glass from my free hand. He tried to smooth over Cho's kick to my ribs. "Bloody hell, Muffcat. JJ never could have done what you have done with your remote viewing abilities. The voices that haunted him were a curse. I knew from the day I laid eyes on the bloke that he was schizophrenic." Through streaming tears, trying to keep my voice from cracking, I whispered, "Nobody knows that better than I do. Now if you will excuse me, Doctor, my ride is waiting for me in the parking lot." I couldn't get out of there fast enough.

Chapter XXXV

As soon as high school ended, my friends and I, wasting not one single second, dove head-on into our drunken rite of passage. It was May of '89 as we took off for Panama City Beach. Our pilgrimage started at 3 o'clock in the morning, with most of the clan, including yours truly, asleep for the first leg of the trip. Parrottville's very own homecoming queen, Miss Leisa Anne Phillips (aka Queenie) took the first driving shift. She drove Momma's station wagon out of Nashville; we were three hours into the journey before Queenie finally admitted to taking I-40 West instead of 65-South when we'd hit the split. We woke up in a strange little town. As our eyes came into focus, we made out the sign, which read: Welcome to Finger, Tennessee! The entire trip was supposed to take eight hours, but Queenie's detour through "third base," along with our teenage attempts to navigate the back roads of nowhere rendered us all petrified and lethargic by the time we hit the sandy beaches of the Redneck Riviera some nineteen hours later. In short order, I wound up getting knocked up after my first shot of tequila in a hot tub with Johnny Glass.

Back home, Queenie was the first to notice my hangover's unusual lingering. Chandra, Camille, Pammy, Aimee, and Julie started their summer jobs and preparations for college while I was left to contemplating what the hell to do. Suffice it to say, Momma was not happy with my demand to have Smokey join Daddy in walking me down the aisle to Rocky Top. I must admit that the bridesmaids did look smashing in their tea-length orange dresses and white cowboy boots. Queenie was my maid of honor. Even with it being a shotgun wedding, she arranged my bridesmaid's tea and gave me the most unusual and special gift. I had always loved the bells at her small church that sits across town next to the oldest cemetery in the Long Hollow Pike community. During the ceremony, which took place underneath the two-hundred-year-old hickory tree on the grounds of The Three Waters, Queenie arranged for a serenade of bells to play my favorite song of all times. Not exactly a melody that most people think about when they recall all the memorable hits from the Beatles. Just as the first note was struck by the campanologist, a cool breeze blew across the entire congregation. "Norwegian Wood" was breathtaking, with just the ringing of the bells in the stifling heat of the southern sun. It is the sweetest memory.

She might not be able to navigate herself out of a pickle jar, but Queenie has always been able to lighten my mood and uplift me from even my darkest despair. Now, instead of that ill-fated wedding, the sound of bells always reminds me of my dearest friend and our teenage mischievous.

*****

I did not even collect my Gucci purse from the Snack Shack before wheeling into the parking lot at the Parrottville Family Fun Center. Once reaching the concrete steps outside, I removed my skates, launching them at the metal building with enough profanity-laced verbosity to move Big D to race from his patrol car. "Don't you fucking dare, David Davenport? You knew all along. Stay the hell away from me! Leave me the fuck alone!"

The detective tried to calm me down, grabbing at my arms as I ran towards the road. "They got to Queenie; come back! Let me take you to see her!" I had no idea where I was going in the middle of the night in a black teddy and barefoot, but I knew I needed to be alone. Big D followed me through the parking lot, barking phrases no pissed off woman ever wants to hear. "Calm down now. Will you stop with your goddamn hissy fit already, and let me explain? At least let me take your stupid ass to the hospital to see Queenie and your grandmother. God! You are so stubborn-headed, Muffcat!"

Turning, I looked David Davenport directly in the eyes, glaring. "Just stay the fuck away from me! What are you some sort of nut job? Do you really want to be associated with a crazy psychic mortician who has a serial killer in her immediate family? Seriously. Tell me, Davenport, what am I to you? A sacrificial token you offered up to the FBI in exchange for them turning a blind eye to the fact that you work for the most backwards ass, unprofessional, goddamn worst excuse for a homicide department there ever was?" I moved away from him, with not one ounce of curiosity as to what the detective's response might be. I ran about ten paces before turning back to add another thought that was tugging at me. "Just when the fuck were you planning on telling me? After you fucked my brains out?"

With that, I made my way to the main road. Big D was still yelling. "Just let me take you to the hospital; please stop! Come on now sweetie!"

There was not one car on the street, after the citywide lockdown. Taking a seat on a bus bench five blocks away from the Fun Center, I cried myself out until I had no more tears. The wind started to pick up.

My whole life had turned out to be one humongous, viscous white lie. Uncle Vernon's secret affair and bastard child; my father turning his five-year-old terrified daughter into the FBI to be some guinea pig; the betrayal of my first husband; the death of Sonny; the parlaying voices; the haunting faces of JJ's victims. And now, sitting alone at the mass transit stop, wearing a fucking porn star teddy, having fake masturbated for the viewing pleasure of my own demented fucking cousin and his perverted girlfriend, that is, if she were still alive; I could not handle knowing that I had been put in the same category as a mass murdering, mentally deranged, sadistic fuck-tard. Who got his rocks off by preying on women, some were my dearest friends.

Guilt crept to the surface of my skin. The kidnappings and murders; the condition of the corpses. Families and friends left devastated, and the entire community's sense of safety forever lost in the wake of these horrific events. Then, there I was, about ready to swing for the rafters with a man I barely knew? My entire family in the protective custody of the FBI, my grandmother on her deathbed, and I was actually considering rolling in the hay with a man who slept with one of my best friends in a threesome? Speaking aloud to myself, I asked, "What the hell are you doing?"

I was on the verge of a full mental breakdown; bells began ringing in the nip of the night sky. I seized the bench and then took a look around me. At first, the chiming was serene and soothing, but no one else seemed to be able to hear them. A woman exiting a bar ran to her car with a paper over her head to block the rain that had started falling. A homeless man took shelter under a streetlight at the liquor store across the street. The tresses of the trees began to sway as the panic attack to end all panic attacks began to paralyze me. My hands started to become clammy. Orange and yellow leaves dropped and scraped across the blacktop, collecting against the wooden fence that held the bar's trash receptacles. Huge thunder clouds made their presence known as they rolled across the night sky, contorting the radiance of the full moon.

Pings of anxiety made it difficult to take in enough oxygen. As the moonlight danced and began to fade into the concrete, the toll of the bell's rhythm was almost ground to a halt. "Does anyone hear the bells?" I screamed like the hysteric I was rapidly becoming. The vagrant with the grocery cart did not answer. He just gathered up his paper bag from his jacket and helped himself to a swig. As the dark clouds crept closer to me, the melody changed, contorted, dissipated into the sound of one lone bell, pitched to a rumbling A long, deep bellowing sparring down from the sky, it vibrated in-between my ears. My thoughts poured from my mouth as if someone was listening, but no one was. "Surely I am not the only one experiencing this?"

Petrified by fear, I tried to yell for help, but everyone was scattering from the parking lot before the eye of the storm blew in. A cook called to someone from the back door of the bar. I waved for his attention, but he didn't respond. He grabbed a cigarette from his coworker then ran towards his car. Heat rose and lingered on my lips like a thousand bees stinging. A single ray of moonlight shone down through the billowing bleakness upon me. As the bells of hell began to ring more luridly, the cries of a thousand voices enveloped my three feet of space, which was illuminated by moonlight.

Labored breath, intense fear, on the verge of blacking out, my silent cries for help continued to go unanswered as I sought shelter underneath a tree. The atmosphere unleashed a ferocious bolt of lightning as the voices became louder. Unable to move or speak, my thoughts turned inward. "Why the hell am I hearing AC/DC?" Brian Johnson's voice was unmistakable. The first verse was conversant, yet increasingly distressing nonetheless. As if the lead singer had been thrust at an angry lynch mob, like some sacrificial lamb. An angry clap of thunder barked like the Devil himself, precisely eight seconds after the flash.

Just as the first chorus bounced off the buildings and echoed in the wind, another voice took over. I was pulled upright by the swirl of the voices as if they owned me. The rain started to pour down on my face as the bells mingled with the bellow of a church organ. The growl of Jonah Wayne Johnson's singing taunted me.

My brain told me to run for safety, but my legs, like the dead roots of a tree that had been petrified for a thousand years, had other ideas. I was trapped; assaulted by sneering voices and unforgiving elements. *"I'll give you black sensations up and down your spine. If you're into evil you're a friend of mine. See the white light flashing as I split the night. Cause if good's on the left then I'm sticking to the right. I won't take no prisoners won't spare no lives. Nobody's puttin' up a fight. I got my bell I'm gonna take you to hell. I'm gonna get ya- Satan get ya."*

Chapter XXXVI

Big D's sedan came to a screeching halt seconds after another bolt of lightning struck the tree overhead. Anyone else would have run from the deafening clap, and yet the detective sprinted towards me. "Muffy Catherine, come on now, run to me, babe!" But, I was motionless. I stared up at the storm, unable to speak or respond. In one fell swoop, the detective grabbed me up as sparks rained down from the branches of the birch tree; we landed on his vehicle, which was sitting sideways in the parking lot.

I looked up to Big D. "He's not done. I swear on my father's grave there will be more victims," I warned. "They caught him, Muffcat. They got him before the tape was even uploaded." I threw my arms against Big D's chest and demanded he let me down. I kicked, flailed my limbs, screamed at the top of my lungs- nothing seemed to work. The detective's grip only got tighter. "Calm the fuck down. God!"

Once out of the direct path of the flames, Big D dropped me flat on my feet. We were next to the driver's door of his sedan when he began screaming in my face. "Now seriously, calm the fuck down, and tell me what you are talking about. Please, you have to know that I believe you, but I never knew JJ was Vernon's son. I swear to you. I swear to God!"

He tore off his flannel shirt while beating at a limb that was burning on the top of his sedan. He then held me by both my shoulders and proceeded to grab my face. "We have to warn the FBI." Our eyes were locked. The rain was picking up. Patrons of the bar were now looking out the front door, making their way into the parking lot. Fire alarms were going off. Two concerned citizens shouted to see if we needed assisted. Big D's gaze was one of bewilderment. I yelled, "He was a decent police officer at one point." I pulled on the handle of the sedan as visions of the First Baptist church exploded and flashed before my eyes. "The church! There are pipe bombs at the church!" It was the only thing I could get out of my mouth.

We were both drenched, and fire was still shooting from the top of the branches of the young birch tree. The detective was groping for me, struggling to calm me down while feverishly attempting to shove me into his vehicle. As I tried to pull away from him, Big D twisted my wrist up the middle of my back. "Stop causing a spectacle. Get your ass in my car, now!" He forcefully crammed my head underneath the doorframe; I must have looked like an under arrest suspect. "Just let me go. Let me go, goddamn it!" He pulled out; I was still eating the floor mat when Big D resumed. "How do you know this? I've already told Pammy that I'm turning in my badge. So, really, please tell me. Now!"

Big D was driving like a maniac back towards the Fun Center. He about took out a service van ahead of us. "I don't know how I know it, but I swear to you I do. The church organ is rigged. JJ was planning on exploding the church at Chandra's memorial. It is his final act of defiance. Please just hand me your phone- I have to warn Betty!"

Now, as he drove 85 MPH on a road riddled with red lights, a flurry of calls went out over Big D's police radio. All about the fire. He flashed his patrol lights. We were less than a block from the Fun Center. Cars parted in the parking lot at the shrill of Big D's siren. There was no controlling my panic. My body was being flung from side to side, but Big D was not about to slow down. We came to a dead stop within inches of the FBI's mobile technology unit. Big D did not even wait for me to exit the car before landing a shot right between Cho's eyes. Within seconds, copious numbers of Jos. A. Banks had him laid out on the payment, face first. J-Laz had her knee in Big D's back. She was in the process of handcuffing him when Giavanna and Dax stopped me from jumping on the pile of suits manhandling Big D. My teddy's straps now ripped, my exposed breast showing, Dax and Giavanna threw me into an idling sedan, sandwiching me in-between their bodies. I fought, as I'm known to do. "I am not going anywhere with you! You cannot hold me against my own free will. There has to be a law against this!"

Nobody else was doing much talking as the meathead in the driver's seat careened towards the interstate. Once on the on-ramp to I-65, Dax handed over his plaid coat. "Are you calmed down now Miss Mansker?" I placed my face in my hands and just crumpled in half. "Bloody hell, do you want to explain what that was all about?" I resisted making any response. Just bawled my eyes out while we sped back towards Parrottville.

Once at our undetermined destination, I recognized the old farm where Sally, or whoever she was, was supposedly renting a studio apartment above the family's garage. The lights to the modest, white farmhouse blazed to life as we pulled into the driveway. With a firm grip and a push by the driver, I was escorted to the door of the main house.

Giavanna extracted her key, but we were greeted by Hollis and Stanley at the door before she got the key in the lock. Hollis' mortician jacket was off. He was recently shaven and wearing a pair of old blue jeans and a hooded sweatshirt. "Come with me." Stanley was still in his crumpled suit, without the jacket. None of the décor in the farmhouse was what you'd expect of a humble Parrottville tobacco farmer. Six or seven men were gathered in a room that looked straight out of *The Bourne Identity*. A long metal table covered in paperwork had some weird contraption lying in the center. The room was dim, but their bank of terminals glowed with camera feeds locked onto my cabin, the funeral home, and the mansion. There was even a camera on the front porch of Aunt Maude's home.

I tucked Dax's plaid coat around my exposed thighs before being thrust down into an office chair. "Now that we have your attention, there is something we want you to see." Dax's pale skin seemed way too young for his years. He dropped a letter down in front of me, onto the metal. Wookiee entered the room and took a seat opposite me on the other side of the table. He was in a suit and had his normally disheveled hair neatly pulled back into a ponytail. "The letter is from your father, Muffcat. He was the one who originally contacted the Stargate project's team." To my knowledge, Wookiee had never uttered a single word, much less a complete sentence. Just when I thought the night could not get any stranger, Eleanor busted through the doorway. She wasn't in a T-shirt proclaiming her sexuality. Her dark gray suit was impeccably tailored, her fanny pack and crunchy sandals nowhere to be found.

I reached for the envelope that had the Bank of Parrottville's logo on the top left-hand corner. Eleanor took the seat beside me and patted my upper thigh. "Muffcat, my involvement with the FBI is a complete secret. Even Pammy is not aware of my undercover status. She won't even look at me after arresting me on the assault charges, but you have to know that my love for her is genuine. Now, my gig over at WSM as a culinary correspondent is the biggest hoax since Martha Stewart resumed the helm of her home accessory empire after serving her time, but I am not, nor have I ever been, a domesticated woman. Been doing this for over twenty-four years now. After my court date, I am going to take a less active role in the Stargate Project. Dax over here is my new boss. We just have some PR issues to clean up. Pammy will have to move forward with my charges. If she doesn't, it will ruin her career, seeing how we are partners. So while I am tucked away at the halfway house, where they are going to have me serve out my sentence, I'll be running The Three Waters for a while."

I looked over at my best friend's lover. The hog farmer was even more striking with the makeup she was wearing. "After the media finds out about me masturbating for a serial killer I doubt Parrottville s going to throw me any grand parade. Just where do you think I'm going? " Eleanor, if that was even her real name, let out a hearty laugh. She slapped her knee before answering. "Well, that video will never be seen by anyone. That's unless you want me to show Big D. He would be more than pleased to see your hot little ass wiz around that rink."

I had to laugh. Finally. The relief, much needed, felt good. The night had been appalling. Wookiee cleared his throat. "We've wanted to have you professionally tested for years, Muffcat. Hell, you have grown up underneath my nose. I've known for a long time you had special talents. Your father was the one who got me into the FBI. He was one of the best undercover agents this agency has ever seen. He had the gift, Muffcat. We sometimes had to make your mother believe he needed a little emotional downtime when he worked on the more complicated cases, but he was a real bad-ass, right up until his untimely death. I swore to him that I would take care of you. Your mother never shared your premonition with him before his procedure; she never knew about his secret life. I really miss that little man. Was one of my dearest friends. Never was able to repay him for getting the help that I needed with my learning disability or assisting me with my status in the Stargate Project."

Watching and listening to Wookiee was freaking surreal. But I had to know it all. "So are you really the midnight miracle? Or was that whole crazy news article just a way to explain your unexpected arrival in Parrottville?" Wookiee stood then rounded the table. He bent down and took my hands in his. "Every bit of the legend regarding my arrival in this crazy world is the truth. If not for the aid of Clyde and your dear grandfather, Mr. Claude, I would have been on a bus back to some orphanage in Mexico. I own my entire life to the kindness your family afforded me."

I had to pull Wookiee into me for a bear hug. Even on his knees, my Mexican Sasquatch towered over me. "What about Uncle Vernon? I guess you knew about JJ being his son?" Hollis stepped up to the table. "Muffcat, after Cliff Johnson found out about the affair and the deception of JJ's paternity, I was forced to claim that boy as my own. I contacted the FBI years ago. When Shelley Danderson turned up dead, I was suspicious. Had my reservations about Jonah Wayne Johnson for a long time. Now just so you know, I really am a lowly mortician. But I never willingly gave that money to JJ. I was forced at the hands of your Uncle Vernon. Come to find out, with his perchance for illegal activities, the TBI have been investigating Vernon Mansker for years. Vernon was the money man behind the moonshiner operation. Tried to appease JJ by getting him involved as a distributor. But when JJ found out there was a lot more to moonshining than hanging around with toothless sex offenders, your Uncle Vernon needed a way to get JJ out of his life for good. Even though I have not one ounce of respect for the lying, cheating sack of shit, the $55,000 was a way to rid your family of the evil that has been haunting the Manskers all these years."

I turned to Giavanna. "So what's your story? Is Simon's going to be hit with some monumental fine for having an unlicensed mortician hacking on our stiffs?" She smiled. Her story was the most surprising of them all. Raphel's story was factual. But Giavana was already practicing medicine in her small village when her son was approached by Sterner Hammond to be tested for the Stargate Program. His death was still very hard for her to discuss, but Giovanna's heart was in the right place. "So, Muffcat, Gawd Bliminy, read the damn letter. We have so many intriguing things to discuss before our plane departs tomorrow." Dax handed me a vodka martini. "No thanks Dax, I've got to slow down on that habit. I've needed a vodka exorcism for years."

I opened up the letter. My daddy's handwriting was hard for me to read. It was not illegible, but the words were so heartfelt. The letter was addressed to Sterner Hammond, who was the religious studies professor and ordained minister Giovanna had encouraged me to talk to after detailing my paranormal encounters. I learned in the first sentence that Daddy was considering having me institutionalized. He, as well as my own mother, was concerned about some "peculiar and odd" behavior. Mother was afraid my actions might endanger her other children. The letter then detailed Tommy's report of witnessing me pushing my sister down the hallway and into the closet. The panic attack my mother experienced when she feared someone had kidnapped her daughters. Father was claiming when they finally discovered us barricaded in the hall closet, I was in some sort of trance.

I began to read the letter out loud to the group. *"Muffy Catherine was begging someone that neither Lucinda nor I could see to call off the "Wind Whispers." The child was manic, almost in a comatose state, viciously slapping and punching at us. Our five-year-old was speaking, but not in the voice of our child. It was as if my princess, my baby girl, was possessed by the Devil himself. This demon or whatever had hijacked her stream of consciousness, claimed my residence was a portal to the underworld. Muffy Catherine spoke of rabid dogs that were trying to drag her soul to hell; flailing her arms, she dropped a packet of Camel unfiltered cigarettes fell to the floor. Sterner, neither Lenore nor I have ever smoked; Tommy was only eight years of age at this time of this episode of madness. The child was inconsolable, frantic, and insistent that many souls had passed through some portal. We only could figure she was describing the gates of hell. Her language was too sophisticated and knowledgeable to be coming from the mind of a little girl. It was like she was reciting Dante's allegory, his guided tour through the afterlife by the Roman poet Virgil himself. Her account was astoundingly comprehensive. We discovered personal belongings of recently deceased clients from my father's funeral home underneath her bed. How does a five-year-old drag a full-length mink coat buried with the body of Thelma Harper into our home without our knowledge? Muffy Catherine was not even in attendance at the funeral. Aunt Maude was with her the entire time Lucinda and I attended the memorial and graveside. Not only was the priceless mink discovered, Lucinda found a pair of boots and a cheap set of earrings rammed into the pocket's lining that belonged to a recent homicide victim, a vagrant that was a known prostitute. No one can explain these artifacts. All of the employees of the funeral home and our B&B have been questioned. They all deny having anything to do with these bizarre events. Tommy claims she walks the halls every night. He's witnessed her corresponding with the deceased daughter of the original owner of the plantation. Nelley Needlemire died in the 1860s during the Confederate occupation of the plantation. There is no way my child would know this woman's name, much less the vivid details of her burial attire we've confirmed through her death portrait. She knows the names of Nelley's deceased's children, their occupations, and their children's names. Muffy Catherine even had the personal diary of the recently deceased Senator Theodore Garson IV amongst her collection. Lucinda caught Muffy Catherine trying to dial the poor widow's residence one night from our parlor's rotary phone. She knew the woman's home telephone number, her date of birth- even her social security number. When Lucinda confronted her the next morning, Muffy Catherine had no recollection of the sleepwalking incident. Please send your recommendations for a place where we can take her to get some help. I'll be at our meeting in Washington. Please contact that intern with the Stargate project and see if he can assist."*

Hollis gave me a few minutes to get my crying jag under control. "Muffcat, your father was inconsolable when you were going through this ordeal. I remember when he questioned me about the mink and earrings, and the pack of Camel's. He was crushed after finding out to whom the items belonged. He tried to have the bodies exhumed, but the Funeral Directors' Association talked him out of it because of the bad press it could bring. Wookiee is right. Your father was really talented, Muffcat." Then, Giavana said, "Dax confirmed your father thwarted many crimes; even an attempt on Bill Clinton's life was defused by his fascinating perception to see into the future. I, for one, am relieved you finally know the truth."

Big D was led into the room by J-Laz, who released his handcuffs before I leaped into his arms. "So, I guess they told you they bamboozled me?" After one incredibly steamy kiss, I pulled back. "You do not know just who you have swooned yet, do you, Detective?" Big D gave me a huge, toothy grin. "Well, I had already figured that one out before they diffused the bombs at the church."

An eternal embrace wouldn't have lasted nearly long enough. "Which one of you crazy bastards is going to drive us home?" J-Laz set my purse down on the table. "We'll keep your boys tied up for the night, you two love birds. But we have some more options we need to discuss with you after your Tina Turner performance tomorrow, Muffcat. So you might want to get some rest before the funeral. We'll take the Lear to Teterboro then pack your bags for a couple of months of training."

Big D handed Dax back his plaid jacket. "Don't call us before 10:00 a.m. I got some real fancy bacon to cook up in the morning for Muffcat." Big D punched Eleanor in the arm. "Don't worry, Clancy. Your secret is safe with me, as long as your knowledge about my own little moment remains a secret from Pammy. She's a keeper. You got lucky."

Chapter XXXVII

Friday, January 18, 2013. JFK airport.

There I was. I'd just had my soul hijacked by a three- hundred pound clairvoyant in a psychedelic muumuu while trying to join the sky high club during a trans-oceanic flight from Heathrow to JFK. Poor Movina. Rosemurta claimed she put up a hell of a fight, but succumbed to the cancer on New Year's Eve. Meanwhile, Big D was still bitching about the damage his back had suffered when Movina decided to go to the other side for a spur-of-the-moment threesome while we flew over the Atlantic Ocean.

Hell, I was practically in liver failure after the monumental week-long private yachting adventure in the southern edge of the Aegean Sea, the guest of J-Laz and her very much older boyfriend (no less than thirty years, but who's counting?) Doctor Dax Tanley. Shit; let's face it. My life was never going to be the same.

After a nice twenty-minute chair massages, during which the talented masseuse had herself quite the time kneading my partner's gorgeous ass, Big D and I boarded our plane back to Nashville, Tennessee. With enough carry-on presents to fund my own angel tree, he and I slid into our first class seats. I knew he was planning something for me, but couldn't put my finger on it just yet. I had other things in mind, like trying to keep my trembling thighs from shaking.

Big D reached for my hand. "So are you sure about this, my little firecracker?" I lay my head on Big D's barreled chest, drinking in his awesome masculinity, and going over everything into my jumbled mind. "I gotta admit, the thought of carrying my own badge is intriguing. But, I think I'm gonna have to pass on Dax's offer. There's no way Gran will be able to handle the funeral home now that Betty announced her retirement. Man, I still can't believe she's decided to run for Uncle Vernon's position. And anyway," I continued on manically, "by the time Clancy serves out her time in the halfway house, I'll hopefully have my license. Well then, so I guess the answer is yes. Eleanor, I mean Clancy, and I are going to start our own PI firm."

Big D kissed the top of my head. "I still can't believe that facility Dax built underneath his estate. Honestly, Muffcat, I knew you were something special from the time you sat your ass in my patrol car, smelling like barbeque. I mean, who does that? But you really do have some wicked extrasensory perception going on in that pretty little head of yours."

A flight attendant pointed to my Harrods's bag and asked Big D if she could store it for him. The perky breasted blonde cooed as she eyed my lover. "Oh swell. I guess I'm gonna have to get used to being jealous. The last man I dated couldn't attract a vulture even if I hosed him down with blood."

Big D snickered as the flight attendant handed over two of our requested liquid Prozacs. "I'm gonna have to hit the gym pretty hard when we get home. You sure you're okay with me moving in, Muffcat?" It did not take me but a second to answer. "Well, that all depends." Big D set his Bloody Mary on the tray in front of him. "Just what the hell does that mean?" I had to giggle. "You really think I want to live with a man who plans my forty- second birthday party at a roller rink and thinks it'd be funny to grease up some pigs to let loose on my family and friends?"

Big D ran his hand through his thick, hair. Oh, that hair. "You never cease to amaze me." After sipping his cocktail, he got down to logistics. "Dylan and Gavin will be meeting us in a limo at BNA."

I lifted my glass and proposed a toast. "Here's to new beginnings." Big D sucked the lemon out of his drink and flipped it around, giving me a big, toothy-yellow grin. He spit the lemon out, then bent over and collected something from his duffle bag. "Well, I cannot pass up the chance for the gig with Metro homicide, but I did get a little something for you after we left Crete. Dax drove me into London while you and J-Laz frolicked over in Paris." Big D's big blue eyes beamed as he handed over a box. I unwrapped the Tiffany box to discover my very own crystal desk name plate: "Muffcat Mansker, Psychic PI." I loved it, and leaned in to give Big D a steamy kiss, after which he whispered "Well, who would have thought a fashion designer turned mortician turned amateur sleuth, who runs a house full of nuts, would wind up with her own PI firm?"

That was a no-brainer. I pointed out the window. "All those angels out there, whose voices are begging me to set their souls free."

Made in the USA
Charleston, SC
28 February 2016